DON'T PANIC, SHE KEPT TELLING HERSELF. DON'T PANIC....

He must have spiked her coffee. She could feel her limbs growing heavy. She went to the dormer window. That terrace should be just below this room. If she could manage to get down to it ...

The window was sealed shut. She could feel herself growing weaker; anything she was going to do had to be done right now. She grabbed a chair and smashed the window. She climbed out of the window onto the small roof. The incline was steeper than it looked. God, how far below?

She shifted her body sideways for a quick look; her hands scrabbled on the tiles as she attempted to get her feet down-slope. Her head was getting muzzy. She stubbed her knee on the gutter, then thought, my knee? The realization that she was sliding came too slowly. Her hands clawed frantically at the rough tiles, then grabbed for the gutter. Then everything went black....

SPECIAL TREATMENT

NANCY FISHER

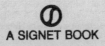

A SIGNET BOOK

SIGNET
Published by the Penguin Group
Penguin Books USA Inc., 375 Hudson Street,
New York, New York 10014, U.S.A.
Penguin Books Ltd, 27 Wrights Lane,
London W8 5TZ, England
Penguin Books Australia Ltd, Ringwood,
Victoria, Australia
Penguin Books Canada Ltd, 10 Alcorn Avenue,
Toronto, Ontario, Canada M4V 3B2
Penguin Books (N.Z.) Ltd, 182–190 Wairau Road,
Auckland 10, New Zealand

Penguin Books Ltd, Registered Offices:
Harmondsworth, Middlesex, England

First published by Signet, an imprint of Dutton Signet,
a division of Penguin Books USA Inc.

First Printing, August, 1996
10 9 8 7 6 5 4 3 2 1

Ⓙ REGISTERED TRADEMARK—MARCA REGISTRADA

Printed in the United States of America

PUBLISHER'S NOTE
This is a work of fiction. Names, characters, places, and incidents either are
the product of the author's imagination or are used fictitiously, and any resem-
blance to actual persons, living or dead, events, or locales is entirely
coincidental.

For my brother Robert, with love.

ACKNOWLEDGMENTS

Many thanks, as always, to my brother, Dr. Robert Fisher, for sharing his impressive medical expertise with me. I'm also grateful to David Dunkel, Assistant to the Headmaster for Physical Education at the Dalton School, for sharing his knowledge and love of the unique game that is baseball, as well as his personal experiences as a ballplayer. Dr. Norman Russell of Cheshire, England, kindly provided valuable tutorials regarding both rugby and the world of Cambridge University. The contributions of my agent, Robert Diforio, and my editor, Hilary Ross, cannot be overstated. And my daughter, Sarah, and my mother, Tema, lavished upon me their usual love and encouragement.

Prologue

Twelve years ago

The line of black umbrellas wavered along the narrow path behind the coffin. Beyond rose the cliffs of the Cornish coast, now wreathed in fog. The rain, mixing with sea mist, tasted of tears.

Before the funeral service had started, there had been much whispering among the mourners assembled in the small stone church. So young, they'd said softly to each other, shaking their heads. So sudden. Poor Catherine.

John and Catherine Fuller entered the graveyard side by side, eyes red, faces stony with self-control, his arm around her shoulder. At the graveside she buckled, but his strong arms caught her, held her up. Cerebral Palsy, they'd told him; a sudden, crippling attack. Yet Andrew had never had any such symptoms before.

The minister's words floated on the air: "... rugby player ... Cambridge ... cut down in his prime...." Everything suddenly seemed unreal. In his mind's eye, John Fuller saw Andrew, mud-splashed, triumphant, charging down the pitch. How many times had he watched his son play rugby? He'd lost count. A local hero, that's what his boy was. And then he'd gone away to Cambridge and it had been the same there. Andrew had written halfway through the year that the coach had told him he'd never seen such fast reflexes, such speed. He'd moved Andrew up to the first fifteen—amazingly good going for a "fresher."

In July, Andrew had gone to stay with friends, but he'd returned home in early August. Of course the local team had to test the new Cambridge star.

Again he saw Andrew running, twisting, and hammering his way down the pitch. Scoring a try, and raising his arms in triumph, a grin on his face. Suddenly staggering, his face contorted in a grimace. Collapsing onto the grass, his body writhing, his arms grabbing at air . . .

He saw himself and Catherine in the emergency room of the small local hospital, and it seemed to him now for the first time that Dr. Trelawney had appeared slightly puzzled, his diagnosis somewhat tentative. Not that it had mattered by then. Not that it mattered now. A single tear traced down his gaunt face. He tightened his arm around his wife.

The coffin began to descend into the damp earth. The wind freshened, and several mourners pulled their coats more tightly around them.

". . . Ashes to ashes . . . ." The rain increased. Beyond the sea of gravestones, the cliffs dissolved in the thickening mist.

PART ONE

Today

Chapter One

April

With a crack that could be heard all the way up in the bleachers, the ball exploded off the bat. The huge Opening Day crowd was already on its feet as Kenny Reese took off for first, his teammates shouting, the Comets' first base coach urging him on. The ball shot out over the left field wall, and frenzied fans halfway up in the stands began jostling for the honor of catching the first home run of Kenny Reese's major league career.

"Scalpel, please," said Dr. Adam Salt. Delicately yet with confidence, he separated the vastus medialis from the patella and quadriceps tendon and dislocated the patella. Adam's deep gray eyes were alive with intelligence and good humor. He inspected the patella carefully, then relocated it. "Turn up the radio, please, Rhonda." The circulating nurse adjusted the volume dial of a small radio on the counter behind the surgical team.

"That's what the papers have been predicting," she said. "Reese and Freeman."

"And Sanchez," said Debbie Stein, the junior surgical resident.

"Sanchez, yeah ... he really is a surprise," Adam agreed. "Lahey clamp, please, Betty." He didn't look up as the scrub nurse slapped the instrument into his outstretched hand.

In his green surgical gown, his shaggy light brown hair concealed by a cap and a sterile mask covering much of his face, Adam Salt looked every inch the prominent orthopedic surgeon. But his scrubs concealed the flamboyant mustache, rugged good looks, and long, lanky frame of an Old West cowboy just in off the range. It was an effect he enjoyed and encouraged. His changing-room locker contained well-worn jeans and a hand-tooled leather belt with a silver buckle. And despite the galoshes he wore in the OR—surgeons can get into a fair amount of gore—Frye boots were his footwear of choice.

At thirty-eight, Adam was already assistant chief of orthopedic surgery at New York General, and sought out by professional athletes for his surgical skill. Being something of a jock at heart, he got a kick out of being on a first-name basis with his heroes.

He worked quickly, continually checking the arthro-scopic monitor as he exposed the patellar tendon, then made two parallel incisions through it to mark the side borders of what would become the bone graft. "I never believe half of what I read in the sports pages," he said. "But Hudson seems to have pulled it off." Morgan Hudson was the Comets' owner. "Never thought the Comets would be any better than middling. Amazing turn-around. Oscillating saw, please."

"Bet Morgan Hudson is one happy camper," said Art Torrence, the senior surgical resident. "These superplay-ers of his are something else!"

On the radio, two well-known sportscasters were en-thusing about Kenny Reese. "From what I've seen, Jim, not just today but during spring training, Reese has a chance to be the first 'over .400' batter since Ted Williams!"

"And he's not only a great hitter, Ron, he's one heck of a shortstop. He was making plays to the left and the right with amazing speed, earlier in the inning."

"Yes, Jim, he seemed to be anticipating exactly where the ball was going to go, and how fast. He looked like he was moving almost before the ball left the bat."

"They're calling them superplayers, and that's what they are. Take Otis Freeman: he can field, he can hit . . ."

"He also seems to know just where the ball's gonna go. Anticipation, that's the name of the game."

"The rest of the team is playing better, too, Ron. Like they're inspired by Reese and Freeman."

"And Sanchez—don't forget Ernie Sanchez. The last three years, he pitched, what? an average of nine wins a season? His best earned-run average was 3.85 during his best season. I have a feeling we're going to see a dramatic improvement in those numbers, starting today. And talk about anticipation, how about that pickoff at second base, at the top of the first inning? No wonder the whole team's inspired."

"They sure are. As I said, I saw them in Arizona, and I still don't believe it! How have the Comets managed to start playing such a hard, offensive game in just a few short months?"

"That's the sixty-four-dollar question. I wish I knew the answer. We all do. Well, here's number thirty-six, Rick Simms, coming up to the plate. Let's see if he can keep the momentum going . . ."

"Now I'm freeing the bone graft," Adam announced, having traded the saw for a scalpel. "Bet these superplayers are costing Hudson a bundle. Worth every penny, too. Wonder why no one's ever heard of Freeman or Reese before? You'd have thought someone would have noticed them in the minors. Now you can just sort of pop up the graft, like this. You follow baseball, Debbie?"

Debbie nodded, somewhat bemused. She was used to music in the OR, not baseball games. Still, Adam Salt was tops in the field of corrective knee surgery, and famous for his unique modification of the Clancy technique for anterior cruciate ligament reconstruction. Debbie knew she was lucky to be working with him.

Adam called again for the oscillating saw and made two parallel cuts through the outer cortex of the patella. "The depth of these cuts is absolutely critical, guys. Too deep and you risk fracturing the patella. Too shallow and the graft may be too thin for fixation in the femoral tunnel."

Debbie peered at the image of the arthroscope on the monitor as Adam extended the knee and directed the senior surgical resident to pull the graft upward as he himself depressed the upper end of the patella. Changing

instruments again, he began making a 1 cm osteotomy.
"You've gotta be careful not to damage or weaken the
patellar tendon graft insertion on the bone here," he
explained as he worked. "What the hell was that?"

"Freeman just stole home!" Rhonda announced excitedly. "Score's three to nothing and it's only the bottom
of the second."

"I gotta go see these guys play," Art exclaimed.

"You know the mayor or the police chief or anybody
important?" Betty asked him. " 'Cause that's the only
way you'll get in. They've sold out the next three games.
I bet you've got your tickets though, Dr. Salt," she
added with a laugh. "In fact, I'm surprised you're in the
OR at all this afternoon."

Adam smiled. "If I'd realized how good those guys
really were, I wouldn't be," he assured her, placing the
graft carefully into a sterile container of lactated Ring-
er's solution and antibiotics. "I'd be at Parker this minute, instead of waiting until tomorrow night's game."

But everyone knew that wasn't quite true. Although
Adam was known to cancel office appointments if offered great seats to important games, he loved doing
complicated knee reconstructions even more than watching baseball.

"Get ready to open that champagne," Morgan Hudson told his personal assistant Jack Ridley, but his eyes
never left the field. One more out and the game was
over—a victory for the Comets, a shut-out for Sanchez,
and a personal triumph and more, for Morgan. Standing
there in the owner's box at the top of the ninth inning,
his whole body frozen in anticipation, Morgan could
sense a similar tension in the crowded stadium just beyond the wide glass window.

Down on the field, Sanchez shook off several signs
from the catcher, then finally nodded. Exuding confidence, he spat neatly on the AstroTurf, wound up, and
let fly. The fastball streaked through the air toward the
strike zone looking deceptively hittable, then slid off at
the very instant the batter leaned in and swung.

"Strike three!" bellowed the umpire.

Comets erupted from the dugout and charged in from the field, their crimson-and-white uniforms bright in the sunlight, their exultant voices drowned by the roar of the crowd.

In the owner's box, Morgan Hudson was on his feet, shouting with joy and jabbing his fists into the air. The intercom telephone rang and he reached for it, yelling happily into the handset. Champagne corks popped as around him, friends and assembled hangers-on offered congratulations and reached to shake his hand or pound his back. "Seven to zip!" "Great way to start the season!" "Wouldn't have thought Sanchez had it in him!" "World Series, here we come!" Impulsive and generous, Morgan was liked and respected, and people were genuinely happy at this turnaround in the fortunes of his team.

Now he turned and grinned across the throng at a pretty, fresh-faced young woman on the edge of the crowd. "Hey, Robin!" he called. "You ought to do another story on me, now. Forget that 'how a self-made toiletries king turned a few patents into a gold mine' stuff, and write about me and my Comets."

Robin Kennedy smiled noncommittally. She knew, as did every reporter and magazine writer in town, that Morgan had been extremely reticent to discuss his superplayers with the press, although he was more than happy to expound at length on the Comets' sudden success. Without some significant new information about the superplayers, it would be just another story.

"You're Robin Kennedy?" inquired a man on her left. "The one who wrote the article about Morgan for *Fortune*?"

Robin turned and nodded as Morgan pushed through the small crowd and arrived at her side. He was a solidly built man of forty who radiated energy. With his deep tan, classic profile, and discreet touch of gray at his temples, he looked every inch the successful entrepreneur. Though only of medium height, his exuberant, forceful personality made him seem larger than life.

"This is the lady!" he exclaimed, laying a suede-jacketed arm across her shoulder. "Beautiful writer. That's why I chose her."

Robin found his nearness disturbing but not unpleasant. "I didn't know you chose me," she said lightly.

He grinned at her, his dark eyes dancing with some secret merriment. "Of course I chose you," he said. "And I'm damned glad I did."

Robin felt a frisson of pleasure. She was suddenly—acutely—aware of his maleness, the smell of his cologne, the feel of his sleeve against the back of her neck. Why hadn't she reacted like this when she'd interviewed him for the *Fortune* story? Perhaps because she was off-duty now, and able to react as a woman, not a reporter ... But what was she thinking? The man was married. Out of the corner of her eye, she glimpsed Felicity, brittle-looking but very beautiful, holding court by the window.

"I wanted someone I could feel relaxed with," Morgan was explaining. "Someone with a good head, but someone fair, someone who doesn't go in for hatchet jobs. I persuaded the magazine to run a few names past me. Yours was one. I read some of your stuff and I liked it."

"I'm flattered." That was true. Although Robin's by-line had appeared in a number of magazines over the past several years, she was by no means considered a heavy hitter. Being selected to write the Morgan Hudson piece had given her her first cover story, and a new prominence.

Morgan grinned expansively. "That *Fortune* story didn't hurt either of us, did it?" He squeezed her shoulder, then released her to reach out for a proffered cigar. Hands offered designer lighters in gold and silver, and he chose one, flaming the tobacco and drawing deeply. Then clamping the stogie between his teeth, he set off through the crowd toward a group of reporters.

Robin's green eyes followed him. That clears up that question, she thought. She knew she was a good writer, but she had no illusions about her rank as a reporter. Well, Morgan was right; the article hadn't hurt either of them. She brushed back the mass of red-gold hair that framed her appealing face, straightened her dark blue blazer, and headed for the champagne.

Morgan glanced toward his wife as he made his way across the room. Felicity was still charming the peasants, rings glittering on her fingers, her slim body encased in the pale green silk pantsuit he hated. Several months his senior, her face belied her age thanks to the ministrations of one of the city's most famous, and expensive, cosmetic surgeons. Everyone thought he was so lucky to be married to the beautiful Felicity. He wondered whose side their friends would take when they learned she was leaving him. Well, screw them. And screw their sympathy, too; he was glad she was going. A few years ago, even last summer, it would have hurt him in more ways than one. But not now. Now the Comets were on their way to being the biggest thing in baseball. And they were all his.

At last, the hopes he'd had when he'd bought the Comets three years before were being realized.

The team had been badly managed back then, the fans had gotten disgusted, and revenues had fallen into the cellar. Morgan had gotten them cheap, certain he could turn the Comets around. He'd tried hard, with infusions of money and key personnel changes, and by the end of that first season, he'd changed managers, and put together a pretty good pitching staff and some excellent coaching. But despite everyone's best efforts, fielding and hitting had not improved sufficiently to overcome the team's legacy of bad management and morale. And really strong fielding and hitting were exactly what was needed to enable the Comets to play more than just a defensive game. And so there they had sat, bang in the middle of the league, for the past two years.

How often he'd wished he could bring in some expensive, high-powered, big-name talent to move the team up in the ratings. But with attendance at just over a million a year the past two seasons, he wasn't seeing a dime of profit. The situation had been impossible.

But not anymore. God bless my superplayers, he thought fervently. Long may they flourish. Chomping down on his cigar, his face wreathed in smiles, he strode over to a group of reporters. "Have some champagne," he told them. "Join the party."

Down in the locker room, the postgame celebration was in full swing. Though well aware that despite today's win, a long, hard season lay ahead, every player was thinking "pennant." Never had the team had such confidence, such heart.

Ernie Sanchez sat with his elbow in a bucket of ice, talking to a group of enthusiastic reporters and milking the experience for all it was worth. He'd never before been hailed as a hero by the press. Of course he'd never pitched a game like today's, never felt the heady adulation of a thousand fans shouting his name.

Across the low, long, brightly lit room, Kenny Reese and Otis Freeman were also surrounded by press people. Kenny and Otis lockered next to each other, and the two men, both new to the team, both in their midtwenties, and both superplayers, had become friends. Now they parried questions from the press while joking and teasing each other and generally putting on a show, especially whenever a question about the supertraining came up. If the way they'd played today was the result of that training—and who could doubt it?—neither man had any intention of talking about it. Although they didn't understand how the super technique worked, they sure didn't want to risk it working for anybody else's team.

"You're very quiet for a young man who has just watched his favorite team make baseball history. Perhaps you liked them better when they were—what is the expression?—'under the dogs'?"

"Underdogs, Agnes," Adam told his old friend with a smile. He swallowed the last of the beer reflectively. "No, I didn't like them better when they were losing. It's just that the new and improved Comets are a little . . . uncanny." Agnes looked at him quizzically, but said nothing. She'd never understood this strange American game, nor the American passion for it.

Adam had just returned from Parker Stadium, where he'd watched the Comets win their second game. Now he sat at one end of the long oak bar in the Polo Grounds, a sports bar named for a long-gone stadium in the Bronx. It was Friday night, and the place was crowded. He signaled the harried bartender for another round, but Agnes covered her half-empty glass and shook her head.

"Now that I am an old lady of seventy," she told Adam in her soft Hungarian accent, "I never drink more than two whiskeys in an evening. I find it slows me down."

"Nothing could slow you down, Dr. Havacek!" said Adam, meaning it.

"Not true," Agnes said sadly. "I needed oxygen at Camp Two. We were only at sixteen thousand feet. So embarrassing."

Adam stole a look at her, but Agnes was perfectly serious. He hid his smile as he slid some money across the bar.

Dr. Agnes Havacek was a genuine character, the more so because it never occurred to her that she was in any way unusual. A brilliant, iconoclastic, fiercely independent woman, she'd emigrated from Hungary in the 1950s at the time of the revolution there. Already a respected research scientist in her native land, she rose to eminence at Johns Hopkins University, and taught at its reknowned medical school. Adam had been one of her students, and her sharp intellect and zest for life had both impressed and charmed him. They had stayed in touch over the years, and when she'd moved to Rockefeller University in New York to pursue her research in brain chemistry some years before, teacher and student had become friends.

Now she finished her whiskey and looked over at Adam sipping his beer and staring into space. "So, Dr. Salt," she said, fixing him with a gimlet eye. "Let me just see if I understand what you have told me about the game you have just seen. The Comets won by eight points."

Adam turned back to her, amused. "Runs, Agnes."

"Runs. Their pitcher struck out several men."

"Twenty-seven."

"And one of the young men ran to the second base without even hitting the ball."

"Kenny Reese. He stole second. Twice."

"Yes. And then that black man caught—"

"Freeman, Otis Freeman."

"—Mr. Freeman, yes. He caught a flying ball—"

"A fly ball that was practically over the fence! Everybody thought it was gone, but Freeman ran back and leaped up and caught it just as it was going over. I've never seen anything like—"

"And there were how many, uh, 'homes'?"

"Homers? Nine."

"Nine. Well, of course I can understand why you should turn to drink."

Adam laughed and swung around on his stool to face her. "You're right, you're right. I should be celebrating. Hell, I *am* celebrating." He leaned his elbows on the bar behind him and gazed at the Friday night crowd, buzzing with the excitement of today's game and the weekend to come. "I grew up with the Comets," he said. "I always rooted for them, even when they were playing godawful ball, even when everyone else had written them off. And now I feel vindicated, you know? I really do. They've turned themselves around, they're playing great ball . . ." His voice trailed off as he thought about the game he'd just seen. All three superplayers had two things in common as far as he could tell. An incredibly fast reaction time. And amazing speed. And that was perhaps understandable in two new young players no one had really studied before. But Sanchez? How had Sanchez suddenly gotten so good?

A roar from the Polo Grounds' assembled denizens brought him back from his reverie. On the big-screen TV across from the bar, highlights of the Comets game were being shown. As Adam studied the slow-motion action replays, he was not surprised to find that the videotape provided dramatic evidence of how amazingly fast the superplayers were at anticipating the play, assessing the pitch, turning, throwing, running. It really *was* as if they knew what was going to happen.

Still, wasn't that precisely what a great ballplayer was supposed to do? Of course it was. He knew athletes, and the limits beyond which they could push their bodies if properly trained and motivated. Someone had simply found a better way to train and motivate these three; that was all there was to it. But why only these three? Why not the whole team?

Again Adam watched Otis Freeman run back for the ball that everyone else assumed was gone; again, he watched the powerful center fielder leap up to make the catch, then immediately throw to first base for a double out. Around him, the Polo Grounds crowd went wild, just as the fans at Parker had done, himself included.

"So how are you finding life after Helen?" Agnes asked. "How long has it been since she moved out?"

"Couple of months."

"And are you dating many women, or none at all?"

"Both," Adam said. "Lots of one-date relationships, but nobody special."

"Give it time," Agnes told him. "You and Helen were living together, what? Two years?"

"A year and a half." He turned and gave Agnes an easy smile. "About eighteen months too long." Though Adam had engineered the breakup, he'd been nervous about how he'd feel when she finally moved out. But there had been no need; her departure had brought only feelings of relief and freedom.

Agnes smiled back. "I never got to see you much when you were with Helen. She didn't like me."

"Sure she did."

"Bullshit."

"Well, don't feel special. She didn't like any of my friends."

Agnes shrugged. "I didn't like her much, either."

"You never said so."

"Of course I said so. I said so several times. You didn't want to hear."

"Actually, I didn't like her that much myself," Adam said. He'd meant it as a sort of joke, but suddenly realized it was true.

"Still, you shared a love of all this, yes?" Agnes said, her gesture taking in the TV screen and its audience. "A love of baseball."

"She hated baseball. And football. And basketball. She hated all sports."

Agnes looked surprised. "Well, you had your work in common."

"Work?"

"She, too, was a doctor."

"A shrink. She never stopped analyzing. Me. Our friends. Our relationship. Drove me crazy."

"I see." Agnes sounded puzzled. "But she was very beautiful, wasn't she? I only met her a few times, but I remember that about her."

"She was all right. Actually, she was a little too perfect. Never a hair out of place. Took hours to dress . . ."

"The sex, then. Surely the sex was . . ."

"She wasn't much into sex," Adam said. He reached for his beer.

"Then why in hell did you stay together for eighteen months?" Agnes demanded.

"I don't know. Inertia, I guess."

"Inertia!" Agnes exploded. "I am very glad it is over!" She looked at him severely. "You do not need a relationship based on inertia. Friendship, shared interests, even sex, this I approve of. But inertia?" She shook her head in disbelief.

On the giant TV screen, Kenny Reese was stealing second base. The bar crowd cheered and Adam turned to watch, his face lighting up. Beside him, Agnes began gathering up her handbag and leather bomber jacket. "I am most happy for your team, my dear Adam," she said. "But it is nearly midnight. Bedtime for old ladies."

Surprised it was so late, Adam dragged his eyes from the screen. Attending rounds were held at eight in the morning on Saturdays, and he still had some paperwork to finish up. "Old lady, my ass," he told her. "How many old ladies go climbing in the Himalayas? Or scuba diving in the Red Sea? Or—"

Agnes slid off her bar stool and grinned up at him. "Okay, Tex," she said. "So I'm not completely decrepit yet. Now, if you can bear to disappoint those two young women over there who have been staring at you for the past twenty minutes, you might help me find a taxi."

Chapter Two

Late June

The thunderstorm that had drenched the city half an hour earlier was now moving out to sea, leaving in its wake discarded umbrellas, flooded streets, and a dramatic medley of towering clouds. From the expanse of windows in his high, elegant office facing the East River, Morgan Hudson could see airplanes reentering the flight pattern for LaGuardia. Beyond the Whitestone Bridge, a shaft of sunlight broke through the cloud cover and illuminated an otherwise nondescript section of the Bronx.

Standing at the wall of glass that stretched behind his desk, his hands in the pockets of his gray cashmere trousers, Morgan sighed with deep satisfaction. The Comets were still astounding fans and sportscasters alike, Hudson & Company was humming along, and all was right with the world, or at any rate, with his world. He wandered over to the mahogany credenza that had been transformed into a small bar. It wasn't too early for a drink, was it? Nearly five, after all. He poured himself a bourbon and soda and sipped, his glance falling on the framed *Fortune* magazine cover hanging nearby. He'd worn a dark Armani suit for the photo session, and a red and white Comets team hat. When he'd first been shown the color proof, he'd been amused to notice that they'd retouched his conservatively colored silk tie to match the cardinal red of the hat. But he'd had to admit they'd been right. Not for the first time, he admired the way the photographer had caught his personality: intelligent, confident, serious, yet upbeat and likable. It was just the way he'd described to the photographer the image he wanted to project, while they were setting up the lights. Morgan smiled to himself as he strolled over to admire the cover once again. It never hurt to make sure people understood what was required.

The *Fortune* article had been completed back in December for publication last February; no one had known then how successful the Comets would be. So the emphasis had been on Hudson & Company, Morgan's wholly-owned toiletries company, with its patented formulations for treatment shampoos and skin care products. The coverage had been good for business in a number of important ways. The piece had also touched on his hobbies and his personal life, and the descriptions of his classy British wife and his passion for light aircraft—he kept a Mooney hangared at the Marine Air Terminal at LaGuardia—had improved both his personal and financial images.

How right he'd been to chose Robin Kennedy to write about him. Such a bright, receptive mind. Quite pretty, too. Brains and beauty. Just like Felicity. Only not like Felicity at all.

Damn Felicity. He felt his stomach muscles cramp at the thought of her, and went and poured himself another drink. A number of their friends had fallen away recently, and he had no doubts why. He shuddered to think what lies Felicity had told them about him.

He downed the drink and set the glass on a side table, then went back around his desk and slumped into his chair. He suddenly felt lonely, and a little old. Don't be stupid, he told himself. You need to get out, meet some new people, have some fun. A little fun, a little companionship. A sympathetic ear. He picked up the phone, then put it down again. Someone new, he thought. A new start. Somebody Felicity doesn't know.

The cover on the far wall caught his eye again, and an idea came to him, but he dismissed it. Then he thought, why not? Why the hell not? She was pretty, she was bright, and she'd only met Felicity in passing. But he didn't know anything about her personal life. He didn't remember a wedding ring, but what if she were seeing someone? Worse, what if she simply turned him down? Then he thought, hell, no; she'd probably be flattered. He pressed the intercom.

"Meg, would you get me Robin Kennedy? No, the reporter who did the *Fortune* article. She'll be in your Rolodex. Thanks." He debated a third drink while waiting, but decided against it. Instead, he glanced through some of the waiting paperwork in his "in" box, but his thoughts drifted. He'd heard Felicity was already seeing someone; she'd even introduced him to their friends. Well, two could play at that game. And Robin Kennedy might be just the person he needed to play it well. Robin was much younger than Felicity; he knew that would hurt.

The intercom buzzed. "Miss Kennedy's on line three," Meg's voice said. "And Mitch Weber called again about the new Dancleer formulation. He says that cheaper synthetic you insisted they use isn't—"

"I know what he says," Morgan interrupted testily. "I have his memo right here." Dancleer was one of Hudson & Company's most popular products. "Tell him I'll call him back in a minute." He took a deep breath and pushed the button for line three. "Robin? Hello! Someone mentioned that *Fortune* article today—it's four months old, but it seems to have made quite an impression—and, er, I thought I'd call and thank you yet again for doing such a great job." As he said the words, he realized how lame they sounded.

But Robin didn't seem to notice. "How nice of you to call," she said with enthusiasm. "And congratulations on the Comets. It was really fun to be there at that first game when it all started."

"Yes, Opening Day was exciting," Morgan agreed. "I'm glad you enjoyed it."

"Oh, I did." Robin paused. Why was he calling her out of the blue, like this? Was he going to ask her out? Wishful thinking, she told herself. And yet, the article had been published months ago; why call her now?

She'd thought of Morgan frequently during the weeks

following the Opening Day celebration at Parker, fantasizing about seeing him again. But she'd admitted to herself that it was unlikely. Despite his attentiveness that afternoon in the owner's box, he no doubt thought of her, if he thought of her at all, merely as a reporter who'd written a good story about him. Besides, he was married.

Then she'd read somewhere that he and his wife had separated, and her fantasies shifted into high gear. She tried to think of an excuse to call him, and was amused to find that in trying to fabricate a reason to make contact with him, she'd actually come up with an interesting pitch for a story. It was a story every sports reporter in the country was after, but she felt she just might have an edge, since Morgan had been so pleased with the *Fortune* article. Although it was a story he'd refused to tell so far, she figured he'd have to tell it sooner or later, if only to clear up some of the weirder conjectures dreamed up by the print and television media in lieu of any hard facts.

For the past several weeks, she'd debated calling him, but had felt rather shy. Robin didn't consider herself a shy person, and she knew her reticence had nothing to do with the article. She was used to making contact with all sorts of people, famous and infamous, in the course of her work. No, it had to do with the way he'd made her feel when he'd put his arm around her at the Opening Day celebration. It would be too disappointing to find out he wasn't as interested in her as she was in him.

But now he had actually called *her*. She pictured his face, his warm brown eyes ... Stop it! she told herself sternly. Be professional.

"Actually, Mr. Hudson—" she began.

"Morgan, please," he said with a smile in his voice. "I thought we'd settled that months ago."

"Morgan." She took a deep breath. Go for it, she told herself. "I've been thinking about calling *you*," she told him, making her tone bright and easy. "I have a story idea I'd like to run by you some time. Maybe I could come to your office—"

"The office is a madhouse these days," Morgan said. "I think I could listen better if we met somewhere else. Perhaps I could take you to dinner one evening?"

His words hung in the air between them.

If it were strictly a business meal, Robin thought, wouldn't he have suggested lunch? Or a drink? But dinner ... Their eyes would meet over their glasses. "You look very beautiful tonight," he'd say. "All these months, I couldn't stop thinking about you."

Morgan, hearing the silence lengthen and fearing Robin had been put off by the suggestion of dinner, quickly backpedaled. "Please don't misunderstand," he said. "It would be purely professional."

Shit, Robin thought. "Of course," she agreed instantly.

"But I really would like to see you again," he added. "I find you very ... interesting. Are you free tomorrow evening?"

"Uh, yes, tomorrow evening would be fine."

"Let's meet at Le Colonial," Morgan suggested. "Say around eight?"

"Le Colonial at eight."

"I'll look forward to it. Until then."

"Until then." Robin slowly lowered the receiver. Get a grip! she told herself. The man finds you interesting. Right. Bet he says that to all the girl reporters. Let's treat this like a business meeting, okay? If he had any idea how you feel about him, he'd probably run like a rabbit.

Morgan hung up and buzzed for Meg. "Make a reservation for two at Le Colonial for tomorrow," he ordered. "Eight o'clock." It was horribly short notice, but Andre would take care of him.

"What about Mitch Weber and Dancleer?" Meg asked. "Should I get him for you?"

"Yes," Morgan answered, "but make that reservation first." He heard Meg disconnect. One of his outside lines immediately lit up as she placed the call to the restaurant. He leaned back in his black leather power chair. He was looking forward to seeing Robin again. Too bad she obviously thought of this as a business dinner. But that could change. His thoughts drifted ... They were drinking Stoli Cristal over ice and eating those little dumplings dipped in spicy sauce ... Now they were in her apartment ... no, she probably wouldn't invite him up to her place. Okay, they were in the back seat of the Mercedes and Ridley was driving. For some reason, she was suddenly unbuttoning her blouse ... she wouldn't do that, would she? Never mind; she was doing it. Maybe it was the vodka. She wasn't wearing a bra, and—yes she was, a tiny one, sheer and black. He could see her—

"Mitch Weber on one."

Jolted from his erotic reverie, Morgan took a moment to compose himself, then picked up the receiver and stabbed the flashing phone button. "Mitch, hang on a second, will you?" Replacing the receiver, he stood and turned toward the window, trying to clear his head. The clouds were gone, and the landscape was bathed in late summer sun. You better keep your pants zipped tomorrow evening, buddy, he told himself sternly. She's a nice kid. Classy. She'd be appalled if she knew what you were thinking. He stretched and turned back to the desk.

Maybe not, though. Maybe she'd like the idea. Women could surprise you. He sat down and hit the phone button. "Okay, Mitch. What's the problem and how are you planning to solve it?"

"So how'm I doing, doc?"

Adam studied the X rays hanging in front of the wall-mounted light box. "Pretty good, Chuck," he said, smiling. "Better than I expected. See this?" With his pen, Adam traced a thin white line on one of the pictures. "That's the bone graft. You can see how well it's healing."

"Yeah?" The bulky quarterback limped over to the light box, favoring his left knee, which was encased in a walking cast. "When can I start playing again?"

"With luck, twelve months. Not this year, that's for

sure." He went back to his desk and sat on it. "Not
unless you want to bust it up for good."

Chuck limped back to his chair and sank into it,
clearly disappointed. "Shit," he said with real feeling.

"Cheer up, buddy," Adam told him. "You're one of
the lucky ones. Most guys with that kind of injury wind
up doing commercials for The Money Store."

Chuck smiled ruefully. "Yeah, I know. And I appreciate everything you've done. I really mean that."

Adam flushed with pleasure. "I enjoyed the challenge." He grinned at his patient. "And I really mean
that." The joint reconstruction had been extremely difficult. "You managing to work out despite the brace?"

"You bet. I gotta stay in shape. And I've been doing
the upper leg exercises, too, just like you showed me."

"Good. But you're not overstraining?"

Chuck shook his head. "I don't think so."

"Well, be careful." Adam reached for Chuck's thick
yellow folder and made some notes, feeling very pleased
with himself. No matter how many procedures he performed, he still got a kick out of using his skill to put
players like Chuck back in the game. "Hang in there,"
he told Chuck as he wrote. "Think positive thoughts.
You'll be playing again."

"That's what they keep telling me down at the Pro
Club, too," Chuck said.

"The Pro Club? That new members-only place for pro
athletes?" Adam looked up, interested. "I've been hearing a lot about that place from my patients. And from
the newspapers, of course."

"You mean because of the superplayers? Yeah, well,
they do work out down there, but they train separately,
you know."

"You ever see where they train?"

"Nah. Most of the Pro Club members are players, too,
one game or another. We try and respect their privacy."

"No curiosity at all?"

Chuck grinned. "They keep the door locked," he said.
"Anyhow, you oughta check the place out, doc, you

being into fitness and all. And you're part of the sports profession, like."

"I might do that."

"Just give me a call and I'll introduce you," Chuck offered, shrugging into his team jacket. "I owe you big time."

"Thanks. And try not to overdo things down there, okay?"

Chuck nodded. "Don't worry. I don't want to blow my chances." He rose and the two men shook hands.

"I'll walk you out," Adam said.

Together they made their way along the beige-carpeted corridor of Adam's private consulting rooms, past the X-ray facility and several examining rooms, and into the tastefully appointed waiting area. The hour was late, and no patients waited. Magazines—*Sports Illustrated, Fortune, Time, Newsweek*, and an assortment of esoteric sports publications—lay scattered on the tables. Chuck's photo smiled up from the cover of a six-month-old edition of *Gridiron*, and he jerked a thumb at it in passing. "Whatsa matter, doc?" he teased. "Couldn't afford to renew your subscription?"

"Oh, we just keep that issue around for Pat to drool over," Adam replied with a wink at the large, motherly nurse seated at the computer station.

"Never mind that," Pat retorted. "I expect two seats to your first game back, Mr. Russell. And they'd better be good ones."

"The best, Pat," Chuck promised. "Right on the fifty-yard line."

"Nice guy," she said as the office door closed behind the quarterback. "You really think he'll play again? That article said he'd never—"

"Actually, his chances are pretty good," Adam told her a tad aggressively. He resented the crepehangers who were always ready with a negative quote. He glanced at his watch: six-thirty. He was due at the New York Athletic Club in an hour. "I thought George Trent was coming in at six-fifteen."

"He called to say he's running a little late."

"With George, that means forty minutes at least."
Putting his hands behind his hips, Adam stretched and
yawned. It had been a long day, and it wasn't over.
"Why don't you go home, Pat? No sense in both of us
hanging around."

"Well, Stan and I were hoping to catch a seven o'clock
movie ..." If she waited until George Trent had come
and gone, she wouldn't get home until half-past. "Are
you sure?"

"Sure I'm sure. Go on." Adam smiled at her encouragingly, then picked up the magazine with Chuck Russell's face on the cover. "Doctors Say Russell May Never
Play Again!" the headline screamed. Not *this* doctor, he
thought angrily. He couldn't wait to prove those rush-
to-judgment bozos wrong. He tossed the magazine aside,
then shuffled aimlessly through the pile on the table.
"Chuck's right, Pat," he said. "Some of this stuff is really old."

"I'll do some weeding tomorrow," she promised. She
shut down the computer and took her handbag from the
desk drawer. "You okay locking up the office?"

"First thing they teach us in medical school."

"Good night, then."

"Enjoy the movie, Pat."

"Thanks."

After she had gone, Adam wandered into the makeshift kitchen for some coffee, but the efficient Pat had
turned off the coffee maker and washed out the pot.
Taking a can of soda from the small fridge, he settled
himself in the waiting room again. Setting aside the magazine with Chuck Russell's photo, he began tossing outdated
issues onto the floor beside his chair. He'd accumulated
quite a pile of throwaways when he came upon an old
copy of *Fortune,* which featured a happy Morgan Hudson in a Comets cap on the cover.

Adam's early discomfort with the Comets' success had
somewhat abated, due primarily to the many stories in
the press, all of which asked the same questions aloud
that Adam had asked himself. He found it strangely
comforting that, despite their best investigative efforts,

nothing terrible had come to light. He told himself that if there *had* been anything sinister to be found, the scoop-hungry journalists would have found it.

True, there had been some wild-eyed speculation, and a number of the more sensational news-magazine programs had aired segments proposing way-out solutions to the superplayers riddle. On the other hand, several sports medicine experts had proposed fairly believable training scenarios for the creation of super skills. And the Comets' general manager had claimed, as had Morgan Hudson himself, that fear of competition was the sole factor keeping them from disclosing their unique training techniques. More to the point, repeated blood and urine testing of the superplayers had turned up nothing untoward: no hormones, no steroids, no drugs. So Adam went to the games, or watched them on TV, and told himself how happy he was that the Comets had finally turned themselves around.

Nevertheless, some part of him held back, wary and suspicious.

Now he paged through the copy of *Fortune* to the article about Morgan Hudson and scanned through it. He read about Morgan's toiletries company; he read about his airplane and his British wife. And he read about the high hopes Morgan had for his beloved Comets. The piece had been published back in February when the general opinion among baseball cognoscenti had been that the Comets would never be any better than middling. Yet no sense of negativism came through; Hudson's hopes of a turnaround were presented as perfectly possible. He wondered why.

The piece was lively and interesting, and Adam turned back to see who had written it. Robin Kennedy, he learned, specialized in neither sports nor business; she wrote mostly about personalities, whatever that meant. A small photo accompanied the blurb about the author, and Adam was just able to make out the long, straight nose, calm, intelligent eyes, and mass of shining hair that fell to her shoulders.

He wondered what she herself had thought of the

Comets' chances before she'd interviewed Hudson for
the article. If she'd done her homework, she surely knew
that the chances of a Comets comeback were slim. So
how had Morgan convinced her to take at face value his
belief in a team that the best professional opinions had
given up on? Had he told her something no one else
knew? But why would he do that? Adam looked again
at her photo. Well, he could think of one reason a man
might be indiscreet.

The office doorbell rang, and he looked at his watch.
Barely six-thirty; George was early. He rose to admit his
last patient.

Dennis Locke was troubled. He stood combing his
thinning hair in the men's room mirror and wondering
what the hell to do about the Comets.

As the newly appointed baseball commissioner and a
longtime fan of the game, he felt keenly the need to
maintain a clean image for the sport. But now, during
his first year—hell, during his first few *months* on the
job, he suddenly found himself in the midst of what was
either the greatest turnaround in baseball history, or a
scandal so big it could kill the game for good. And he'd
run out of ways to determine which one it was.

All the testing of the superplayers had turned up nothing, and that was good. But the press wouldn't let up,
and he couldn't really blame them.

And here he was, caught in the middle.

Well, better get on with it, he thought, pocketing his
comb. Let the members of the New York A.C. honor
me as the new baseball commissioner. Let the mayor of
New York present me with a plaque. What choice do I
have? I can't stand up and say, "Listen guys, I think
there's something seriously fishy about the Comets but
I can't prove it, so let's cancel the season until we figure
it out." Damn. I need a drink. He fixed a smile on his
face and pushed through the door.

The crowd in the Grill Room had grown; members in
black tie and their women in a variety of evening attire,
drank, laughed, and greeted one another across the

mock-Tudor room overlooking Central Park. Locke's progress toward the bar was slowed by people stopping him to offer a few words of welcome or to attempt to involve him in a discussion about baseball in general and the Comets in particular. He fought his way to a gin and tonic, then toward Tripp Overman, his host. Tripp was deep in conversation with a tall, rangy young man with shaggy brown hair and a flamboyant mustache. An actor? Locke wondered. A reporter? But then Tripp noticed Locke and waved him over, and he found himself being introduced to Dr. Adam Salt.

"Chief of orthopedic surgery at New York General . . ." Tripp said.

"Assistant chief," Adam interjected.

". . . and a serious fan of the game," Tripp continued. "Some would call him a baseball fanatic, but that's because they don't love the game as much as we three do." He gave Locke a significant look.

So this was the doctor Tripp Overman had said he might find useful. Locke looked at the young man more closely as he extended his meaty hand. "I've heard of you," he told Adam, noting with amusement that the man was wearing snakeskin boots with his tuxedo. "Aren't you the guy who's going to get Chuck Russell playing football again?"

"That's my plan," Adam said, accepting the hand and shaking it. Locke's grip was very strong. Adam studied the stocky, gray-haired, ruddy-faced man with interest, thinking how much smaller he was in person than he appeared to be on television, and recalling what he'd heard about him. The first new baseball commissioner in nearly a decade, Dennis Locke had a reputation for scrupulous honesty barely tempered by tact. His knowledge and love for baseball were legendary, and he was respected by owners and players alike. But he was also famous for his short fuse and his impatience with bullshit. The Comets situation must be very difficult for him, Adam decided.

"I hope you can pull it off," Locke was saying. "Russell's a powerhouse. The Giants need him badly."

"Doing my best. But Fanelli's no slouch. I think the Giants can have a good season next fall, even without Russell ..."

"I don't know that I'd agree with that," Locke responded. "Fanelli's inconsistent."

Satisfied that the two men had hit it off, Tripp slipped away to greet the mayor, who was coming through the doors at the far end of the room.

"True. But with Russell out, Fanelli's got more pressure on him to deliver."

"Maybe so. Trouble is, Fanelli's an arrogant son of a bitch. The fans don't like him much."

"Fans can change," Adam said. "So can players, given the right circumstances. Take Sanchez."

"Sanchez?" There was no one named Sanchez playing for the Giants.

"Ernie Sanchez. The Comets pitcher."

Those damn Comets again, Locke thought. "Yes, Ernie Sanchez certainly has improved," he said testily. "And no, I have no idea why."

"Hey, take it easy," Adam laughed. "I was just making conversation. I know you're taking a lot of heat just now. I didn't intend to add to it."

Locke took a pull at his drink. "It never lets up," he said. "Questions from the press, questions from the owners of the other teams. Questions I've asked myself."

"Me, too," Adam assured him. "I love the Comets, always have. But ... the blood and urine tests really came back negative?"

"You think we'd lie about it?"

"Of course not. It's just ... well, I was kind of hoping you might have found something that was ... not illegal, just ... unusual."

"No, there was definitely nothing like that. No irregularities whatsoever." Locke swallowed the rest of his drink in one impatient gulp. "I wish to hell there *had* been," he said. "At least we'd know where we stand."

Adam looked at him in surprise. "I thought you were satisfied," he said. "When NBC Sports interviewed you, you sounded so positive."

"I'm the baseball commissioner for chrissake. What am I supposed to say? 'Cancel the season, something stinks'?" People nearby glanced at them, and Locke put his hand on Adam's arm and drew him over to the large window. Dusk had fallen, and beyond the glow of streetlights along Central Park South, the park was shadowy and forbidding. "Sorry," he said. "I didn't mean to bark at you."

"That's okay," Adam replied lightly. "You're only saying everything I've been saying to myself for the last few months. Besides," he added, noting the press that had infiltrated the room since the mayor's arrival, "I'm probably one of the few people here it's safe to bark at."

Dennis Locke was silent for a moment, thinking. There was something very likable about this young doctor. And Tripp had assured him that Adam Salt could be trusted. "What do you think it could be?" he asked at last.

"It . . . ? You mean, how they're doing it?"

"What the fuck else are we talking about here? Uh, sorry, I'm wound tighter than a bedspring."

"I have no idea," Adam said honestly.

"You're a doctor, a sports doctor . . ."

"I do knee surgery," Adam protested. "I work with a lot of pro athletes, but . . . steroids, drugs? Not really my area."

"I know, I know. Tripp told me." Adam's eyebrows rose. "Look, Tripp says you love this game as much as I do." Adam nodded, intrigued. "Dr. Salt—Adam—I need your help."

"I don't think I understand."

"Sure you do." Dennis set his empty glass on the windowsill and stared out at the park. "The superplayers work out at a place called the Pro Club."

"I know. A number of my patients—"

"Exactly. Your patients are athletes. They go places, hear things. And I bet many of them belong to the Pro Club."

"Chuck Russell does," Adam said thoughtfully. "We

were talking about it this afternoon. He says the super-players train in a locked room."

"That's right. It's off-limits to the other members, but my office checked it out. The techniques are a little strange—'New Age,' I think the expression is. But we didn't find anything illegal."

"They let you in?"

"They had to, didn't they? If they wanted me to let the superplayers play." Dennis turned back from the window. "The thing is," he said carefully, "everything seemed kosher. But we could have missed some subtle clue. Something a medical man might recognize."

"Surely you had a medical advisor on the inspection team."

"Two. But it might be different if someone like you were there on a regular basis. Not as an inspector, but as a member, a friend. One of the guys."

"You asking me to spy?" Adam said stiffly. He had a certain sympathy for Locke's position, but professional ethics were involved here.

"No, no, not spy, exactly. But you could talk to your patients, see what they've heard. Go over to the Pro Club, try and join. You've got a great reputation in the field, you've worked with a lot of the guys. Sniff around. See what you can find out. Besides, it's a helluva club. You'll love it."

"I'm not comfortable with this, Mr. Locke. I'll have to think about it."

"Call me Dennis. Listen, this'll be just between us. No one else has to know."

"Tripp will know."

"Tripp will *suspect*. He won't *know*, because I won't discuss it with him. Or with anyone else. Hey." Locke draped an arm around Adam's shoulders. "I'm not ask-ing you to do anything that would go against your pro-fessional ethics. Or your personal ethics, come to that. All I want to know is whether there's anything illegal about how the superplayers got that way. Steroids, drugs . . . something we haven't been able to find. Whatever you might accidentally learn about the other players is none of my business."

Adam was silent.

"I'm not asking you to help me personally," Dennis told him. "It's baseball that needs your help."

Across the room, the mayor moved toward the microphone and Tripp beckoned to Locke. Dennis took a few steps toward the podium, then turned back to Adam and fixed him with a steely gaze. "You've spent years helping the players," he said. "Now I'm asking you to help the game."

Chapter Three

"... and they were paying me a ton of money to write stuff like, 'Now get everything you wash springtime-fresh, and get a free towel, too!'" Robin laughed. "Actually, it was a lot of fun."

"Why didn't I know you used to be in advertising?" Morgan smiled fondly at her, and signaled the waiter to refill her glass. He was finding Robin refreshingly different from most of the women he knew.

Robin shrugged. "You never asked," she said nicely. "Why would you? The *Fortune* article was about you, not me." She sipped the cold white wine and smiled back.

All Andre had been able to come up with on such short notice were two love seats and a low table in a corner of the upstairs lounge, but in a way, Morgan decided, it was better than the dining room. Less formal. More ... intimate. He dipped a vegetable roll in hot sauce and popped it into his mouth. "Go on," he said. "Then what?"

"Well, I wrote for myself on the weekends and in the evenings, and I started submitting ideas to magazines. Eventually I sold a couple of articles. It was great to see my work in print, but it didn't pay the bills. So one day, I sat down and thought about what I needed to do and what I wanted to do. And it occurred to me that maybe I was going at the thing backward."

"How so?" She'd done something new with her hair, or maybe it was just longer. She looked even better than Morgan remembered her. He was very glad he'd called her.

"There I was, a full-time copywriter and a part-time magazine writer who wanted to be a full-time magazine writer. So why not be a part-time copywriter? I could quit my agency job and go freelance. I'd probably make enough money to survive, and I'd have time to give the magazine writing a fair shot."

"Sounds risky."

"I guess it was. But I had some savings and a good strong sample book. I figured if the freelance didn't pan out, I could always get another job. So I got up my courage and quit. Everyone at the agency thought I was nuts." Robin grinned like a naughty child. "The creative director went ballistic. I mean, he actually yelled at me, told me I was an idiot, and I'd be back begging for my old job in a month."

"Nice guy."

"Ah, but there was a reason. See, he'd been working on a novel for eight years, and he was always telling everyone that one day he'd quit the agency business and finish it, but everyone knew he never would. So he was furious with me for doing something he knew he wasn't brave enough to do himself." Robin sighed. "If he hadn't been such an asshole, I would have felt sorry for him."

Morgan laughed. "And you've made it work," he said.

"Pretty much. I don't make a fortune, but I manage. And I'm doing a lot more of what I want to do." She took a sip of wine, aware of his eyes on her.

"You have the spirit of a real New Yorker," Morgan told her with a smile. "Did you grow up in Manhattan? Do you still have family here?"

Robin sighed. The inevitable questions, she thought. God, I'm so tired of telling the story.

When she'd first come to New York at the age of twenty-one, on the run from an abusive three-year marriage and hoping to find work as an actress, she'd made a conscious decision to reinvent herself. Right there on the bus north, she'd written out a slew of possible names, then created around her choice a whole new version of who she was and where she'd come from. Although

Robin considered herself an honest person, she'd figured she rated a fresh start.

"Oh, native New Yorkers are a myth, didn't you know?" she now said lightly. "We all come from somewhere else."

"I suppose that's true." Morgan smiled. "I come from Chicago by way of the London School of Economics."

"Really? How interesting."

"Not really. Tell me more about *you*. Where did you go to college?"

"Saint Albans," she said quickly, the lie coming automatically after so many years. "It's a small women's college outside New Orleans. Very exclusive. I wanted to come East to college, but grandmother insisted." Robin had discovered that people in New York knew little about the Deep South, and cared less. No one had ever checked. Now, of course, no one had any reason to.

"You don't sound like you grew up in the South," Morgan said.

"I studied acting when I came to New York," Robin explained. "The drawl had to go!" That much was certainly true. She'd worked hard on her accent, and no one ever suspected she'd grown up dirt-poor in a small shitkicker town in East Texas, or that she was the first in her family to finish high school. As a child, she'd spent most of her time at the small county library, in part to escape the grim realities of life with an alcoholic mother, four rough-and-tumble siblings, and an abusive stepfather. After high school, a local junior college and marriage to popular, fun-loving Tommy McGee had seemed to offer a more permanent means of escape. But Tommy had always been a drinker, and marriage seemed to make it worse. He'd stay out late, then come home and beat up on her. And when she lost the baby . . .

"Tell me more about growing up," Morgan said fondly. "I want to know all about you."

No you don't, Robin thought. "My mother's from one of those old southern families," she said brightly. "The kind they make movies about . . ." Her years in New York had taught her that the most sophisticated people could be rather naive; people wanted to believe that somewhere, somehow, someone's life was more exotic than their own. "The family didn't approve of my father. See, he played banjo on a Mississippi riverboat called the *Delta Queen*. Sort of a tourist version of the old-time paddle wheels. He was a renegade from an Old Boston family, sort of the black sheep . . ." It all sounded so lame in her ears; how could anyone believe it? But they always did; they lapped it up. If only she'd been strong enough to be herself. Now she was trapped in her own lies.

Morgan's eyebrows rose. "You mean . . . ?"

"Oh, no, I'm sure not! Kennedy's not that uncommon a name in Boston. Anyway, he was a rogue but a real charmer. When my mother's family forbade her to see him, they eloped; very romantic. But it turned out that my father was a terrible gambler. I mean, it was like a sickness with him. He couldn't help himself. After he was shot—" She glanced at Morgan to see if he was buying it. He was. "After my father was killed, my mother and I went to live with my grandmother— Grandfather had died by then—in the old family mansion out in the country." She'd told the story so many times, she could actually picture the columned portico, the porch swing, the live oaks lining the long drive. "When I graduated from college, they expected me to get married and start a family. But I wanted more. So I managed to convince my grandmother—she was the one with the money—to stake me to a year in New York."

The old stories were getting harder to tell, harder to feel comfortable with. Why had she invented such complicated lies? She'd needed them when she'd first arrived in New York, broke and scared and alone, her self-esteem in the cellar. She didn't need them now; in fact, she hated them. But so many people knew her as Robin Kennedy, daughter of the antebellum South and graduate of St. Albans, it had become impossible to tell the truth.

"You were lucky to have the support of your family,"

Morgan told her. "New York can be a pretty rough place if you have no money."

Tell me about it, Robin thought, remembering the roach-infested one-room walk-up with the bathtub in the kitchen, the part-time waitressing jobs that were her only source of food. Until Jeremy had picked her out of an open casting call for a soft drink commercial. It was Jeremy who'd refined away the last vestige of her southern drawl and convinced her to dye her nondescript brown hair a reddish gold; Jeremy who'd taught her about the advertising business, who'd discovered her diary and told her she could write.

"I *was* lucky," Robin said. Lucky and smart. Smarter than poor Jeremy, who'd gotten heavily into cocaine and then heroin. Jeremy, who'd died of an overdose in the apartment they'd shared, three weeks after she'd started her first copywriting job . . .

With an effort, Robin wrenched her mind back to the present. She was with Morgan Hudson in this lovely restaurant, drinking white wine, and feeling very happy. The past was dead. The future lay before her. Robin Kennedy's future.

"Well, I'm glad you decided to abandon the agency business," Morgan told her. "Otherwise, you might never have written the *Fortune* article. And I would never have met you." Their eyes met and held, and he reached over and lightly touched her hand. She flushed slightly but didn't draw back. Should he kiss her? Better not move too fast. She's quality, he thought with satisfaction; definitely a class act. But he recalled his erotic daydream of the day before and felt a hardening in his groin. Her silk skirt was fashionably short, and he had a sudden urge to slip his hand between her legs. Instead, he smiled, removed his hand from hers, and relaxed back against the sofa cushions. "Now, what was that story idea you wanted to pitch me?"

Robin was confused. Morgan had been pleasantly formal when she'd joined him at the restaurant, ordering drinks and food and making small talk as though she were a client or business associate. But as the evening progressed, he'd warmed up noticeably. And a moment ago he'd been about to kiss her, she was sure of it. Yet now he was pulling back. Well, she thought, I have two choices: I can lean across the curried prawns and kiss *him*. Or I can pitch him my story idea. The second option is safer. She centered herself and began to speak.

"I'm not a sports writer," she said. "But I do know baseball. I don't know my way around a locker room. But I do know my way around the owner's box, thanks to you. Now, there's a baseball story out there that every reporter in the country is after, and you know what it is because your team is at the center of it. You're going to have to tell it to someone, sooner or later, if only because the press won't let you alone until you do. You and I have already worked together, we like each other, and I hope we both feel we can trust each other. So I'm asking you to give that story to me."

"The story being my superplayers?"

"Bingo."

Morgan sighed. "Robin," he said, "I know you're going to find this hard to believe, but there's really no story there. Not in the way you and all the other press out there mean."

"I'm not 'all the other press out there,' Morgan."

Morgan nodded, "I know, I know. I'm sorry. What I mean is, everyone's looking for the big story, the scoop, but there *is* no scoop. I can't tell you why my guys are such great players, but I can tell you two things: One, whatever they're doing down at the Pro Club, it's not illegal. And two, it has to be kept confidential, or the competition could get in on it and kill us."

"But it does seem strange," Robin mused, "that you could make that kind of change in a player without drugs or steroids or something."

Morgan spread his arms wide. "That's the whole point!" he exclaimed. "That's why the competition would love to know the secret, whatever it is."

"Whatever it is? Come on, Morgan. Are you telling me that the owner of the Comets doesn't know how his own superplayers got that way?"

Morgan took a sip of vodka. "That's exactly what I'm telling you," he said. "The specifics of the technique, exactly how and why it works, are secret, even from me. But I can promise you this, Robin: steroids are not involved."

"How can you be sure, if you don't know the specifics?"

"Because I've made damn sure of it. You think I would knowingly involve my players in anything illegal? I'd have to be crazy. I love that team."

"Then let me do the story," said Robin, sitting forward on the sofa. "You can read it over before I submit it, correct any errors, make sure I don't give away any trade secrets. Give me an exclusive and it will get the other reporters out of your hair."

"Well . . ."

"Do you like all those wild stories circulating about the superplayers? Wouldn't you prefer to at least try to set the record straight?" Morgan was silent. Robin pressed on. "Take the Pro Club," she said. "All that mystery. They've refused to talk to reporters, but if you called them, told them you'd approved my doing a story—"

Her face was flushed with enthusiasm, her eyes bright and eager. She looked so young. Maybe the story wasn't such a bad idea, Morgan thought. "I have no formal connection with the Pro Club," he cautioned. "I can't make them talk to you. But I do exert a certain influence."

He's going to say yes, Robin thought. I've done it.

"Okay. You can do the story. I'll call over there and tell them you've got my clearance."

"When?" Robin asked without thinking.

Morgan grinned at her. "Not too anxious, are you? I'll be in Cleveland for a couple of days, but I promise I'll call them before the end of the week. Soon enough for you?"

Robin nodded. Her first exclusive. And what an exclusive! "Thank you, Morgan," she said happily. "You won't regret it."

"I'm sure I won't. You'll have to follow up with Connor Egan on Thursday. He runs the place."

"I will. Oh, and I'll want to interview the superplayers ..."

"No problem. Just let me know ahead of time so I can arrange it."

"Uh, okay."

"And you'll have to clear what you write through me," he added. "We should probably meet on a regular basis to discuss your progress. Would you mind that?"

"Not at all," Robin said.

"Neither would I," Morgan told her. He leaned close to her and took her hand again. God, she was attractive. "I wouldn't mind it at all. In fact, I think it could be fun."

"I think so, too," Robin said softly, her heart fluttering. It had been four years since Jeremy died, four years of self-protection, insulation. She'd run from relationships, scared of being hurt again. But Morgan made her want to let down her guard, to allow herself to feel again.

Gently he brushed her lips with his, then slowly increased the pressure and inserted the tip of his tongue. To his surprise, he felt her mouth open immediately in response and draw his tongue inside. Desire rose in him like a knife as the kiss intensified. Robin moaned very softly and moved against him, but he forced himself slowly, reluctantly, to pull back. Restaurant scenes were no good.

"Let's get the hell out of here," he murmured.

The wailing of a car alarm brought Adam instantly awake at seven-forty, and in a foul mood. There were few mornings he could enjoy the luxury of sleeping in, and this was one of them. At least it had been, until a minute ago. He shoved the hair out of his eyes and staggered to the window of his third-floor apartment. Across from the brownstone in which he lived, a red Pontiac nearly pulsed with sound, its owner nowhere to be seen. Going back to bed was obviously not an option.

He stripped off the T-shirt he'd slept in and flung it onto the large sleigh bed, then padded to the cheerful, well-equipped kitchen to put on a pot of coffee. While the coffee was perking, he headed down the hall to the john for a shower and shave, then back to the bedroom again. From the antique pine armoire which held his clothes he chose a pair of black chinos and his famous silver-tipped tooled belt. From the high oak dresser he took a freshly laundered red T-shirt with a gaudy picture of a cowboy riding a bull and the words CHEYENNE RODEO—BEST IN THE WEST printed boldly underneath. Having actually been to the Cheyenne rodeo, Adam felt justified in wearing the shirt even though he'd never actually ridden a bull. He'd patched up too many smashed knees to even think about it.

The two-bedroom apartment was a pleasant, eclectic mix of country antiques and Southwest charm. Adam had grown up in Westchester, a suburb of New York City, but he'd gone to college in Colorado and still had many friends scattered between Denver and Santa Fe. An avid collector, he'd chosen everything in the apartment himself, from the furniture to the linens to the hand-woven Indian rugs, and considered it less than a compliment when visitors asked for the name of his interior decorator.

Back in the kitchen, he poured out a mug of strong, hot coffee, spooned some food into a dish for Gargantua, his tiny orange cat, then decided he was hungry, too. He sliced the remains of a two-day-old baguette and put it to soak in milk and egg while he sautéed a few thin slices of Black Forest ham in a smidgen of butter and a dash of orange juice. Adam enjoyed cooking almost as much as he enjoyed eating. Flipping the ham out of the pan and the soaked bread in, he reflected that it was only his steady regimen of physical exercise that allowed him to keep doing both. He wasn't due at the hospital until four; maybe he'd grab an hour or so at the New York Athletic Club gym around midday.

Carrying his plate and mug into the comfortable living room, he settled himself on the sofa and began to eat. Following the scent of ham, Gargantua jumped up next to him and began carefully tracking the ham's path from plate to fork to mouth, her nose twitching. Adam laughed and fed her a small piece. Then, remembering how Helen used to hate it when he fed the cat from his plate, he grinned and gave her some more. The undersized feline had adopted Adam during a rainstorm several years back, but despite copious feedings and proper veterinary care, she'd refused to grow so much as an inch.

The car alarm had finally died while Adam had been cooking, and he turned on the TV and watched the news while he ate. The Comets were playing in Seattle tonight, and that brought to mind his conversation with Dennis Locke.

What should he do? he asked himself yet again. Locke's plea that he help the sport as well as the players had been well-aimed. But there were ethical considerations. He wiped his plate with the last of the French toast, and went back to the kitchen for more coffee. Although he'd called Chuck Russell the previous day to take the quarterback up on his offer of an introduction to the Pro Club, Adam still hadn't decided whether to use it. He poured the last of the coffee into his mug, added milk, and sipped. No harm in wandering over and having a look at the place, he thought. I don't have to commit myself to anything. Hell, I could join the Pro Club if they'd have me, and still not commit myself. As long as I don't promise Locke anything, as long as I do any investigating on my own terms, there really isn't a problem here.

And the Pro Club was supposed to be a terrific facility. Adam considered himself a connoisseur of gyms, and he had to admit he was eager to check out this new one.

Setting his coffee back on the kitchen counter, he gave the dishes and frying pan a quick wash, then checked the time: just past nine. Ten o'clock seemed a good time to arrive, and it shouldn't take him more than thirty minutes to walk the twenty-five blocks downtown. Plenty

of time to finish his coffee and have a look at the
sports page.

The morning was perfect for a stroll, sunny and warm,
with no hint of the humidity that had plagued the city
earlier in the week. Adam ambled downtown along
Third Avenue, glancing at store windows and enjoying
the playing-hooky feeling he always got whenever he
found himself with a few unscheduled hours in the middle of the workday. The Gap was having a sale, which
reminded him that he needed some denim shorts and
perhaps a light sweater, which reminded him of cool
evenings in East Hampton. This, in turn, reminded him
that, with Helen now out of his life, the chances of her
brother inviting him to spend the Fourth of July Weekend at his beach house were nonexistent. He turned east
on Sixty-eighth Street, mentally scanning a list of other
acquaintances with vacation homes from whom he might
cadge an invitation, and nearly missed the Pro Club's
discreet entrance.

The appearance of the building that housed the gym
took him by surprise. He'd expected new construction
with a high-tech exterior; lots of glass and chrome. Instead, someone had joined two wide town houses, re-
taining much of their original charm. Even the doors
that concealed what was obviously a garage that had
been scooped from the bottom of the right-hand town
house had been covered with a veneer that matched the
building's stonework. To the right, the double building
was flush up against a large office block that had gobbled
up the half block from there to the corner, but to the
left, the Pro Club's premises were separated from its
neighbor, a squat four-story building housing a fortune
teller, nail salon, and Korean grocery, by a short, narrow
alley running back from the street. Large tubs of flowering plants were set at intervals along the frontage,
while solid white-painted shutters mounted inside every
window shielded those within from prying eyes. Classy,
Adam thought. But—a serious gym? Mentally shrugging
his shoulders, he climbed the stone steps to the solid
oak door and rang the bell.

"Please insert your key card," a disembodied voice told him.

Adam looked around for the intercom, located it along with a video camera that was mounted above the door and was obviously transmitting his image to person or persons unknown, and spoke. "My name's Adam Salt. Uh, Dr. Salt. Chuck Russell said to come by."

"One moment, please." A pause. A soft metallic click. "Come in, Dr. Salt."

Adam pushed through the door into a small, square, deeply carpeted hallway. Facing him was a wood-paneled wall; to one side, a windowed door led to a stairwell.

"Please take the elevator to the fourth floor," the voice told him, and a concealed panel in the wall in front of him slid open. Amused at the histrionics, Adam stepped inside and pushed the button marked "4." The elevator was carpeted and paneled to match the hallway; it smelled of sweat. The car ascended fast, then settled, pinging four times to tell him he'd arrived.

The door slid open and Adam stepped out into another world.

He was in a glassed-in reception area that was cantilevered out over the gym. The effect was breathtaking and somewhat dizzying. Beyond and below, the interiors of the buildings had been joined and gutted to a height of some sixty feet. Specialized glass-enclosed areas—a weight room, a Nautilus setup—were terraced out from the other three walls and hung at different levels over the main space which itself was divided by movable walls. Changing rooms and showers were, presumably, below the gym floor level. Adam looked up, expecting a giant skylight or some dramatic ceiling treatment. But the flat ceiling boasted nothing more than ordinary-looking oversized lighting fixtures that shed a flat cool glow over everything. Similar lighting units were fixed beneath each of the overhangs to illuminate the areas beneath them. Narrow metal stairways gave easy access from level to level.

"Impressive, isn't it?"

Adam turned. An extremely well-built young man with white-blond hair and an air of propriety extended a hand in welcome. "I'm Connor Egan," he said. His voice was surprisingly deep, his grip painfully strong. "I manage the Pro Club. Have a seat." He indicated a leather seating area off to one side, and Adam obediently went and sat down. "Chuck Russell says you operated on his knee," Connor said, a note of uncertainty in his voice. He'd heard of Adam Salt—most people involved in professional sports had—but this guy sure didn't look like a doctor. He looked like an athlete himself. And that shirt . . .

Adam nodded. "I do a lot of work with athletes."

"You do a lot of work on yourself, too," Connor said.

"Uh, yeah," Adam said, faintly embarrassed. "I like to keep in shape. Er, that's why I'm here."

"No place better. I've heard of you, of course. I mean, even before Chuck called."

"Oh?"

"You've got an excellent reputation in the field. But I still had to ask some of the guys about you. See, we're—I hate to use the world 'exclusive' but we *are* a private club. We're not open to the public. And we're pretty small. Most of our members are pro athletes, and they require a certain amount of privacy. We have to protect them from the general public. Not you," he added quickly. "You're part of the sports world, and the guys respect your work. They also say you're discreet. And I see that you're serious about your body," Connor added. "That's real important. We're not some cute little place the secretaries go to after work, you know?"

"You mean, it's men only?"

"Not in today's world," Connor told him. "That wouldn't be legal. Or necessary. We do have woman members, but they're all serious athletes: two top-seeded tennis players, an Olympic skier . . ."

"Athletes and doctors," Adam said with a wry smile. "An interesting combination."

"Not that many doctors," Connor replied, missing the

humor. "Most doctors aren't seriously into fitness, like we are here." He stood. "Ready for the grand tour?"

"You bet."

Starting at the top, Adam followed the muscular, white-haired young man through the facility. Everything was new and squeaky-clean, and the equipment professional and state-of-the-art. The pale wooden floors were unscratched, the mats stacked in several corners were still bright and fresh. Clean, rolled-up towels were piled on small carts strategically placed at intervals throughout the gym. Bottled-water coolers stood along the wall on every level. Members, all men this morning, were working alone or with trainers; several looked up, eyed him inquisitively or nodding a greeting, but most ignored him and concentrated on what they were doing. Adam recognized several faces.

"No superplayers today," he said conversationally as they reached the main gym floor. "In Seattle for tonight's game, huh? But I guess they wouldn't be training out here with the rest of us, anyway."

Connor gave him a look, but Adam kept his expression innocent and friendly. "Sure they train out here," he said. "It's just the special training that happens in the Supertraining Room."

"And where is that?"

"Downstairs," Connor said briefly. "Beyond the changing rooms. But it's off-limits, even to members."

"Okay, okay," Adam said, laughing. "I promise not to peek."

Connor smiled bleakly and pushed open a door set flush with the wall. "These are the stairs down to the lower level," he said. "The elevator goes down there, too."

The stairs opened into a small lounge area: boxy white pine chairs with brightly upholstered seats, matching coffee tables, a magazine rack, and a small, simple reception desk. The lounge opened directly into a juice bar with eight stools, and a row of public phones. The dressing and locker rooms beyond were well-lighted, carpeted, and freshly painted. The walls of the showers and bathrooms were covered with imported matte-white tile. Somebody's spent a lot of money on this place, Adam thought. He noticed at least four different doors set into the walls of the changing room. Which one led to the Supertraining Room? he wondered. Never mind; he'd have plenty of time to work it out once he was a regular here.

"I'm confused," he said aloud. "I thought there was a garage down here. It looked like a garage door from the street."

"There is," Connor told him. "At this level, the two buildings are still divided. We keep the private training van next door."

"This is one helluva place," Adam told him sincerely. "Where do I sign on?"

"Let's take the elevator up to my office."

Connor's office was a tiny room to one side of the elevator shaft at the fourth-floor level. Its window, fronting the street, was permanently shuttered closed, and Adam realized that what had looked like wooden panels from the outside of the building were actually metal, presumably steel. The desk, small, white, and laminated, held a diary, some neatly stacked papers, and a complicated-looking telephone/fax. Several filing cabinets, three rather good antique-style wooden chairs, and a bright kelim rug completed the furnishings.

Signed photos of athletes, the superplayers among them, were mounted on the walls. Adam wandered over and read the inscriptions. "All those hours really paid off! Kenny Reese" "I couldn't have done it without you. Otis Freeman." Hmm . . .

Connor pulled some papers from a desk file and pushed them across to Adam. "Initiation fee is five thousand dollars. Yearly dues are three thousand dollars. You can pay by check or credit card."

Eight thousand big ones; Adam winced. Maybe he could deduct it as a business expense. "I'm afraid I didn't bring my—"

"You can pay next time you come in," Connor said. "You'll need to fill out these papers, too, and bring them back. Just give me a call before you come, and I'll have your locker and key card ready." He stood, and Adam stood, too. The two men shook hands again, Adam trying not to wince. "Welcome," Connor told him. "I'll walk you back to the elevator."

"I'm sure you hate it when people want to talk about the superplayers," Adam said casually as they waited for the elevator. "But I really have to compliment you on the incredible results you've had with them."

"Thanks," Connor said. "It's been very exciting."

"It must be," Adam enthused. "To actually work with them, one-on-one, and then to see them go out and use what you've, er, given them to turn a whole team around. I bet it feels great."

Connor grinned. "You've got that right," he said. "I love it."

So Connor's the one who's actually doing it, whatever "it" is, Adam reflected. "But why just the Comets?" he said aloud. "I mean, I can understand why you wouldn't want to give the training to another baseball team, but why not a couple of football players? Or basketball? How do you decide?"

Connor looked surprised. "I don't," he said. "The owner does."

"Owner? You mean, the owner of the team? Morgan Hudson?"

Connor laughed and shook his head. "The owner of the Pro Club," he explained.

"And on what does he base that decision?" Adam asked, keeping his tone light and jocular. The elevator arrived and he stepped in, holding the door open with his foot.

"He bases it on whatever team he happens to be rooting for at the time," Connor told him. "The Comets got lucky, I guess." He reached in and pressed "L." The door panel began to close, sliding Adam's foot out of the way.

"And who exactly owns—" Adam began, but the panel slid closed, shutting off his words, and Connor's darkening expression.

Chapter Four

For the second time that week, Robin awoke to the scent of roses. These were a delicate white, and had arrived the afternoon before in a long cream-colored box tied with ribbon. She'd drifted in and out of a series of confused and anxious dreams all night, but now, as she opened her eyes and breathed in the scent of flowers, she remembered. Everything was going to be all right.

But the morning after that first dinner with Morgan, Robin hadn't been so sure. Although the kiss in the restaurant had aroused her deeply, once at Morgan's town house, she'd pulled away, unable to follow through. Despite the months she'd spent fantasizing about him, the reality of a physical commitment was suddenly too frightening. Morgan had been puzzled and angry, but as she struggled to explain, he'd become surprisingly patient and gentle. He understood, he said. It was happening too fast. She needed time. Robin was grateful for his patience, but she knew he didn't really understand. How could he? She didn't fully understand it herself.

They'd finished their drinks and he'd taken her home, promising to call her soon. She hadn't really believed him, but the next morning, red roses had appeared, accompanied by a warm note.

Yesterday evening he'd returned to the city, preceded by the white roses, and swept her off to the theater and dinner. Again he'd embraced her, and again she'd responded up to a point and then pulled away, angry with herself for not being able to do what her body was urging her to do. But again, Morgan had been patient and understanding. They'd work it out, he assured her. Meanwhile, he just wanted to be with her.

She moved through the apartment, collecting her notebook, a pen, and the Post-it on which she'd scribbled the address of the Pro Club. *Sports Illustrated* had agreed to pay her a small fortune for the exclusive rights to the finished article, and her appointment with Connor Egan was at noon today. But the excitement of consolidating her position as a writer paled before the excitement of being involved with Morgan. Everything would be all right, she told herself yet again. All she needed was time.

She showered, then pulled on a pair of soft brown trousers and a silky, pale pink shirt. Padding barefoot to the kitchen, she put on some coffee, then went back to the bedroom for her pink Dock-Siders. Dreaming there on the edge of the bed, one shoe on and the other in her hand, she caught sight of her face in the mirror over the dresser and laughed aloud at her sappy smile. It had happened so fast. She and Morgan Hudson, a couple. Amazing.

But sipping coffee at the small kitchen counter, Robin's smile faded. It *had* happened fast. Was that why she was having so much trouble with the physical side of things? She'd thought—she'd *hoped*—she was over all the old, bad stuff by now. I've been living like a nun for four years, Robin thought impatiently. How much longer until I can have a normal life?

Jeremy had suggested that some emotional trauma could be at the root of her problem, and of course he was right. Although she'd refused to discuss her past with him, his insights and friendship had led her to begin to sort out her feelings. But then poor Jeremy had died the horrible death of an addict there in the living room, and suddenly Robin was right back where she'd started. Putting herself at risk again emotionally was still very hard, even with someone like Morgan. The physical and mental pain she'd experienced in her short life had left a veneer of self-confidence and strength that concealed a deep vulnerability.

A glance at her wristwatch brought her out of her

reverie with a jolt. Ten minutes to twelve! Abandoning her coffee, she ran for the door, grabbing a linen blazer from the hall closet, and praying for a taxi.

... thirty-seven ... thirty-eight ... hang in there! Adam told himself ... thirty-nine—shit. The weights descended with a clang. Adam exhaled forcefully, then looked around, embarrassed. Real men didn't clang the weights.

"Don't push it, Dr. Salt," said a voice by his ear. "Here, I'll back it off a notch, okay?"

Adam's flush was lost on his already overheated face. "Sure, Connor. Thanks."

Connor went around behind the apparatus and began fiddling with the weight key, leaving Adam staring up into the eyes of a tall, very pretty young woman. She looked familiar, but he couldn't place her. "Hi," he said, sitting up and swiveling around to face her. "You a new member?"

The woman smiled. "No, I'm a reporter. Robin Kennedy."

A reporter ... ? Suddenly it clicked. "You wrote the piece about Morgan Hudson in *Fortune*, right?"

"Right."

"Just giving her the tour," Connor said, having finished adjusting the weights. "For a new article she's writing. Robin Kennedy. Dr. Adam Salt." Adam started to offer a sweaty hand, then thought better of it and pushed the hair out of his eyes instead.

"You're Adam Salt? But I was going to call you next week!"

"I'm delighted but confused," Adam told her.

"Morgan's, uh, Mr. Hudson's given me an exclusive on his superplayers," Robin explained. Adam's left eyebrow rose; this could be interesting. "*Sports Illustrated* suggested I talk to you," she continued. "They said you're one of the best-known sports doctors around, and you know a lot of athletes personally." She eyed his light brown hair and muscular, half-naked torso gleaming with sweat. "I thought you'd be, uh, older."

"Stick around," Adam said. "A few more rounds with this machine and I'll walk out of here an octogenarian."

Connor glanced pointedly at his watch. "Ms. Kennedy?" he said tentatively. "We really need to keep going, here. There's a session in the Supertraining Room at one." And you showed up twenty minutes late, his tone said.

"Of course," Robin said. "Sorry. Nice to have met you, Dr. Salt—"

"Adam. Uh, you're going to watch a superplayer training session?"

"No, of course not!" Connor said quickly. "Just a fast tour of the room before the session starts. Ms. Kennedy understands that the actual training session is never open to anyone."

"No, of course it isn't," Adam agreed. Then putting on his most ingenuous look, he turned to Robin. "Perhaps I could come with you, Ms. Kennedy. I mean, since you're planning to involve me in this story of yours." Connor's face darkened, but Adam ploughed on. It was the first he'd heard of anyone other than the superplayers being shown the training room. Even Chuck Russell hadn't been inside. "It's not as if you were going to watch an actual session. And how can I talk to you about a training room I've never seen?"

"I doubt Ms. Kennedy is planning to ask you about the training room," Connor said quickly. "She doesn't need you in there; she's just going to see where—"

Robin's chin went up. Who was Connor, to make her decisions for her? Adam was right; he *should* see the room. She wasn't sure how far Morgan's influence extended around here, but there was one way to find out. "I think that's an excellent idea, Dr. Salt. You can keep me medically correct." She turned and smiled at Connor. "Let's go."

Connor shook his head. "I really don't think—"

Adam rose from the exercise bench. "Would you excuse Connor and me for a moment?" he asked Robin. He draped an arm around Connor's shoulders and walked him a short distance away.

"I may be the new boy," he said, keeping his voice low and conspiratorial, "but I realize how important discretion is—in my business as well as yours. Now, I don't know how that reporter got permission to look around the special training room. But I do know there are a lot of wild-eyed stories out there on the street. And we don't want any more of them. Right?" Connor nodded. "So," Adam continued, "I could sort of guide her, you know? Try and tone down any, uh, inappropriate ideas she may get in there."

"*I* can do that," Connor said.

"Not long-term, you can't," Adam replied. "But I *can*, since it seems I'm going to be consulted on this story of hers. Besides," Adam lowered his voice still further, "I think your refusals are starting to look a little funny to her."

Connor reflected. He'd been surprised and dismayed when his boss had told him he'd agreed to Morgan Hudson's request for this reporter's tour. To Connor's mind, some unofficial control of what she wrote would be quite welcome. But he wasn't delighted at having anyone else in the room with her. Still, Pro Club members who'd had dealings with Adam had said he could be trusted. Then he thought, if the woman is really planning to involve the doctor in her story, she'll describe the training room to him afterward. He nodded slowly. "I guess it'll be okay. But there's no time for you to change your clothes."

The two men rejoined Robin, and, feeling rather naked, Adam grabbed a towel and draped it around his shoulders. They followed Connor into the elevator and down to the lower level. He led them to the rear of the dressing area and past the four white-paneled doors that Adam had eyed so suspiciously on his first visit but which he'd since come to realize concealed only a linen room, a small workshop, and two equipment closets. Connor disappeared around a short freestanding wall of lockers and Robin and Adam followed. Immediately before them was yet another door, steel this time, with no visible keyhole. Motioning them back, Connor hit a button set into the wall beside the door and spoke into a small metal plate just above it. The voice-activated lock clicked, and Connor pushed open the heavy steel slab. "After you," he said graciously, allowing them to precede him, then stepping inside himself and pulling the door firmly shut.

The room they entered was long, narrow, and high-ceilinged, and bathed in strange blue light. Mats covered the pale wooden floor, and huge video monitors were built into the side walls. Large machines of unfamiliar design were placed at intervals throughout the room. Of red plastic and shining silver metal, with protruding fixtures of unrecognizable purpose, they appeared faintly sinister.

"What *are* those things?" Robin asked Connor. "They look lethal."

Connor frowned. "Biofeedback," he told her sternly. "Our own design. We use them to improve hand-eye coordination and increase reaction speed."

Robin nodded and made a note while Adam wandered over for a closer look at one of the machines. Biofeedback? Well, it could be.

"And the monitors?" Robin asked. "Do they study videos of their games?"

"Sometimes," Connor agreed. "But we also use them for the MIEs. Our Mental Image Enhancement exercises."

Bullshit City, Adam thought. "Sounds interesting," he said. "How does it work?" This ought to be good.

"We use speeded-up images of various plays—depending on which player we're working with—along with these MIE machines over here, to train the eye to follow faster and faster action. We've found that when the eye decodes faster action, the brain reacts faster, causing the body to move faster."

Robin frowned. "I would have thought it worked the other way," she said. "The eye decodes faster because the brain is working faster."

Not just another pretty face, Adam thought. He smiled approvingly at her, then realized Connor was

staring at him. "You're right, up to a point," he said to
Robin, allowing a touch of condescension to creep into
his voice for Connor's benefit. "But if I'm understanding
it correctly, this MIE technique is a form of biotraining,
a method of schooling the brain to cause the body to
react more and more quickly to specific visual stimuli
through the conscious imaging of those visual stimuli
that the brain is being trained to detect and react to on
the playing field. Do I have it right, Connor?" And was
any of that even in English?

"That's exactly right, Dr. Salt," Connor replied, obviously relieved.

Robin turned to Connor. "I still don't exactly understand—"

"I'll take you through it later," Adam interrupted.
"With diagrams. I think diagrams will help." He nodded sagely.

Is he pulling my leg? Robin wondered. But no, he
seemed quite serious.

Connor led them quickly through the room, talking
rapidly of vitamin therapy, meditation, breathing techniques, and motivational chanting. Robin took notes fe-
verishly; Adam smiled and nodded, but his eyes missed
nothing. Soon they arrived back at the door again, and
Connor, checking his watch, quickly ushered them
through it. He himself remained inside. "Perhaps Dr.
Salt will see you out, Ms. Kennedy," he said. "My session starts in just a few minutes."

"Of course," Adam agreed. "Whatever you say, Connor. And I must tell you, I'm very impressed. I've never
seen anything like it." God knows *that's* true enough.

Connor beamed, shook Adam's hand, shook Robin's
hand, and closed the door firmly behind them.

They headed through the dressing room area toward
the elevator, and Robin put her notebook back in her
shoulder bag. As they passed the stairs to the main exercise area, she turned to Adam. "Please don't bother to
see me out, Dr. Salt," she said. "Go on back upstairs.
I'll be fine."

"No problem," he told her. "I think I've had it for today."

"Then why don't you join me for coffee? Or lunch? It's nearly one o'clock."

Adam debated for about one second. "I'd love to," he said. "But my treat. And only if you start calling me Adam. I'll grab a quick shower and be with you in ten minutes. Is that okay?"

"Fine. I'll meet you in that juice bar area. I have a few phone calls to make."

A quarter of an hour later, they were sitting across from each other in a small neighborhood bistro, roast chicken salads and iced teas in front of them.

"So what did you think of that weird room?" Robin asked.

"What did *you* think?"

"Well, I'm just a layman, I don't really understand it the way you do. But ..." Robin ate a forkful of chicken thoughtfully. "The thing is, I've read about biofeedback, and I know that it works ..."

Adam nodded. "Yes, it often does. Not always consistently, but it's certainly a legitimate behavior modification method."

"But the way Connor described it, well, it sounded backward to me. You understood it and explained it, although I'm not sure I understood your explanation any better than Connor's ..."

Adam took a long drink of tea. "It's kind of hard to—"

"That's okay. You can draw me those diagrams later." Robin grinned. "It doesn't really matter whether I understand it, as long as I can write in my article that *you* do."

Adam looked up, alarmed. "What?"

"Well, you do, don't you?"

"I, uh, sure. Er, yes." Shit. "But I hope you won't quote me directly."

"Top medic, asked about the special training room, said, 'I, uh, sure, er, yes.' Sounds like a great quote to me." She smiled. "Don't worry. I am planning to quote you, but only with your permission—and only when you say something worth quoting."

Adam nodded. "Fair enough."

"Good." Robin pushed her half-eaten salad to one side and reached for her notebook and pen. "So tell me what you thought about that strange blue light everywhere."

"Well, as Connor said, certain colors tend to influence mood. There are all sorts of pseudoscientific ideas out there these days; aromatherapy, color therapy ... So now there's blue-light therapy, too." He shrugged.

"And vitamin therapy? Oxygen therapy?"

"Both are recognized to some extent by the medical profession, although not exactly in this regard."

"How about meditation and breathing?"

"We physicians definitely recommend breathing. You can quote me on that."

"Very funny. You ever meditate?"

"No, but I once knew someone who did. He swore by it. And of course there's Zen tennis."

"Excuse me?"

"You don't hit the ball, 'it' hits the ball, 'it' being your brain which, if you can manage to get out of its way, will do a better job than you will."

Robin looked at him quizzically. "You believe that stuff?"

"Actually, that particular stuff, I do. I've experienced it myself, and not just playing tennis. You probably have, too. Ever been driving for a long time and suddenly realize you're driving on automatic? Driving perfectly well, but not aware of driving? Who's at the wheel? 'It.' "

"Right."

"And then *you* suddenly take over and the car wobbles a little bit and doesn't drive quite as smoothly and accurately as it was doing before. That's you getting in 'its' way."

"So we should all drive in a state of meditation?"

"No, of course not. Look, athletes in many different sports can tell you about special moments when they're playing incredibly well and time suddenly seems to slow right down, and they don't know how they're doing what they're doing, and they don't feel like they're the ones doing it. . . ."

"This is all a little New Age for me," Robin said. "I like things nice and clear around the edges." Ouch! Adam thought; that's usually *my* line. "Can you," Robin continued, "give me one scientifically sound reason that room we saw could produce a superplayer?"

"I can't give you one scientifically sound reason it couldn't," Adam said.

"That's not the same thing."

"I know. But the truth is . . ." Adam trailed off. The truth was, he was caught right in the big middle. "What I'd like to do is think a little bit more about what we saw today, maybe do a little reading. . . . I assume we'll be meeting again to talk about the story." Let me buy some time here, he thought. The fact was, he was at a loss as to what he could give her that would be both quotable and correct. He sighed and swirled the ice cubes around with his straw. He didn't want to mislead Robin with untruthful praise of the supertraining techniques Connor had described, or what they'd seen in the room. But he also couldn't afford to have his real opinion quoted in the press, much less to Morgan and Connor. Tell her he was certain that three-ring circus Connor had shown them today couldn't actually produce the superplayers' reflexes and speed? Forget it! Any advantage he now had as an inside observer, whether for the baseball commissioner or for his own curiosity, would be blown sky-high.

Misunderstanding Adam's silence, Robin tried again. "All I want is the truth, Adam. I'm not writing an ad here. Just an article."

"Are you sure Morgan Hudson knows the difference?" Adam said, then wished he could call the words back. The last thing he wanted was a confrontation with this pretty woman who'd just taken him into that off-limits training room.

"I don't know whether Morgan does, but *I* do," Robin

told him firmly. "I used to work in advertising, and believe me, I know! Look, it's true that Morgan got me into the Pro Club, and gave me an exclusive on the team. But I *am* a journalist."

Morgan's journalist, Adam thought. "I shouldn't have said that," he apologized. "I have nothing but respect for Mr. Hudson. By the way, I thought your *Fortune* article was very good." He smiled at her. It wasn't hard.

She smiled back at him, forgiving him. "Thanks."

"Is that how you two met?" he asked her.

Robin's eyes grew soft. "Yes. Yes, it was."

I was right, Adam thought, but I'd rather be wrong. Too bad. Neat lady. But I can't compete with Morgan Hudson. He reached for his tea, drained it, and set the glass down. "Interesting man, our Mr. Hudson," he said. "At least, he seems so from all I've read about him. Self-made. A private pilot. And dedicated to the Comets. I'm dedicated to the Comets, myself."

"Everyone is, these days."

"No, I've been a Comet fan for many years. Way before all this. I've always admired Morgan for everything he's tried to do for that team. I'm glad he finally succeeded."

"So am I," Robin said.

"So what's he like?"

"Well, he's . . ." A certain tension came into her face, Adam noticed. "He's very . . . understanding," she said. "He's generous. He's . . . good at running his business."

And he's in love with you, Adam thought. Who can blame him? "I'd really like to meet him sometime," he told her.

"Maybe I can arrange that," Robin said.

The check came and Adam insisted on paying. They exchanged business cards. Out on the sidewalk they parted, Adam heading uptown to his office, Robin crosstown to her apartment. Each had a sudden urge to look back, but neither did.

In the special training room, Kenny Reese's session had gone well. Connor had seemed especially pleased with the way he'd done his MIEs today. Now he sipped the special energy tonic, tartly sweet with a sort of herby smell, and watched the motivational lecture on one of the giant video monitors. How lucky he was to have been plucked from the bush leagues and given this incredible opportunity. How very fortunate to be given this unique training, to become a superplayer.

And what a great facility this was, not just the training room, but the whole darn place. Everything was so clean and new and high-tech. And people so friendly and helpful. Especially Connor. Not that he couldn't be tough on you, if you weren't doing things exactly right.

He'd laughed at it all at first—not out loud, of course. He'd never imagined baseball training would be anything like this. But then, he'd never imagined the results would be anything like this, either.

Connor approached. "Time for the deep breathing and meditation," he said.

Obediently, Kenny set aside his drink and folded his legs into a semblance of the lotus position. He placed his hands, palms up, on his knees and stretched his neck around until his head felt comfortably balanced.

"Center yourself," Connor said softly, "and then begin."

In through the nose, out through the mouth. In through the nose . . . The yoga breathing technique that had seemed so foreign at first now came without effort.

"Find your mantra." The meaningless Sanskrit phrase sidled into Kenny's brain and skittered around. "Don't chase it," Connor said softly. "It will settle."

Kenny felt himself moving slowly into that strange state of being that meditation sometimes, but not always, produced. His breathing was strong and steady, his body position rock-solid.

Connor moved to a small area behind a half wall, where the sound and video controls were mounted. The first time he'd seen it, the setup had reminded Kenny of the scene in *The Wizard of Oz* where Dorothy discovers the Wizard is doing it all with smoke and mirrors. But unlike the movie, Connor's smoke and mirrors were

right there in the open for all to see. They also seemed
a lot more effective.

The blue light dimmed to a hazy midnight as Connor's
fingers played the controls like a piano. He spread his
hands across the switcher and the giant video monitors
lit up; he closed his fists over the rheostats and brightly
colored abstract images chased each other across the
screens. In through the nose and out through the mouth
and let the mantra settle. He pushed buttons and turned
knobs; strange music curled out of the hidden speakers
and a rhythmic pulsing began beating softly at the air.
Let the energy flow through you. Let it flow. Now.

Chapter Five

July

"There. Just above that line of trees. Do you see it?"

Robin looked out across the rolling countryside beyond the car window. A thick stand of trees curved away into the middle distance. Set high into the hillside above was a large white house, chimneys rising into the blue sky. Even from this distance it was obvious the house was a beauty.

"It's enormous."

Morgan smiled. "You can't see it from here, but there's a pool and an English garden in back. You'll love it."

Robin looked over at him fondly. "Who wouldn't?"

"I'm glad you decided to come this weekend. I haven't been up here for weeks, not since . . ." Not since that bitch Felicity walked out on me, he thought, and turned me into a figure of fun. Well, the party we're throwing this weekend will take care of that. "Never mind. On to better things."

Uncertain how to respond, Robin said nothing.

"We'll swim and golf—do you play?"

"Not really."

"That's okay. I'll teach you. And the fishing's terrific. I'm sure we can find one of Felicity's old rods for you." Felicity had wielded a mean fly rod.

"Afraid you'll have to teach me that, too," Robin replied lightly. "I can shoot squirrels, though." She gave him an impish look.

Morgan looked startled. "You mean with a gun?"

"That's the usual way."

"And what do you do with the squirrels?"

"You eat them."

Morgan made a face. "Sounds delicious."

"Actually, it's not bad. Depends how hungry you are."
Morgan looked over at her in surprise. "The caretaker
on my grandmother's plantation taught me to shoot
squirrels," she added quickly. "It was our secret."

"All these things I'm learning about you," Morgan
said affectionately. "So what do you shoot with? A
shotgun?"

"A shotgun, a rifle, a pistol ... And I ride, too. I
really am a country girl, despite the fishing."

"Well, I'll have to be careful how I treat you," Morgan said. "You might decide to blow my head off."

"Not funny."

"No, I guess not. Look, there's the airport we'll fly
into next time." He indicated a short asphalt runway set
at right angles to the road and flanked by a number of
small outbuildings. About twenty small planes of various
makes were tied down in the field beyond the small
airstrip.

"I was looking forward to that part of the trip," Robin
told him sincerely. She'd never ridden in a small plane
and it seemed rather glamorous.

"So was I," Morgan said. "I'd much rather fly up here
than drive. But they're waiting on parts." A short way
beyond the airport, Morgan turned right onto a small
country road, and they lost their view of the house. "Not
much farther."

"And where's the river from here?"

"The Hudson? About three miles that way." Morgan
pointed over one shoulder. "You can see it from the top
of the house."

"Sounds glorious."

"It is. The countryside around here is really beautiful." He looked over at her and smiled. "You compliment it perfectly."

"Thank you, kind sir."

"I wasn't sure what we'd feel like doing tonight, but
I booked a table at The Old Forge, just in case. They

fill up pretty quickly on Friday evenings. It's a wonderful country inn, quite old. And the chef is very talented. In fact, they're catering the party tomorrow."

Robin felt her stomach knot. Why had Morgan felt the need to throw a huge party this weekend? What would she say to his friends? What would they think of her? She imagined them shaking their heads as they gathered on the stairs or in the hall: "She's nothing like Felicity." "No, but then, who could be?" "Felicity's so beautiful. So accomplished." "Such a wonderful golfer." "And she's really great at killing fish." Robin giggled.

"What's so funny?"

"Just thinking about the party. It'll be fun." Of course they'd like her. Felicity might be the greatest thing since sliced bread, she told herself, but Morgan had left Felicity.

Morgan reached over and patted her thigh. "It will be," he said. "And I want to show you off." He swung the car onto a long tree-lined drive. "Nearly there."

Robin stretched the stiffness from her neck and shoulders. She was ready for a little R&R. The past few weeks had been busy ones. She'd interviewed all three super-players—that Kenny Reese was really a sweetie, she reflected—and she'd begun contacting what she'd refer to in her article as "industry sources"—managers and trainers from various teams. She'd even had a talk with the baseball commissioner, not that he'd given her much material.

Perhaps best of all, she'd spent a number of evenings getting to know Morgan, all of them fun and pressure-free since, by mutual unspoken consent, they'd avoided the issue of sex. So Robin had felt relatively comfortable accepting his invitation to spend the weekend at High House, though rather guilty at her inability to consummate their relationship.

"Here we are," Morgan announced, bringing Robin out of her reverie. The car pulled up in front of a rather grand-looking white colonial house bordered by flowering shrubs. Tall windows flanked the entranceway. Everything looked fresh and clean.

With the engine turned off, Robin could hear the bird-song. While Morgan unpacked their bags from the trunk, she simply stood there on the pale pebbled walk, en-joying the smells and sounds. "Come on, country girl!" Morgan told her. "Let's get this stuff inside, and I'll show you your room."

The interior of the house was a blur of chintz and country antiques, rather feminine, Robin thought, but very appealing. The house had been built with two stair-cases—one for the servants, Morgan explained. The ground floor held the formal rooms and a large country kitchen, the floor above, the major bedrooms. "The ser-vants lived on the third floor, back when the house was first built," Morgan told her, "so the rooms up there are rather small, but we've made them quite charming. Of course, everything's been redone."

By the lovely Felicity, Robin thought. Well, why should I care? I'm here and she's not. "I love it all," she told him.

He led her to a sunny bedroom overlooking the gar-dens. The walls were covered in a butter yellow and white stripe, and a Spanish rug in yellow, white, and powder blue covered most of the polished wide-plank floor. "This is your room," Morgan told her. "I'll be just across the hall, in case you get lonely."

Robin flushed slightly. "It's a beautiful room," she said. He put his hands on her face and kissed her lightly on the mouth. As she responded, his lips drifted down to the curve of her neck, then lower still, to the curve of her breast where it met the scooped neckline of her light cotton sweater. Suddenly he stopped and stepped back. "A swim first, or lunch?" he asked.

"What?" Robin stared at him in confusion.

Morgan smiled at her. "I want this to be a really nice weekend," he said. "I'm not going to pressure you. But I can't keep on starting to make love to you and then stopping. It's too . . . difficult for me."

Robin felt the guilt well up inside her. "I'm really sorry," she said softly.

"God, don't apologize!" Morgan told her. "It's not your fault."

Of course it is, Robin thought. What's wrong with me? She leaned over and kissed his cheek; she could feel his hardness against her leg. "Thank you," she whispered. "Thank you for . . . for being so—"

"Enough," Morgan told her. "Go dig out that swimsuit. I'll meet you by the pool." He took her by the shoulders, turned her toward her room, cupped her fanny in his hands, and gave her a little shove. "March!"

They swam, they ate the lunch of cold chicken and salad that Margaret, the local woman who cleaned and cooked for Morgan, had left for them, and sunbathed on chaises set around the freeform pool. Later they took drinks into the garden, and Robin filled baskets with cut flowers for their bedrooms. Dinner at the Old Forge was delicious, and the staff was friendly and attentive. Morgan placed a possessive hand around her shoulders as they entered and left the restaurant, and reached to take her hand several times during the meal, but aside from a quick kiss outside her bedroom door, he made no attempt to touch her once they'd returned to the house. Robin was vaguely disappointed but grateful, and when she finally crawled between the butter-colored sheets, she felt happy and confident, and ready for a party.

She slept late the next morning, awakened by the sound of the crew erecting the giant party tent. She dressed hurriedly and went downstairs, where Morgan, who'd been up for hours, found her gazing bemusedly at the white canvas structure taking shape on the lawn. He kissed her lightly, brought coffee and pastries to her at the pool, offered her a choice of newspapers, and rushed off to deal with the chair rental people. A short time later, Jack Ridley, Morgan's personal assistant, arrived to take over, and Morgan joined Robin.

"This place is a madhouse," he announced. "Let's get out of here."

They spent the rest of the morning exploring the nearby village, then bought sandwiches to eat by the river. When at last they returned to the house, it had been transformed by flowers and fairy lights, and three caterer's assistants were busy in the kitchen.

"One drink, and then we should change," Morgan told Robin. "A glass of champagne on the terrace?"

"Wonderful."

"You go on out. I'll be right back."

She'd just settled herself at one of the stone tables, now sporting a pale pink cloth and an artful arrangement of flowers, when Morgan returned bearing a bottle, two glasses, and a large dress box.

"This is for you," he said, handing the box to her. "For the party. I hope you like it."

"I'm sure I will—oh, Morgan, it's gorgeous." The dress was obviously expensive, the material thin, soft, and clingy, the color a perfect match for her blue-green eyes. "I'll go and try it on!"

Morgan laughed. "Finish your wine first. There's plenty of time."

The first guests were arriving as Robin descended the polished staircase, feeling a little self-conscious. He'd gotten the dress size right, but the cut was lower and tighter than she would have chosen. It emphasized her bust and showcased her rear, and if it hadn't had a designer label inside, she'd have felt a little cheap in it. Still, Morgan had obviously planned on her wearing it this evening; at least she could give him that.

In retrospect, she could barely remember the details of that evening, except that it was magical. Names and faces, too many to recall ... Morgan's arm around her waist, shepherding her through the crowd, introducing her to fascinating people, leaving her with this group or that but always returning to move her along ... the looks of interest, curiosity, and envy from the women as Morgan, handsome and debonair, smiled into her eyes; the expressions of sheer lust on the faces of the men as he let his hand slip casually onto her rear or dangle low off her shoulder, just touching her breast ... After several glasses of champagne, the faint embarrassment she felt over this public display turned to pleasure that he was claiming her as his own.

Depositing Robin among a small crowd surrounding the CEO of a well-known bond trading company who owned a small castle several miles away, Morgan took a glass of wine from a passing waiter and stepped out into the cool night air to light a cigar. Several couples drifted across the darkened lawn toward the terrace. Soft music whispered from speakers hidden around the compound.

Morgan drew deeply on the smuggled Monte Cristo, well-pleased with the evening. Everyone who mattered had come tonight. And Robin was making a hit in the dress he'd chosen so carefully for her. The darkness above him glittered with stars; as he watched, one shot out from the others and threw itself across the sky. A good omen, he thought.

"I see that Felicity's departure hasn't slowed you down any," said a masculine voice behind him. He turned; Sandy Morrison, short, portly, and extremely wealthy, grinned up at him. Some fifteen years older than Morgan, Sandy was a commercial shipbuilder, originally from Scotland, who sold or leased his supertankers to the major oil-producing nations of the Middle East. He and his beautiful wife Britt had been friends of Morgan and Felicity's for some years, but they hadn't seen much of each other since the parting with Felicity. Britt was a good friend of Felicity's.

Morgan turned and clapped Sandy on the back. "She's something, isn't she?"

"She is indeed. There's not a man in there who wouldn't like to rip that rather revealing dress right off her nubile body. Is she as hot as she looks?"

Morgan smirked. "Hotter," he said. "We haven't been out of the sack all weekend."

"She'll wear you out, lad," Sandy cautioned. "Still, what a way to go! Does Felicity know about her?"

"No, but I expect Britt will take care of that."

Sandy guffawed. "Yes, I expect she will. Who is she, anyway? Where did you find her?"

"She's that journalist I told you about. The one who wrote the *Fortune* article."

"*That* girl? She's got one helluva body for a journalist."

Morgan smiled. "True. But there's more to her than sex, wonderful though it is."

"Who *needs* any more?"

"You're a pig, Sandy."

"I know. But a happy pig. So what else does she have besides a great set of knockers?"

"She's clever, she's witty . . ."

"Oooh, just what you need in bed. Good conversation."

". . . and she's from a rather famous family."

"You mean, she's a Kennedy Kennedy?"

Morgan nodded. "It's all rather hush-hush. Some sort of scandal with her father. Her mother's family's been estranged from them for years. I'm going to do a little sleuthing, see if I can bring them all together again."

"Very noble," Sandy said dryly. "You know, marrying a Kennedy doesn't have quite the cachet it used to, old boy. Unless there's money involved, of course."

"Don't be vulgar, Sandy. Besides, I'm not even divorced yet."

"Of course. Forget I said anything. Listen, I'll be in Stockholm next week, but we might meet for lunch the week after."

"I'd like that."

"My secretary will call yours. And now I'd better join my lady wife. And you'd better rescue the fair Ms. Kennedy. When I last saw her, Alan Lindell was plying her with champagne and tales of insider trading." He winked at Morgan. "Keep taking that vitamin E, lad."

Morgan turned to watch Sandy disappear back inside the tent, and a faint smile played across his lips. He gave the man a few minutes to lose himself in the crowd, then he ground out his cigar and went in search of Robin.

"Run that again in slow motion."

"That *was* slow motion."

"Jesus!"

Adam had been studying videotapes in the darkened

editing suite for an hour now, trying to analyze what the superplayers were doing and how. Even in slow motion, the men seemed to be reacting instantaneously.

Seated at the client desk, a stack of videotapes beside him and a cold beer in his hand, Adam shook his head in disbelief. "Go back about two minutes and play it again, Frank," he said. "Can you slow it down some more?"

"Sure thing." Frank Jacoby, the videotape editor, sat at the Grass Valley switcher, a printed shot log beside him. He hit a few buttons and the videotape rewound, paused, and began to play again. "You want another Coke, help yourself," he told Adam. "I think there's more pizza back there, too." The remains of their impromptu dinner littered a low table at the rear of the small, windowless room.

"I'm okay," Adam told him. "You?"

"Sure, I'll have one more. Big time Saturday night, you know?"

Frank was a tall, rangy man in his midforties. He and a partner had built up a lucrative post-production facility that catered mainly to advertising agencies. Housed in a loft in the Chelsea section of Manhattan, VideoPort boasted the latest in digital editing technology. With the technical "toys" at his disposal, there was nothing the man couldn't do to a video image.

Together they watched Ernie Sanchez pick the man off at second again. Even in very slow motion, he was moving pretty damn fast.

Looking thoughtful, Frank finished his cola and aimed the empty at a nearby wastebasket. The can hit the rim, bounced up, and plopped inside. Adam rose and stretched, then searched through the detritus of dinner for an unopened can. He tossed the soda to Frank, who popped the top and sipped, then reached over and set it carefully on Adam's desk. Food or drink anywhere near the switcher was a recipe for disaster.

"Where'd you say these tapes came from?" Frank asked.

"I didn't. Actually, Dennis Locke got them for me."

"The baseball commish?" Frank said, impressed.

"Er, yes. A friend of mine knows him, asked if he'd help me out with this, uh, research project of mine."

"Uh-huh." Frank's curiosity had been piqued when Adam had called him about viewing tapes of the superplayers. He'd offered him free use of one of the studios, with Frank as his editor, if Adam could work on a weekend night when the room wasn't booked by a paying customer. Now, as he watched the footage with Adam, he realized there was more here than Adam was willing to talk about.

"Hey, you still racing?" Adam asked. An avid dirt biker, Frank had banged up his knee in competition some years back, which was how the two men had met.

"Yeah, some. Susie's always at me to give it up. Says I'll kill myself one of these days. Probably right. You want me to give you a frame by frame of this play?"

"That would be great."

Frank hit some more buttons, and the image of Ernie Sanchez jerked across the screen one frame at a time . . .

"Will you look at that?" Frank exclaimed. "They both started moving at the same time."

"Huh?"

"Here, I'll run it again . . ." Frank's fingers flew across the switcher buttons. "See? The runner's just starting to move his right foot, and Sanchez's arm is already going back . . ."

"You're right. Jesus."

"Let's check out that double out of Reese's in the game against Cleveland last month," Frank said, excited now. He shuffled through the shot log which listed in detail the material on each of the videotapes. "Hand me tape three-oh-seven." Adam slid the plastic cassette across the desk and Frank slipped it into one of the playback machines. He scanned forward quickly, looking for the time code number that matched the one in the log, then pushed "play." "First, let's look at it in normal speed."

"Pretty impressive."

"No shit. Now I'll slow it down and run it again . . ."

Almost before the ball came off the bat, they could see Kenny Reese moving to his left, heading toward where the ball would eventually arc down, his glove angled just right to scoop it out of the air.

"How the hell did he know?" Adam demanded.

Frank just shook his head. "Watch," he said.

With absolutely no pause, Reese whirled around and threw to third to make the second out.

"There was no one on second," Frank said. "The runner at third didn't have to go. There was no reason to think he'd go; look at his stance. But Reese didn't even hesitate. He didn't even look at third before he threw!"

"Actually, he *did* look," Adam corrected him. "Take it back and run it frame by frame. See? See there? Reese looked over at the runner on third all right, but so fast, he couldn't have taken in what he saw, processed it, and turned it into action."

"He couldn't, but he did."

"Yeah, he did." Adam paused, thinking. "It's not just that he's reacting faster. It's like he's actually *thinking* faster."

"Anticipation is the name of the game."

"So all the sports announcers keep telling us. But this isn't just anticipation we're seeing here, Frank. It's ... something else."

"You mean he really *is* thinking faster?" Frank asked. "Like, he's taking in information faster and processing it faster? Is that possible?"

"I don't know," Adam said slowly. "But ... it's like that amazing catch of Freeman's in the second game of the season, remember? When everyone—on the field, in the stands, on the bench—*everyone* thought it was gone, a home run, no question? But Freeman made this amazing leap and caught it halfway over the fence. It took him about a nanosecond to make up his mind to go after the ball. A second, and I mean *one second* later, and that ball was gone!"

"Let's run some of the at-bats again," Frank said. He riffled through the shot log. "Tape three-thirty-one and thirty-two ..." But Adam sat motionless. "Something wrong?"

"Look, Frank," Adam said slowly. "About what we're doing here tonight. I don't want to read about it in the newspaper or hear about it on the street, okay? We need to keep this just between the two of us. Are you okay with that?"

Frank swung around in his chair. "Adam," he said, "we do a lot of work for advertising agencies. We create animatics that test new campaign ideas. We make commercials they use to pitch new accounts. If we ever talked about what goes on here, every day of the week, we'd be out of business in five minutes." He took a swig of soda and set the can down on the desk again. "Now let's run some of those at-bats, okay?"

For the next half hour, they ran all three superplayers' at-bats; then they ran more fielding tapes. They slowed them down, speeded them up, single-framed them, blew up the images for close-ups; they even ran them in reverse. There was no question about it. At bat, all three superplayers knew instantly where the ball would come in over the plate, how fast it would be traveling, what the angle would be. No wonder they were all batting over .300. In the field, they knew in a flash exactly how the ball would come off the bat, where it would go, and how long it would take to get there. They decided within seconds precisely where to throw the ball, and they threw it there with speed and accuracy. They consistently made good, fast, defensive and offensive plays, and they made them look easy.

It really does seem like they're thinking faster, Adam mused. Like something's happening in the brain. But what? Meditation? Vitamin therapy? MIEs? I don't, I won't believe that. What am I missing here?

"So what do you think, Adam?" Frank asked at last. "Steroids?"

"They've tested negative for all drugs, steroids included."

"That why the commish put you onto this?"

"I never said that."

"You didn't have to." Frank glanced at his watch. "It's ten-thirty. You want to keep going, or what?"

Adam sighed. "I guess not. We've seen everything there is to see. Buy you a beer?"

"Thanks, but I'd better head home." Frank began the process of shutting down the switcher, while Adam packed the Comets cassettes into two cartons. A VideoPort messenger would return them to Dennis Locke in the morning.

"I'm heading up to the Lincoln Tunnel," Frank said. "Drop you somewhere?"

"I think I'll walk for a while."

Frank punched his arm lightly. "You worry too much, man. I mean, you know they're not on drugs, right? Maybe they're just really good."

Adam smiled. "You're probably right. Thanks again for the studio time."

"No problem." Frank waved and headed for his parking garage, and Adam walked slowly north. Maybe Frank's right, he thought; maybe they *are* just really good.

Good enough to bat .375 his first season, like Reese was doing? Good enough to change from a lackluster pitcher into a no-hitter hero in six months, as Sanchez had done? Good enough to reach up and pluck home runs out of the sky without even thinking, as Freeman did?

Bullshit, he thought. Nobody's that good.

Chapter Six

"You didn't waste any time," Felicity said dryly. She speared a shrimp and cut it neatly in half.

"Neither did you," Morgan reminded her.

Felicity shrugged. "Caleb and I are just friends."

Morgan swallowed the retort that rose to his lips and instead shifted his gaze to the elegant, intimate room in which they sat, and the decorative garden beyond. Housed in a brownstone on East Fifty-fourth Street, Raphael had long been one of his favorite restaurants. Trust Felicity to remember that, and to arrange to meet him here and ruin it for him.

She swirled the shrimp around in its pink sauce. "I'm not sure I like the idea of you bedding your mistress in my house."

"*Your* house?" Morgan exclaimed, swinging around to face her again. "High House is mine."

"Only temporarily. I might decide to sell it." Felicity popped the shrimp into her mouth and chewed meditatively. "Too bad you're such a bad money manager, Morgan."

"That's not fair. I needed the money to—"

"Yes, yes, I know. You always have a good reason for needing more of my money." She sipped her Perrier and blotted her lips delicately with the starched white napkin. "Britt says she's very beautiful."

Morgan allowed himself a small, self-satisfied smile. "I think she is," he said.

"And very young. And a journalist. Do you think that's quite wise?"

"Which part?"

Felicity fixed him with an icy stare. "Don't play silly buggers with me, Morgan," she said. She dipped another piece of shrimp in sauce and ate it. "You've looked over the papers?"

Morgan sighed and nodded. "You're rapacious," he said.

"You don't have to sign."

"I wish that were true."

Felicity pushed back her plate and reached into the large i santi handbag beside her on the banquette. "I've brought three clean originals that I've already signed." She held out the papers. "And the check, of course."

"God, Felicity, can't I finish my lunch first?"

"Suit yourself," Felicity replied, replacing the documents in her bag. "You were the one who was so very anxious to do this."

Morgan cut into a softshell crab, then changed his mind and reached for his Scotch. His appetite was gone. "Okay, hand them over."

"Whatever you say," Felicity replied cordially as she pulled out the papers again. Morgan drank deeply, then set down the glass and took out his silver pen. "The third copy's yours," she told him brightly. She watched carefully as he signed the three sets of documents and passed two back to her. She placed them carefully in her handbag, then pulled a long white envelope from a side flap. She slid it across the table toward him. "A pleasure doing business with you."

"I'll bet." Morgan opened the envelope and pulled out the check. It was pink, and covered with drawings of flamingos. "Cute," he said.

"You didn't used to be so critical of my checks," she said, "back when I financed your company. Or when you sold me your share of High House. Or when—"

"Okay, okay. Enough." Morgan tossed the empty envelope on the table and shoved the check in his jacket pocket.

"With you it's never enough." She looked around for the waiter. "Coffee?"

"I don't think so," Morgan told her.

"Oh, keep me company. A cappuccino," she told the young man.

"Yes, madam. Anything for you, sir?"

"Nothing, thank you." When the waiter had gone, Morgan turned back to Felicity. "We've had our differences," he said earnestly. "But we don't have to be enemies, do we?"

"I don't know, Morgan. Do we?"

"I hope not."

Felicity reached over and patted Morgan's hand. "You've got it wrong again, dear," she said. "You're supposed to say that before I give you money, not after."

Morgan pulled his hand away as though he'd been burned. Damned woman.

"Unless you think you're setting me up for next time," she continued, "in which case you needn't bother. This is it, Morgan. This is the last of my money you're going to get."

"I hope it's the last I'll need."

"I hope so, too. You have nothing left to sell me."

"This is a loan, Felicity. A loan against my shares of the company as collateral."

"Of course. My mistake. Although you've never been very good at paying back loans, have you?" She smiled. "I would say that, oh, six months from now, when the first payment is due me, I'll own rather a lot of Hudson and Company stock." Her coffee arrived, and she sipped it slowly. "Caleb thinks it would be an interesting idea to take it public."

"Public?" Morgan flushed with anger. "You tell Caleb to keep his fucking hands off my company."

"Well, it *is* what he does. And it really isn't your company anymore, is it? At least, it won't be, once you miss that first payment."

"I won't miss it," Morgan told her grimly.

"Well, I can't imagine where the money's to come from," Felicity said pleasantly. "Caleb's studied your company thoroughly." She turned and signaled to the waiter. "Check, please."

Morgan sat fuming. So he'd miss the first payment,

would he? Felicity had no idea of the amount of money he could get for the Comets if they won the pennant. And they would; they had to. The Comets were his only hope.

The waiter placed a leather wallet containing the check in the middle of the table. With a slim, polished forefinger, Felicity pushed it over toward Morgan. "Thank you for a lovely lunch, dear," she told him.

"Fuck you."

"Every word a poem." Felicity rose, gathering up her hat and her handbag. "Take good care of my company," she said. Before he could answer, she was gone.

The dun-colored concrete cubicle was more like a bunker than an office. Down beneath the stands and just off the team dressing room, the office shared by the manager and several coaches was packed tight with desks, chairs, and a small spartan sofa. At Morgan's request, Jim Warfield, the Comets' general manager, had commandeered it for the Kenny Reese interview. That interview was nearly over now, much to Warfield's relief. He'd heard that Robin Kennedy was involved with Morgan romantically, but she was still a reporter. And Warfield had been warned repeatedly to be wary of reporters. How far was he supposed to let her go with Reese? Morgan had supervised the interviews the woman had done with Freeman and Sanchez; Warfield would have felt more comfortable if Morgan had been available for this one, too. Never mind, he told himself; Reese had batting practice in fifteen minutes. He turned his attention back to the young player, seated at one of the desks across from Robin and talking animatedly. Kenny's ability to charm the press as well as his fellow players had become legendary. Yet there was nothing put-on about it. The boy was naturally good-natured and friendly.

"Doesn't it get lonely?" Robin was asking. "Do you miss your family?"

Kenny nodded. "It does and I do," he said. "But Amy and I talked about it when the offer first came. And we decided it would be best if she and the kids stayed out West. We didn't know how this superplayer thing would go, and we didn't want to uproot everybody if ... if things didn't work out."

"But things have worked out very well, wouldn't you say?"

"Yeah, just great. So far."

"You sound a little unsure," Robin said nicely. "Anything wrong?"

"Of course nothing's wrong," Jim Warfield said quickly. "Kenny's just a little tired, right, fella? He's been playing hard lately."

"I always play hard," Kenny replied. His tone was neutral, but his eyes made it obvious that he resented Warfield's hand-holding. "And I'm not tired. It's just, well, sometimes it feels too good to be true." He gave Robin a wide, ingenuous smile. Warfield scowled and made a note on the pad in front of him.

"But it *is* true," Robin said. "So do you think you might change your mind and bring your family East next season?"

"Life in Boulder is very different from life in New York City," Kenny said. "Amy's happy out there, the kids are happy. I'm on the road so much, and busy training ... I'd love to have them here, but I have to think about what's best for them. Not that it's easy," he added wistfully.

"How old are your children?"

Kenny beamed. "Two and four. One boy, one girl."

"I bet they're proud of you."

"They call me after every game. Hey, when is your story going to come out, Ms. Kennedy? Amy's keeping a scrapbook."

Robin smiled, flattered. "I'll get you some nice clean reprints," she promised. She consulted her pad. "Well, we seem to have covered most of my questions ... One last thing: I wonder if you could talk a little about your personal opinion of the special training. Those strange MIE machines I saw, for example—"

Warfield was on his feet. "I don't think this is really

necessary, Ms. Kennedy. Kenny's already given you twenty minutes this afternoon—"

"I don't mind talking about it, Mr. Warfield," Kenny said. "The MIEs are really—"

"Kenny, please. We'd really prefer that you not discuss the training with the press."

"Sure, Mr. Warfield," Kenny said, his blue eyes innocent and friendly. "I know that. Only, I thought she was different from the other reporters. She's already seen the training room, and Mr. Hudson said—"

"I know what Mr. Hudson said," Warfield told him. "But she's still a reporter, and you can't be too careful what you—"

"Hey, there's no reason to insult the lady," Kenny said pleasantly. "I'm sure Ms. Kennedy wouldn't write anything you didn't want her to." Shit, Robin thought. I'm back in the advertising business. "And she doesn't try to trap you into saying things you don't want to, like those other reporters sometimes do," Kenny continued. He turned to Robin. "Ernie and Otis said you were real nice to talk to."

"Thanks, Kenny. I enjoyed talking to them, too." And Morgan wouldn't let me bring up the training with them, either.

"Anyhow, Mr. Warfield, I know when to talk and when to shut up," Kenny said earnestly. "I don't want some other team reading about our techniques."

"I know you don't," Warfield said. "And you're right; I was out of line. Ms. Kennedy, I apologize. Now, Kenny's got batting practice in a few minutes, but I have a thought. Why don't you write down any questions that didn't get answered today, and I'll get you written responses."

Like hell you will, Robin thought. But of course she had an inside track with Morgan, she reminded herself. She'd just have to make him understand that she needed freer access to the superplayers. Surely she could convince him. Hadn't he already gotten her inside the Pro Club? "Good idea," she said. She rose and held out a hand to Kenny. "Thanks so much for your time. Is it okay if I watch you practice?"

He beamed at her. "Sure!" he said. "Uh, if it's all right with Mr. Warfield." Warfield nodded. "Good. See ya out there!"

Warfield stood, too, and together he and Robin made their way along the dark concrete corridors and out onto the field. He seated her in the third row of stands just above and to the right of the batting range.

The warm sunshine felt good to Robin after the dark innards of the stadium. She and Warfield made small talk until Kenny appeared, smiling and high-fiving the other players. Together they watched him amble toward the batting coach. He chose a bat, swung it several times, and moved toward the backstop. Suddenly he paused, an expression of pain on his face. He dropped the bat and put his hands to his head. The batting coach took a step toward him.

Robin leaned forward. "What's wrong?" she asked. "What's happening?"

"Nothing," Warfield told her lightly, but his eyes were serious. "Please stay here." He moved quickly down the steps and out onto the field.

Kenny waved the coach away and reached down for the bat, shaking his head as though to clear it. The coach hesitated, then walked up to Kenny and put an arm around his shoulder, his face solicitous. But Kenny shook him off angrily, an expression of pure rage on his face, and, lifting his bat menacingly, he began to shout. Robin could hear the crude words carried on the breeze. The coach quickly backed off. Everyone else on the field seemed frozen, stunned not so much by the language as by the fact that it was coming from Kenny Reese, Mr. Congeniality.

Then as suddenly as it had started, it stopped. Kenny dropped the bat and looked around in bewilderment. He began to speak softly. Robin couldn't hear the words, but it was obviously an apology, because the mood on the field perceptibly lightened. With an embarrassed smile, Kenny picked up the bat again and took up his position in front of the backstop.

Warfield came bounding up the stadium steps. "Just a little headache," he reported. "Came on suddenly, then went away. Pure stress. These guys work hard!"

"He didn't seem like a guy under stress."

"Probably keeps it all inside," Warfield said. "Worst thing you can do. But he's just fine now. See?"

Out on the field, Kenny was swinging away, sending balls deep into left field. The batting coach called out to him, and he grinned and gave the man a thumbs-up. The next ball went speeding down the first base line.

Warfield glanced over at Robin. "Everybody gets headaches now and then," he said. "Bet you do, yourself." Out on the field, Kenny was laughing and joking and attempting to balance the bat on one finger. Warfield settled back in his seat and folded his arms behind his head. "Believe me," he told Robin with a friendly smile, "you and I should be as healthy as Kenny Reese."

Chapter Seven

Late July

Adam tossed his bloody scrubs into the red plastic-lined bin and yanked open his locker. The procedure had taken longer than expected, and he was running late. He hoped Robin would understand. Helen never had.

He exited the room at a trot, smoothing his hair with his fingers. The elevator was slow as usual, so he opted for the stairs, taking them two at a time and arriving at the orthopedics department offices on the third floor twenty minutes late and only slightly out of breath.

"I put her in your office and got her some coffee," Beth, the department secretary told him. "How'd it go?"

Adam gave her a thumbs-up, brushed his mustache with a fingertip, and pushed through the door. As assistant chief of the department, Adam rated a small but cheerful cubicle, complete with phone, computer terminal, desk, and three comfortable chairs. Robin was seated in one of them, reading, Adam was amused to see, his recent copy of the *Journal of Orthopedics*. She looked up expectantly as he entered.

"Please forgive me," Adam said. Her skin was lightly tanned and her bright hair was pulled back and gathered in a green band that matched her printed cotton dress. "You look far too lovely to be kept waiting this long."

"You're forgiven," she assured him with a smile. "But if this is a bad time—"

"Not at all." Adam started around his desk, then thought better of it and chose the chair next to her. "The patient's in Recovery and I'm all yours. How's the article coming?"

"Pretty well, I think. Considering."

"Considering what?"

Considering the fact that someone carefully coached the superplayers before I was allowed to ask them about the training. Considering the fact that everything I've got feels somehow hollow. Aloud she said, "Considering I haven't finished my research."

"Haven't you spoken with the superplayers yet?"

Robin nodded. "Oh yes, several times. They were a little guarded about the special training at first. But I explained to Morgan that I needed to be able to talk freely with them, and he was very helpful."

"So you've met the guys," Adam said. "Sanchez ... Freeman ..."

"Yes, and Kenny Reese. He's my favorite."

Adam laughed. "He's everyone's favorite. I've gotten to know him a little through the Pro Club. Nice guy. And an excellent ballplayer."

"That's the understatement of the year. Did you see that triple he hit last week?"

"You were there?" Robin nodded. "More research?" he asked with a smile.

"You could say that."

Of course, Adam reminded himself; she's Morgan Hudson's girlfriend.

"Actually, I've seen more baseball these past few months than I have in my whole life," Robin exclaimed. "It's a great game." She pulled a manila folder from beneath the orthopedics journal, and offered it to him. "Now, I know you're busy, so I'll try to be brief. This is the rough outline of the article, with your quotes marked in yellow. I don't want to misquote you, and I'd also appreciate your opinion of the rest of it. Especially what I say about the special training. It's a delicate issue."

"I don't see how it would be."

"I don't just mean the need to protect trade secrets," Robin said quickly, "although that's important, too. But Morgan will advise me about that. What I want your help with is the way I explain what's happening, uh, scientifically."

"I understand," Adam said, reaching for the envelope. He took out the pages and began skimming through them. "I'd like to make a couple of changes to some of these quotes," he said at last. "Would you mind if I made a copy of this? I could revise the quotes and send it back to you."

"You can keep that copy," Robin told him. "And if you have any suggestions about the rest of the article, I'd really like to hear them. Maybe you could call me when you've had a chance to go through it."

"I'd be delighted to." He set the papers aside and leaned back in his chair and smiled at her. "Morgan Hudson's a lucky man," he said, then immediately thought, God, what a stupid thing to say.

Robin colored slightly. "Yes, the Comets just keep on winning."

"The Pro Club's not doing badly, either," Adam said quickly. "New members keep popping up every day. You planning on interviewing the owner?"

"The owner of the Pro Club? Are you kidding? The man's a recluse."

"Morgan tell you that?"

"Yes," Robin said, bridling at his tone. "He's apparently a very private person. Ever see him at the club?"

Adam shook his head. "I asked Connor about him a couple of times, but he went all quiet and distant."

"Morgan says he's fabulously rich. He invests his money secretly, and hates publicity." She paused. "The press has been trying to get hold of him for months, you know."

"Sounds mysterious."

Robin shrugged. "Not nearly as mysterious as the way that supertraining works," she told him, surprised to hear herself give voice to the thought. There was something about Dr. Adam Salt that inspired both confidence and confidences.

It was Adam's turn to look surprised. "You explained it pretty well in this article," he said, tapping the folder.

Robin nodded. "Yes, it sounds good on paper, but ... I guess what's bothering me is that it seems sort of ... flaky."

"Flaky? May I quote you, Ms. Kennedy?"

Robin laughed. "Please don't! It's just, all that stuff about meditation and light patterns ... it's so ... sixties. But maybe I'm thinking too narrowly. I mean, Zen tennis works; you said so yourself. Why not this?"

"Why not indeed?" Adam said noncommittally. It would be pretty stupid to reveal his own misgivings to Morgan Hudson's girlfriend, charming though she was. Certainly not if he hoped to learn more about the superplayers. He felt a pang of shame at the idea of using this lovely, rather trusting young woman. But I'm not doing it for myself, he thought. I'm doing it for baseball. That made him feel a little better, but not much.

Robin rose and reached for her straw bag. "Well, I'll look forward to your opinion of what I've written." She paused. Should she mention that sudden headache of Kenny's? she wondered. But Adam seemed to have such faith in the technique. Those MIE machines had actually made sense to him when they'd toured the training room together. He'd probably laugh it off, tell her she was being silly. We all get headaches, he'd say. And he'd be right. "Well, I've taken up enough of your time." She reached out her hand to shake his.

He stood, too, and took her hand in both of his. Her skin was smooth and pleasantly warm. "Not at all. In fact, if you're free for lunch ..."

"I'm afraid not," she said, disentangling her fingers. "Maybe another time." In fact, Robin had nothing on her calendar until three o'clock, but Adam's comment about Morgan being a lucky man, the way he'd taken her hand, the way he was looking at her now, all made her more than a little uncomfortable. She wondered whether she would feel the same discomfort if Adam weren't so attractive.

"Well, it was a pleasure seeing you again," he said. "I'll call you when I've looked over this material, and we can arrange to meet and discuss it."

"That would be very helpful," Robin answered. Again she paused. There was something terribly likable about Adam. But she was quite happily involved with Morgan, thank you very much. How could she make him understand her position without being rude? An idea occurred to her. "Morgan and I are having a party at his town house, two weeks from Saturday," she told him, "to celebrate the Comets' winning streak. Perhaps you'd like to come."

That puts me in my place, Adam thought, amused. And quite right, too. "I would, very much," he said easily. "I have nothing but admiration for the way Morgan's turned my favorite team around. I'm looking forward to meeting him."

"I'll send you an invitation," Robin promised. "Feel free to bring a date."

"Oh, I think I'll batch it," Adam said with a smile. "Let me walk you to the elevator."

When Robin had gone, Adam attacked the paperwork piling up on his desk, and returned the many phone calls that had come in while he'd been in the OR. It was a good morning to get such things out of the way. His first private patient wasn't due until three, and the hospital was only four blocks from his private office.

By one-thirty his stomach was telling him in no uncertain terms that it was time for lunch. The hospital cafeteria or a sandwich from the deli? Easy choice.

Out on the street it was hot and humid, with dark clouds lowering. Adam stripped off his white hospital jacket and slung it over his shoulder as he made his way through the midday crowd. He'd picked up a cheese and tomato sandwich at a local deli and was still several blocks from his office when the clouds burst, sending pedestrians scattering. In seconds his brown bag disintegrated, landing his lunch in a puddle. A national bookseller had recently opened a megastore just down the block and Adam ducked into it, drenched and annoyed.

The smell of fresh coffee filled his nostrils. To one side of the large, carpeted and paneled store, two women were dispensing cappuccino. Adam immediately felt better.

Soon he was leaning against the brass rail that separated the coffee bar from the books, sipping the foamy brew gratefully. Outside, the rain was still pelting down. Surely it couldn't continue at that rate, he thought. He decided to wait ten minutes and make a run for it.

Meanwhile, a bookstore was a good place to be. He finished his coffee and, unfamiliar with the layout of the store, began to roam the aisles. Perhaps the new Robertson Davies book was in. Adam didn't have much time for reading fiction, but Davies was special. And what was that book Dr. Jameson had recommended, something about chemistry and conscious states . . . ? He'd just passed Computers and was coming up on Psychology when he saw a familiar figure. Hunched down in an effort to be inconspicuous, his smart blue blazer spotted with rain, Kenny Reese was scanning the Chemistry section. He held a crumpled paper in his hand. Adam watched him refer to the paper, then back to the shelves, and finally shake his head in defeat.

"A little light reading?" Adam asked, coming up beside him.

"What? Oh, hi, Dr. Salt, uh, Adam. Yeah, I've got this reading list, but they don't seem to have a lot of the books here."

"May I see it?" Adam studied the list. "Are you sure you want to read these?" he asked. "Some of them are rather . . . complicated."

"You think I can't understand them?" Kenny asked a touch belligerently.

"I didn't say that," Adam assured him. "Actually, we probably have some of these in the medical library at the hospital. I'll borrow them for you if you like."

Kenny was immediately all smiles. "Would you? That'd be great."

"Sure. Only I'm curious. Why is one of the world's greatest baseball players interested in reading chemistry textbooks?"

"I was a chemistry major in college. You look surprised," he added, seeing Adam's expression. "I graduated from Colorado State. Someday, I'm going back to grad school." Kenny studied Adam for a moment, as if trying to determine his attitude. "I keep in touch with several of my old professors. They send me reading lists now and then ... chemistry, biology." He looked at Adam hopefully. "I'd really appreciate your help with these books."

"I'll be happy to do what I can." Kenny passed Adam the list and he put it in his pocket, glancing at his watch as he did so. "I've got about half an hour before my next appointment. You want to grab a bite? I'd like to hear more about your studies." And about the Supertraining, he thought. But I better not rush things.

Kenny hesitated. "I've got a meeting with my agent and my attorney at two-thirty, but the office is just around the corner. Actually, I could go for some pizza."

"Good. There's got to be a place nearby." The two men started toward the front of the bookstore. "Big doings?"

Kenny beamed. "The biggest. I'm about to sign a terrific endorsement contract." He lowered his voice. "I can't talk about it until it's been announced in the press. You understand."

Adam nodded. "Congratulations on whatever it is. You've earned it."

"Thanks. Uh, Adam, about those books ..." Kenny gestured vaguely at the shelves around them. "Don't mention it to anyone, okay?"

"Okay," Adam said. "But why?"

Kenny shrugged. "It's just the way I feel about it."

"It's your call," Adam told him. "Let's go get some food."

There was a small pizzeria down the street from the bookstore, and the two men hurried to it through the rain. People turned and stared as Kenny went by, and the pizza chef and counterman both asked for his autograph.

"Must be tough to have a private life," Adam said when they were seated. "Doesn't it get to you?"

"I try not to let it," Kenny said. "I'm so lucky to be playing pro ball, and making all this money. I'd feel like a shit if I didn't give something back."

"You do, Kenny. You give something back, every game you play."

"I guess. But autographs and interviews and being stopped in the street come with the territory, you know? Anyone who chooses to play pro ball, they have to know what they're getting into." Kenny took a large bite of his regular pizza with extra cheese. "What's that stuff you're eating?" He looked over at Adam's plate. "Doesn't look like any pizza I ever saw."

"Sun-dried tomatoes, broccoli, and fresh buffalo mozzarella."

"You've gotta be kidding."

"Want a taste?"

"Not me." Kenny signaled the counterman for another slice, regular, and sipped his Diet Coke. "It was nice running into you like this," he told Adam ingenuously. "I don't get to see many people who aren't in the game, just other players, managers, coaches, trainers ... They're pretty nice guys, most of them, but sometimes I feel kind of ... isolated. Not that I'm complaining," he added quickly. "It gives me more time for my books."

"Chemistry and biology?"

"That, too. But what I meant was, I've been making a thorough study of the games and the players. I have about a dozen notebooks filled with my observations."

"Really?"

"Oh, absolutely. See, everybody has his own way of playing. Sure, we all operate on instinct to a certain extent, and on what we've learned about the pitchers we've faced, and so forth. But we all have our own individual styles. Me, I'm a ... cerebral player. At least, that's how the college paper used to describe me. Cerebral." Kenny grinned and took in a mouthful of pizza, chewing and swallowing vigorously. "I study the pitchers I'm likely to face," he continued. "I study the other teams' fielders. I'm taking notes all the time. I write down the observations after each game I play. I do the same thing when

I watch games on TV. And I'm constantly reviewing what I know. So when I walk up to the batter's box, I can practically tell you what the pitcher had for breakfast." Adam laughed appreciatively. "And after every game, I inspect my bat. I mean, I really study it, check where the marks are on it so I can see exactly where I made contact with the ball. Than I clean it with alcohol, so I can see the new marks next time."

Adam shook his head in admiration. "Whatever your system is, it sure works." He smiled at the enthusiastic young shortstop. Catchers, center fielders, and shortstops tended to be the brightest players in baseball, and Kenny, a shortstop, was no exception. "And you still find time to read chemistry textbooks?"

"I love the game," Kenny said, "but I have to think of the future."

"Plenty of time for that," Adam assured him. "You've got a long, illustrious career ahead of you."

But Kenny's eyes were serious. "I could get injured," he said. "I could lose my edge." He finished his soda, checked his Rolex watch, and reached for his wallet. "Nobody plays forever."

The elevator opened silently and Kenny stepped out and looked around, immediately impressed. Previous meetings with his new attorney had taken place at Goldman and Associates, the foremost representative of athletes in the country and Kenny's agent. But the offices of Butler, Donofrio, and Shea made Randy Goldman's place look small-time.

Yards of expensive broadloom separated him from the vast semicircular reception area whose windows overlooked some of the most expensive real estate in the city. As he approached, an imposing receptionist in a tailored maroon suit and silk blouse smiled coolly at him from behind her walnut desk amid the antique tables, plush custom-made Chinese carpet, and deeply upholstered sofas and chairs.

"Kenny Reese, for Mr. Donofrio," he told her diffidently.

"Of course, Mr. Reese," she said pleasantly but impersonally. "Please have a seat. Mr. Goldman's already here. I'll tell them you've arrived."

Kenny glanced nervously at his watch. He wasn't late, was he? No, he was right on time. Goldman had gotten here early because he'd wanted to review the contracts one last time; he'd told Kenny that on the phone this morning. Relax, he told himself.

He smiled at the receptionist and wandered over to the sweep of windows. Man, what a view. Must cost plenty to have an office in this building. But of course Butler, Donofrio, and Shea were the best. He was lucky to have them acting for him. That thought, plus the impressive view, made him feel nervous again. Come on, guy, he told himself, don't be so awed. It's your money that's paying for this.

That made him feel better. He went and sat down in one of the overstuffed chairs, chewing the bubble gum he'd popped in his mouth after lunch. It was a habit he's picked up once he'd started playing for the Comets. Nearly everyone on the team, players, coaches, and managers, had something in his mouth most of the time. Kenny found it amusing the way the generations divided over the chew of choice. The older guys favored Red Man and Skoal Bandit, what they called 'smokeless tobacco'; they'd sit in the office or the locker room during strategy meetings, spitting into paper cups. The younger players shunned the sticky brown stuff, opting instead for Bazooka Bubble Gum or David's Sunflower Seeds.

Maybe he should get rid of the gum before he went into the meeting, he thought. He spat the gum into his hand and looked around for an ashtray, but there weren't any. No wastebaskets, either. Maybe the receptionist had one. He was just about to ask her when Larry Donofrio himself came out into the reception area.

"Kenny! Nice to see you." Donofrio exclaimed, offering his right hand in greeting.

"Hiya, Larry," Kenny said. The gum lay stickily in his right hand.

Donofrio stood waiting, hand extended, smiling at his

famous client. Kenny debated shoving the gum in his pocket, but decided the movement of his hand would be too obvious. Where were the goddamn ashtrays? Didn't anybody smoke anymore? Donofrio's smile was starting to wilt around the edges, and a puzzled look crept into his eyes. In desperation, Kenny gestured to the windows with his left hand. "Will ya look at that!" he exclaimed. Donofrio swung around and Kenny immediately dropped his right hand, pressed the sticky wad onto the side of the antique leather chair, and quickly wiped his damp fingers on his pants leg. "Amazing view," he finished lamely, standing and offering his now-gumless hand to Donofrio.

A long green marble table ran the length of the conference room. Around it were set twelve pale, upholstered chairs. A carafe of coffee and an assortment of sweet rolls had been placed on a side table. Larry Donofrio knew Randy's weakness.

Randy Goldman sat before a stack of contracts, a halfeaten cinnamon bun—his second—and a cup of coffee before him. Unlike Donofrio, who at fifty-six was slim, soft-spoken, and elegantly tailored, Goldman at thirtyfive was short and chubby, with unruly black hair and a penchant for wildly patterned ties. He laughed loudly and spoke his mind freely. Kenny was in awe of Larry Donofrio, but he liked and trusted Randy Goldman.

"Grab a chair, Kenny," Randy told him. "Coffee?"

"Sure." Kenny went and poured himself a cup, added sugar and cream, and sat down across from Randy. "Everything okay with the contracts?"

Randy grinned at him. "Everything's just great. Sponsor'll be here in half an hour for the signing."

"They're bringing a photographer," Larry said. "To immortalize the deal."

"And a nice fat check," Randy added, grinning. "Four million over two years. Make you a rich man, Kenny."

"You, too," Kenny said. Randy got fifteen percent of everything Kenny earned.

Randy laughed good-naturedly. "Good for all of us," he said.

"That reminds me," Larry interrupted. "You bring those eight by tens?"

Randy dug into his Mark Cross briefcase, a birthday gift from his wife, and extracted a manila envelope. "Clients always want autographed headshots for their walls," he told Kenny. "You'll wanna write something deeply personal. Like, 'To my good friend George, I'll never forget those nights in the turkish bath.'"

Donofrio gave Goldman a look. "Careful, Randy," he said. "The kid might take you seriously."

"He's hardly a kid, Larry," Randy told him. "And he's not stupid."

Larry scowled. "I was joking, for chrissake." He checked his 18-carat gold Omega Seamaster Professional Chronograph, waterproof to a depth of one thousand feet, so useful for practicing law in Manhattan. "Tempus fugit, Randy. I think you better tell him."

"Tell me what?" Kenny looked from Larry to Randy.

"Just something we have to get straight," Randy murmured. "Larry, would you mind stepping out of the room?"

"I've already told you I need to be present," Larry answered. "He's my client, too. Legally, I want to be able to say that I heard him being warned."

"Warned?" Kenny was on his feet. "Warned about what? What's going on?"

Randy sighed. "Sit down, Kenny. You're making me nervous."

"*I'm* making *you* nervous?"

Larry removed a newspaper clipping from a file in front of him and slid it across to Kenny. "Remember this?" he asked.

Kenny glanced at the article. "So what?" he said. "It happens to everybody."

"No. It doesn't happen to everybody," Larry said sternly. "And it especially doesn't happen to the clean-living, golden-haired, all-American spokesperson for Goodtimes Cola. Tell him, Randy."

"Go on, Randy," Kenny said. "Tell me. Tell me how a little fight in a bar in some jerkwater town that didn't even get into the papers aside from this local rag, is anybody's business but my own."

Randy sighed. "Kenny, you know better. You're in the spotlight these days. And once this endorsement contract's signed, it'll get worse."

"Yeah, well, the guy insulted me. He insulted the team."

"And you nearly killed him." Randy shook his head. "I don't understand it. You're one of the best-liked players in baseball; even-tempered, good to your mother, kind to animals ... Then all of a sudden, one night in a bar you jump on some poor asshole who's trying to look big in front of his friends, and you pound his head on the floor till the guy's unconscious. You know how much it cost us to hush that up?"

"You didn't do a very good job," Kenny said moodily, shoving the clipping in Randy's direction.

"You see it in the *New York Times*?" the agent demanded angrily. "The *Boston Globe*? The *Washington Post*? We did the best we could."

"He's right," Larry said. "As your attorney, I have to advise you in the strongest possible terms: curb your temper."

Kenny shook his head as if to clear it. "I don't remember the fight real well," he said. "The guy made a crack and something just sort of came over me. I ... I don't think I meant to hurt him. I'm sorry."

"I think you probably are," Randy told him sternly. "I've known some real shits in this business, and you're not one of them. But stress can do funny things to people. Fame, too. Success. If that's your problem, get some therapy, get a hooker, get something. But don't get angry. Are you listening, Kenny? You could lose your endorsements."

"Not to mention your Comets contract," Larr chimed in. "Fans are the lifeblood of the game. And they don't like a brawler."

"I'm not a brawler!" Kenny slammed his fist on the marble table. It made a satisfying sound but it hurt like hell. "What about Freeman? He gets in more fights than

I do. And how about when Sanchez went after that pitcher that nailed Jack Sandusky with a fastball last week? If we hadn't pulled him away, he would have—"

"Freeman and Sanchez are not my clients!" Randy roared, pulling himself upright. "*You* are my client. And I'm telling *you,* not Freeman or Sanchez or Sandusky or the goddamn man in the moon: control your fucking temper!"

In the angry silence that followed, the knock at the door sounded very loud. A secretary poked her head into the room. "Mr. Donofrio, the Goodtimes people are here."

Larry nodded. "Right on time. Is the champagne ready?"

"Two bottles on ice, Mr. Donofrio."

"Good." He turned back to Kenny and Randy. "Time to smile for the nice people who are about to pay us four million dollars."

Randy looked over at Kenny. "Sorry I yelled," he said.

"Yeah, me, too."

Larry beamed at them both, then turned to the waiting secretary. "Please ask the gentlemen with the deep pockets to join us."

The rain had stopped, but clouds still shrouded the late-night sky when Connor exited the darkened Pro Club and made his way toward the corner of the building. He stopped at the narrow, unlit alleyway that bounded the east side of the clubhouse. He glanced around at the quiet street, then slipped into the shadowy recess, moving quickly, his jacket brushing against the wet brick on either side. By the time he'd reached the halfway point, he could just make out the faint greenish glow of the control panel set into the right-hand wall some distance away. Green meant that Barrett had disarmed the system in anticipation of his arrival. Connor sighed with relief. He hated this place with its high, dark, enclosing walls. When the light glowed red, as it sometimes did, it meant that Barrett had forgotten. Then

Connor would have to wait in this narrow slit of an alley until Barrett got himself organized. Waiting in the alley always gave Connor the heeby-jeebies. Sadistic bastard, he thought. There was a perfectly good door to Barrett's quarters on the top floor of the Pro Club, carefully camouflaged and locked from the inside. Connor knew this because he'd lugged in the equipment for Barrett's personal gym that way. But Barrett had forbidden him to use it after that.

He closed his eyes and repeated his mantra several times to quiet his jumpy nerves, then pressed the talk button and identified himself. The lock released with a click, which echoed in the narrow canyon like a pistol shot. Pushing through the steel door camouflaged to look like the surrounding brick, he entered a minuscule foyer of cinderblock and cement.

Connor always found the interior stairs leading out of the foyer nearly as nervous-making as the alley. The stairway curled tightly around itself like a thin metal serpent, its narrow steps barely illuminated by low-level bulbs set at wide intervals along its sinuous length. A slow-moving two-person elevator ran in a narrow shaft set into the wall behind the spiraling stairs, but having tried it on his first visit, Connor had vowed never to enter it again. It was like being trapped in a vertical coffin.

He was breathing hard as he reached the fifth-floor level, but more from stress than exertion. A thin line of light bled from under the thick steel door before him. As he stepped onto the straw doormat, a blast of cold blue light hit him from above. He blinked in the sudden glare, turning to face the video camera bolted to the wall beside the door.

"Hello, Mr. Barrett," he said.

"Come."

Machinery hummed and the door slid open. Connor stepped inside.

The room he entered was low and dark, lit by antique wall sconces in the shapes of torches, and several desk and table lamps with shades of colored glass. The furniture, old and of excellent quality, was shabby and scratched and dirty. Wet glasses had left rings on the Chippendale desk, and stuffing leaked from beneath the pale cut-velvet upholstery of a Victorian sofa. Bach's Goldberg Variations played softly through the built-in speakers.

Picking his way through the books and files and packing cases that littered the floor, Connor made his way to his accustomed seat, a high-backed wooden chair with carved arms and ball-and-claw feet. The room was empty, but he was used to that; the boss liked to make an entrance.

No sooner was he seated than an interior door at the far end opened, an electrical hum filled the air, and Paul Barrett, who had watched Connor's entrance on his closed-circuit video system, rolled into the room.

Barrett wore a tight-fitting brown pocket T-shirt that emphasized the bulky muscles of his upper body, the result of frequent workouts with the exercise equipment he'd ordered Connor to install. But his pale eyes were cold and bitter. No workout ever invented could improve the withered legs that lay, pale and useless, beneath the plaid blanket.

He steered the wheelchair toward Connor, stopping to face him a short distance away. An angry scowl deepened the ugly lines that years of rage and jealousy had etched on his once-handsome face. "So the doctor's still here," he said. His voice, rarely used, was low and raspy, but his accent was clipped and precise. "You are a fool."

"Salt's okay," Connor assured him.

"Salt's a doctor. And you showed him the room." Barrett spun his chair away in anger. "You showed him the bloody room!"

"I told you, I had to. The girl insisted. Look, let's not keep going over this, okay? They bought the story."

"Maybe. Anyway, the girl doesn't matter. We can deal with her. But Salt . . ." Barrett brushed back his thinning hair, once thick and chestnut, now lank, faded, and graying.

"I tell you, Salt's okay. He's a member. The guys like him. Everyone says he's discreet."

"Salt's a doctor, dammit!" Barrett exclaimed. "A *sports* doctor. And you showed him the room."

"But he bought the story. I already told you what a help he was in selling it to the girl."

The older man shook his head impatiently. "Doesn't matter. He had to know better. Fools. I'm surrounded by fools." He sent the wheelchair trundling over to the cluttered desk. From a side drawer he drew a battered metal box, unlocked it with a key he dug from his shirt pocket, and raised the lid. He reached inside and withdrew a fistful of crumpled bills. Slowly he began to count out the money ... one hundred ... two ... "I don't know why I keep paying you," he said. "What good are you to me, anyway?"

Connor gripped the arms of his chair tightly. Ignore the old bastard, he told himself. Take his money and let him rave.

"The competition is dying to know how we do it," Barrett continued, reclosing the box and shoving it back inside the scarred desk. "So is the press. And so is the baseball commissioner—the first of your guided tours, as I recall." He began gathering up the wrinkled bills from the desktop.

"Be realistic, Mr. Barrett. I couldn't refuse the baseball commissioner."

"Well, you damn well could have refused Adam Salt." Barrett stared at the money in his hands, then looked over at Connor. "Secrecy is absolutely vital," he said sternly. "If Salt starts talking ..."

"He won't," Connor said.

"How in the bloody hell do you know?" Barrett demanded. He shoved the hand control sideways, then forward, and the heavy metal chair lurched around and headed straight for Connor, stopping abruptly when their knees were an inch apart. The first time Barrett had done this, Connor had leapt up in panic and Barrett had laughed. These days, Connor steeled himself not to move. The mean son of a bitch, he thought. One of these days, I might surprise him.

"You listen to me, lad," Barrett told him, eyes burning. "Nobody goes into that room but you and the superplayers from now on, get that? Nobody else."

"I only let the girl in because you said it was okay," Connor protested.

"I told you, the girl doesn't matter. Keep your eye on Salt."

Connor nodded resentfully. Barrett suspected everybody, hated everybody. Locked away up here like some crazy hermit, how could he know whether or not Salt could be trusted?

"You like money, Connor. I know you do. And if you want it to keep coming, you'll keep your mouth shut and do precisely as I say. Do we understand each other?"

"Yes, Mr. Barrett." Stupid bastard, Connor thought. He needs me as much as I need him. No, he needs me more.

Paul Barrett smiled unpleasantly. "There's a good lad." With a sudden convulsive movement, he tossed the fistful of crumpled hundreds in Connor's face. Some landed in his lap, others on the floor. "July," he said. "For services rendered. Go on, then. Don't you want it?"

Connor gripped the chair hard, his anger a white hot ball in his stomach.

"Well, if you don't want it . . ." Barrett reached over and plucked a bill from Connor's lap and waved it in front of Connor's face.

Connor's right hand came up fast, immobilizing Barrett's wrist in an iron grip. "It's my fucking money," he said. With his left hand, he plucked the bill from Barrett's fingers.

"For now," Barrett told him. "As long as you behave yourself." His eyes bore into Connor's as the two men stared at each other. Then slowly Connor released Barrett's wrist and dropped his hands into his lap. Barrett smiled mirthlessly and sent the wheelchair careening backward, his strong hands working the controls. "Pick up your money and get out."

Connor studied Barrett for a long quiet moment. Then he bent over and began gathering up the hundred-dollar bills.

Barrett watched disdainfully as Connor collected the bills, counted them, and shoved the wad in his pocket. Then he reached beneath his blanket for the hand-held radio control he used to unlock his front door.

The steel slab slid open and Connor was nearly through it when he paused and looked back. "Mr. Barrett," he said softly, "I'm sorry about your legs. But insulting me won't make them better." Barrett didn't reply. "I don't deserve to be treated like this."

"You don't deserve to run the Pro Club?" Barrett demanded angrily. "You don't deserve to be paid all that money?"

"You know what I mean," Connor said quietly. "Each time I come to see you, it's worse. Please, Mr. Barrett. Don't make me—" But here his nerve failed him, and he turned and scurried through the door. Barrett could hear his footsteps echoing down the dark stairway as the door slid closed behind him.

For a moment Barrett sat staring at the closing door. Then he swung around and headed back to the inner room from which he'd emerged. He hated Connor, hated his youth, his health, his strength; hated his wholeness.

Once he'd been like Connor, he thought bitterly: strong and fit, with muscular legs that carried him down the muddy playing field to score again and again. He gazed up at the photographs that covered the walls of his inner sanctum. Himself in the green-and-white uniform of his youth, running the ball toward the goal line, crashing through the opposition's defense, displaying the scars and bruising that were so much a part of that violent form of football called rugby . . .

. . . Himself, whole and strong, hearing the cheers of the crowd, basking in their adulation. Until that final, awful scrimmage when they carried him off the field for the last time, paralyzed below the waist. Hatred had boiled within him then and every day since then; it boiled within him now. Hatred of every man who could do what he could not.

A glass of wine sat on a nearby table; impulsively he hurled it at the wall in front of him. The glass shattered, raining shards onto the floor and splashing the photographs with red liquid. Shocked at what he had done, Barrett stared at the ruined pictures, and a guttural cry rose from deep within him. Sobbing, he levered himself half-out of the wheelchair and dabbed at the stains with a corner of his blanket.

Damn Connor, he thought fiercely. Damn all athletes. Damn their perfect bodies and the strength in their legs. I could have been better than any of them!

Chapter Eight

August

Another day, another party, Robin thought guiltily but happily, as she checked her makeup in the antique mirror that dominated one wall of Morgan's dressing room. She had recently turned down a lucrative freelance copywriting offer because it meant spending two weeks in Dallas, away from Morgan. And her article about the Comets was languishing on her desk at home, although it wouldn't take much to finish it. It wasn't that she didn't need the money, or that she was having too much fun to think about work. It was that, for the first time ever, Robin was giving herself permission to simply enjoy life. At least, she was trying to. For years, Robin had poured all her energies into learning and earning. Putting fun first was a new and pleasant experience, she reflected, but it took some getting used to.

She adjusted the neckline of Morgan's latest fashion fantasy. As usual, it was too tight and too low-cut, but, grateful for his continuing patience with her sexual incapacitation, she didn't have the heart to reject it.

People were beginning to arrive; she could hear the murmur of their voices filtering up the paneled stairwell. She wondered if Adam was downstairs, and whether, despite what he'd said about coming alone, he'd brought a date. She found herself hoping he hadn't, but then thought, why should his social life matter to me?

Carefully, she opened the black silk box and removed the antique earrings Morgan had just given her. She pushed the thin platinum backings through one earlobe, then the other. The small, delicate sapphire and diamond dewdrops exactly matched the blue of her cocktail dress. She'd never owned anything like them, never imagined she ever would. She loved them, loved Morgan for giving them to her. And yet she'd happily take Morgan without the earrings, she told herself. It was Morgan, not his money, that had attracted her.

And what had attracted him to her? Lately she'd begun to wonder. It was one thing to be shown off to his friends, another to be exploited, she mused, tugging the neckline of her dress upward again. But no, that was unfair. Morgan couldn't be sweeter. Or more patient. Still, there were times when, remembering what she'd written in the *Fortune* article, Robin wondered whether she'd been a little too dazzled by Morgan, a little too accepting of everything he'd told her. The replacement part for his private plane was taking forever to arrive, and the *New York Times* Business Section had carried a small piece about recent substitutions of cheaper ingredients in the formulas of some of Morgan's toiletries which some felt would reduce their efficacy. Could Morgan be short of money? She fingered the earrings—no, of course not. He was just a shrewd businessman. And airplane parts could well be scarce. Besides, he owned the most successful baseball team in the country.

Which brought her back to the unfinished Comets article.

The magazine was clamoring for it, but the truth was, she had misgivings about submitting the piece as it stood. Not that it was inaccurate, at least not so far as she knew. But she'd been getting strange vibes lately, first from Adam, who'd carefully watered down his quotes but been overly noncommittal about the rest of the piece, and then from Morgan, who was taking an inordinately long time to react to it. Surely, he wanted the article published; he'd been enthusiastic about the idea. Well, she'd sit on it a little while longer, she decided. She'd keep going to the home games and talking to the players ... She'd talk to Adam, maybe talk to Connor again ... see if she could develop any new insights into her own resistance to the story as she'd written it. The superplayers would be at the party this evening; maybe she'd be able to grab a moment alone with one of them. She gave the neckline a final tug and headed for the stairs.

Adam had indeed arrived. Drink in hand, he was talking animatedly with Kenny Reese and Otis Freeman. All three men had dressed for the occasion, but over his tailored trousers and silk shirt, Otis wore his trademark team jacket, customized with hundreds of shiny metal studs. Adam hailed Robin and, greeting the players, she took him away to meet Morgan.

Despite the friendliness of their smiles and the firmness of their handshakes, the two men studied each other carefully.

"I'm so pleased you could come, Dr. Salt," Morgan told Adam, his tone warm and welcoming. "I've heard a lot about you, and not just from Robin. You're quite a figure in the world of sports medicine, they tell me."

"Please call me Adam. And I've heard a great deal about you, too. Congratulations on the Comets."

"Thanks." Morgan flushed with pleasure. "It's an exciting time for all of us. By the way, I'm delighted you're helping Robin with the Comets article."

Are you? Adam wondered briefly, then pushed the idea from his head. Morgan certainly *looked* delighted. "My pleasure," he said, "although 'helping' is a little strong for the small contributions I've made."

"You're modest."

"Not at all. Anyway, I should be thanking you. I've been a Comets fan for as long as I can remember. This winning streak is a real thrill for me."

Morgan grinned. "For me, too. Hey, any time you want tickets to a game, just let me know."

Adam thanked him and the two men made casual conversation for a few minutes. Then Morgan excused himself to greet a recent arrival, and Adam turned to Robin. "Nice guy," he said, surprised to find he actually meant it.

"Yes, he is." Robin smiled.

"Nice place, too."

"You should see the rest of it. I didn't realize people actually lived this way."

"Some people do." Adam softened the remark with a smile. "So when will your article be published?"

"I'm . . . not sure. I want to do a little more polishing before I submit it." She'd taken a glass of champagne from the tray of a passing waiter; now she sipped it and looked around. Morgan stood at the center of a small crowd, laughing loudly. A group of Comets players stood off to one side, sipping soft drinks. They seemed a little self-conscious, out of place in the showy crowd, but pleased to have been included. Kenny Reese was alone at the buffet table. Perhaps this would be a good time to—

"Well, I'd love to monopolize you," Adam told her, "but I'm sure you want to circulate." He, too, had noticed Kenny alone at the buffet. "Great earrings, by the way." He touched her earlobe lightly, sending a thrill down her spine. For a moment, their eyes met. "Catch you later," Adam said softly. Reluctantly, he turned away.

Robin watched him amble toward the buffet table. What just happened here? she asked herself. Whatever it was, it was nice. Then she thought, Nice? What kind of reaction is that? You're in love with Morgan.

"Robin?" She turned. Morgan was smiling and waving her over. "You've got to hear this!" Returning his smile, she moved toward him through the crowd.

"So how are you getting along with those textbooks?"

Kenny looked up from the smoked salmon. "Hey, Adam. I meant to thank you, man, but I've missed you at the gym."

"My schedule got a little crazy the last couple of weeks," Adam told him.

"And the team's been traveling. Anyhow, thanks."

"You're welcome." Adam forked some salmon onto his plate. "Looks good."

"Only the best around here." Kenny's glance took in the paintings, the furniture, the guests.

Every seat in the large drawing room was occupied,

so the two men took their filled plates over to the rather grand stairway and sat on the steps. From this vantage point, Adam idly watched the crowd ebb and flow. Across the room, Morgan, addressing a group that had gathered around them, snaked an arm around Robin's body and pulled her against him. Then he said something that made everyone laugh. Even at that distance, Adam could see that Robin looked faintly embarrassed.

He turned his attention back to Kenny. Supplying the young player with textbooks had not been a completely unselfish act. Ever since that day in the bookstore, he'd made it a point to seek out Kenny at the gym, hoping that the growing trust between them would allow Kenny to speak to him about the supertraining. Now he began drawing Kenny out about the recent games the Comets had played, and the chances of a pennant win. Kenny responded with enthusiasm. After a few minutes, Adam mentioned he'd been consulting with Robin on her article about the Comets. Kenny had been interviewed by her, hadn't he? Yes, several times, Kenny said; he'd found her very easy to talk to.

"Of course, you can't tell a reporter everything, can you?" Adam asked. "About the special training, I mean."

Kenny looked puzzled. "Well, she's already seen the training room," he said. "But I don't go into the details, no."

"Why not?"

Kenny looked surprised. "You know why not, Adam. The competition finds out how we do what we do, they're gonna start doing it, too."

"I'm not so sure," Adam said. "Not everyone wants to take such chances."

"Chances?"

"With drugs. Steroids. Whatever it is they're giving you guys."

"Hey!" Kenny's face darkened. "What the hell—"

"I'm sorry I said it that way," Adam said quickly. "It's just ... look, I'm a doctor, and I've seen that training room. You and I both know those machines couldn't really produce those incredible reflexes, that—"

"I can't believe this!" Kenny exclaimed. "Are you accusing me of doing drugs? I thought you were my friend."

"I *am* your friend. But think about it, Kenny. just between us, nothing else makes sense."

"Sure it does. We have the MIEs, the—"

"—and the giant video screens and the meditation. Right. Sure. Listen, Kenny, you've studied chemistry and biology. You know damn well the so-called Supertraining couldn't possibly—"

"I'm not doing drugs!"

How hard should I push? Adam asked himself. How mad should I get him? He didn't want to lose Kenny's friendship, but pushing him to the limit was the only way he felt he could gauge how truthful Kenny was being with him, and how much he actually knew. "Come on," he said, putting a hand on Kenny's shoulder. "Level with me. What is it? A new kind of steroid that can't be detected on a standard test?"

Kenny stood, upsetting his empty plate. The fork bounced down the steps and clanged onto the marble floor. "Fuck you, Dr. Salt," he said angrily, his blue eyes blazing with indignation.

Adam got up and grabbed his arm. "I'm sorry. I apologize. But you've been to college, Kenny. You have a scientific background. You have to know there's more to this than the New Age crap. The other guys may believe it, but not you. You're too smart. You have to know better."

"Fuck you! I don't know anything." A blinding pain shot through his head and he staggered, then grabbed the banister to steady himself.

"What's wrong?" Adam asked quickly. "What's the matter?" He reached out a hand to help, but Kenny shoved him away, then leaned heavily against the railing, his eyes shut tight with pain.

Good going, doctor, Adam told himself angrily. You turn a new friend into an enemy and give him a cerebral hemorrhage into the bargain. Maybe you should go kick Morgan Hudson in the butt and poison the wine, just to round off the evening.

But Kenny was recovering quickly. He shook his head to clear it, and knelt to pick up his plate and fork. When he turned back to Adam, his face was calm and his eyes were clear. "I can understand why you think we're using drugs," he said softly. "But we're not. I promise you, we're not. I've taken science courses in school and yes, I agree that the supertraining seems, well, a little strange. But sometimes you just have to take things on faith, you know? Like our friendship. You've just accused me of something pretty slimy. But you also got me those textbooks. And you're helping Robin with her article. She's a real nice person, and Morgan Hudson trusts her and she trusts you. So I'm going to try and forget what you said today." He started for the drawing room, then stopped and turned back again. "But don't ever, ever, accuse me of taking drugs, Adam. You understand?" Adam nodded, and Kenny disappeared into the crowd.

So what did we learn from that little encounter? Adam asked himself. One: I believe Kenny's telling the truth, at least as far as he knows it. Two: Kenny's a very forgiving guy. And three: I don't think Kenny's ever going to discuss the training with me again. For a private investigator, I make a very good surgeon.

Kenny pushed through to the bar, requested a Coke, and downed it quickly. The headaches that had started after being hit in the head during that first brawl in Jacksonville had been getting worse since the fight in the after-hours club in Seattle, but he didn't dare tell anyone. As his agent had predicted, Morgan and the club manager had been furious with him when they'd heard about the Jacksonville incident. If word got out that he'd been fighting again, they might bench him. And there were his endorsements to worry about.

He rubbed his shoulder where the guy had smashed him with a pool cue last week. Well, he'd given as good as he'd gotten. Better, in fact. What had they been fighting about, anyway? It was all a sort of blur. Funny, he'd never thought of himself as a brawler. Must be the stress, he thought. God, he missed Amy.

He got himself another Coke and sipped it slowly, feeling lonely and depressed. How could Adam accuse him of taking drugs? Of course he wasn't taking drugs. He slumped into a vacant chair and watched the passing throng. I don't belong here, he thought. I belong back in Colorado with Amy and the kids, teaching high school chemistry and coaching Little League.

Don't be stupid, he told himself quickly. You know how lucky you are to be playing pro ball and making this kind of money? To be a superplayer? To be getting the special training?

The special training that Dr. Adam Salt, a highly respected sports doctor, had just called "New Age crap."

The other guys may believe it, but not you. You're too smart. You have to know better.

Kenny frowned. But I don't know better, he thought. I don't know anything at all.

"I saw you. At Morgan's party last week."

"I was drinking Coke!" Otis's eyes were wide and innocent.

"Yeah, Coke and whatever it was you poured into it from that flask in your pocket." Connor shook his head in anger and frustration. "You know the rules, Otis. No drinking, no drugging."

"Plenty of other guys on the team drink," Otis protested. He grabbed a towel from the cart and wiped the sweat from his face. "Why pick on me?" He turned angrily and began to walk away.

"We're not finished here." Otis swung around belligerently, but Connor's tone, low and dangerous, held him in check. "This training session is not over. And, to answer your question, you know fucking well why I'm picking on you, as you put it. You're a superplayer, dammit. You know the rule: No booze."

"Yeah, well, you listen to me, man," Otis retorted. "This team's playing better ball than it has for years, and a lot of that's due to me. So what if I break a goddamn rule now and then? What're they gonna do, trade me?"

"No, Freeman," Connor answered softly. "They won't trade you. They'll just stop giving you that special training."

The two men stared at each other for a beat. "They do, and I'll tell what I know," Otis said.

"And what, exactly, do you know?"

Otis waved a hand at the giant screen. "All this. How to do it."

"That would be a big mistake," Connor told him.

"Yeah, your mistake."

Connor studied the tall, powerfully built young man in front of him. He'd been such a nice, polite kid when Connor had first found him, modest about his athletic talent and so very grateful to be asked to join the Comets. But that had gradually changed over the past several months, and Connor found it troubling. He'd noticed a similar progression in the other superplayers; with success had come belligerence. Was this what happened when you became rich and famous? Aloud he said, "You think you could tell someone how to build this training room? You think you could do what I do?"

Otis shrugged, aware he'd gone too far.

"You listen to me, Otis. You're a helluva player. But you can't do it alone. Nobody can. You can't play alone, you can't train alone. You're part of a team. The Comets. The Pro Club. We win or we lose together. The rule about booze is a team rule. And if people break it, they're working against the team. Now, you're a superplayer, which means you're a very special, very important member of the team. And that means you have to be even better at following the rules. You're a leader on the field, and you have to be a leader off the field, too."

Otis lowered his eyes, abashed or resentful, Connor couldn't tell. Still, he gave Otis a small, encouraging smile. He really was a good kid underneath. But the boozing had to stop. "Now, you do those MIEs, then you take a shower, then you go home and empty all your liquor bottles down the toilet, you hear me?"

The MIE session progressed well, if silently. Otis was subdued and faintly hostile, but he followed Connor's directions without comment.

"Do I have to do the meditation today?" Otis demanded, once the MIEs were finished. "I hate that part." He finished his energy tonic and tossed the empty at Connor, who just managed to catch it.

"You like the results well enough," Connor answered more forcefully than he'd intended. What had gotten into Otis today?

"I guess."

"You guess?" Connor prided himself on his patience, but this was too much. "Why, without the meditation, you'd—" Shut up, he told himself fiercely. Just shut up.

Otis shrugged—he hadn't really expected Connor to let him off—and settled himself cross-legged on the mat. "Okay, man," he said. "I'm waiting."

The lazy insolence of his tone stung Connor. I do all the work, he thought, and the players get all the glory. And they're not even grateful. They're rude.

His fingers stabbed angrily at the controls, sending the bright images scurrying across the giant screen. Just like Barrett. So Barrett thought up the damn technique. So what? It isn't worth shit without me. I run the gym, I do the training, I deal with the players . . . and I get less out of this than anyone. Less money. Less respect.

The pulsing sounds increased, the images faded. "Center yourself, Otis," he said tersely. "Concentrate on the mantra. You know what to do."

Otis looked over at Connor and gave him a big, friendly smile. "I'm sorry I gave you a tough time today," he said. "You're just doing your job." Connor nodded, only slightly mollified. Otis placed his hands on his knees and closed his eyes.

From somewhere nearby, a buzzer sounded. "Ignore it," Connor instructed. "It's just the van coming back." The garage was on the other side of the training room wall. Otis nodded; his eyes were closed, his brow furrowed, his breathing deep and regular.

Connor watched him for a few minutes. Then he reached beneath his shirt for the long gold chain around his neck. From it hung a small, oddly shaped key. Silently he crossed the exercise floor, inserted the key, and disappeared through a small, unobtrusive door.

Chapter Nine

"... the bid stands at one hundred and forty-five thousand ... do I hear one hundred and fifty? One hundred and fifty thousand, anyone?" The silver-haired auctioneer looked out over the crowd. "All done at a hundred and forty-five?" He glanced inquiringly at the two representatives taking phone bids, but they shook their heads. "Going once ..." he began the familiar chant, "going twice ..." He brought the gavel down smartly. The bid was almost twenty thousand above the reserve. "Sold at one hundred and forty-five thousand to paddle number three-oh-seven."

Morgan craned his neck, trying to locate the successful bidder, as two men in beige aprons stenciled with the name of the auction house carefully removed the exquisite nineteenth-century Dutch flower painting from its stand. Two others carried in a colorful painting of later date and set it up carefully on the wooden display easel.

"Who bought it?" Robin asked.

"I don't know," Morgan said. "I couldn't see."

"The next item, number two-eight-six in your catalogs, is an early Rockwell Kent...." The well-dressed Sunday afternoon crowd consulted catalogs and notes and shifted in their seats for a better look. Rustlings and low murmurs accompanied the arrival of some people, the departure of others.

"It was so beautiful," Robin said. "I don't know how you could have gotten tired of it."

"I've had it a long time," Morgan said shortly. "I needed a change."

"Maybe you'll find something here," Robin suggested. "There's a Milton Avery coming up later."

"No rush," Morgan said lightly. "In fact, there's really no reason to stay any longer." He checked his watch. "Let's go and have a late lunch somewhere." He rose from his seat on the aisle and, taking Robin's hand, led her from the room.

In the hallway just beyond, a blond woman in a lavender suit stood at the cashier's window, a paddle in her hand. A pale, round-faced conservatively dressed man in his late thirties waited beside her. Morgan glanced at them, looked again, and stopped dead, letting Robin's hand drop.

Felicity turned and smiled. "Hello, Morgan," she said. "And you must be Robin. How charming to meet you. I don't believe you know Caleb Nordeman . . ."

Robin took a tentative step forward, glad she'd rejected Morgan's dress of choice in favor of a conservative skirt and blouse, but Morgan advanced upon Felicity, a suspicious look on his face, and grabbed the paddle from her hand. The numbers 307 gleamed whitely against the dark green background. "Damn you," he growled. "I should have known it was you."

But Felicity merely shrugged. "I've always loved that painting," she said. "Caleb insisted I have it."

"And that's why you're paying for it."

"Let's not be vulgar, dear. You'll get your money whoever of us writes the check." She glanced over at Caleb, who made a hurry-up gesture, then slid the paddle through the slot in the window and reached in her purse for her credit card.

Morgan stood by, fuming but powerless to stop the transaction. Caleb eyed him with some amusement.

Robin went and took Morgan's arm. "Let's go," she whispered. "Let's just leave." But he shook her off roughly. "Go outside," he ordered. "Wait for me outside." Embarrassed and hurt at both his tone and his words, Robin stalked out the door.

Felicity followed Robin's departure with her eyes.

"Not very gallant," she told Morgan lightly. "I expect she'll make you pay for that."

Morgan scowled. "She's not like you."

Ignoring the insult, Felicity signed the credit card charge slip, slid it back to the cashier, collected her receipt, and tucked it away in her purse. Then she turned back to Morgan. "I know you think I'm being a bitch," she said. "But I really do love that painting. I'm sorry if my buying it upsets you, but look at it this way: thanks to me, it sold well above its reserve, which means more money for you."

"You could have told me. You could have offered to buy it from me privately. Or at least told me you were planning to bid on it."

"But I didn't know you were selling it until I saw it in the catalog," Felicity protested. "As for telling you ahead of time ... frankly, I wasn't sure how you'd react. Obviously I was right to be cautious." She put a conciliatory hand on his arm. "I truly didn't mean to be secretive about it."

"Didn't you?" Morgan snorted. "You're the one who was always so fond of secrets, as I recall. You're the fucking queen of secrets."

Felicity's face tightened. With a glance at the waiting Caleb, she linked her arm firmly through Morgan's and led him away from the cashier's window. "We really should make an effort to be more polite to each other," she said softly. "Common courtesy aside, we share too many secrets, you and I, to be constantly at odds with each other."

But Morgan shook himself loose. "You were the secretive one," he said, "not me."

Felicity only smiled. "Until now," she said knowingly. "Until now."

"Then don't tell him," Felicity said brightly into the telephone. "Are you two joined at the waist? Don't you have a life of your own anymore?" Her tone was bantering and playful.

"I just wouldn't feel right about lying to him," Robin replied.

"Who said anything about lying? Just don't tell him." Felicity laughed. "If you're not careful, Morgan will take you over, wrap you in a silk cocoon, and before you know it, you're living his life, not yours."

Robin was silent, but Felicity's words had hit home. Her life had been completely keyed to Morgan's these last few months. It was pleasant, but was it healthy? She'd been furious with Morgan when he'd ordered her to wait outside Sotheby's yesterday, but she'd gone outside and waited, which had made her furious with herself. Maybe Felicity had a point. But lunch with Felicity hardly seemed the ideal way to assert her independence. Besides, Felicity was . . . Felicity.

Felicity laughed her tinkling laugh again. "I don't think it's Morgan's feelings you're worried about," she said with a smile in her voice. "You're not too comfortable with the idea of lunching with your boyfriend's soon-to-be ex-wife, are you?"

"Frankly, I'm not."

"I thought that was it." Felicity's amused tone made Robin feel provincial and unworldly. "Well, I'll admit that I am curious about you," Felicity continued. "That's perfectly natural under the circumstances, isn't it? But you have nothing to fear from me, dear. I was the one who initiated the breakup of my marriage. Perhaps Morgan told you?"

"No . . ."

"Well, he wouldn't, would he? Men are like that. The point is, I'm actually quite grateful to you for coming along when you did and making Morgan happy again. It makes me feel less guilty about having left him for Caleb, the man you met at Sotheby's yesterday. Well, almost met. By the way, Caleb and I were both so embarrassed for you. 'Go wait outside,' indeed! Morgan has a tendency to treat women like children. You mustn't let him."

"He was upset," Robin said loyally. In fact, she agreed

wholeheartedly with Felicity; she'd been shocked at the way he'd spoken to her.

"He was upset with *me*. Why take it out on you? Never mind, Morgan gets like that, sometimes. Listen, do come and have lunch. I'd feel so much better if all four of us could be friends. Or at least not enemies. You and I can start the process. They'll thank us for it, believe me."

Which was how Robin came to be sitting at Felicity's scrubbed pine kitchen table the following afternoon, drinking Bloody Marys and eating cracked crab.

She'd taken Felicity at her word and dressed informally in a pair of forest green chinos and a nubby beige top, but she'd still been surprised by Felicity's clothes: old stonewashed jeans with a hole in one knee, and a faded madras shirt. With her hair pulled back in a ponytail and her face nearly devoid of makeup, Felicity looked quite young and completely nonthreatening.

And she was excellent company. Robin's initial diffidence soon evaporated in the warmth of Felicity's personality, and soon the two women were chatting and laughing and trading Morgan anecdotes as if they'd known each other for years. Of course Robin had to tell her "Daughter of the Old South" lies, but she offered a very abbreviated version, and then encouraged Felicity to talk about herself.

By the second pitcher of drinks, they were laughing nearly nonstop at Felicity's amusing stories of what she termed her terminally boring youth and adolescence, spent at Roedean, England's socially preeminent girls school, and on her family's country estate near the sea. Felicity's expression turned serious as she talked about the death of her father in a hunting accident when she was in her early twenties, and of the responsibilities of managing her inheritance. But she soon had Robin laughing again as she described her chance meeting with Morgan in London thirteen years before on one of her jaunts up to town to stay with friends, and the mistakes she'd made while trying to adapt to New York living.

"But I finally got it worked out." She laughed. "And I wouldn't live in England again if you paid me."

"And have you become a baseball fanatic, too?" Robin asked. "That's how I'll know you've really adapted."

"God, no," Felicity said. "I find team sports nearly as dull as team players."

It was nearly four when a woman named Audrey ("More money than sense," Felicity told Robin, "but terribly sweet.") telephoned to remind Felicity of a fashion show she'd promised to attend with her at five that evening. Felicity pressed Robin to come with them.

"I can't afford designer clothes," Robin protested.

"Who can?" Felicity laughed. "We're just going for the party." She studied Robin critically. "You're a little taller than I am, but we're the same body type. I've got tons of things you can wear."

Giggling like schoolgirls, they ransacked Felicity's closets and dresser drawers. Felicity did Robin's makeup and showed her an elegant new way to put up her hair.

As they stepped into the limo Audrey had sent, Robin felt cool and beautiful, like someone in a play. Felicity patted her arm. "You'll love Audrey," she whispered. "And let's have lunch again soon."

"I'd love to," Robin answered happily. She felt a pang of anxiety at the thought of Morgan's anger if he knew that she and Felicity had become friends. But then she thought, Felicity's right. Morgan and I aren't joined at the waist. I have a right to my own life.

PART TWO

Chapter Ten

Late August

The noise in the Comets' clubhouse was unbelievable. Morgan had once told Robin that you could always tell how well a team had played by the noise they made after the game. Judging by today's decibel level, Robin thought, the Comets must be batting a thousand. Which indeed they were. Thanks to the superplayers, the team was now near the top of the league. But it wasn't only the abilities of the superplayers that had produced such success. It was the way their playing inspired every member of the team to pull together.

As the Comets' manager liked to tell reporters, when a player is thinking about his salary, he plays for himself. But when he's thinking about the pennant, he plays to win. "It's a different mind-set," Warfield would explain. "You hit behind your teammates to move them up. You stop thinking about your personal statistics and start thinking about winning the game." This was the first time in years that the Comets had a shot at the pennant. And their style of playing reflected their new confidence and unity.

Team members filled the small lounge, clustering around the training table, and helping themselves to drinks from the cooler. Morgan had closeted himself with Warfield, and Robin moved through the crowd of players, media people, and hangers-on, looking for someone to talk to. The Comets had come to accept her presence in the clubhouse both as Morgan's girlfriend and as a reporter. But the very reasons for her acceptance also made them just a little cautious of her.

She spotted Ernie Sanchez and waved. He waved back, then waggled a cold beer in her direction. She grinned and nodded, and he tossed it over. She caught it and started toward him, but a *New York Post* reporter got there first. She exchanged some banter with several of the other players, but the noise and the crush of so many hot, sweaty bodies was getting to her, so she wandered back toward the empty dressing room, sipping her beer. Being "backstage" the first few times had been a thrill, but it got a little old after a while. She sank onto a bench, leaned back against a closed locker, and put her sneakered feet up on a metal stool. She finished the beer and was wondering where to put the empty when she heard the moan.

It was a deeply plaintive sound, like an animal in pain. She got to her feet and looked around, but saw no one.

The moan came again, louder; it seemed to emanate from somewhere just beyond the lockers across the room. Someone, or something, was in the underground corridor that led from the dressing room to the dugout.

Cautiously she made her way to the doorway and looked out into the semidarkness. There, hunched against the wall, his back toward her, was a shadowy figure. She took a few nervous steps into the corridor. As her eyes became accustomed to the gloom, she realized that the figure was wearing a baseball uniform. A cap had been flung onto the floor by his feet, and he gripped his head with rigid fingers. The number on his jersey read 39. Kenny Reese.

"What's wrong?" Robin exclaimed, hurrying forward. "Should I get a doctor?"

But Kenny waved her away without turning around. Another low moan issued from his throat.

"I'll get Warfield," Robin said, stepping back, but Kenny's hand reached back and grabbed her arm. "No," he whispered. "Please. No."

Robin moved around in front of him. Even in the dim light of the corridor she could see how badly he was suffering. "Let me help you," she said. "Lean on me. We'll get you inside where you can lie down."

But Kenny shook his head violently. His hand held her arm in an iron grip. "They'll bench me," he said.

"What? Kenny, you need help."

But already the pain was lessening. Kenny straightened up and raised his eyes. "Shit!" he said, recognizing her. "Of all people, it had to be you." Robin stepped back, hurt and puzzled. "A reporter *and* Hudson's girl. Shit." He slumped back against the wall.

"I'm only trying to help," Robin said. "What's Morgan got to do with it? Or my being a—" She paused, feeling foolish. It was obvious that Kenny was afraid she'd talk or write about this encounter. But ... talk or write what? That he wasn't feeling well? Everyone felt lousy now and then. "Listen to me," Robin said firmly. "I promise you I won't breathe a word. Not to Morgan, not to Jim, not to anyone. And I won't write about it. But please, let me help you."

"I don't need your help," Kenny told her roughly. He started to push by her, then stopped and swayed dizzily. "Damn."

Robin reached out a hand and steadied him. "How long has this been going on?" she asked. "I saw you grab your head like that during batting practice last month. Was it the same thing?" Kenny nodded. "Come inside and sit down," she said, but Kenny again shook his head. "Okay, we'll talk here. As I said, I won't tell Morgan. You can trust me."

"I guess I have to," Kenny said grumpily. "I mean, what choice do I have?"

"No choice," Robin assured him. "So you've been having headaches."

"Yeah."

"Why not talk to the team doctor?"

"I can't." Kenny sighed. "I got in a fight in a bar about a month and a half ago. Got hit in the head. That's when it started. Now every time I'm in a fight, it gets worse. I've already been warned about fighting. There's a lot of pressure on the superplayers to keep their noses clean. If all this comes out, they'll fine me, maybe bench me, I could lose my endorsements—"

Robin shook her head. Kenny, a brawler? It didn't seem to fit. But even if he were, she doubted he'd lose his endorsements or his spot in the lineup just now. He was too important. "They need you," she assured him. "You're a superplayer. They wouldn't pull you out with the pennant in sight. They couldn't afford to—"

But Kenny shook his head. "They could stop giving me the Supertraining," he said. "They could give it to someone else, and send me back to Colorado."

"They wouldn't do that."

"Wanna bet?" Kenny replied bitterly. "I sure don't."

Robin decided to try another tack. "Here's an idea," she said. "If you're afraid to confide in the team doctor, why not see someone on the outside?"

"Yeah, like it still wouldn't get leaked."

"Doctors don't talk about their patients," Robin said.

"No, only the famous patients," Kenny said cynically. "Anyhow, I wouldn't know who to go to. I wouldn't even know who to ask. And if I did ask someone, then that person would know—"

"Be quiet and let me think," Robin said.

"I'm thirsty," Kenny complained. "I want a beer."

"In a minute. Look, why don't you call Adam Salt? He's a sports doctor, and you already know him. Adam says you work out together at the Pro Club."

"You're a friend of Adam's?"

"He's consulting on my Comets article."

"Yeah, that's right. Well, Adam does have a real good rep with the players. But he specializes in knees and shit. What good is that to me?"

"Give him a chance. At least it's a place to start. What's the matter?"

"We had, well, a little argument. At that party Hudson threw." Kenny looked embarrassed. "I haven't seen much of him since."

"An argument? What about?"

"It isn't important." Robin waited. "Okay, maybe you're right. Maybe I'll call him. Can I go get my beer now, Ms. Kennedy?" Fully recovered, he gave Robin the full force of his wide blue eyes.

"Promise me you'll call Adam. Promise you'll call him tomorrow."

Kenny shrugged. "I guess I better see somebody," he said softly. "The pain's pretty bad. And if it happened during a game ..."

"Call him tomorrow."

"And you promise you won't mention this?"

"Not as long as you call Adam."

Kenny gave her one of his thousand-watt smiles. "You drive a tough bargain, lady."

". . . and that's why I'm here," Kenny finished. "I was kind of afraid to call you, after what you said to me about using drugs, but ... I didn't know where else to turn." He sipped the soft drink Adam's nurse had brought him from the small office kitchen, and shifted self-consciously in his chair.

"I never should have said what I did," Adam said. "I apologize. And let me reassure you about something else. Whatever happens in this office is strictly between you and me. It's called patient confidentiality. You have my word. So let's start at the beginning ..." Adam opened the file folder Pat had prepared and quickly reviewed Kenny's medical history; everything appeared normal. "And you're not taking any medications, any drugs—"

"I already told you!" Kenny rose from his chair.

"I meant prescription drugs," Adam protested mildly. Kenny relaxed back into his chair. "No, nothing."

"Okay." Adam thought for a minute. "Do you eat or drink anything at the Pro Club? Anything unusual? Maybe something the regular players don't get?"

"Just the energy tonic," Kenny said. "We drink it after the workup and before the meditation. But the others might get it, too, I never noticed." He leaned forward in his chair, suddenly alarmed. "You think they're putting something in the energy tonic?"

"Of course not," Adam reassured him. "I was think-

ing you might be having an allergic reaction to something in it, that's all." He hesitated. "Maybe you could
bring me a sample, and I could check it out."

"I could try," Kenny answered doubtfully. "They tell
us not take it out of the training room."

"Try anyway," Adam told him. "Just so we can rule
it out."

Kenny shrugged. "Okay."

They moved to the examining room, where Adam
checked Kenny's heart and lungs, Kenny provided a
urine sample, and Pat drew several tubes of blood.

"Show me where you were hit, that time in Jacksonville," Adam said. Kenny rubbed a spot just above his
right ear. "This hurt?" Adam palpated the area lightly.

"No."

He parted Kenny's hair and checked the scalp. A pink
scar showed where the skin had been broken. The
wound had not been deep, and it had healed cleanly.
"Looks okay," he told Kenny. "When you get the headaches, do they start on this side—or hurt more over
here?"

Kenny shook his head. "It's an allover pain," he said.
"Like my head's being squeezed all around. Hurts like
hell. Afterward, I feel a little dizzy for a coupla
minutes."

Adam made some notes in Kenny's folder. "I think
the best thing I can do is to refer you to—"

"No referrals."

"Kenny, this isn't my field, and—"

But Kenny shook his head. "I don't want to see any
strange doctors," he said. "Isn't there anything *you* can
do?"

Adam was silent for a moment. The chance of doing
some medical research on a superplayer had a lot of
appeal, especially in light of his decision to help Dennis
Locke. God knew, he hadn't been much help so far. On
the other hand, he had no right to play fast and loose
with Kenny's health. His commitment and responsibility
as a doctor meant he owed Kenny the optimum treatment available.

"I strongly recommend that you consult a neurologist," Adam told Kenny firmly. "There are a number of very fine people here in New York—"

"I won't," Kenny told him flatly. "Let's just forget the whole thing." Angrily, he began buttoning his shirt.

"That's my strong recommendation," Adam repeated. "But if you're absolutely dead set against a consult, maybe there is something I can do." Kenny looked up hopefully as Adam continued. "I'd like to arrange for a test that could give us a clue to what's happening. After that, we can talk again."

Kenny brightened. "Sounds good to me," he said.

"Okay. Here's what we'll do." Adam was scribbling notes on the pad in the folder. "I'm going to send you for an MRI—"

"What's that?"

"Magnetic Resonance Imaging. Known informally as a brain scan."

"Jesus, you think I have a brain tumor?"

Adam shook his head. "Let's not get carried away here," he said lightly. "A brain scan is standard procedure in cases of head injuries that result in continued, severe headaches. The MRI will show us if there's anything abnormal going on in there, any swelling or injury. Headaches can have many causes, Kenny. Especially when you've been hit in the head." He smiled reassuringly.

"A brain scan . . . Does it hurt?"

"Not at all. But it needs to be done in a hospital. I'm on staff at New York General, so I'd like you to go there for it. I'll arrange for your records to be kept extremely confidential. Wherever possible, I'll identify you only by your first name. Pat will make all the arrangements."

"You trust her?" Kenny asked dubiously.

"Unto death," Adam assured him. "Now, how fast can we get this done? Can you spare two hours some time this week? No? Well, next week, then."

Kenny had departed and Adam was back in his office when Pat buzzed him to say that Robin Kennedy was on the phone.

"Did he call you?" she asked as soon as Adam picked up.

"He not only called me, he came into the office today."

"Good. And?"

"Are you asking as a reporter or a friend?"

A brief silence. Then, "That's not a very nice question," Robin told him.

"But it's a necessary one. Kenny's very concerned about this whole thing getting out, and there is the matter of patient confiden—"

"Hey, I was the one who made him call you," Robin protested. "I've already promised him I wouldn't talk or write about it. Adam, I'm worried about him. He was in such pain. Can you do anything for him?"

"I recommended a neurologist but he refused. I'm sending him for an MRI—a brain scan. If there's been an injury to the brain because of the fight he was in, the MRI will show it to us."

"Do you think there's been an injury to his brain? I'm asking as a friend."

"The truth is, I haven't the slightest idea. The symptoms he's experiencing could indicate brain damage of some sort. But without the scan, who knows?"

"And if there has been damage, then what?"

"Well, it depends on where and what kind."

"Would he have to stop playing?"

"Let's not get ahead of ourselves. I don't know anything yet." And when I do, I'm not telling a reporter. Or Morgan's girlfriend.

"I really hope he'll be okay."

"So do I."

Robin paused. "Could Kenny's headaches be caused by stress? By bottling up the stress of being a superplayer?"

"I wouldn't have thought Kenny was particularly stressed out. In fact, he seems to be handling the whole thing rather well."

"Aside from those fights he seems to get into."

"Aside from those," Adam conceded. "The answer to

your question is, yes, stress can cause headache. But my gut feeling is that Kenny's headaches have a physical cause."

So much for Warfield's hypothesis, she thought. "Like what?"

"That's what I'm hoping the MRI will tell us."

"I see. Okay, next question: do you think Kenny's headaches could be connected in some way with the supertraining?"

Adam paused. "Why would you think that?"

"I'm not saying I do. I'm just asking if *you* do."

"No ... not really," Adam said slowly. "I don't see how they could be." Not yet I don't.

And you probably wouldn't tell me, if you did. "I have one more question. As a reporter this time, but off the record."

"About the MRI?"

"No, about baseball in general. The thing is, I can sort of understand how a Comets scout could find a couple of hot young players, give them some special training, and turn them into superplayers. But what about Ernie Sanchez? How unusual is it to see this kind of improvement in a guy like him?"

"You mean, because he's older than the others?"

"Yes, partly. But also because he's a known quantity. Most people never saw Kenny play before he joined the Comets; he might have been fantastic even before the special training. But Sanchez has been playing for years, and was only average."

"Any way you look at it, I'd have to say the improvement in Sanchez is pretty unusual," Adam admitted.

"So what's actually causing it?"

"Have you asked Morgan Hudson? And now *I'm* asking as a friend."

"Of course I've asked Morgan," Robin replied hotly. "He doesn't know any more about it than we do. He just says its the supertraining. Well, we *know* it's the supertraining. What I want to know is, *why* is it the supertraining?"

Adam laughed. "Speaking as a medical man," he replied pleasantly, "I have no idea. But as a fan, I'm delighted." How he wished he could sit down with this smart, pretty lady and tell her of his own fears and suspicions, and solicit her help in uncovering the superplayers' secret. But of course that was impossible. It wasn't just that she was a reporter; he somehow believed that Robin truly wanted to learn the truth for its own sake, and would deal responsibly with it. No, it was her close connection with Morgan. Not that he mistrusted Morgan; he had actually liked the man when he'd met him at the party. No, it was simply that Morgan was too close to the superplayer process, and Robin was too close to Morgan. Her first loyalty would be to him, and secrets always came out in the bedroom. Still, he wished he could be open with Robin. She had a good head, and—

"The hospital on line three," Pat's voice came through the office intercom, interrupting his thoughts. "It's the duty nurse on G-five. She say it's important."

"I'm terribly sorry," Adam told Robin. "An emergency. Perhaps we could continue this discussion another time?"

"Sure," Robin told him. "I'll check in with you in a few days, see how Kenny's doing. As a friend, Adam, as a friend."

Adam chuckled and disconnected, leaving Robin confident that Kenny was in good hands, yet with the uncanny feeling that Adam knew more than he was telling her.

After he'd dealt with the hospital problem by increasing one medication and discontinuing another, Adam turned to the video monitor on the credenza behind his desk. He'd found the VCR setup useful for reviewing complicated surgical techniques performed by others, and had even arranged to have several of his own procedures taped for future study. But the video he now slipped into the machine had nothing to do with surgical procedures.

As he studied the latest tape Dennis Locke had supplied, Adam froze specific plays, as well as close-ups of the superplayers' faces and bodies, playing them back using the frame-by-frame control button. While not nearly as effective as Frank's professional system, the makeshift technique enabled him to study eye movements, the clenching of hands around a bat, the sudden swivel of an arm to scoop a ball out of the air, and other sequences of reactive action.

No question about it, he decided. Something was actually speeding up the thought processes of the superplayers. And that, in turn, was speeding up both their anticipation of other players' actions and their own reaction times.

But it's more than that, he mused. Somehow, the relaying of messages from eye to brain, and from brain to reactive nerves and muscles, is being speeded up, too. But how?

"We know it's the Supertraining," Robin had said. "What I want to know is, *why* is it the Supertraining?"

Why indeed? Perhaps the MRI—and Agnes Havacek—would provide a clue.

"Forty-love," intoned the referee. Morgan grinned and got ready to serve again. A dedicated but by no means superior tennis player, he'd never gotten close to the semifinals until today. He fired the ball high and fast across the net, and his opponent smashed it back, sending the ball into the far corner of the court. Morgan found himself running almost before the ball left his opponent's racket, returning it with speed and power, much to the surprise of his opponent. Confident that Morgan wouldn't have anticipated the direction of the ball, or moved fast enough to reach it in time, he was caught off guard by the fierce return.

"Game," the referee announced, "and set."

To his joy and surprise, Morgan won the following match set, as well. His place in the finals now a certainty and his face wreathed in smiles, he trotted over to the center court sideline where Robin waited with a bottle of designer water and a towel.

It was quite cool for the last weekend in August, and Robin had a light sweater draped across her sleeveless dress. She pushed her sunglasses back onto the top of her head and kissed Morgan lightly on his wet nose. "Remind me never to play tennis with you again," she told him as he began toweling the sweat off his face and neck. "How did you get so good?" Her praise was honestly meant. She and Morgan had played tennis together a number of times here at the country club, and she'd thought them fairly even matched.

He grinned. "Good clean living's what does it," he told her. "No booze, no tobacco, no sex—hey, it's just a joke," he added quickly, seeing her expression. "I wasn't even thinking about .. I don't mean anything personal." He slung a sweaty arm around her waist. "Now how would you feel about a tall, cool drink on the terrace?"

"How would you feel about taking a shower first?" Robin replied, laughing, her good humor restored. "And then you can tell me how Morgan Hudson, Captain of Industry, turned himself into Andre Agassi."

"Promise you'll wait for me?"

"Forever. Well, twenty minutes," she teased.

Morgan grinned. "Order me a Tom Collins. I'll be back before it gets to the table."

Robin looked around. Nearly all the spectators who had gathered to watch the semifinals seemed to be heading for the outdoor bar. "With this crowd, that's a pretty safe bet," she told him.

"Okay, ace, what's your secret?" Robin asked a short time later as they sat over drinks at the table she'd managed to secure. She stirred her strawberry daiquiri with her straw. "How did you get so good so fast?"

"I made someone an offer he couldn't refuse," Morgan told her.

"You bribed the referee?" Robin said in mock horror.

"Better. I bribed Connor Egan," Morgan replied. "Actually, it wasn't a bribe, just a payment for services rendered." Morgan's eyes were dancing with excitement. "I got permission from the owner of the Pro Club to—this has to be just between us," he cautioned, his expression turning serious. She nodded, frowning. "Connor's giving me the special training! Isn't that terrific?"

"You mean supertraining? Like Kenny and Otis and—?"

"Lower your voice." Morgan looked around furtively at the press of people on the terrace. "I've always dreamed of winning the club's singles tournament," he said, turning back to her. "But no matter how hard I try—lessons with the best coaches, lots of practice, intensive tennis seminars—I never even make the semifinals. But about two months ago, it occurred to me that what works for my superplayers might work for me, too. And of course it does."

"But I thought . . . you told me the training was very restricted. Only the three Comets players—"

"That's right, that's right. But I decided they just might give the owner of the Comets a little special consideration. Which, after I threw enough money at them, they did."

"But . . . if Connor can be bought," Robin said slowly, "why couldn't anybody just throw money at him and get the training? The owner of the Phillies, for example?"

But Morgan shook his head. "It's not Connor I threw the money at."

"You told me the owner of the Pro Club was very rich. Why would your money make a difference to him?"

"Well, it did," Morgan replied testily. "As for selling the training to my competition, he wouldn't dare."

"How can you be so sure?" Robin pressed.

"I just am, dammit!" Several people turned to look in their direction. Morgan took a pull at his drink and stared out at the golf course irritably, but when he turned back to Robin a moment later, he was smiling again. "Sorry I barked at you. Now tell me you're happy for me."

"I'm happy for you," Robin said. "I really am. So what's the training like?"

Morgan looked surprised. "It's exactly what Connor showed you, that day in the training room with Adam."

A disturbing thought occurred to Robin and she

opened her mouth to speak, then realized she was bound by her promise to Kenny Reese. Instead, she lowered her eyes and stirred her daiquiri, concentrating on the swirling fluid. If Kenny's headaches were connected to the Supertraining in some way, as she'd suggested to Adam, then Morgan . . . But no, Adam had told her he didn't see how they could be. Well, that was a relief.

"Penny for them," Morgan offered. Robin looked up, puzzled. "Your thoughts. You look so serious."

She smiled up into his eyes. "I was just wondering what to wear to the tournament dinner," she said lightly.

"Maybe I can help you there." Please, no, Robin thought. "And I might have another little surprise for you before too long. I've got someone working on it right now."

"That sounds mysterious," Robin teased. "Won't you give me a hint?"

"Well, it's got something to do with—no, I really do want it to be a surprise. But I promise you'll be pleased." Best not to tell her just yet, Morgan decided. The company he'd hired was having a little trouble tracing the connection with the Kennedys, and it would be a shame to have to disappoint her.

Chapter Eleven

The beginning of September

TELEPROMPTER SCRIPT: SIX O'CLOCK NEWS—SEPT 2
PAGE 12 OF 17

DISSOLVE FROM JOHN TO SKIP. CUE SKIP.

Thanks, John. Yes, the big story in sports tonight is the fight between Comets fielder Otis Freeman and Detroit catcher George Smits. It started on the field, and then moved into the stadium parking lot after the game.

ROLL FILM.

Apparently it began with an argument between the two during the changeover in the middle of the fifth inning. It quickly escalated into a shoving match, and their teammates stepped in and separated them--that's Kenny Reese over there on the right, grabbing Freeman's arm. But it erupted again later as the players left the stadium. An ABC camera crew caught this footage of Freeman and Smits going at it in the parking lot. Comets owner Morgan Hudson refused to comment, but we understand Freeman has been fined three thousand dollars, and other sanctions have been applied.

CUT TO STILL OF FREEMAN. SUPER STATISTICS.

Will Freeman be playing in Atlanta next Thursday? You betcha. With 48 home runs to his credit so far this season, and 131 rbi's, the Comets can't afford to bench him, not with a pennant win a real possibility . . .''

COMETS TAKE ON BOSTON, ATLANTA, UMPIRE

Special to The New York Post–September 7

Talk about your close calls. The Comets nearly lost their number one pitcher for the rest of the season. But his teammates moved fast and managed to stop hurler Ernie Sanchez from getting his hands on the umpire late in the second game of last night's double-header in Boston.

The score was six to zip in favor of the Comets. Boston's Larry Knight was on deck with a full count and bases loaded. Sanchez threw a change-up, low and inside, and the umpire called ball four. Sanchez was very unhappy, and he wasn't the only one. Fans yelled and threw debris onto the field as Knight walked in a run, costing Sanchez his shutout. As the runner cleared home, Sanchez went straight for the umpire's throat. Catcher Bob Nettles grabbed him from behind and brought him down, but Sanchez fought him off and started for the umpire again. He finally had to be carried off the field.

Sanchez has been fined, and suspended for five games.

How his suspension will affect the Comets' pennant chances remains to be seen. Sanchez has 245 strikeouts to his credit already this season, and a nice low-earned run average of 2.02 runs per game. He's also set a record for the most pickoffs of runners on base. This violent behavior is new for Sanchez, whose friendly disposition over the years has earned him the nickname 'Easy Ernie.' But pennant-win pitching is also new for him this season, so nobody in the Comets camp is complaining, at least not publicly.

Maybe it comes with the job. Sanchez is by no means the first superplayer to go rogue, on the field or off. Last week, strongman Otis Freeman threw a punch at Detroit catcher George Smits. And Kenny Reese, always the first one to break up a fight on the field, has a rather different reputation once the game is over....

These and stories like them broke in the media the week after Adam's examination of Kenny Reese. Later that same week, Adam walked an extremely nervous Kenny through the MRI procedure at New York General.

Using various subterfuges to shield the identity of the young player, he managed to preserve his anonymity from everyone except the carefully chosen radiology technician, an older East Indian gentleman who found all sports tedious in the extreme and didn't know Kenny Reese from Kenny Rogers.

For the patient, undergoing an MRI is like being sealed up inside a small tin can. The procedure takes about twenty minutes, during which the patient must remain as still as possible as he or she lies there in total darkness. Even for those who are not claustrophobic, it can be a harrowing experience. Kenny was glad Adam was there to talk him through it.

When the procedure was finished, Adam took the ballplayer out through the radiology department's back entrance, leaving the technician to pack up the films and messenger them across town to Rockefeller University.

Returning to his office, Adam found more videos from Dennis Locke's office waiting for him. He watched them on his office VCR, and then he took them over to Frank's videotape editing studio. The professional slow-motion on Frank's machine was far better than the frame-by-frame at the office, and as Adam watched Sanchez's recent attack on the umpire, he noticed something he realized he never would have picked up on his office set.

"Run that part again, will you?" he asked Frank, who hit some buttons. Adam glued his eyes to the screen as the action inched along in slo-mo. Yes, there it was: a sudden, convulsive tremor just before Sanchez went for the umpire. How curious, he thought. How very curious.

"Frank, let's run that other tape where Freeman jumps on the Phillies player in the parking lot," he said, intrigued. "There's something I want to check out." Frank ran the second video forward to the appropriate place, and Adam watched the playback carefully, certain he'd see Freeman's body give the same convulsive twitch. But the elation he felt at his discovery was checked by the realization that he had absolutely no idea of its significance.

Robin was seated in the crowded departure lounge at La Guardia Airport in New York, reading a follow-up story on the Comets fracas in the *New York Post* and waiting for the weather to clear. Poor Kenny, she thought. And it had been worse for Sanchez and Freeman. Still, the fact that all three of the superplayers had been fighting did seem to give credence to Jim Warfield's stress theory.

It was Friday afternoon, and the airport was crowded. Robin was on her way to Minnesota to do a human-interest piece for *People* magazine about a well-known explorer and his upcoming expedition to Antarctica. It had taken a real effort of will for her to accept the three-day assignment, and that troubled her. Was she really willing to give up her fledgling career as a writer to become Morgan's appendage? None of Morgan's friends' women, be they wives or girlfriends, worked at anything. Their job, it seemed, was to be available to their men, to go where they went, play the sports they played, party when they partied.

As she sipped her diet soda, she glanced down at the ring Morgan had given her, five small diamonds in a fancy gold setting. She'd loved it until she'd seen similar rings on the hands of the girlfriends of four of Morgan's buddies. The Girlfriend Ring, she thought angrily. I've become The Girlfriend.

But was that quite fair? She and Morgan weren't like the others, were they? After all, he'd given her the exclusive on the Comets' supertraining story before they'd started dating, so he must respect her as a writer. And he seemed proud of her abilities when he introduced her to his friends as a reporter.

Although he hadn't been very pleased at the idea of her spending three days in Minnesota, she recalled. In fact, he'd been quite annoyed. She'd tried to explain that she couldn't keep turning down assignments or people would stop offering them to her. But he'd obviously felt that being in town on Saturday night for that old goat Sandy Morrison's party was more important. And so it was—to him.

Being Morgan's girlfriend was fun, she decided, but it wasn't enough. It was all too easy to float away on champagne and expensive gifts and weekends in the country, and forget what she really wanted from life. Love, yes, but love with a man who valued her talents, accepted her independence, applauded her drive to be successful. She'd thought Morgan was such a man. But his selfish reaction to the *People* magazine assignment had made her reconsider.

Or was she being too hard on the relationship? She really did care for Morgan. And he was being so patient with her, so understanding of her problems in bed. She owed him at least the same patience, she decided. They'd work out everything, in time.

"Flight forty-eight direct service to Minneapolis/Saint Paul is now ready for boarding through Gate Seven . . ."

At last, Robin thought. Around her, travelers, mostly businessmen on this Friday afternoon, began gathering up their belongings and heading toward the gate. Outside, clouds were still scudding across the sky, but the large dark mass of cumulonimbus had moved off and the rain had diminished. Robin finished her soda, hefted her carry-on bag, and headed down the corridor. Passing a newsstand, she noticed Kenny's photo on the cover of some magazine. She'd already called Adam's office and been told the MRI results weren't in yet. I must try him again when I get back on Monday, she thought. Surely he'll have had them by then.

But it wasn't until Tuesday, five days after the procedure had been performed, that Agnes Havacek called Adam. "We have been so very busy, my dear Adam,"

she apologized. "And one is on vacation and another is
sick . . . Can you come this afternoon?"

In contrast to the frenetic pace of New York General, Rockefeller University's neuroscience labora-
tories were a sea of calm and quiet reflection. A lab
assistant escorted him along a long hallway to a set of
double doors labeled NEUROCHEMISTRY in large yellow
letters. Inside was a large, bright, well-equipped research facility with the latest in computer equipment.
The air-conditioning was going full force. Agnes rose
from her desk inside a small open cubicle just beyond
the door. She wore a white lab coat over slacks and a
sweater. "You're looking well," she told Adam, kissing him on both cheeks.

"You, too." He looked around. "What's different?"

"We've finally been renovated, thank goodness," she
said. "And painted. The conference room is through
there, now. We'd better get started." She took his hand
and led him through the lab. "Lu has to be somewhere
in half an hour."

"Lu?"

"Dr. Luyen Chou, our consulting neuroradiologist.
He's the best."

Adam was impressed. Agnes was incredibly demand-
ing of the people who worked for her; if she said Chou
was the best, he was. "So what have we got?" he
asked.

"Something interesting, perhaps."

They entered the conference room. A fiftyish man in
whites was clipping a series of MRI images in front of
a long wall-mounted light board.

Agnes introduced the two men, who shook hands
while Agnes settled herself in a chair. "Sit here," she
told Adam, patting the seat beside her. "Let's show him
what we've got, Lu."

Smiling shyly, Dr. Chou led them to the wall and
began to take them through the films. "Everything is
well within normal limits here. No sign of damage to the
brain tissue, no sign of edema, no fracture, no hema-
toma . . ." His small hand flew across the black-and-

white images. "Even over here, at the site of the blow to the head which you described, there is nothing unusual at all."

Adam's shoulders sagged. No damage, no abnormality, no swelling, no blood clots. Could it really be plain old stress, then? But Agnes had said they'd found something interesting. He looked over at her; her eyes were sharp and amused.

"Show him, Lu," she said.

"It's the thalamus," Dr. Chou told him, pointing. "There's something funny about it."

"Funny?" Adam repeated.

Agnes laughed. "Don't throw jargon at him, Lu. Explain it so he can understand."

Dr. Chou grinned. "It's too small," he said. "The thalamus is too small."

"What's the significance of that?" Adam asked.

"Maybe nothing," Dr. Chou told him. "The thalamus is a sort of biological black hole. We know very little about its function. But I can tell you that this thalamus is significantly smaller than normal."

Adam looked at Agnes. "The thalamus is too small? That's it?" He shook his head in frustration. "So what do we do, Agnes, get him a thalamus transplant? Give me something to work with here."

"Patience, Adam. Show him the other thing, Lu."

The neuroradiologist picked up a film from the pile on the table and clipped it in front of the light board. Its label read DETAIL: CORTEX, UPPER RIGHT QUADRANT. "Over here," he directed, pointing to a tiny spot on the picture. Adam moved closer. "There's a small lesion on the cortex, and it's a strange one. It's obviously not a tumor, but what is it? This we do not know."

"We don't?"

Dr. Chou shook his head. "I have never seen a cortical lesion like this before," he told Adam solemnly. "Never."

"Could it be an artifact?" Adam asked.

"That was my first thought," Dr. Chou replied. "But

it also appears on images thirteen, fourteen, and fifteen." He pulled more films from the table as he spoke and clipped them to the light board. "Here, you see? And here . . . and over here. It's definitely something real."

"But you say it's not a tumor?"

"Absolutely not," Agnes declared. "Your patient, this Kenny with no last name, he does not have brain cancer."

"That's good," Adam said.

"Very good, yes," Dr. Chou agreed.

"But why is he having these headaches?"

"That is what we must find out."

"So what now?" Adam asked. "Any thoughts?"

Agnes was looking from one image to another, her finger tracing the shadows. "I want a sample of spinal fluid," she decided. "Will your mystery patient submit to a spinal tap?"

"I'll ask him."

"Don't ask him," Agnes said sternly. "Order him. It could be important."

Adam nodded, but his mind was racing. Seizures . . . Didn't he dimly recall something about seizures from medical school? Something about seizures and rage . . . ? On the video, he'd seen Sanchez's body convulse just before he attacked the umpire, with a muscular twitch that was more like a seizure than a temper tantrum. "Easy Ernie" had been ferocious, Adam recalled; he'd gone blindly for the umpire's throat. And Freeman in the parking lot. And Kenny, too, probably, in that Jacksonville bar. A sudden convulsion followed by rage . . .

"I'm a little rusty on all this," Adam told Agnes, "but aren't there seizures that *mimic* rage?"

Agnes smiled approvingly. "Indeed there are. And such seizures often suggest brain cell damage in the cortex." She tapped the strange cortical lesion. "Has your patient had such seizures?"

"Er, that's privileged information, Agnes."

Agnes's expression turned stormy. "Privileged from *me*?"

"Uh, I'm sorry, Agnes, but my patient—"

"It is no good!" Agnes exclaimed angrily. "I cannot work like this. Who is this Kenny-with-no-last name?" But Adam just shook his head. Agnes shooed Dr. Chou away, then turned to Adam fiercely. "One more thing I will do for you, Dr. Salt," she said. "Because we are old friends and because I am curious about this case, I will analyze the spinal fluid. After that, if you still want my help, you must tell me everything you know about your mysterious patient. Otherwise, I cannot help either one of you anymore."

"Okay, Agnes."

"Okay you will tell me?"

"Okay I will explain the situation to my patient and get his permission."

"Explain, too, that I need that spinal fluid. Tell him not to wait too long." Adam nodded, but she put a hand on his arm. "You must make him understand," she insisted, her eyes deep and troubled. "The brain is a very delicate organ. And there are many ways it can die."

Robin slept late on Tuesday, then phoned Adam's office to inquire about the results of Kenny's MRI. Her call was fielded by Pat, who explained that Adam was out of the office and that she herself had no information about the test results.

Pushing Kenny and the superplayers to the back of her mind, Robin spent the afternoon sorting through her Minneapolis interview notes and outlining her article. Later, she treated herself to a long bath and Chinese takeout in front of the TV. Morgan had claimed a business dinner that evening, and Robin found herself glad of the opportunity for some private time. She hoped his appointment would go well; he'd seemed preoccupied when they'd met for dinner the night before.

* * *

Darkness had fallen as an ill-humored Morgan made his way along Fifth Avenue. His destination was a mere eight blocks north of his East Sixty-ninth Street town house, but as he waited for the light at Seventy-second Street, he was already sweating in the stifling heat. He shrugged off his jacket and folded it over his arm, then loosened his tie. The hell with it, he thought; he pulled it off and stuffed it into a trouser pocket. God, what weather.

By the time he reached the high white building, moisture was trickling down his temples, and circles of sweat ringed his armpits. But in the lobby, the air-conditioning was going strong, and when the elevator man let him off on the nineteenth-floor landing, he was beginning to recover. He raised a finger to the bell but the door swung open before he could ring.

"You look exhausted," Felicity told him. She herself was crisp and cool in a pale skirt and striped blouse. "Don't tell me you walked here."

"It's only eight blocks," Morgan said belligerently. He strode into the living room of Felicity's apartment, looked around, and headed for the drinks trolley beside the sofa. "May I?"

"Of course." Felicity settled herself in a wing chair. A magazine and a half-finished glass of white wine sat on the lamp table beside her.

Morgan began filling a glass with bourbon, soda, and lots of ice. "You're looking very well," he told her.

"Thank you, dear. Living without you has done wonders for my complexion, not to mention my temperament."

Morgan muttered something under his breath; he wandered over to the window and looked out. "Go ahead," he told her. "It's your dime."

"Excuse me?"

Morgan circled around behind her chair and peered through an open door. It led to the kitchen. "It's an expression," he told her. "It means *you* called *me*. You do the talking." He ambled across the room toward a lithograph hanging behind the sofa.

"For God's sake, settle somewhere," Felicity exclaimed impatiently. "You're making me dizzy."

Morgan shrugged and sat down on the white linen sofa. "So why am I here?"

"I asked you to come because we need to talk about money."

"Don't we always?" Morgan answered dryly. "What is it this time?"

"The Comets."

Morgan's eyes narrowed. "We have nothing to discuss," he said roughly.

But Felicity shook her head. "We have a great deal to discuss, actually. Like the distribution of the profit."

Morgan rose angrily. "Not a chance," he replied forcefully. "You agreed the Comets wouldn't be part of any settlement between us." He slammed his glass down on the coffee table. "Dammit, Liccy! You've got the country house, you've got a chunk of company stock, Caleb's ready to put my company on the auction block—"

"He's encountering a little problem with that, actually."

"Yeah, like I'm going to be able to make the payments on the loan." Morgan settled back into the sofa. "Sorry to disappoint you."

But Felicity shook her head. "That doesn't worry us," she said calmly. "It's only a matter of time until you start missing the payments. That's more of a delay than a problem. No, the problem is that you've been messing around with the formulations."

"Messing around with—I've been updating things, economizing, increasing profitability. I would have thought that would please your money-grubbing friend."

"Well, it doesn't," Felicity replied coolly. "Caleb says increasing profits is fine, but not at the expense of market share. Sales are slipping, Morgan."

"That's not true."

"Bullshit." Felicity held out her empty wineglass. "Refill this for me, would you, dear?"

"Fill it yourself," Morgan growled.

Felicity shrugged, then rose and replenished her drink. "Caleb's gotten hold of some rather alarming figures for the last quarter. And by the way, when did you put that huge mortgage on the town house?" Morgan was silent. "Fairly recently, I'd guess." She sighed. "You've borrowed an awful lot of money from me over the years, Morgan. And our divorce settlement was quite generous. I only hope you're good for all of it." She resumed her seat in the wing chair and sipped at her wine.

"Come on, Liccy. You're not hurting for money."

"Actually, I am. Oh, not hurting-hurting. But not all my investments have been wise ones, I'm afraid."

Morgan smiled complacently. "Caleb's been making mistakes, has he? Not quite the wunderkind you thought he was?"

"These are investments I made before I met Caleb," Felicity explained. "Caleb's helping me dump the worst of them, but I've taken some unexpected losses. So you can understand why I raise the issue of the Comets."

"Now it's my turn to say bullshit, Felicity. We had an agreement. You get a piece of everything else, but the Comets are mine."

"But I agreed to that when I thought everything else was worth something," Felicity protested. "Now it looks like only the Comets are worth anything."

Calm yourself, Morgan told himself. He took a pull at his drink before he spoke. "The team's begun winning," he said at last, "and that's just great. Certainly their winning streak makes them a more profitable team to own—"

"You misunderstand me. I'm not concerned with the day-to-day revenues. I'm talking about profit from the sale of the team."

"I have no intention of selling the Comets," Morgan told her firmly.

"You will, eventually. And when you do, I want—"

"The team is not for sale," Morgan exclaimed. "And I don't give a goddamn *what* you want."

"Then you'd better start," Felicity replied heatedly. "If not for me, the Comets would still be in the cellar. If not for me, there wouldn't be any superplayers."

Morgan paled. "Let me remind you of the rest of our little agreement," he said, his voice deep with tension, his eyes dark and dangerous. He moved quickly to where she sat and grasped her shoulders so hard she winced with pain. "I agreed not to contest the divorce. I agreed to give you a much bigger share of our joint assets than you had any right to. And you agreed to keep your mouth shut."

"That's right," she conceded. "And now I want a piece of the Comets." She shrugged her shoulders in an attempt to free them from Morgan's grasp. "You're hurting me."

"Good. Forget the Comets."

"No, Morgan. I want a piece of the team, or *you* can forget the Comets."

"It won't do you any good. I won't sell them."

"I'm prepared to wait."

Morgan's hands moved up and encircled Felicity's neck. It would be so easy . . .

"No, Morgan," she said, reading his thoughts. "It wouldn't." But her eyes were frightened as they bore into his. When the phone rang suddenly, they both jumped. Morgan sighed and removed his hands; they were shaking with the effort of controlling his rage. With a small sigh of relief, Felicity slid away from him and reached for the phone. She spoke briefly, then handed it to him. "It's Jack Ridley," she said with distaste; she'd never cared for Morgan's personal assistant. Morgan had been able to move Ridley into the town house only after Felicity had moved out.

He took the phone from her and listened for a moment. "It's okay," he said into the receiver. "You were right to check. Tell him to call me here right now." He hung up, but kept his hand on the instrument. Thirty seconds later, it rang again and Morgan picked it up, gesturing to Felicity who shrugged, retrieved her wine-glass, and left the room.

Once in the hallway, she quickly made her way down the carpeted corridor and entered her bedroom. Setting down her drink, she went to the bed table and silently picked up the telephone extension.

Chapter Twelve

Vivaldi's "Four Seasons" seeped from the wall speakers, and pools of soft light illuminated the low, cluttered room as Paul Barrett worked the hand-held mechanism that would admit his anticipated guest to his inner sanctum. Barrett was prepared to be flattered, charmed, threatened, and cajoled; it didn't matter. The outcome of their conversation would be the same; he held all the cards.

Now he dropped the portable radio control mechanism into his lap as his visitor hurried in out of the dark stairwell and looked around with an expression of distaste. "Nice place."

"I like it. You don't have to." He rolled to his desk and reached for one of several bottles that stood there. "Have a drink," he suggested. "Help you calm down."

"I *am* calm." But a hand reached for the tumbler Barrett filled with the strong red wine. "I came here to make you change your mind. There's too much at stake. You can't stop."

Barrett watched with faint amusement as the contents of the glass disappeared. "I'm afraid I must," he said. He drained his own glass and set it down on the desk while he uncorked another bottle.

"I don't think you understand."

"Really? Explain it to me, then." Not that it will do you an iota of good.

Over an hour later, having been charmed, cajoled, threatened, and flattered, and having played his guest like a fish on a line, Barrett decided he'd had his fun. Cutting off the fiftieth repetition of "You can't! You

mustn't!" with a wave of his hand, he spoke with an air
of finality. "The fact is," he said, "the decision's been
taken out of my hands."

"What do you mean?"

"The problem has proved to be too great." Barrett
refilled his glass yet again. He'd been drinking steadily
all evening, and his face was flushed, but he spoke softly,
almost reflectively. "I've been over and over it, and it's
just no good. Much as I hate to admit it, it appears I
was wrong."

"Wrong? But the technique's been working."

Barrett seemed not to have heard. "I thought if I
threw enough money at it . . ." he mused. "But I couldn't
undo it. I'm afraid it's irreversible."

"And what's wrong with that?" his guest demanded.
"The Comets will get better every year . . ."

Barrett smiled thinly. "I'm not talking about athletic
ability," he explained. "It's not the super reflexes that're
irreversible. I mean the process itself. That wonderful
process that turns out to be so utterly destructive. Not
that I give a damn. Jocks." He spat the word out angrily.
"Well, we've all had our fun. Now it's over. You'll see.
Hell, you're seeing it already, if only you had the brains
to look."

"See what, for godsake? All I see is that the Comets
are finally winning. Put it in English, will you?"

"Plain English? All right. Every superplayer will soon
fall victim to the very process that turned him into a
superplayer. Plain enough? But I really did think I could
fix it," Barrett continued in his strangely detached tone.
"I tried, truly I did. Ah, me, so it goes. More wine?"

His visitor had risen, incensed. "Are you saying the
special training puts superplayers in danger? And you
knew about this all along? You knew the training was
harmful?"

"It kills, actually," Barrett answered mildly. "I've seen
it happen before. But I was so sure I could find a way
to reverse it, given proper funding and time."

"But . . . how could you?" his guest spluttered. "How

could you keep this terrible thing a secret? And from me, of all people?"

"I'd never have gotten the funding if it were known. Besides, I was so sure I could reverse it." He drained his glass, and began to refill it. "Well, it was good while it lasted. We all had a good run. I don't know why you're so upset."

"You don't know why— My God, if I'd known this from the start, I—" The agitated words were suddenly bitten off.

Barrett looked up from the half-filled glass and noted the cunning expression, the narrowed, dangerous eyes. Despite the solid desk between them, he instinctively rolled his wheelchair backward a few feet.

When the voice spoke again, the tone was menacingly calm. "This is a shakedown, isn't it?"

Barrett shook his head vigorously. "No, no . . . I assure you—"

"You don't assure me of anything; in fact, you make me damn nervous. I never should have trusted you and your promises." A pause for breath. "I think I'm beginning to understand now," the voice continued. "There *are* no side effects, are there? This is all about money, isn't it?" The visitor stood and began pacing energetically, righteous anger growing. "Blackmail. A blatant attempt to up the ante." A side table went over with a crash. A lamp followed.

"You're wrong—"

"No wonder you insisted on keeping control of the whole process." A chair splintered against the wall. "And now you think you can blackmail us? Blackmail *me*? You pathetic cripple."

If Barrett was frightened, he concealed it well. "Aren't you getting your cut?" he replied. "Haven't you all used *me*? Well, now it's payback time."

"But there's no more money, don't you understand? Living up here in the Black Tower, you've lost touch with reality. Unless the process continues, there's nothing. You have to keep going!"

"It's not money I want," Barrett replied. "It never

was, really. It's revenge." He smiled mirthlessly at his
frenzied guest. "And revenge is truly sweet. Once the
story gets out—and it will; it has to—no amount of
money will save you."

"You can't be serious. You're in this yourself, right
up to your neck. Whatever happens to us happens to
you." But Barrett remained calm, his eyes mocking. "Or
perhaps you have other plans, is that it? Like doing a
runner?"

"How could I possibly?" Barrett protested mildly. "A
pathetic cripple like me?" But he realized he'd gone
much too far. Nervously, he fiddled with the portable
radio control device in his lap; one of the buttons was
programmed to dial 911.

But his guest saw the motion and moved quickly, grabbing the device from his hands. "I'm right, aren't I?
You're planning to dump us all in the shit and
disappear."

Grabbing the armrest control, Barrett spun the wheelchair around and began to retreat, but his guest was
faster. An unopened wine bottle smashed down repeatedly on Barrett's fingers, and then on the controls, ren-
dering all useless. The wheelchair was spun around and
shoved up against the desk, trapping Barrett, who was
crying out in pain. "Barrett, you bastard. You set us up."

"No, no—" Barrett protested.

"Then continue the process."

"I won't."

"Don't, then." The wine bottle descended again.

Chapter Thirteen

"Have you seen it?"

"The police called me around seven this morning," Morgan replied. "I couldn't believe it."

"Me, neither. God, it's awful." Robin gripped the phone tightly. It was barely nine o'clock and she'd already fielded calls from three publications and two TV news shows about her relationship with Morgan and her insider status with the team. Like sharks, she thought, circling a story, smelling the blood in the water. "It doesn't seem real, does it?"

"But ... you didn't know him, did you?" Morgan sounded puzzled.

"Of course I know him. I interviewed him twice, and I've talked to him plenty of times, unofficially."

"You what? When? Who introduced you?"

"You did, Morgan." What's wrong with the man? she wondered. "Otis and Kenny and—"

The light dawned. "You've been talking about Otis Freeman? I thought you meant Paul Barrett."

"Barrett? You're the one who knows Barrett. Uh, knew him. I can't believe Otis killed him, can you?"

"I can't believe *anyone* killed him," Morgan answered.

"You must be terribly upset. Did you know Barrett well?"

"I didn't know him at all," Morgan replied. "I only met him maybe twice, briefly. Everything, even the original offer of the training, was done through Connor Egan."

"I guess that figures," Robin said. "The newspapers are saying Barrett was a recluse. It seems so spooky that

he was living above the Pro Club all that time and nobody but Connor knew he was there.''

"Barrett didn't get around much,'' Morgan said dryly.

"Yes, he was a paraplegic. A spinal injury when he
was twenty-one, it says here.'' Morgan heard the rustle
of newspaper pages. He'd already read the early-morn-
ing editions and watched the TV reports. "It happened
when he was playing rugby at university,'' Robin continued. "In England.''

"Rugby's a rough sport.''

"So it seems. Well, I guess it's no wonder he wanted
to help other athletes.''

"Yeah,'' Morgan said. "He was a real sweetheart.''

"And he was from your alma mater.''

"The London School of Economics?'' Morgan asked,
surprised.

"No, Cambridge. Did you know him there?''

Now it was Robin's turn to listen to the rustle of newspapers as Morgan replied with some asperity, "I just told
you I didn't know him. Cambridge isn't like Princeton
or Harvard. It's actually thirty-one separate colleges.
And my degree was in economics, not biochemistry.
Anyhow,'' he added, having found the information he
was looking for, "Barrett was thirty-seven, according to
the *Times.* That's three years younger than me. I would
have been long gone before he got there.''

"A simple 'no' would have done it,'' Robin told him,
a smile in her voice. "So what will happen to the special
training program, now that Barrett's gone?''

"I expect it'll continue. Connor Egan really runs the
show, after all.''

"Poor Connor,'' Robin said. "It must have been horrible for him, finding Barrett like that. Imagine walking
through the gym before it opened—he says he did that
every evening—and suddenly seeing a secret door on the
top floor standing wide open ... did you know about
the door?''

"Of course not.''

"... and then going into Barrett's apartment,'' Robin
continued, "not knowing whether an intruder was still

in there ... finding Barrett with his skull crushed ..."
She shivered.

"That was pretty stupid of him," Morgan said testily.
"He never should have gone inside. He should have
gone straight back to his office and called the police."

"You're right," Robin agreed. "Well, the person we
have to think about now is Otis."

"You bet. We're so close to a pennant win. I don't
know if we can pull it off without him."

For a moment, Robin was speechless. Was that the
only aspect of the situation that worried Morgan? Didn't
he care that Otis was facing a charge of murder? But
she bit her tongue and merely asked, "You've got him
a good lawyer?"

"Uh, sure. I'm working on that right now. But—"

"But what? Surely you don't believe Otis is guilty."

Morgan paused. "Frankly, I don't know what to
think," he said slowly. "His jacket was found by the
desk, and his name was written in Barrett's appointment
book for yesterday evening. The newspapers have been
full of stories about his violent attack on George Smits
in the stadium parking lot the other week. I understand
Freeman's a drinker, and don't think the press won't
find that out any day now." He sighed. "Who knows
why he met with Barrett, or what transpired? Did Freeman get drunk and lose his temper? It's certainly
possible."

"You can't be serious."

"Believe me, I don't like the idea any better than you
do. We'll do everything we can for him, of course. And
I'll go and see him this morning."

"Can I come with you?" Robin asked.

"I don't think that's a good idea," Morgan replied
firmly. "Not just yet. Uh, much as I love talking to you,
sweetie, I'm going to have to head down to the office
now. I've got enough to take care of today without all
the damn newspaper people camped outside my front
door. And it's only going to get worse."

"You sound tired."

"I am. My business dinner ran late, I didn't sleep well,

and then the phone calls started this morning. I've got a raging headache and I think I'm starting a cold. In fact, would you mind terribly if we cancel dinner tonight?"

"No, of course not. But we don't have to go out. I could come over and cook something—"

"That's nice of you," Morgan said quickly, "but I'd be lousy company. Listen, I'm flying to Atlanta tomorrow to catch the game there, but I'm coming back Friday morning with the team. How about dinner Friday night? We'll go someplace special."

"Sounds like fun."

"Good. I'll pick you up around eight. Oh, and Robin? Don't talk to any reporters."

"I *am* a reporter," Robin replied with a smile. But Morgan had already hung up. Slowly she lowered the receiver. The phone immediately began ringing, but she ignored it as she collected up the newspapers that littered her living-room floor, folded them neatly, and stacked them on a side table. She listened as the answering machine clicked on; sure enough, another TV news show was calling. She didn't need Morgan to tell her not to talk to reporters.

She went to the kitchen for some coffee, and then back to her desk. The phone began ringing again, and again she waited for the answering machine to pick up. To her surprise, she heard Felicity's voice.

"Just calling to see if you were planning to come tomorrow evening. I hadn't heard, and I—"

Robin reached over and picked up the receiver. "Felicity, it's me. Sorry about the machine; I'm trying to dodge the press. Isn't it awful about Otis Freeman?"

"Terrible," Felicity agreed. "Do you think he really did it?"

"I don't," Robin said slowly. "But Morgan seems to."

"Does he? That's interesting. Never mind, we can talk about it tomorrow. You did get my invitation?"

"No," Robin said, "I'm afraid I didn't."

"But I mailed it over two weeks ago," Felicity protested. "Damn post office. I'll be so disappointed if you're not free. Caleb's throwing a huge birthday bash

for me at his place. Tons of people, rivers of champagne
... And he has the most spectacular terrace in New
York; you must see it. Please say you can come."

Robin hesitated. One night on her own had been a
nice break. But today was Wednesday, and Morgan
wouldn't be free until Friday. Three nights in front of
the tube were two too many. Although she didn't quite
believe Felicity's story about her invitation being lost in
the mail, she decided she didn't really care. It sounded
like a good party. "I'd love to come," she answered.

"I'm so glad. Come around eight. Do you have a pencil?" Robin dutifully copied Caleb's Park Avenue address into her diary. "Bring a date, if you like."

"A *date*?" Robin laughed.

"Good God," Felicity exclaimed. "What was I thinking? No, *don't* bring Morgan, please."

"Don't worry. He'll be out of town with the Comets."

A pause. "Well, if there's anyone else you want to
bring," Felicity offered, "a friend, I mean ... please
feel free."

"I'm comfortable coming on my own," Robin said,
amused. She'd known plenty of women who wouldn't
dream of attending a social function without a male es-
cort; she'd always felt rather sorry for them.

"Then we'll see you tomorrow. I'm so glad. We've
both been so busy lately; it will be fun to have a good,
long chat."

Robin doubted that a good, long chat would be possible, let alone a priority, at such an evening, but she
agreed that, yes, a chat would be fun, and they said their
good-byes.

Over the next hour and a half, Robin worked on the
People magazine article; she'd promised to deliver a first
draft to her editor on Monday. The phone rang so often,
she'd nearly decided to disconnect the damn thing when
she heard a voice she knew.

"Robin, it's Adam. Sorry to take so long to get back
to you—"

She lunged for the phone, nearly knocking over her

coffee mug. "I'm so glad you called," she said. "How's Kenny?"

"The MRI was pretty much within normal limits," Adam said. He'd thought hard about how he could answer her question without contravening doctor-patient confidentiality. "Pretty much" and a change of subject were the best he'd been able to come up with.

"Thank goodness for that. Does he know?"

"I only got the final results yesterday afternoon. I left a message on his machine, but he didn't call me back, and now the team's away until Friday. I'll probably hear from him then."

"He'll be so relieved. But ... what about his headaches?"

Adam sighed. "I know you want to help," he said, "and I hope you won't take this the wrong way, but this really is between Kenny and me, doctor and patient. It would be wrong of me to discuss his case with you without his consent."

Robin was silent. Of course Adam was correct. She had no right to ask such questions. "I understand," she said at last. "And I'm not insulted. I'm sorry if I've put you in a difficult position."

"Not at all," Adam said kindly. "I'm glad you were there to push him to seek medical treatment. It was the right thing to do. And don't worry; we'll get to the bottom of it."

"Good." Robin hesitated for a moment. "I assume you've seen the papers this morning."

"You mean the murder at the Pro Club."

"Yes. Adam, you've talked to the superplayers, you've worked out with them at the gym. What do you think? Could Otis Freeman really be guilty?"

It was a question Adam had been debating ever since he'd turned on the TV that morning and learned about Barrett's murder. He'd gotten to know the young player through occasional meetings at the Pro Club, and he was finding it hard to believe that Otis was capable of bludgeoning another man to death with a wine bottle. Yes, he had a short fuse sometimes, and he'd been involved in his share of brawls recently, like the one in the stadium parking lot that had gotten so much publicity. But there was a vast difference, Adam felt, between a fistfight with an opposing player, and the violent murder of a cripple in a wheelchair. As a scientist, Adam was used to dealing with facts, and in this case, the facts pointed to Otis's guilt. But somehow it didn't feel right. And as a doctor, he had come to rely on his instincts as well as his information.

Aloud he said, "I don't know. I hope not."

"Me, too. What can we do to help?"

"I'm hoping to visit him tomorrow. As a friend, not a doctor," he added quickly. "But it's really up to the lawyers."

"Morgan's seeing him today."

"Good. Uh, did Morgan say what would happen to the supertraining?"

"He seemed pretty sure it would continue," Robin answered, "since Connor's been doing it all along."

Interesting, Adam thought. "Terrible about Barrett, isn't it?" he said aloud.

For the next few minutes they discussed the murder and their reactions to it. Adam was gently probing into Robin's earlier conversation with Morgan when Pat interrupted him with an incoming call. Promising to catch up with her later, Adam hung up, leaving Robin wondering whether Adam's visit to Otis was motivated by something other than friendship.

Otis Freeman was being held downtown, a few blocks from the old courthouse. Adam arrived around two that afternoon as arranged, and was walked through security clearance by the medical examiner, an old friend from medical school who was there to interview another prisoner. An armed guard escorted him through several sets of double security doors—the lock on the door ahead didn't click open until the lock on the door behind had clicked closed—and deposited him in a large waiting room in need of a paint job. Some ten minutes passed before a different guard led him through more security gates and into a small visiting room divided into cubicles.

A clear, bulletproof partition, ceiling-high and solid, divided the room lengthwise from wall to wall, neatly bisecting each cubicle. Headsets—earphones with small attached microphones—lay on narrow counters each side of the cubicles. Adam sat down and put on his headset as the guard spoke briefly on an internal telephone. Minutes later, Otis Freeman was brought into the room.

Adam studied the powerfully built player as he seated himself, nodded to Adam through the clear partition, and fumbled with his headset. He looked awful. "I need lawyers, not doctors," Otis said. His tone was not unfriendly; he was simply stating the obvious.

"I'm not here as a doctor," Adam explained with a small smile. "I'm here as a friend."

"Yeah, well I can sure use some of those," Otis agreed. His face was haggard.

"How're you feeling? Any, uh, headaches or anything?"

Otis ignored the question. "I didn't do it, man," he stated. "I didn't."

Adam nodded. "Have you talked to a lawyer?"

"Yeah, late yesterday. Morgan got me this guy, he's supposed to be real hot. He says they can't hold me. There's no real evidence, it's all, uh, circumstantial."

"Like your name in Barrett's diary?"

"Yeah, like that."

"Well, I'm glad to hear it. So, er, what were you and Barrett planning to talk about?"

"Hey, I didn't even know the man."

"But you had an appointment with—"

"I never had any damn appointment. I didn't even know there was anyone living up there. Did you?" Adam shook his head. "I can't help it if Barrett wrote my name in his book. Nobody told me anything about a meeting with him."

"And your jacket?"

"I think maybe I left my jacket in the gym that morning after the training session. I remember looking for it in the dressing room after the game, and I couldn't find it." Otis shifted in the hard wooden chair. "Anybody could have dragged it up there. That's what the lawyer says."

"That's good," Adam told him. He wasn't sure how many more questions he could get away under the guise of friendly chatter, but he decided to press on. "And of course your lawyer's checking out your alibi." He tried to make the question sound matter-of-fact.

Otis lowered his eyes. "Uh, that's a problem," he said softly. Adam waited. "See, a bunch of us went out drinking after the game, celebrating, you know? And, well, there was this girl ..." Otis shook his head as though to clear it. "I went off with this girl, and at some point she wanted us to go back to her place. I remember it was dark, and we were climbing all these stairs and I kept stumbling around in the dark and falling down and laughing ... I was really tanked. Anyhow, I must have passed out 'cause the next thing I remember is, it was light and I was lying on this filthy mattress, and the girl was gone and so was my money and my watch. Well, I got myself out of there somehow, and went home—"

"Did you take a taxi? They can check the trip sheets and—"

"Nah, I felt too sick. I walked for a while, then I got on the subway. I finally made it home, I don't know, around five in the morning, and I guess I passed out again, because all of a sudden the police were pounding on my door."

"But surely the girl will come forward."

"After she stole my money and my watch? Oh, you bet." Otis massaged his temples and his scared and tired eyes. "Connor told me not to drink," he said at last. "He warned me. Now look where it's got me."

"It's all circumstantial," Adam reminded him. "Your lawyer—"

"Yeah, right. Meanwhile, there's a white man murdered and a black man with no alibi and his name and his clothes all over the damn place—"

"But no fingerprints," Adam told him. "They haven't found your fingerprints on the bottle or the glass. Or anywhere. The *Post* broke the news an hour ago."

Otis looked up, suddenly hopeful. "One for the home-boys," he said.

Felicity had been right, Robin decided; this *was* the best terrace in New York. She sipped her champagne and watched another airliner lift off from La Guardia Airport, its navigation lights twinkling. The terrace was huge and extensively landscaped, and tonight it had been filled with beautiful and fragrant flowers.

"Incredible, isn't it?" Robin turned to see Felicity, re-splendent in black and silver, coming through the French doors from the magnificent drawing room. "From way up here, you can almost forget what a terrible city this is." Felicity sighed. "I still can't get over the murder of that poor Mr. Barrett. I simply don't understand who would kill a recluse and a cripple. Or why." She settled herself at a delicate wrought-iron table. "Come and sit," she said. "I love your dress, by the way."

Robin laughed. "Felicity, you can't possibly love this dress." As soon as she'd entered the high oak-paneled entrance gallery, Robin had realized she was horribly underdressed. Nearly all the men were in dinner jackets, and the cost of the women's designer gowns alone could have supported a small nation. Aside from the jeans, skirts, and blazers that formed the bulk of her wardrobe, Robin's closets held several outfits foisted upon her by Morgan, and two "dressy" dresses bought on sale at a well-known discount store. She'd been quite fond of those two dresses until this evening.

"No, really," Felicity insisted as Robin joined her at the small table. "You look lovely. You're young and slim and pretty, and I promise you half the women in this room would trade places with you like that." She snapped her fingers and grinned. "Not me, of course. I've had enough of Morgan Hudson."

A waiter came by and refilled their glasses; Felicity took a tiny sip, then set her glass on the table beside a decorative silver bowl and idly plucked a violet from the mass of flowers that filled it. "Don't mind me, dear," she said, suddenly contrite. "I know you care deeply for

Morgan. Maybe your experience will be better than mine. Maybe this time he's not just—" She broke off abruptly, leaning back in her chair and toying with the small purple flower. "It really is glorious up here," she said with a vague gesture that encompassed the starry sky and the carefully landscaped greenery. "Like a weekend in the country. I do hope you're enjoying yourself."

Maybe this time he's not just—what? Robin wondered as she assured Felicity that it was a lovely party and she was having a wonderful time. In fact, she'd found the few people with whom she'd managed to strike up a conversation self-involved and a bit dull. Not for the first time, she wondered why Felicity had bothered to invent that lie about her invitation being lost in the mail, and to press her to come. Why did Felicity want her as a friend at all, come to that? Could it be that she was still in love with Morgan, and that Robin was her way of keeping an eye on him? But surely that couldn't be right; Felicity had left Morgan for the wonderful Caleb.

Maybe this time he's not just what?

"And how is Morgan taking this whole thing?" Felicity asked, breaking into her thoughts. "The murder, and the arrest of one of his star players . . ."

"He's very upset, of course."

"Yes, I expect he would be. It's all so mysterious, don't you think?"

"It's troubling, of course, but . . . mysterious?"

"The man's jacket and his name in the diary, but no fingerprints," Felicity said. "Isn't that mysterious?"

"He could have worn gloves, I suppose . . ." Robin said doubtfully.

"Well, I expect the police will get to the bottom of it. They've probably already found out things that we know nothing about." Felicity took another small sip of wine. "Perhaps they've told Morgan."

"Morgan? Why would they do that?"

Felicity shrugged. "Oh, I'm just talking," she said. "Otis is a Comet and Morgan owns the Comets and Otis trains at the Pro Club . . . Well, whatever Morgan knows or was told about the murder, I expect you know, too. Or will." She gave Robin a conspiratorial smile. "You have the inside track."

"But, Felicity, I don't know a thing about the murder," Robin protested. "And if Morgan does, he hasn't said a word to me."

Felicity studied Robin across the table for a moment. Then she smiled brightly, tossed the crushed violet aside, and stood up. "Well, I'd better get back to my guests, I suppose," she announced, turning toward the drawing room. "Oh, look—there's Britt and Sandy. I wasn't sure they'd come." She took hold of Robin's arm casually. "Britt's one of my very dearest friends," she explained in a low voice, "but Sandy's an old buddy of Morgan's, and doesn't approve of me." She laughed lightly. "Over here, Britt!" She waved, and, catching sight of her, the two late arrivals redirected their steps toward the French doors.

Shit, Robin thought.

"You both look divine," Felicity was saying as they stepped out onto the terrace. "Britt, Sandy, I'd like you to meet—but how silly of me. Of course you already know Robin Kennedy, don't you?"

Chapter Fourteen

"What in hell are you playing at?" Morgan stood framed in the doorway of Robin's apartment, his face flushed with anger, his eyes hot and accusatory. "How could you be so disloyal?"

"It was only a party," Robin protested feebly. Some dinner this is going to be, she thought.

"*Felicity's* party. Felicity and that asshole Caleb Nordeman."

"You were out of town and Felicity called—"

"And it wasn't the first time, either. Damn you!" He shoved past her into the living room, slamming the door shut with a bang. His hands in fists, he turned to her again and she backed away fearfully. She'd known from the moment the Morrisons had stepped onto the terrace last night that Morgan would hear of her presence at Caleb's apartment and be furious. But she hadn't expected him to physically threaten her. Not Morgan. He'd always been so gentle with her.

Morgan moved toward her, shouting abuse. Don't hit me, she begged him silently, her eyes wide. Please. No. Suddenly all the old feelings she'd thought she'd left behind—the terror, the sense of worthlessness and guilt—came flooding back. This was all her fault. She had provoked it. She was to blame. She deserved what she got.

Then suddenly she thought, no. I don't deserve this. Nobody deserves this.

Quickly she backed away, her right hand behind her, until she felt the wall unit. Keeping her eyes on Morgan, she fumbled along the shelf for the heavy metal statuette, a copy of a Degas dancer, that she'd bought at a junk shop years ago. She'd barely closed her fingers around it when he grabbed her shoulder, swung her around, and threw her across the room. Despite the torrential rain that had begun around five that evening, she'd put on a tapered silk dress for her dinner with Morgan. She felt the skirt seam rip as she fell hard against the sofa but she was up in a flash, the statuette in her fist.

"Keep away from me," she warned as he moved toward her. She raised the statuette threateningly. "I mean it, Morgan." It was hard to keep her voice steady but she knew it was important to try.

Breathing hard, he stared at her with furious eyes, but he didn't come any closer. Inwardly trembling, she pressed her advantage. "Sit down and we'll talk about it," she said firmly. "Over there." With the statuette, she pointed to a chair placed between the windows at the end of the room and her position near the sofa. That would leave a clear run back to the door if she needed it.

Morgan stomped over to the chair, positioning himself behind it, his hands clenched. "I'm sorry I grabbed you like that," he said, his eyes hard and unrepentant. "But dammit, Robin, it was a shitty thing to do!" He pounded a fist on the chair back for emphasis.

"And grabbing me, as you put it, was also a shitty thing to do. Now, can you talk calmly, or shall I call the police?"

"The police?" The word seemed to shock Morgan out of his anger. "No, don't do that." He took a deep breath and exhaled slowly. The flush was slowly fading from his face. "I just want to know why my girlfriend and my ex-wife have become such buddies."

"Sit down." Reluctantly, Morgan sat; Robin remained on her feet, wary and watchful. "Felicity invited me to lunch the day after we met at the auction," she stated. "I don't know why I went; maybe I was curious. We've seen each other maybe twice since then, including last night. I know it's a little awkward for you—"

"A little awkward?" Morgan was on his feet again.

"It's insulting. It's treacherous. And you didn't even tell me yourself. I had to find out from Sandy and that bitch wife of his. I can't tell you how embarrassing it was."

He's right about that, anyway, Robin admitted to herself. I probably should have mentioned the party to him; he'd have found out eventually, even without the help of the Napiers. Perhaps Felicity had even planned it that way. But why would she bother? Again, Robin wondered whether Felicity was still in love with Morgan.

"Felicity's a snake," Morgan declared. "The thought of her befriending you, telling you lies about me . . . and you telling her my business—"

"I wouldn't do that," Robin assured him. "Anyway, we didn't talk about you." Well, not much, anyway, she told herself. "I guess I can understand your being upset about my going to Felicity's party, but there's no reason we can't all be civilized about—"

"I guess your idea of civility and mine are vastly different," Morgan interrupted.

"Yes, they are," she replied stiffly. "I don't believe in hitting people when I'm angry at them."

Morgan looked embarrassed. "Neither do I," he said. "I . . . I don't know what came over me." He frowned. "I owe you an apology for that, Robin. . . . But try to see it from my side."

Robin sighed. "I can," she admitted. "I can see that Felicity's hurt you deeply. And my having lunch with her and going to her party makes me seem like I'm siding with her against you. But that's not at all what I intended." Morgan seemed much calmer. She decided to risk sitting down, and chose a straight-backed chair opposite and at some distance from him, laying the statuette in her lap. "After that awful scene at the auction house," she continued earnestly, "Felicity and I thought it would be better if we could all be—well, maybe we couldn't all be friends, but at least we could . . . not be enemies. We wanted to make it easier for you."

"How very kind." Morgan stood abruptly, and clutching the statuette, Robin did, too. But despite his snide tone, his anger seemed spent. "Just two little do-gooders."

"That's not fair."

"Listen, Robin. You don't know that woman the way I do. In fact, there's a lot you don't know about Felicity and our marriage and— If you really want to make things easier for me, stay away from her, okay? Just stay away from her." He started toward her; she raised the statuette and he laughed hollowly. "I'm not going to hit you," he promised. "I've never hit a woman in my life. I can't think why—" He shook his head in puzzlement. "I'm really sorry I grabbed you like that. Please forgive me. It's just that it caught me by surprise, your socializing with Felicity, and it upset me." He put his arms around her and hugged her gently, kissing the top of her head. "September's a tense month in baseball, kid. I guess my nerves are shot." He pulled back and studied her. "We still on for dinner?"

Robin didn't answer right away. Gently disentangling herself, she went to the wall unit and placed the dancer in its accustomed spot, turning it this way and that until she was satisfied with its position. Finally she turned back to him. "I don't think so," she replied softly. "Not tonight."

"Tomorrow?"

She shook her head.

"I said I was sorry," he said somewhat belligerently. "What more can I do?"

Robin sighed. "I accept your apology. That isn't it. I just think maybe we need a little ... distance."

"Distance."

"Yes."

Morgan's mouth turned hard and his eyes turned bitter. "You've got it." He strode to the door, yanked it open, and walked out.

"Paul Barrett invented the supertraining. He was killed by a person or persons unknown, possibly Otis Freeman, but there's probably not enough evidence to hold him. The superplayers will continue to train at the Pro Club." Dennis Locke looked over at Adam accusingly. "I've learned more from the goddamn newspapers than I have from you."

Adam shrugged. "All that was news to me, too."

"Then why've you been avoiding me? I've been calling you since the story hit the papers Wednesday morning."

"Give me a break, Dennis. I've been spending more time inside the OR than out of it." He glanced disconsolately at the summer rain pelting the sidewalk and running down the plate glass window of the delicatessen in which they sat. Why did weekend rain always seem so much wetter and gloomier?

The waitress arrived with their food; a pastrami sandwich for Dennis, vegetable soup for Adam. "Hell of a lunch," Locke told Adam, looking over at the floating carrots and celery with distaste.

"I could say the same of yours. Clog your arteries worse than the Lincoln Tunnel at rush hour."

"Doctors." Locke took a large, defiant bite. "Haven't you learned anything that could help?"

"About the murder, absolutely not. About the supertraining . . ."

"Yes?"

"Not exactly."

"What the fuck does that mean?"

"It means I'm working on it."

"The man was a biochemist, for godsake," Locke exclaimed. "I had my people quietly rip the place apart all over again, and you know what we found? Zip. Zilch. Nada." He lifted the top slice of bread, drenched the beef with mustard, and clamped the sandwich back together. "The media's having a field day with this thing, I have to keep saying there's no evidence of anything illegal . . ." He picked up the sandwich, mustard leaking onto his fingers. ". . . and you? You're working on it."

"Calm down, Dennis. With your temper and that sandwich, you're gonna give yourself a stroke. Look, I've found something that may be connected in some way to the supertraining, or it may not be. I don't know yet."

"What is it?" Dennis demanded. "Drugs? Steroids?"

"No, nothing like that, and keep your voice down."

"Are you kidding? I can barely hear *you*," Dennis protested, but he spoke more quietly. The family restaurant held more than its share of children this Saturday morning, and the noise level was high, but Locke conceded that Adam was right to be cautious. "So what did you find?"

"One of the, uh, guys consulted me about ... well, about a physical complaint," Adam explained softly, leaning across the small table toward Dennis. "An MRI showed a couple of brain abnormalities. These have no direct connection to the man's playing skills as far as I can tell, and I have no idea what's causing them. But it's ... suggestive."

"Of what?"

"I'm not sure."

"And?"

"And nothing. That's all I know."

"Some fount of information you are," Dennis said morosely.

"Be fair, Dennis. I can't tell you what I don't know."

"And when will you know something?"

"I have no idea."

"But you'll tell me if it turns out to be important, right?"

"You know I will."

"Of course, that might not be for ten or twelve years, but what's the hurry?" Locke attacked his sandwich angrily. "You realize they're about to win the pennant, don't you?"

"I've got twenty bucks on them," Adam replied, smiling.

Dennis Locke sighed deeply. "You leave me no choice," he said. "I'll have to step up my current plan of action."

"Which is?"

Dennis shook his head in disgust. "Doing nothing."

The rain continued all weekend long, matching Robin's mood. Even the two dozen white roses that arrived on Saturday accompanied by a note in Morgan's own handwriting failed to cheer her or put to rest the doubts and questions that had begun to assail her. He'd nearly hit her; he'd certainly grabbed her in anger and sent her reeling. She began to question how well she really knew him, and what she really meant to him. Just how deep did their relationship go? she wondered. What was it he wanted from her, as a woman, as a reporter? Did he have some ulterior, unknown motive for allowing her to write the Comets story? Why was he so eager to believe that Otis Freeman had murdered the owner of the Pro Club?

And then there was Felicity: why had Felicity befriended her? What were her true intentions? Could she still be in love with Morgan? What had she been trying to learn from Robin, out there on the terrace?

To escape these unanswerable questions, she threw herself into her work; the first draft for Monday's meeting with the *People* editor, thank-you letters to people who'd been helpful to her in Minnesota, a complete reorganization of her Comets notes. But her thoughts kept intruding. By Sunday night, she was exhausted; she tucked herself into bed around nine and fell into a deep sleep.

When she awoke Monday morning, the sun was shining and the rain had washed the city clean. Despite the bruise blossoming on her upper arm where Morgan had grabbed her, her spirits rose.

Her meeting with the editor went well; only a few changes were suggested, all of which, Robin felt, would improve the piece. Buoyed up, she hurried on to her next appointment, a meeting with Bill Thomas, a senior editor at a popular daily tabloid, who had an article to propose. Robin had never done any newspaper writing, and she was both flattered and puzzled. The paper had a number of highly regarded columnists on staff; why call her?

Thomas's small cluttered corner office was filled with memorabilia: photos, footballs, even a framed baseball jersey, all signed. A sports story, she thought sadly, knowing what was coming. Thomas welcomed her with praise and coffee, but two minutes into his pitch her fears were confirmed: it was her relationship with Morgan, not her writing skills, that Bill Thomas was after.

"We want to present the real story about Otis Freeman and this terrible murder," he assured her. "The truth as only an insider would know it. I don't mean to presume on your personal relationship with Mr. Hudson ..." (the hell you don't, Robin thought angrily) "... but you certainly are in a position to know where the bodies are—er, what really happened."

"I think not."

"You talk it over with Mr. Hudson," the editor insisted. "Tell him our attitude is friendly, not confrontational. Make him understand—"

"I will do no such thing," she stated. "Any time you have a real story you'd like me to cover, I'd be delighted to talk again. But—"

"Hey, we have real reporters on staff here for those stories. I only called you because you and Morgan Hudson are—"

Flushed with anger and embarrassment, Robin mustered the shreds of her dignity and strode from the office. Unseeing, she hurried through the press room and out into the hallway. A "down" elevator was just closing and she ran for it, colliding with a man who was coming out. Papers scattered.

"Shit."

"Sorry. Here, I'll help."

"Robin? It *is* Robin, isn't it?"

"Lee? When did you leave the agency?" Lee had been a senior media planner when Robin had worked in advertising.

"Three months ago. I'm running the advertising department here."

"That's great!"

"How about you? You doing a story for us?"

"Not a chance," Robin said firmly.

"You have time for some coffee? My office is up on fifteen. Or there's a canteen just down the hall."

"The canteen will be just fine."

The windowless beige room was furnished with Formica tables and orange plastic chairs, all empty at the moment. Self-service coffee and tea urns were set out along one wall. Lee and Robin settled themselves at a corner table and brought each other up to date.

"Don't mind Bill Thomas," Lee told her as she sipped her tea. "Even the male chauvinists around here think he's a pig. So you're dating Morgan Hudson. Must be exciting, especially with the Comets about to win the pennant. I can see why Bill wanted a story from you."

"Yeah."

"His approach leaves something to be desired, I admit. But it's common knowledge that the press has been denied access to the Supertraining room but you've been inside. I don't suppose you'd tell a friend, off the record . . . ?" Robin smiled and shook her head. "Didn't think so. Anyway, there's that, and then there's your personal involvement with Hudson, which is how you got to go inside the training room in the first place—"

"Actually, that's not the way it—"

"—and now there's this murder at the Pro Club. Bill Thomas can smell a hot story. Everyone can."

"Well, they won't get it from me. Not yet."

"So there *is* a story."

"I didn't say that," Robin replied quickly.

Lee eyed her speculatively. "Planning a book?"

"I have a deal with . . . a magazine."

"Good for you," Lee said. He drank some coffee. "I can see it now: 'Murder in the Locker Room, Mystery on the Mound.' Hope they're paying you plenty." He grinned at her.

"Lee, that magazine deal was made weeks ago," she protested. "Well before Paul Barrett's murder."

He held up his hands in mock defense. "Okay, okay," he said, laughing. "More tea?" Robin shook her head, and Lee went to refill his coffee cup. "It's too bad about Freeman being, uh, out of action," he mused. "Even so, Hudson's gotta be smiling all the way to the bank. I mean, with attendance at what? just under three million so far this season, he's gotta be coining it for a change."

"For a change? Morgan's business has always done well."

"Maybe, although my wife's at Chase and she says there are rumors ... But I meant the Comets. The team's got to have cost him a bundle over the years, but now with those superplayers bringing in the crowds ..." Lee stirred his coffee thoughtfully. "Wonder how they'll do without Freeman?"

"Yesterday's paper said the evidence is very circumstantial," Robin reminded him. "They won't be able to hold him."

"That's probably right." Lee drained his cup and checked his watch. "Guess I'd better get back to work." He gathered both their cups and dropped them into the trash basket. "Funny how fame changes people," he remarked. "All those superplayers seem to have developed some pretty hot tempers. They'd better be careful they don't spend the rest of the season on the bench. Come on, I'll walk you to the elevator."

Later, walking home in the brilliant sunlight and mulling over the events of the morning, Robin found herself getting angry all over again. So everyone thought she'd gotten the Comets scoop just because she was sleeping with Morgan. It was not only terrible for her fledgling career, it was blatantly untrue. She'd gotten the exclusive because ... because ...

Her pace slowed, then stopped. Why *had* she gotten the exclusive? Come to that, why had she been assigned that original article on Morgan for *Fortune*? Because Morgan wanted to sleep with her? That might explain the Comets exclusive, but not the *Fortune* article. Because she was the best writer *Fortune* could get? Hardly. Besides, Morgan had chosen her. And not because he was attracted to her; he hadn't even met her then. So, why?

A woman bumped into her, a man eyed her strangely, but she was oblivious.

Because I was young and inexperienced, she thought.

Because Morgan figured he could control me and what I would write. And he was right, wasn't he? He dazzled me, the assignment dazzled me, and I accepted whatever he told me. Every time I asked him for research materials, backup information, he supplied it with a smile, and I took what I was given. I never had to do any digging myself. He made it so easy for me. Too easy.

But why would he do that? What did he have to conceal? Lee had mentioned rumors in the financial community that Morgan's business was less than sound. That would easily explain why he'd wanted a neophyte to write the *Fortune* article. And the Comets piece?

She began walking again, her mind racing. His motivation for giving me the Comets exclusive must have been the same, she thought: control of what I write to make sure I won't rock the boat. Why? Well, it's understandable that as the Comets' owner, he'd want the super-training technique kept confidential. That didn't mean there was anything wrong with the training; he just didn't want to know about it if there was. So he gave the exclusive to a writer who knew nothing about sports or medicine. It all came down to money. And there was the bonus of maybe getting me into bed. She smiled ruefully. Of course it hadn't worked out quite that way. Morgan didn't know then that she had problems in that area. Or was she misjudging him? He'd been so understanding when she'd explained that she couldn't—

Again she stopped short and a kid on Rollerblades swerved to avoid her. It had suddenly occurred to her why Morgan might have been so patient, so understanding: sex with her could simply be a way for him to assure her loyalty, her blind devotion; another way to keep control of her and the Comets story she alone was allowed to write. Sure he'd take the sex if he could get it. But being understanding about her sexual hang-up would work just as well as the real thing to co-opt her, to tie her to him emotionally. To keep her on his side.

Was that what Felicity was trying to tell her? Maybe this time he's not just—using you?

Robin sighed deeply. Who knew what Felicity had re-

ally been about to say? She trudged on down the street.
Maybe I'm reading too much into all this, she thought.
Maybe it's just my famous low self-esteem trying to convince me that a man like Morgan Hudson couldn't possibly be attracted to me without an ulterior motive.

But facts are facts.

I accepted whatever information Morgan deigned to
give me for the *Fortune* story. And now I'm doing it
again. I never really pushed for the truth behind the
supertraining room; I just accepted it all on faith.

Not that I would have known where to start or what
to question. I've never done any investigative reporting.
I have no background in sports or science. Yes, and
that's precisely why he gave you the Comets exclusive.
You don't know enough to smell a rat.

Maybe not. But I sure know enough to smell a story.

She squared her shoulders and stepped up her pace.
There had to be a pay phone around here somewhere.

Large metal colanders masquerading as light fixtures
allowed faint illumination to pool on the paper-covered
tabletops. Young people, mostly in jeans, laughed and
called to one another across the small room, their voices
bouncing off the roughly plastered buff-colored walls.

"It's not fancy," Adam said, "but it's good. Also out
of the way, as you requested. You sure you're okay with
Tex-Mex?"

"I grew up on it," Robin said, smiling.

"Really? Where was that?"

Robin froze. If I say New Orleans, I'll have to tell all
the old lies again, and I'm sick of lying. But if I say East
Texas and he ever talks to anyone else I know— "Down
south," she said. "How's the green chili here?"

"Four-alarm, but wonderful. The margaritas are good,
too."

"Okay, but one's my limit if you want intelligent
conversation."

Adam chuckled. "I'll keep that in mind. Why don't
we order, and then you can tell me how I got lucky
enough to take you to dinner tonight."

Both Robin and Adam had dressed carefully for the evening, Adam in a new western-style silk shirt, jeans, an old tweed jacket, and his snakeskin boots for luck. Robin had chosen a full-length printed cotton skirt and matching pink short-sleeved sweater. They studied the menu and, surreptitiously, each other; both liked what they saw. As she had that day in his hospital office, Robin had the strong impression that Adam Salt was a man of openness and honesty, a strong man capable of gentleness, someone she should trust.

As before, Adam was impressed by her intelligence and humor, and beguiled by her beauty. But he had no illusions that it was his own unique appeal that had been the cause of her phone call to him that afternoon, requesting a chance to talk, and he was very curious. Once the ponytailed waiter had taken their order and gone off to fetch their drinks, he looked at Robin expectantly. But Robin found she wasn't quite ready to broach the reason for this meeting. "Tell me about Otis," she said instead.

Adam obligingly described his visit to Freeman, now out on bail, and recounted the player's version of his movements the night of the murder.

"Think he's telling the truth?" Robin asked, sipping her margarita.

"Yes, I do," Adam hesitated. "At least, I *want* to believe him."

Robin smiled ruefully. "It's easier to believe what you want to believe, isn't it? To convince yourself . . ." She broke off as two huge plates of food arrived, steamy and fragrant.

"Hope you're hungry," Adam told her.

"Ravenous," Robin replied. The way the first sip of margarita had hit her empty stomach reminded her that she hadn't eaten all day.

"Dig in, then." He smiled at her. "And between bites you can tell me what's up."

Where to start? Robin wondered as she ate a spoonfull of chili. "As a reporter, I have some serious questions . . ." No. "As Kenny's friend, I wonder whether . . ." But she wasn't a close friend of Kenny's, despite her interest in his well-being. "As Morgan's girlfriend, I've been lied to and manipulated ..." To her embarrassment, tears came to her eyes.

"I warned you about that chili," Adam teased. Then his eyes grew serious as he realized chili was not the problem. "What's wrong?"

"I need your help."

"You've got it." He reached for his hanky and passed it over to her. "What is it? Are you ill?"

"No, nothing like that. I'm just being stupid." She dried her eyes and looked around self-consciously.

"They'll think it's the food," he assured her. "Happens all the time." She gave him a weak smile and he smiled back encouragingly. "Tell me how I can help."

"It's about the superplayers."

Crying over the superplayers? Not likely, Adam thought. Did Morgan dump her? Aloud, he simply said, "Go on."

Robin began to talk, slowly at first, then with growing animation as the words came tumbling out. She didn't mention her fight with Morgan or the suspicions her interview with Bill Thomas had forced her to face—that was all too personal. But she expressed her feelings of being manipulated, her doubts about the special training, and her decision to finally begin digging in earnest for some answers to the questions she kept asking herself.

"For example?"

"Well, for a start, all three superplayers have suddenly become very angry young men. Did you know they used to call Sanchez 'Easy Ernie'?" Adam nodded. "Could a personality shift like that be caused by the training in some way? And if it could, does that mean Otis really could have killed Barrett after all?"

"Well ..."

"And Kenny's headaches," she continued. "We assumed they were caused by some physical injury, but could they actually be connected to the Supertraining?" Adam smiled at her use of the word *we*, but his smile faded as she described the practice session she'd seen during which Kenny apparently had experienced both a headache and a temper tantrum virtually at the same time. If the headaches were connected to the tantrums and the tantrums to the training . . .

"So you see, I have to start digging," Robin declared, "not only as a reporter, but as a responsible citizen. For the good of the players. For the good of the game."

She was using the same arguments on herself that Dennis Locke, the baseball commissioner, had used on him, Adam noted. Still, she was Morgan's girlfriend; discretion was called for.

"How about Morgan?" he asked. "Does he share your convictions, your need to dig?"

"Morgan's always cooperated in the writing of my Comets article," she said too quickly. "He got me into the Pro Club training room."

"That's not what I asked."

Robin sighed. "Morgan's heavily invested in the Comets' success," she said. "That doesn't mean he'd approve any training that would harm them. But if I were in his position, I wouldn't go looking for trouble. Would you?" Adam shrugged; she was probably right. "I've been through the training room, I've talked to the superplayers and the staff and Connor Egan, everybody who's close to the technique—"

"Except Paul Barrett."

"I'm afraid so, yes. Too late for that now. But my point is, everyone I *have* talked to has been as open and cooperative as possible, given the legitimate issue of keeping information from the competition. But somehow, I'm getting the feeling that what I've been writing is only what I'm supposed to write, and what I've been seeing and hearing is only what I'm meant to see and hear." She paused. "As I said, I'm beginning to feel manipulated."

"By Morgan?"

Robin flushed. "This has nothing to do with Morgan," she said flatly. "And I'm not here as his . . . representative. And I don't intend to go running to him with information."

"Again, that's not what I asked."

"I know." Robin ate a spoonful of chili. "Morgan wants a positive story," she said at last. "It's good for business. He decided months ago that I'm the writer who can give it to him."

"And what do you want?" Adam asked, fixing his eyes on hers.

"I want the truth. I want you to help me find it."

"And then you want to publish it."

"Yes."

"So we have a little problem."

"Why? Aren't you after the truth, too? Don't you want to help Kenny?"

"Of course, and that's exactly the point. For me, knowing the truth and using it to help my patient is what's paramount. There are issues of confidentiality here, but more than that, I'm not interested in being part of a newspaper investigation."

"Then let me be part of your medical investigation," Robin offered. "An editor I talked to today wanted me to write a messy little exposé about the Otis Freeman situation, because I had the inside track. I turned him down, of course, but he's right. I do have an inside track, and so do you, with Kenny."

"I talked to Kenny yesterday. He says his headaches have stopped. He refuses to come in for any more—" Adam broke off abruptly.

"More tests? But you told me his MRI was normal." Adam shrugged and looked vaguely embarrassed. "I know, doctor-patient confidentiality. But that just proves my point. I can probably get to Kenny more easily than you can right now. Maybe I can convince him to come and talk to you. Adam, we're stronger as a team than we are alone. Let's work together."

"But Robin . . ." Adam put his hand lightly on hers. "We can't work together if you're planning to use everything I tell you in an article."

Robin fell silent, intensely aware of the warmth of his hand. So what was the solution? She knew she couldn't find all the answers on her own, or interpret them correctly if she did. She needed Adam's knowledge of medicine and sports. But she was close to Morgan and the Comets, so Adam needed her, too. "Let's compromise," she suggested. "I won't submit anything for publication without your agreement. And you'll seriously consider the issue of publication again, after we know whatever there is to know. Things may look different then. You may actually want certain facts to be known. And frankly, I wouldn't want to write anything until then, anyway. What do you say?"

"You're counting on being able to change my mind?" He smiled.

"No," she answered, her expression serious. "I'm trusting you to consider the issue fairly."

"And I'd be trusting you with privileged information. I'd be trusting you not to disclose anything either of us may learn, or even suspect. Not to Morgan, not to anyone."

"Yes."

"So it all comes down to trust."

"Doesn't everything?"

They looked at each other across the remains of their dinner, Adam's hand still resting on hers. She's a reporter after a story, he thought; there was every reason not to trust her word. But somehow he did, absolutely.

The restaurant became fuller and noisier, but they never noticed as they sat over coffee and talked into the night. Adam told her the truth about Kenny's MRI, and the need for a spinal tap. He cautioned her that the atrophying thalamus and cortical lesion might possibly be tied to the headaches, but there was nothing to connect them with the supertraining. Although the seizure implications were suspicious, no other players had complained of persistent headaches.

They agreed on their next steps: Robin would make contact with Kenny under some pretext and bring him together with Adam; Adam would spend some time at the Pro Club and try to get Connor talking.

Adam spoke of his work and Robin asked intelligent questions; Adam asked about her writing career and she set him laughing with tales of the world of advertising. But underneath the banter, each was keenly aware of having made a commitment of trust to the other. And although Adam had removed his hand from hers when the coffee arrived, and Robin hadn't told him in so many words that her feelings for Morgan had cooled, they were both aware that the friendship that was growing between them that night was an excellent start to whatever might happen next.

Chapter Fifteen

"I don't know why we couldn't have done this over the phone," Kenny protested, sliding into a gilt chair opposite Robin. "Or at the stadium. Or you just could have sent me a copy of the article." Yesterday had been taken up with a boring photo shoot for Goodtimes Cola, there was yet another press party this evening, a meeting with his agent tomorrow morning, and, of course, baseball games to win. He had barely any personal time these days and it was starting to get to him. He looked around with disapproval at the cavernous, gilded Plaza Athenée dining room, empty aside from the two of them. "Don't you have an office?"

"No, I don't," Robin replied pleasantly. "And to answer your other questions, the stadium's too noisy, sending you the article would take too long, and for privacy, you can't beat a hotel dining room at two-thirty in the afternoon." *And Adam's office is just around the corner.* "I promise this won't take long."

A small, white-haired waiter, resplendent in his dinner jacket, arrived with the menus. "I'm afraid you're too late for the full lunch," he said apologetically, "and too early for the set tea. But all the cold selections are available. And the desserts."

"I'll have a beer," Kenny told him sullenly.

"Holstein? Beck's?"

"Bud." Kenny's eyes dared the man to challenge his choice.

The waiter remained placid. "Very good, sir." They'd send a runner around the corner to Gristede's; it had happened before. "And for the lady?" In his youth, he'd been trained to address all women as "madame" or "mademoiselle," but these days, who could tell?

"A cappuccino, please. And the apple tart. Are you sure you don't want to eat something, Kenny? A sandwich?"

"No thanks. Just the brew."

The waiter nodded and departed, and Robin gave an inward sigh. True, she'd had to pressure Kenny to meet her here, but she'd never expected this surliness. She hated to think what would happen when Adam arrived.

As if catching her thought, Kenny gave her a hundred-watt version of his thousand-watt smile. "I'm just a little stressed out these days. I didn't mean to take it out on you."

"Apology accepted." She pulled out the typewritten mock-article she'd prepared for this meeting and put it on the table. "There are just a couple of things . . ." she said, flipping the pages. "Uh, how are you feeling these days, Kenny? How are the headaches?"

"They're gone," he said briefly. He glanced at his watch. "You said this wouldn't take long."

"That's right. There are a few points I'd like to clarify . . ." For the next twenty minutes, Robin went over the answers to questions Kenny had already supplied during previous interviews with her. Their order arrived as they worked, and Kenny downed his beer and looked around, signaling to the little waiter for another. Robin was relieved to see that the beer seemed to relax Kenny; he stopped looking at his watch and started smiling more.

She knew Adam had arrived when she saw the smile freeze on Kenny's face.

"Hey, Kenny, is that you?" Adam exclaimed, his voice echoing in the empty room. "And Robin, too. What a surprise."

"Surprise, hell," said Kenny, rising. "You set me up." He looked angrily from one to the other.

"Set you up?" Adam repeated innocently. "How could you possibly—"

"Of course we set you up," Robin said firmly. "We care about you. Now sit down and listen."

"I don't have time for this bullshit—"

"You better make time," Robin told him. "Adam's worried about you. He thinks you may have a serious medical problem. But unless you cooperate, he can't help."

"I don't need any help," Kenny insisted loudly. "The headaches are gone." He turned toward Adam, aggrieved. "I already told you that on the phone."

"And I told you that the MRI had turned up some strange things," Adam replied calmly. "We have to talk about this, Kenny, face-to-face. It's important."

"And it'll be great material for that article, right, Robin? No thanks."

"This article's a sham," Robin told him. "And I've put the Comets exclusive on hold. Anyway, I wouldn't write about your medical condition without your consent. It wouldn't be ethical."

"Since when do reporters have ethics?"

Robin flushed at the insult, but remained calm; the remark was so unlike the Kenny Reese she'd gotten to know. "You have my word," she said firmly. "If you like, I'll leave you two alone so you can talk privately."

"Good," Kenny replied flatly.

Adam sighed. Unrealistic though it was, he'd been hoping Kenny would view Robin as his advocate and insist on her being included in the discussion. The confidentiality issue had been troubling him ever since he'd told her about Kenny's MRI the other night. Having Kenny's agreement to disclose would have made Adam feel a lot more comfortable. But it was not to be. He looked over at Robin. "Would you mind?"

"Not at all."

She collected her papers and reached for the check, but Adam got to it first. "I'll take care of this."

Kenny stood up as she did, and put a tentative hand on her shoulder. "Sorry if I was rude to you."

"It's okay."

Both men watched her leave the room; then Adam turned back to Kenny. "Sit down. Please." Kenny shrugged, and with a great show of looking at his watch, resumed his seat. "I'm glad your headaches are gone," Adam began. "But that doesn't mean everything's now okay. Whether or not the headaches were the result of the fights you were in, they caused us to do an MRI. And as I told you on the phone, the MRI opened up more questions."

"But I feel fine."

"I know. But that doesn't mean you'll keep feeling fine. I urge you to let us do that spinal tap."

"I'm sorry I started this whole thing," Kenny declared. "I got in a fight, I got hit in the head, I started having headaches, the headaches went away . . ."

"I don't think those headaches were caused by getting hit in the head," Adam said slowly.

"Oh yeah?" Kenny said belligerently. "What do *you* think caused them?"

"I don't know, but . . . maybe the Supertraining."

Kenny stared at him. "The training? That's impossible."

"Is it?"

"If the training caused the headaches, how come the other superplayers haven't been having headaches?"

"I don't know."

"And how come the headaches went away?"

"I don't know that, either. But Kenny, you're too smart not to realize that the way you've been playing can't be due to stuff like meditation and biofeedback. You were a science major. You have to know better."

"I don't want to know better," Kenny said firmly. "I don't want to stop the training. I want to keep playing."

"Nobody's going to make you stop doing anything," Adam assured him.

"Damn right."

"All I'm saying is, let's do the spinal. Let's try to find out what's going on inside that brain of yours. Maybe it's something we can fix, or at least arrest." Adam hesitated. "You're not the only superplayer, remember. If it *is* caused by the training, it'll happen to your teammates, too, eventually."

Kenny leaned back in his chair and closed his eyes for

a long moment. When he opened them again, he looked weary and confused. "Don't you think I've wondered why the supertraining makes us play so well?" he said softly. "But it's kinda like the goose with the golden eggs thing. I have too much to lose if I start questioning things. Besides, I haven't done anything wrong."

"It's not a question of right or wrong."

"I haven't taken any drugs or anything," Kenny continued, "and the only thing they give us at the Pro Club is the energy tonic—"

"Which you were going to try and get a sample of."

"Yeah, but it can't be that," Kenny protested. "I've seen Connor drink it."

"Look, it's perfectly possible that the things we saw in the MRI weren't caused by the supertraining," Adam said. "It could be something else entirely. But unless we do more tests, we'll never know. And if we don't know what caused that cortical lesion, we can't treat it, we can't keep it from happening again."

"But it's not bothering me."

"Not at the moment, no," Adam agreed.

Kenny looked at him fearfully. "You think it will? You think something's gonna happen to me?"

"I don't know. Please. Have the spinal tap."

"I don't want to stop playing," Kenny said softly.

"I don't want you to stop playing," Adam replied. "You've lifted my favorite team into a pennant race for the first time in eleven years." He smiled encouragingly. "You're my hero, kid."

"When the coach finds out . . . and Morgan Hudson . . ."

"Nobody's going to find out."

"She'll tell them." Kenny flashed a glance in the direction in which Robin had departed. "She's Hudson's girlfriend."

Adam shook his head. "She won't tell him."

"Don't get me wrong," Kenny said. "I like Ms. Kennedy. She was so worried, that day in the locker room. She practically blackmailed me into coming to see you. I know she means well. I'm just afraid . . ."

"I swear to you, she won't tell anyone. No one will know."

Kenny studied Adam for a long moment. Apparently he sensed the same qualities in him that Robin had, for he leaned toward the older man and nodded. "Okay," he said softly. "I trust you. When do you want me to come in?"

"As soon as possible. Tomorrow?"

"It'll have to be late; around seven?"

"I'll set it up." He reached for his wallet and the check. "You're doing the right thing."

Kenny gave him a crooked smile. "Like I have a choice."

"I'm so dreadfully sorry about the other night," Felicity said. "I had no idea they'd actually show up. I assure you, Sandy Napier avoids me whenever possible."

"It doesn't matter," Robin said tiredly. "Morgan would only have heard about it from someone else." The phone had been ringing as she'd come through the door after her meeting at the Plaza Athenée; now she switched the receiver from one ear to the other as she pulled off her suit jacket and slung it over the back of a chair.

"But it *does* matter," Felicity insisted. "We've become such friends, you and I; I wouldn't want you to think I'd put you in such an embarrassing position on purpose."

Robin recalled Felicity beside her on the terrace, waving and calling to the Napiers through the French doors. Aloud she said, "Of course you wouldn't."

"That's settled, then. So, are you free for lunch one day this week?"

Robin hesitated. "I don't think I should," she said. The phone had a long cord; she carried it over to the coffee table, kicked off her shoes, and settled herself on the sofa. "Morgan seems to take my friendship with you as a personal affront, and I guess I can understand his, er, discomfort."

"Discomfort?" Felicity hooted with laughter. "Fury's more like it. Apparently he met that toad Sandy for a drink around six on Friday, and Sandy couldn't wait to tell Morgan he'd seen his girlfriend and his wife having a heart-to-heart. Morgan was on the phone to me in minutes. Such language. Then, after he'd finished insulting me, he forbade me to see you again, actually forbade me. 'We're not *dating*, for God's sake,' I told him. Can you believe it?"

"Actually, I can."

" 'She's not a child, Morgan,' I told him. 'She's not a chattel. You don't own her.' " Felicity paused. "He doesn't, does he?"

"What, own me? No, of course he doesn't."

"Then let's have lunch."

"Felicity, I . . ." Robin paused. There was an undercurrent here she didn't fully understand. "Actually, I'd love to," she said, phrasing her response carefully, "but it will have to wait at least a week, maybe two. I've got a deadline coming up and I'm working like a demon."

"Sounds like a terribly polite excuse," Felicity said, sounding amused.

"No, really—"

"Not that I blame you. Morgan can be quite frightening at times, can't he? You'd never know he had such a temper."

"I'm working. Honestly."

"All right, I believe you. But I'm not letting you off the hook." Felicity lowered her voice. "He didn't hit you, did he?"

"No . . . no."

"Because I'd feel so absolutely awful if my little party were the cause of any serious unpleasantness between you two. Now, we will have that lunch, won't we? You promise?"

"I promise. Once I get this work done."

"Good. Then I'll look forward to talking to you soon. Bye, sweetie."

Robin slowly lowered the receiver. What a strange conversation, she thought. And what odd timing. Felicity claimed Morgan had called her on Friday, yet she'd waited four days to call Robin. And what was that business about Felicity accusing Morgan of treating her like a child, or a chattel?

Was it possible, she wondered, that Morgan wasn't the only person trying to manipulate her?

"Business as usual in there?" Adam asked, tucking a faded blue T-shirt into his white exercise shorts.

"More or less," Howard Finkel replied. The beefy cardiologist stripped off his drenched sweats and tossed them into a plastic bag. "The crowd's dropped off a little and the rumors are flying."

"What kind of rumors?"

"About what you'd expect. Will the place really stay open? Is Freeman really innocent? Does Connor know something he hasn't told the police? Did Barrett leave a will?" He wrapped a towel around his waist. "The superplayers are still training; Sanchez was leaving as I came in."

Adam felt it as soon as he entered the main workout space; a subtle undercurrent of tension. Though the weight bars rose and fell with their accustomed regularity and the rhythmic slap of the light bag echoed from the cantilevered space above his head, he could sense uncertainty and doubt in the stances and expressions of the members around him. Everyone was wondering what had really happened. And what would happen next.

He lay on his back doing bench presses on the Nautilus and watched Connor descend the open stairs from the penultimate level. Although out of his sight line, Adam knew that bright yellow police tapes proclaimed the top floor, with its secret entrance to Barrett's living quarters, off-limits. The club had been closed all weekend while detectives swept it for clues, but it had opened on time Monday morning, much to Adam's surprise.

Connor arrived at the main level and looked around, apparently pleased that most of the regulars hadn't deserted the Pro Club just because of a little murder. Adam gave him a strained smile, and purposely let the weight bar clang down. Connor shook his head and headed over.

"Too much weight, as usual," he said disapprovingly. "It's the reps, not the pounds, that build strength." He went around and pulled out the key. "I'm taking it down to thirty-five, okay?"

"Whatever you say." Adam sat up and swiveled around to face Connor. "Personal service. That's part of what makes this place so great. I'll miss it."

Connor looked up. "What do you mean?" he asked suspiciously.

"I just meant . . . that is, I assume with Barrett, uh, gone, this place can't keep going indefinitely, can it?"

Connor stood and came around the bench to face Adam. "Sure it can," he said.

"But how?"

Connor shrugged. "Who cares? All I know is, the estate attorneys have told me to keep the place open while they sort things out."

"But then what? There are all kinds of rumors. It's bad for morale."

"Do you think I don't know that?" Connor sounded aggrieved. "I tell people, but they just don't listen. They'd rather imagine all sorts of disaster scenarios. The truth is, the estate will either keep the place running or sell it to someone who will. Think about it: who'd be stupid enough to close down a successful place like this? We train the superplayers."

"The attorneys told you this?"

"Yes, of course. I don't know what everybody's so upset about."

"Funny how murder makes some people so nervous," Adam said. Connor gave him a look, but Adam kept his expression bland. "You knew him well?"

"Who?"

"Paul Barrett, our reclusive ex-benefactor upstairs."

Connor's mouth tightened. "I met with him sometimes," he said. "I didn't know him well."

"What was he like?" Connor didn't reply. "A crippled ex-jock locked away above a gym," Adam continued, "and other people benefiting from his discovery . . . He must have been a saint."

"Uh-huh."

"Or a real bite in the ass."

Connor got up. "Whatever he was like," he said grimly, "he's dead now. Don't change the weights." With a gesture toward the rear of the exercise machine, he began to move away, but the beeping of a cellular phone stopped him. Reaching into his pocket, he extracted the instrument, flipped it open, and put it to his ear. Adam saw his shoulders slump as he listened.

"Yes, I see," he heard Connor say. "Okay, okay. Tell them I'll be right there." He put the phone away, the action turning him back toward Adam, and stood a moment in unhappy contemplation. Then, almost in spite of himself, he tilted back his head and looked up toward the ceiling. Adam followed his gaze. There on the topmost exercise terrace stood two burly men in suits. Connor stared up at them for a very long moment. Then he slowly made his way back to the open stairway and climbed up toward the waiting police detectives.

Chapter Sixteen

Mid September

"And this is Robin Kennedy, a . . . colleague of mine."

Agnes studied Robin for a moment. "Colleague? You are a doctor?"

"Robin's a medical writer," Adam said quickly, giving the cover story he and Robin had concocted earlier en route from his office to Rockefeller University. "She's doing a story on modern diagnostic techniques." He felt bad about lying to Agnes, but until he was ready to tell her who Kenny was, Robin's role had to be withheld, too.

"Of course." Agnes nodded. "There's such a need for material in that area." She glanced sharply at Adam as she spoke; he knew as well as she that the field had been overwritten. Well, it was his patient they were about to discuss; if Adam was indiscreet enough to include a writer . . . a very pretty writer . . . The light dawned. She turned back to Robin, all smiles. "I am so very happy to know you," she said. Then, giving Adam a broad and knowing wink, she led them into the lab. Adam raised his eyes to heaven, and Robin grinned in amusement.

A Macintosh Power PC was set up at one end of the long Formica-topped counter; reports, printouts, slides, and miscellaneous paraphernalia were arranged neatly along the rest of its length.

"First, the results of the spinal tap," Agnes said. "And then I will tell you about that mysterious liquid you refused to identify for me." Kenny had managed to sneak out a little of the energy tonic and Adam had sent it to Agnes for analysis along with the spinal fluid.

Agnes typed several commands on the keyboard; the screen saver graphic of flying neon-colored brains disappeared ("My assistant made that. Amusing, no?"), and the monitor screen came to life.

"We can rule out meningitis and any sort of unusual virus," Agnes began, scanning through the data on the screen. "In fact, everything is perfectly normal—"

"Normal? But you said on the phone—"

"Don't interrupt, Adam," Agnes told him firmly. "Everything is normal except for two things." She counted them out on her fingers. "Number one, there is an abnormally high protein level. As you know, this could indicate a degenerative disease of some sort. Number two—"

"Why do high protein levels indicate disease?" Robin interrupted.

"When cells are destroyed," Adam explained, "protein is released. So high levels of protein in the spinal fluid could indicate the destruction of brain cells." He turned to Agnes. "But in this case, the high protein levels are a stand-alone. There are no symptoms that would indicate a diagnosable physical problem, and the nervous system appears to be functioning normally. Degenerative brain disease seems like a long shot to me."

"I assume you have examined this patient recently?"

"I did a complete physical when he came in for the lumbar puncture. He's strong and fully functional. His headaches are gone and he says he's feeling fine."

"Then I agree," Agnes said. "Degenerative brain disease is doubtful." She typed briefly on the keyboard and new data appeared on the monitor. "I said there were two abnormalities," she continued. "The second abnormality is more interesting to me." She turned back to Adam and Robin, ready to enjoy the effect of her announcement. "We have here the presence of an unidentified hormone."

"An unidenti—" Adam stared at her. "What the hell *is* it?"

"As I said, it is unknown, something new. But I believe it is linked to the atrophying thalamus. And now I have another little surprise for you. Come." Agnes led an openmouthed Adam and a confused but fascinated Robin out of the lab and down the corridor. "I have managed to isolate this hormone from the spinal fluid," Agnes told them over her shoulder.

"You're amazing, Agnes," Adam told her sincerely.

She stopped at a small unmarked door, withdrew a set of keys from the pocket of her lab coat, and inserted one into the complicated-looking lock. As she pulled the heavy door open, a cold vapor swirled out and Robin stepped back. Agnes smiled at her. "It is only the refrigeration," she said. "No ghosts here."

The small cold room was lined with steel cabinets. Agnes pulled out a narrow drawer and beckoned them over to look. Inside nestled a small glass vial filled with a clear pale fluid.

"My God," Adam breathed. "What is it?"

"I believe," Agnes answered slowly, "that we are looking at an unknown thalamic hormone, very powerful." Her eyes glittered with excitement. "The contents of this tube is, I believe, the reason your patient's thalamus is atrophying. This hormone is replacing, probably in much larger doses, something the thalamus produces naturally."

"Something no one's identified."

"Until now, yes. So mysterious, the thalamus. Still today, we know so little about it."

"That's true." Adam thought for a moment. A heretofore unidentified thalamic hormone, but not produced by Kenny's thalamus ... the duplicate of a hormone naturally produced by the thalamus, only much stronger ... But what was its function? And why was it present in Kenny's spinal fluid? "I think it's time I told you who my patient is," he said.

"It is past time," Agnes agreed solemnly.

"But not in this refrigerator."

Agnes led them back to her small, tidy office and settled them in chairs around her desk. Then she looked at Adam expectantly.

"Kenny Reese is a baseball player," he told her. "He

plays for the Comets. You know who the Comets are, Agnes?"

"Who does not? My assistant talks of them all the time. And I seem to recall you speaking of them, too, one night last spring."

"That's right," Adam said, remembering. "Freeman made that incredible catch in the second game . . . Well, Kenny's a superplayer, one of the three Comets players who have been specially trained at a place called the Pro Club. The superplayers are, well, they're amazing ballplayers. They react faster, they anticipate plays practically before they're made, their reflexes are—"

"Why didn't you tell me this before?" Agnes interrupted angrily. "Really, Adam, it is most annoying."

"I'm sorry, Agnes—"

"You ask me to help you and you keep the most important fact from me."

Adam grinned. "You mean, that my patient's a celebrity?" He found this new side of Agnes amusing.

But Agnes snorted. "Oh, yes, I am so interested in famous people. No, Adam, the fast reaction time, the reflexes. That is the important fact." She stood and began pacing with excitement. "Yes, now it becomes clear."

Robin looked over at Adam questioningly. Adam shrugged. "What becomes clear, Agnes?" he asked.

But Agnes shook her head. "I must think." She wandered back and forth across the small room several times before turning back to Adam and Robin. "Much of this you already know, my dear Adam," she began, "so you will forgive me for stating the obvious." She came around and perched on the edge of her desk. "The premotor area of the brain has subcortical connections with the thalamus." Adam nodded. "The thalamus is involved in recruiting nerve pathways for the transmission of cortical motor function information."

"And you think this hormone could help speed up those transmissions?" Adam asked eagerly. Faster information transfer could speed up the motor functions, which would explain—

But Agnes shook her head. "No, not directly. But nitric oxide could."

"You're losing me."

"An unusual little molecule, nitric oxide," Agnes mused. "It's an uncharged molecule with an unpaired electron, which makes it an ideal messenger molecule. It can walk through walls."

Robin laughed, but Adam looked puzzled.

"I mean, my dear Adam, that the nitric oxide molecule moves freely across cellular membranes. It drifts in and out of cells, Robin. And its unpaired electron makes it highly reactive; it lasts only a few seconds before decaying into nitrite. We know it's an important catalyst for interneural communications." Agnes turned to Robin again. "That means the transmission of impulses across the synapses linking one neuron to another." Robin managed a nod; synapses sounded vaguely familiar from high school biology, but that was as far as her knowledge extended. Sensing this, Agnes elaborated. "I'm talking about the way that neurons—nerve endings—send messages to each other; the way the nervous system controls the actions of the body. Is that a little clearer?"

"Yes, thanks." Robin smiled gratefully.

"Now, nitric oxide is a known enhancer of neural connections. So," Agnes went on, "increased levels of nitric oxide could mean better neural communications, faster neural communications. And *that*," she concluded triumphantly, "could very well lead to faster transmission of cortical motor function information, and thus, faster reaction time."

"But you didn't say you found increased levels of nitric oxide," Adam pointed out. "You said everything except the protein levels and this new hormone was normal."

"We can't calibrate nitric oxide levels. Its half-life is too short. It spontaneously transmits its signal and then decays, all in a matter of seconds."

"Let me understand this," Adam thought aloud. "You suspect that the hormone you found is increasing the level of nitric oxide in the brain, right?" Agnes nodded.

"And that could be speeding up impulse transmission time."

"Yes. But that's not all that's happening. Have you ever heard of a neural mechanism called LTP?"

"LTP? No, I don't believe so."

"LTP stands for long-term potentiation. There's been an explosion of research in this area since 1987. The LTP effect is what happens when the transmission of impulses over and over again between two neurons produces positive feedback. This positive feedback effect means that future transmissions between those neurons become easier and easier. We believe the LTP effect is produced by a signal being sent from the neuron that's receiving the impulse, back to the neuron that transmitted it. We call that signal 'the retrograde messenger.' Experiments at Stanford suggest that the retrograde messenger just might be nitric oxide."

"Which means?"

"If you increase the level of nitric oxide, you increase neural learning and memory. The corollary could be that you reduce information processing time and reaction time."

"So Kenny could see the ball coming off the bat the same way any other player would," said Adam, "but his brain would process that information faster and his body would react faster."

"And," Robin added slowly, working it out, "the more often he did something—the more often he batted, or fielded—the faster his reaction time would be, because the LD, uh, LP—"

"LTP effect," Adam prompted.

"Right. It would make the information transmission in his brain easier and easier, each time."

"Exactly." Agnes's eyes sparkled with approval. "And LTP isn't limited only to the particular synapse that's sending the messages back and forth. Research at Stanford, Columbia, the University of Alabama, the Planck Institute, all indicate that nitric oxide's LTP effect extends to neighboring synapses as well. It can even enhance transmissions between neural pathways that aren't directly connected."

"That's incredible."

"Yes, but Adam, you must understand that much work remains to be done. For example, it is believed that nitric oxide may be involved in coordination and balance. But how? Also, although we have identified the discrete neuronal groups in which nitric oxide occurs, the specific brain pathways in which it is involved are still unclear."

"Okay, I can understand that increased nitric oxide could boost interneural communication time. But nitric oxide is toxic." Adam shook his head. "It's toxic, Agnes. In large amounts, it works on pathogens like bacteria and viruses, but it also knocks out healthy host cells. It's an indiscriminate killer."

"Exactly!" Agnes exclaimed. "It is all clear now, yes?"

"No."

"Adam, you're not thinking. If this new hormone is increasing the amount of nitric oxide beyond the normal level the brain is equipped to handle, if it is increasing it to a toxic level, then that toxic level of nitric oxide would cause the nerve cells to begin to digest themselves."

"Which would explain the high protein levels in the spinal fluid."

"Precisely."

Adam turned to Robin. "You getting any of this?"

"Not all of it, but enough to know we're on to something."

"He will explain it carefully later," Agnes said, "so you can write about it in your article." She looked from one to the other. "If there really is an article."

"There isn't," Robin said. "I'm not a medical writer. I was actually writing an exclusive about the Comets and the superplayers, but I've stopped. At least for the time being," she added with a glance at Adam. "Until we find out what's really going on."

Agnes fixed Adam with a severe look but her eyes twinkled. "And why could you not tell me this? Why did you not simply tell me, here is Robin, a very pretty woman whom I like very much, who is helping me to— what exactly is your part in this investigation?"

"I . . . I have a sort of inside track with the team, the players . . ."

"She dating the owner of the Comets," Adam said flatly. "She has access to people and places that I don't."

Agnes's face fell. Too bad. She had hoped . . . Well, working together as they were, things could change. She'd noticed Robin's look of faint displeasure at Adam's announcement of her involvement with the Comets owner; that was hopeful.

"Now, how do we explain the seizures?" Adam asked, attempting to bring the conversation back on track.

"Seizures?" Robin asked. "Who's been having seizures?"

"All the superplayers, I suspect," Adam said. "Those temper tantrums, the sudden rages . . . I think they're actually a kind of seizure that looks like rage."

"You mean Kenny's brawls were really seizures?" Adam nodded. "What caused them?"

"Let's think about what could be happening inside Kenny's brain," Agnes suggested. "This mysterious hormone increases the production of nitric oxide to toxic levels. As a result, the brain cells in the cortex are continually being irritated and destroyed by these high levels of nitric oxide. In such a case, spastic seizures might occur. In fact, I believe they'd be quite likely to occur."

Adam nodded. "Remember that game against Boston, when Sanchez tried to attack the umpire?" Robin nodded. "Well, I had a videotape of the game, and when I slowed it down, I could see Sanchez give a sort of convulsive twitch at the start of his attack."

"A spastic seizure?" Robin asked.

"It's certainly possible," Adam said thoughtfully. "But the big question is, where's this hormone coming from?"

"It certainly isn't being made by Kenny's thalamus," Agnes said. "It must be being introduced from the outside, somehow."

"The energy tonic!" Adam exclaimed.

"The what?" Agnes stared at him suspiciously.

"Uh, the fluid I sent you for analysis."

Agnes sighed. "Again, you keep the facts from me." She returned to her desk chair and hunted through some papers on her desk. "The report was delivered only this morning," she said, drawing forth a stiff blue folder. "I have not had a chance to read it." She opened the folder and scanned the sheet of paper inside. "Oh, this is interesting," she exclaimed. "This is very, very interesting."

"Come on, Agnes, tell us," Adam pleaded.

"Well, basically, what we have here is . . . Gatorade," she announced.

"Gatorade?" Adam looked at her in disbelief.

"Water . . . glucose . . . lemon juice . . ." Agnes read from the paper. "Yes, I would definitely say Gatorade. Lemon Ice, I believe the flavor is called. One of my favorites." She grinned at them. "Oh, there is one other ingredient. Rather a strange one."

Adam and Robin leaned toward her eagerly.

"Dried, finely powdered sage." Agnes chuckled. "Don't be disappointed, Adam," she said kindly. "A hormone such as we have discovered cannot be given by mouth. Surely you know that. It would be digested."

"When I sent you the energy tonic, I didn't know we'd find a thalamic hormone in Kenny's spinal fluid," Adam said defensively.

"Of course you didn't. Now listen to me, because I need your permission. I want to study the effect of this hormone we have isolated. I want to inject some of it into the spinal fluid of laboratory animals; rats, I think. Do I have your permission to do that, Adam?"

"Absolutely. How soon will you start?"

'Immediately."

"Good."

"There is something else you should know about nitric oxide, Adam. Although it appears to alleviate the neurotoxicity of the excitatory transmitter glutamate, which is released in large doses during a stroke—uh, it reduces stroke damage, Robin—nitric oxide also constricts the blood vessels, causing cerebral ischemia. Not only could that counteract its ability to reduce stroke damage, but in very large, continuous doses, I believe it is possible that nitric oxide might actually produce a stroke."

"You mean—"

"Kenny could be at risk."

"Jesus. And there's nothing we can do?"

Agnes shook her head. "Not with what we know right now."

"We can make him stop training," Robin said fiercely. "We can make them all stop training."

"Ten days before the pennant game?" Adam exclaimed. "Not a chance. Besides, we have no proof that the training and the hormones are connected."

"None at all," Agnes agreed sadly. "Despite the spastic seizures—the rages—of the other players, we can show no actual, provable connection between the training and the presence of this hormone. We don't even know if it's present in the spinal fluid of the other superplayers."

"You're sure the only thing they give the superplayers is the energy drink?" Robin asked Adam, who nodded. "No injections? Maybe something they told Kenny was a vitamin shot?"

"Kenny says absolutely not. I don't think he'd lie to me. Not now. Besides, an injection wouldn't do it."

"Why not? Don't doctors give people hormone injections all the time?"

"It's true that hormones are traditionally delivered by injection," Adam answered patiently. "But they can't pass through the body's blood-brain barrier."

"The—what?"

"The blood-brain barrier. It's one of the ways the body protects the brain from injury. The blood-brain barrier stops waste products and other poisons from passing through the cranial blood vessels and reaching the nerve cells of the brain. It's the reason medication that needs to get into the brain is usually injected directly into the spinal fluid."

"Well, maybe that's how they're doing it."

But Adam shook his head. "I saw no evidence of earlier punctures when I did the spinal tap. And Kenny says he's never had any injections at the Pro Club."

"Maybe he forgot."

Adam smiled at Robin. "A spinal injection hurts like hell," he said. "I don't think he'd forget it."

"Then we have nothing," Agnes concluded. "Well, who knows? The training may actually have nothing to do with the presence of this hormone ... no, I don't believe that, either. It all fits together too neatly." She sighed deeply. "It is so difficult. Yes, by all means, tell Kenny to stop the training if you wish, but remember, we have no idea how the training could be causing this hormone to be present in the spinal fluid. Whatever we may suspect, we have no knowledge and no proof. And if we accuse the Supertraining of causing a hormonal imbalance—which is the most we could say—and we then learn that we are wrong, that the training is not the cause, then we are in serious trouble." Adam slumped in his chair, and Robin looked stricken. "That doesn't mean the connection does not exist. It simply means we do not yet know enough to say what it is." She sighed. "I wish I could be more helpful."

"You've been enormously helpful, Agnes," Adam assured her. "I can't thank you enough."

"It is the kind of puzzle I like, normally. But not when lives are at stake." She rose. "On to the rats. I will call you as soon as I have anything significant to report. And meanwhile, Adam, Robin ..."

"Yes?"

"Be careful."

Robin was very quiet as they left the building. The implications of what she had just learned were very troubling, yet these new facts explained so much. Morgan's recent violent behavior, for example; couldn't the supertraining he'd recently started be causing him the same sudden rages the superplayers were experiencing? And if that were so, didn't she have an obligation to tell him? But Morgan's reaction hadn't been a sudden, out-of-the-blue thing, she reminded herself. It had been the direct result of his hearing about her friendship with Felicity. And hadn't Felicity referred to Morgan's shortness of temper in their phone conversation? No, she couldn't blame Morgan's rage on the supertraining. But that didn't excuse her from warning him, did it?

She glanced at Adam; he, too, was deep in thought, his rugged, good-looking face solemn, his gray-green eyes serious. A light summer breeze ruffled his shaggy brown hair. She found herself wondering what would it be like to be kissed by him, then flushed as he turned and smiled at her.

"How about some coffee?" he asked. "There must be a place around here."

It was midmorning and the coffee bar was nearly empty. They brought their cappuccinos to the counter beside the window and sipped awhile in companionable silence, looking out at the tree-lined street.

"Now what?" Robin asked at last.

"Now I talk to Kenny again," Adam said. "Or try to."

"I thought he'd decided to cooperate."

"You mean because he agreed to the spinal tap? No, with Kenny, it's one step forward, two steps back. He's still in denial about this whole thing. He's terrified."

"I don't blame him."

"Neither do I, I guess. But as a doctor, I can't help him unless I know what's going on."

"And even then—"

Adam turned to face her. "Yes, even then, I don't know if I, if anyone, can help him." He sighed. "I was so excited back there with Agnes. I mean, it *is* exciting: the discovery of a new hormone, the connection with nitric oxide ... We know what's happening chemically now, and that's a real breakthrough. Next I'd like to do a PET scan—positron emission tomography. The read-out will show us exactly what part of Kenny's brain is working when he's playing. Or when he's thinking about batting and making plays."

"You can actually see that?" Robin exclaimed. "That's amazing."

"Yeah," Adam agreed. "But the PET won't tell us

how the hormone got into Kenny's spinal fluid. It won't help us tie it to the Pro Club or the supertraining. And Kenny will still be at risk. Shit." He drank some coffee, wiping the foam from his mustache with a paper napkin.

"Tell Kenny to stop the supertraining."

"You think I haven't?" Adam shook his head. "He can't, Robin. Not unless we can prove a direct connection between the hormone and the supertraining. Frankly, I don't blame him."

Robin stared at him. "You don't?"

Adam smiled at her astonishment. "I'm a jock at heart," he explained. "I love sports. I love to play them, watch them, read about them. And I know a lot of the pros through my work. Professional ballplayers are amazingly dedicated people, Robin. They routinely play through pain, through illness, through personal tragedy. And the Comets have a lot of heart these days. The pennant's practically theirs for the first time in years, and the World Series is coming up fast. There's no way any Comets player is going to choose to stop playing right now. And for the superplayers, refusing the training means choosing not to play." He paused. "I don't even know if Kenny'd be allowed stop the training. It's probably in his contract."

"Unless we can prove that it's making him sick."

"Which we can't. Another cappuccino?"

Robin shook her head. "What do you want me to do?" she asked.

"Damned if I know," Adam told her. "See what you can find out from your boyfriend, I guess." Is he still my boyfriend? Robin wondered. Despite the flowers he'd sent the next day, she hadn't actually spoken to Morgan since a week ago Friday when he'd raged at her about Felicity's party. "And stick close to the Comets," Adam added. He stirred the remains of his coffee, then drained the cup and set it back down on the counter. "Despite what Agnes just told us, we don't actually know zip."

Robin put a hand on his arm. "We know a lot," she said. "We know there's a strange hormone that's causing the superplayers to play like they do. And we know it gives them seizures that look like rage."

"Yeah," Adam conceded. "But we don't know how the hormone got there, or how to make it go away. Not that anyone involved wants it to."

I'll call Morgan as soon as I get home, Robin decided. If there's a connection between the supertraining and the hormone, Morgan's at risk, too. Besides, I'm sure he wouldn't approve of anything that would hurt his Comets. He loves those guys.

As if reading her thoughts, Adam turned to her, his face serious. "One of the reasons I suggested having coffee was because there's something I want to say to you." He paused, arranging the words carefully in his mind. "I realize that you and Morgan are very close," he said at last. "But I'm trusting you to be discreet. When you asked if we could work together on this, you assured me you weren't Morgan's representative, and you wouldn't go running back to him with information. I trusted you then, and I still trust you. But after what Agnes told us today, you could be thinking that by telling Morgan, by getting him involved, you can help Kenny and the others."

"I wasn't—" Robin started to say, then fell silent. It was precisely what she'd been thinking.

"Of course you were," Adam told her. "It's a perfectly natural reaction. But you mustn't do it. I'm not saying Morgan doesn't care about his team; of course he does. But until we know what's really happening, telling Morgan could cause everyone a lot of grief."

"Why?"

"Well, suppose he stops the training and the Comets lose the pennant. And then we find out the hormone had nothing at all to do with the supertraining."

"Is that possible?"

"Anything's possible, Robin. I don't think it's probable, but it's certainly possible. In that case, Morgan's hurt, the team's hurt, the Pro Club's hurt, Connor's hurt . . ." He took her hand and looked deep into her eyes. "And I'd be hurt, too."

"You?"

"Yes. Because you made a promise to me, Robin, and I trusted you to keep it."

Robin nodded slowly. Whatever her personal feelings, Adam was right; telling Morgan was out of the question. "You can trust me," she said softly.

Adam gently squeezed her hand. "I never doubted it."

Chapter Seventeen

"Goddamn it, Ray," Morgan's voice boomed through the intercom speaker on Meg's desk. "What is this shit?" Ray began to protest but Morgan overrode him. "These are the old numbers," he bellowed. "I told Megan to send you the new ones two days ago. Damn woman."

At her desk beside the door to Morgan's private office, Meg bristled with righteous indignation.

"She did send them," Ray Goetz was explaining. "But I thought it would be better if we—"

"I don't pay you to second-guess me," Morgan roared.

He used to be such a nice boss, Meg reflected; good-tempered, polite, thoughtful. But he'd been impossible lately, just impossible. And he refused to listen when she tried to talk to him about it. That's why she'd secretly begun switching on the intercom speaker on his desk whenever she had the chance. She rarely heard anything interesting, but it put her one up on this rude man. Now her desk phone rang and the interoffice extension lit up. She carefully lowered the volume button on the intercom box before taking the call, then listened, spoke briefly, and slowly replaced the receiver. Great timing, she thought. Not. She hit her intercom "talk" button and pressed the buzzer.

"I thought I told you," Morgan's angry voice boomed through the intercom speaker. "No interruptions. Don't you listen?"

"Robin Kennedy's here," Meg said calmly. Maybe she should just quit. Last Sunday's *Times* had had lots of listings for experienced executive secretaries.

"Who? Robin's *here*?"

"In reception. She's not on your calendar."

"Of course she's not on my calendar. I wasn't expecting her, dammit." Yes, she would definitely quit, Meg decided. Just as soon as she found another job. She'd start looking tomorrow. "Ask her to wait," Morgan barked, then changed his mind. "No, we're nearly finished in here. Bring her through."

But raised voices were still issuing from Morgan's office as Meg led Robin in from reception. She'd never actually met Robin before, though she'd spoken to her on the phone several times at Morgan's request. She seemed nice, but nervous. Meg wondered if she was finding Morgan's new temperament as difficult as everyone at the office was.

"I guess I came at a bad time," Robin said, her eyes drifting toward the closed door. "Maybe I should just go."

"Oh, it's always that way when he meets with Sales and Marketing," Meg explained, embarrassed for her. "I, uh, think they're nearly through. Would you like some coffee?"

The office door banged open, disgorging Ray Goetz and three other men in shirtsleeves, all looking frazzled. Behind them came Morgan, a scowl on his flushed and handsome face. "Tomorrow," he called after their retreating backs. "First thing." He spotted Robin and his expression softened. It had been nearly two weeks since the blowup in her apartment, and he'd missed her. She looked especially pretty today, he thought. The dark green of the light summer dress set off her bright hair, and the soft drape of the material accentuated her bust. He felt a stiffening in his groin. "What a delightful surprise," he told her, all smiles, taking her hands in his. "When you didn't return my calls, I thought you'd—" He glanced over at Meg, seated at her desk and taking in every word. "Why don't we go inside." He drew Robin into his private office and closed the door. Meg turned up the volume on the intercom box, and sat back to listen.

"I'm sorry I didn't call you back," Robin said, seating

herself on the leather sofa. "I had a tight deadline on
that explorer article, and—"

"I forgive you," Morgan said, settling himself very
close to her. "As long as you've forgiven me, too."
Robin nodded. The nearness of him was making her
uncomfortable. "See what you can find out from your
boyfriend," Adam had said. How could he know that
her feelings for Morgan had definitely cooled? Still, her
friendship with the Comets owner could be important in
unraveling the mystery of the superplayers. She had to
reestablish contact of some kind with Morgan.

But not this kind, she thought, as Morgan leaned
closer, tracing his finger along her cheek, around the side
of her mouth, and down her neck. Why hadn't she called
him and suggested lunch, instead of coming here to his
private office?

"Let's kiss and make up," he whispered. He pressed
his lips against hers, moving his hand rapidly down her
neck and onto her breast. Her scoop-neck dress opened
at the front, and before she could stop him, he had the
top two buttons undone. Swiftly he pushed her bra aside
and bent to take her nipple in his mouth.

"Don't, Morgan. Please—"

Now he was pressing her back against the sofa, his
hand between her legs, his fingers insinuating themselves
beneath her panties. He took her nipple between his
teeth and bit it gently, then harder.

"Stop," she told him, struggling to right herself, pushing at the hand between her legs, the mouth on her
breast. "Please stop!"

Morgan grabbed her hand and thrust it against his
crotch. "Show me that you forgive me," he mumbled.

"No, Morgan. I can't—"

Morgan lifted his head and looked at her. "You
can't what?"

"I can't do this." Robin shoved herself upright, trying
to button her dress with one hand; Morgan still held the
other tightly against his groin. "I'm sorry, Morgan. It's
not my fault."

"And it's not mine. I have needs, Robin. A man has

needs." He studied her for a beat, then dropped her hand and withdrew his own from between her legs. "I thought you forgave me," he said accusingly.

"I did. I do."

"Well?"

"Not here," she protested. "Not in your office."

"It'll be fun. Something new." His voice was soft but his hands became insistent again.

"Morgan, let go of me!"

"Maybe what you really need is to be forced," Morgan told her. "Maybe a little roughness will turn you on." He grabbed her hair and jerked her head back hard. She cried out with pain but he ignored her, pinioning her on the sofa with one strong arm while shoving his other hand up under her dress again. His finger stabbed deep inside her, hard and angry.

"Stop it, Morgan!" The more she twisted away, the more it hurt.

He withdrew his hand and began undoing his fly, shifting his body on top of hers. "This is what you've wanted all along, isn't it?" he whispered, his eyes blazing. "All that bullshit about not being able to—"

A knock at the door. "Mr. Hudson?"

Morgan froze. "Go away, Meg."

The door opened slightly. "I'm sorry, what did you say?" Meg asked. Morgan jumped up from the sofa as though stung. "Oh, am I interrupting something?" The door swung back to reveal Meg poised on the threshold, pad and pencil in hand. Morgan strode toward her, his face a mask of fury and thwarted lust. Meg held her ground. "Was that you buzzing me?" she asked innocently. "The system's been acting funny lately, and I wasn't sure—" She sneaked a look past Morgan; Robin was on her feet, back turned, adjusting her clothing.

"No it wasn't me," Morgan told her. "Get out."

"I'm not *in*, Mr. Hudson," Meg protested. "I just wanted to make sure, in case you needed me ..." Beyond him, Meg could see Robin turn and hurry toward her.

"I think I'd better go," Robin told Morgan softly as

she moved past him toward Meg. Morgan reached out and grabbed her wrist; Meg saw her wince.

"That will be all, Meg," he said, his eyes furious.

But Meg was enjoying herself. "Sure, Mr. Hudson." She turned to Robin. "I'll just show Ms. Kennedy out."

"She can find her own way—"

"Yes, thank you, Meg," Robin said gratefully. Strands of hair had come loose from the silver hair clip, and her lipstick was smeared.

Just in time, Meg thought. The bastard.

Robin turned and stared at Morgan for a long moment. Then she pulled free and walked past him through the doorway into the outer office. He watched in fury as Meg led Robin back toward the reception area.

"You want to freshen up, there's a ladies' room just down that hall," Meg told her.

"No, I'd better just leave," Robin replied uncertainly.

"Nonsense," Meg told her. "I'll stay right here until you come out. Uh, to make sure you find your way to the elevators."

Robin locked herself inside a stall and began to shake. Stupid, stupid, stupid, she railed at herself. You walked right into it. But a visit to the office had seemed so safe, so impersonal. Eventually she managed to bring herself under control, and went to the sink. Your fault for coming here, she told her reflection silently as she repaired her makeup. How could she have known Morgan would suddenly try to rape her? He'd never attempted to force himself on her before. It's not your fault, she told herself sternly. You have to stop thinking like that. She combed her hair and reclipped it. Well, there goes my inside track, she thought.

She finally emerged and headed for the bank of elevators, and only then did Meg return to her desk. Morgan's door was closed. Meg turned down the volume button on the intercom box through which she'd listened with growing fury to the scene inside his office. She wondered idly when he'd realize his fly was undone, and who would tell him. She smiled and began to clean out her desk.

Inside his plush, paneled office, Morgan slumped in a chair, his head in his hands. How could he have treated Robin like that? Why was he so angry all the time? He stood and went to the window, staring out at the city below. What was happening to him? After some minutes, he shook his head to clear it, and checked his watch. He had a training session at the Pro Club in half an hour. That always made him feel better.

All three of the superplayers were in the Pro Club this afternoon, and the mood was electric. The decibel level rose with each new arrival; everyone wanted to congratulate the heroes on their latest triumphs and wish them luck in their final sprint for the pennant next week. Adam could feel the excitement in the locker room, on the workout terraces, in the juice bar. Everyone was high on the Comets' unabated winning streak. World Series, here we come. He'd tried to catch Kenny's eye as he passed the Nautilus machines but failed; the man seemed determined to avoid him. Can't blame him, Adam thought; all he's ever had from me are uncomfortable medical procedures and bad news.

The presence of the superplayers in the gym seemed to inspire everyone to do some extra reps, put an extra five pounds on the machine, work through the pain a little longer. Adam was no exception, and forty-five minutes of maximum effort had exhausted him. Time to pack it in, he decided.

As he tossed his wet clothes into his gym bag, he thought he heard faint rhythmic sounds emanating through the wall that separated the special training room from the changing area. This was surprising since all three superplayers were still out in the gym. Who was in there?

He showered and dressed, then perched on a stool at the juice bar and ordered a carrot and celery cocktail. While he sipped it, he watched the entrance to the locker room. Kenny was still out on the floor, and Adam was determined to try and talk to the player when he came in to change.

He'd finished his drink and started a second one when Kenny finally appeared, heading for the locker room.

Adam called to him, but Kenny gave him a hostile glance and continued on. Adam slid off the stool and followed him.

"Leave me alone," Kenny hissed over his shoulder as the two men entered the empty locker room.

"I have news about the spinal tap," Adam said quickly, following him to the back of the room. "You've been dodging my calls again, so I assume you don't want to hear it. But as your doctor, I owe it to both of us to try."

Kenny yanked open a locker. "You're right. I don't want to hear it."

"Okay. I won't tell you about the strange hormone we found. Or how it's related to the way you play. Or those fights you get into."

Kenny turned and eyed Adam suspiciously. "What hormone?" he said.

Adam looked around. Two men had entered the room and were heading for lockers halfway along the wall. Kenny glowered at them, and they hesitated, then turned and went out again. Kenny sat down on a bench and began unlacing his sneakers. "What hormone?" he repeated.

As Adam told him what Agnes had discovered about the hormone and the energy tonic, and what she and Adam hypothesized, Kenny's fingers became still. He leaned back against the lockers, his eyes troubled.

"So Agnes is running some tests," Adam concluded. "And I'd like to do a PET scan."

"What's that?"

"Positron emission tomography. They inject an isotope, usually radioactive glucose, and put you in a scanning machine, sort of like the CAT scan tunnel. Then I ask you to concentrate on, say, batting. Or fielding. The PET scan shows us what part of your brain is working when you're thinking about baseball."

"Yeah?" Kenny asked, interested despite himself. "How?"

Adam grinned. "Actually, it's kind of cool. The area of the brain that's working starts to glow. Uh, we would do it at Rockefeller," he said, pursuing his advantage.

"Not New York General?"

"No, the PET uses a cyclatron. We don't have one. Rockefeller does."

"So the PET will tell you what part of my brain thinks about baseball," Kenny said. "So what?"

"Well, I think we'll find that the cortical lesion—remember I told you about the spot on the MRI film?— the lesion is on the part of your brain that thinks about baseball."

"And then what?" Kenny said testily. He pulled off his sneakers and tossed them into the locker behind him. "Will the PET test help you cure it?"

"Uh, not exactly. But—"

"So it's useful for writing a paper about my case, maybe get it published in the AMA journal or someplace, but it's not going to help me one bit. No, I don't think so."

"But, Kenny, we can't help you if—"

Kenny jumped to his feet. "You can't help me at all," he exclaimed, slamming the door of the locker. The crash echoed through the room. "You and Robin Kennedy, claiming you care about me when all you care about is a story! Fuck you, Adam! I won't—" Suddenly he crumpled onto the bench, his hand to his head. "Shit."

Adam went cold; the headaches were back. He touched Kenny's shoulder, but Kenny shrugged him off, moaning.

Five minutes passed as, helpless, Adam watched Kenny wrestle with his pain. Finally the spasm subsided. Adam filled a paper cup at the water cooler in the corner and Kenny drained it in two gulps. "They're back," Kenny said fearfully. "God, what am I going to do?"

"Can you stop the training?"

"No, it's in my contract. Anyhow, I thought you said

it was this hormone that was messing me up. What's the connection with the supertraining?"

"We don't know yet," Adam replied. "But it seems logical. Stopping the training would be the prudent thing to do."

Kenny shook his head. "I can't." His eyes were scared but his voice was steady. "We're gonna take the pennant. And then we're gonna take the Series. You have any idea what that means to any team, let alone a team like the Comets?"

"Yes, I do."

"Then you know I can't stop. I can't let the guys down." He stood and opened the locker door. "And it's not just the team. I want it, too. Shit, I want it so bad I can taste it."

Adam nodded. "Look, we don't really understand why the hormone's there. Maybe its presence has nothing to do with the training. It's possible." Kenny looked around hopefully. Poor bastard, Adam thought. He's going to go on with this, whatever I say. At least let me give him a little comfort. "Maybe the headaches'll go away by themselves; they did before."

"You think so?"

"I don't know. Anything's possible. Maybe when Agnes does her tests . . ."

"You're not angry about the PET scan?" Kenny asked.

Adam shook his head. "I'm just trying to find a way to help," he said. "So is Robin. Believe me, publishing an article is not the intention here."

"I know that," Kenny said. "I just got mad. I get mad a lot these days." He pulled off his sweaty exercise shirt and stuffed it in a canvas bag. "I'm glad Robin made me call you."

"Call him about what?" said Morgan Hudson. Both men spun around.

"Uh, hi, Mr. Hudson," Kenny said nervously.

But Morgan's eyes were fixed on Adam. "I know you, don't I?"

"We've met," Adam replied easily, though his pulse

was racing. "I'm Dr. Adam Salt. Robin Kennedy consulted me about her article on the Comets. You and she were kind enough to invite me to that party you threw in July . . ."

"Of course, of course. You're a member here?"

"Yes. Great place, isn't it?" A movement beyond Morgan caught Adam's eye; Connor was shutting the door to the supertraining room. But Adam was certain it had been closed when he and Kenny had come into the locker room. No wonder Morgan had appeared so suddenly; he'd been inside the supertraining room. He was the reason for the rhythmic pulsing Adam had heard through the wall. Now that was interesting.

"You haven't answered my question, Kenny," Morgan said pleasantly. "Why did Robin Kennedy want you to call Dr. Salt?"

"It was about the article," Adam said quickly. "Robin thought it would be helpful if I spoke with Kenny directly."

"She was wrong," Morgan told him, his eyes on Kenny. "All interviews go through my office or Warfield's. Kenny knows that."

"And now *I* know it," Adam said brightly. "My fault entirely."

Several people entered the locker room, laughing loudly. Morgan glanced over at them, then turned back to Kenny. "Helluva good game yesterday," he said loudly. He beamed at Kenny and slapped him on the back. "Keep it up, son, and we'll all be in the history books. Nice to see you again, Salt."

Both men looked after Morgan as he headed for the showers. How long had he been standing there?

"Thanks for the quick save," Kenny said quietly.

"No problem."

The door to the special training room opened and Connor emerged. "Kenny? We're ready for you."

For a tiny moment, Kenny hesitated. Then he squared his shoulders determinedly. "I'd better get going," he told Adam. "You coming to the game next week?"

"Wouldn't miss it."

Kenny gave him a thumbs-up and his famous grin. Then he turned and followed Connor into the training room.

Robin sat on a bench overlooking the East River. Behind her, Carl Schurz Park resounded with the shouts and laughter of children. A Circle Line boat chugged past, its passengers staring out at this strange island with its quaint and colorful natives. For a moment she wished she were out on the river with them, admiring the superficial glitter of the city, oblivious of its dark heart.

She realized that Morgan's behavior could be due to the supertraining, but that didn't make it any easier to deal with. The feelings of violation and helplessness and shame persisted. She knew those feelings all too well; she'd lived with them for most of her life. Tears sprang to her eyes; all the old, bad stuff was coming back fast. Get a grip, she told herself. This is not then. You're a different person. You have independence, a career, even a new name. You can handle this. Better, you can simply walk away from this whole mess. Let Adam deal with it. You never have to see Morgan again, never have to talk to him.

But I do, she thought. That's my part of the bargain I made with Adam. Besides, I can't spend my life running away.

Restless, she went and leaned on the wrought-iron railing and looked down into the murky water. Adam wouldn't want you to go on with it under these circumstances, she told herself. He'd be the first to tell you to forget it.

But I can't just forget it, and it's not only because Adam and I made a deal. The thing is, I'm a journalist, or at least I'm on my way to being one, and I have a responsibility to myself and to my profession. I want to learn the truth about the superplayers.

And perhaps also the truth about my own strength and commitment.

She turned away from the setting sun and left the

park. When she got home, her answering machine was blinking. One of the messages was from Morgan. She took a deep breath, picked up the receiver, and began to dial.

Chapter Eighteen

Late September

"We did it! We fucking did it!"

The wild celebration that had started in the Comets' dugout at Parker Stadium several hours ago was continuing with undiminished vigor in Morgan's huge town house living room. Players, coaches, and managers, their friends and lovers, and a select group of invited press, laughed and shouted, chugalugged champagne, and replayed every highlight of the game that had just won the team the league pennant.

". . . and Reese here takes off and I think, this time they're gonna nail him. But no, he not only beats the throw, he sets a new record for base-stealing." The Comets' catcher slapped Kenny hard on the back, spilling his drink on his shirt.

". . . so I was worried about Colberg getting a hit off Sanchez and bringing Thompson home," the head coach was explaining to a petite blonde. "But pitching on the corner, especially when you're ahead on the pitch, is the difference between the majors and the minors, and sure enough, Ernie struck him out. That brought up Havermeyer. Now, Havermeyer's erratic . . ." The blonde smiled and nodded and looked around for her date.

". . . and when that ball went sailing over the wall in the seventh with two on and only one away," Jim Warfield exclaimed for the twentieth time to anyone who would listen, "I knew the only question about this game was how much we were going to win it by."

Morgan, his face flushed with excitement and champagne, laughed and nodded and speared the air with his stogie as he accepted the congratulations of the milling throng. From the corner of his eye, he saw several new arrivals come through the arch between the living room and entrance gallery, but Robin was not among them. Jack Ridley approached, carrying a brown envelope. Morgan excused himself and drew Ridley to one side. "Have you seen her?" he asked.

"No, but this just came."

Morgan scanned the label as he took the envelope. "About time," he muttered. "Here, get rid of this for me, will you?" Handing Ridley his half-empty glass, Morgan started for the privacy of his den, but Connor Egan, resplendent in black silk, intercepted him in the hallway. "Jack said you wanted to talk to me."

Morgan hesitated, then clapped an arm around the younger man's shoulder. "So I did," he said heartily. "Let's go into my office. It's quieter."

The small den, deeply carpeted and elegantly paneled, was cool and silent. Gesturing Connor to the burgundy leather sofa, Morgan settled himself in a club chair across from him and smiled. "I've just bought the Pro Club," he announced.

Robin stood on the sidewalk outside Morgan's elegant limestone town house. Although heavy tapestry curtains shielded the interior from view, she could imagine the boozy, noisy scene inside. I'm not sure I'm up for this, she thought.

Yes, Morgan had apologized abjectly and repeatedly for what he termed "that unforgivable incident" in his office. And yes, she'd crossed her fingers and assured him that she'd forgiven him, all the while making plausible excuses for not seeing him. What else could she do, having decided she needed to maintain some sort of relationship with Morgan for the sake of her and Adam's investigation?

Which was why she was standing there on the pavement, staring up at the tall, opaque windows. Having deflected Morgan's invitation to accompany him to the stadium today, she'd had to promise to come to the party if the Comets won. But staying on the right side of Morgan, albeit at arm's length, was only part of the reason she'd come. The other part was guilt.

Though her ardor for Morgan had cooled, and despite the incident in his office, she couldn't bring herself to view him as an unmitigated cad. She preferred to believe that since his violent behavior might have been caused by the supertraining, he wasn't really responsible. And that made her feel guilty about her promise not to tell Morgan what Agnes had discovered in Kenny's spinal fluid. Yes, Morgan had used her to control the press stories about him and his team, and she resented it. But he was still a human being. Shouldn't she warn him that he might be putting himself in physical danger by continuing to take the training? She sighed. She'd wrestled with the question and been forced to the conclusion that she couldn't risk telling him what she and Adam had learned. There was the promise of confidentiality she'd made to Adam, of course. But beyond that, she realized that they simply didn't know enough yet. Going public now could cause far more harm than good, while compromising their investigation. Besides, Morgan hadn't been taking the training for very long; his erratic behavior could have any number of other causes.

All of which made the idea of being face-to-face with Morgan even more uncomfortable.

She pushed through the low wrought-iron gate, then paused. Don't be a ninny, she told herself firmly. She crossed the tiny courtyard and began to climb the stone steps leading up to the intricately carved front door. It's a huge party, for godsake. There'll be hundreds of people around. How bad can it be?

"I've just bought the Pro Club," Morgan repeated. "From Paul Barrett's estate. I want you to continue running it. I'll raise your salary and pay you a percentage. Interested?"

Connor's eyes widened. "You bet." He'd been worried about his future ever since Barrett's murder. But this could solve everything. "What are you going to do with the place?"

"Oh, I'm not planning any changes," Morgan said. "I want to keep it just the way it is."

Connor's expression tightened. "You mean, continue the supertraining?"

Morgan nodded. "And the regular programs as well, of course. The place is quite a moneymaker, I gather."

"I, uh, wouldn't know about the financial end," Connor said quickly. "But about the supertraining—"

"Yes?"

"I'm not sure how much you know about the supertraining, uh, how much Mr. Barrett told you."

Morgan laughed. "I'm taking it myself," he said.

"Yes, of course. But there are things you may not—"

"Listen," Morgan interrupted, "I'm not interested in the details. Just keep doing whatever it is you do. Frankly, the fewer people who know, the better." Connor glanced at him sharply. " 'Loose lips' and all that. I didn't buy the Pro Club in order to help the competition."

"Absolutely not."

Morgan hesitated. "I understand you were questioned by the police."

"That's right."

"Any, uh, problems there?"

"Problems? No, no problems." Connor paused. "I explained that I was going around checking the gym early in the morning before we opened, the way I always do. I saw the door to the stairs between Barrett's apartment and the gym standing open."

"I never even knew that door existed," Morgan mused.

"Most people didn't. Of course, most people didn't know about the door in the alley, either. Mr. Barrett was big on security, and he liked his privacy." Connor paused, remembering. "He didn't even let *me* use the door from the gym when he wanted to see me," he said resentfully. "He made me go outside and walk all the way around to—" Catching himself, he shot a look at Morgan and continued in a more neutral tone. "That's why I was so surprised to see it open that morning. It was real unusual. So I went up to have a look and, well, there he was."

"And you immediately called the police."

"Of course." .

"Good." Morgan shook his head. "A terrible thing. And Otis Freeman's jacket . . . Believe me, I'm delighted Freeman was released, but . . . I just don't understand how his jacket got there. Or why Freeman's name was in Barrett's diary if, as he claims, he didn't go to see him. Do you?"

"No idea."

Morgan sighed. "Never mind," he said. "What's done is done. You're not superstitious, are you?"

Connor laughed. "You think people will have a problem with the Pro Club because Barrett was murdered there?" He shook his head. "Believe it or not, business is better than ever."

"No, I was wondering whether you'd like to live at the Pro Club. In Barrett's old apartment."

Connor's face lit up. "It's a lot bigger than my place. Must be expensive, though," he added, his smile fading. "I don't know if I can afford—"

"I meant rent-free, of course," Morgan assured him. "Think about it."

"I don't need to think about it, Mr. Hudson. Thanks."

"Somebody from my office will call you to work out the details." He rose and Connor did, too; the two men shook hands. "Glad to have you aboard. Now go on back to the party. Enjoy yourself." He swung the door open, glancing at the waterlogged lime slice nestled in the bottom of Connor's empty glass. "Have another gin and tonic."

"It's Perrier. I never touch alcohol. The body is a temple—"

"Whatever." Morgan ushered Connor out into the hall, then swung the door shut behind him. He retrieved the envelope Ridley had given him and, settling himself in the club chair again, ripped it open. Perfect timing, he thought. Despite Robin's assurances that she'd forgiven him, her manner had been rather cool recently. This report was exactly what he needed to make it up to her. She'd probably be here any minute. Smiling with anticipation, he withdrew the single sheet of plain white paper and began to read.

Robin moved through the crowd, looking for Morgan. I'll have one drink, say congratulations, and leave, she thought. A glass of champagne was thrust at her; a waiter offered chicken on skewers. Lighten up, she told herself. It was really very exciting to be able to celebrate the Comets' amazing victory with the Comets themselves. Adam would love it, she reflected, unaware that she was smiling. Adam was often in her thoughts these days. And the thought of him always made her smile.

A long bar had been set up along one side of the living room. Ignoring the red-coated bartenders stationed behind it, Kenny was refilling his glass from an open champagne bottle. As Robin started toward him, she saw Connor, muscles rippling under tight black silk, approach him and begin a conversation. She continued toward the two men. Here was a chance to congratulate Kenny while reestablishing contact with Connor. She wanted a private chat with Mr. Egan sometime soon. As she got closer, she was shocked at how haggard Kenny looked. It was obvious he'd been celebrating hard; his eyes were glassy, his movements slurred. But the tiredness in his face spoke of illness rather than drink. She saw Connor put a hand on Kenny's shoulder; he spoke softly and she couldn't make out the words. Kenny's answer, however, was both loud and clear.

"I'm fine, goddammit," he snarled, shoving Connor's hand away. "Leave me the fuck alone."

Connor drew back, startled. "I only said you look tired."

"Well, who the fuck made you my mother? Why don't you go screw yourself?" Kenny's voice was muzzy from alcohol and exhaustion.

"Hey, calm down—"

"*You* calm down, you son of a bitch." Kenny drew

back a fist and swung awkwardly at Connor, but Connor moved fast, grabbing Kenny's arm and pinioning it behind his back. Kenny suddenly noticed Robin. "What the fuck are *you* staring at?"

Robin colored. "I just came over to say congratulations on a great game."

"Yeah? Well, thanks a shitload."

Robin opened her mouth to speak but Connor glanced at her and shook his head. Several people had turned to stare. Connor grinned at them as if this were all some huge joke, and they smiled back and turned away. Connor turned back to Kenny. "Let's go get some coffee, shall we?" Still grinning, he frog-marched Kenny out of the room.

It was the alcohol talking, Robin told herself. Don't take it personally. She went to the bar and traded her champagne for a club soda, then angled her way back through the seething mass of people. Where was Morgan? A sudden shove nearly knocked her off her feet, but a hand grabbed her elbow. "Sorry about that," said a stocky, dark-haired young man. "Chain reaction." He removed his hand from her arm and extended it toward her. "Richard O'Gorman, *New York Observer.*"

"Robin Kennedy."

"Yeah, I thought I recognized you. Some game, huh? The fans sure got their money's worth today." Robin nodded. "So, you figured out how they're doing it yet?"

"How they're doing what?"

O'Gorman grinned knowingly. "Yeah, right." He took a sip of champagne, then wrinkled his nose. "Damn stuff's warm. So, the Comets are the new league champions. Hard to believe, after all these years. Don't suppose you'd care to let me in on the secret of their success?"

"The team's got a lot of heart," Robin said.

O'Gorman raised a sardonic eyebrow. "Heart," he said. "You bet." He glanced at his watch. "Well, along about now, folks start throwing up on other folks' shoes, so I guess I'll be going. Nice to have met you."

"And you," Robin replied. "Actually, I ought to be leaving, too. If I could just find Morgan . . ."

"Hudson? Isn't that him over by the door?"

Robin looked; Morgan stood framed in the archway between the living room and the entrance gallery. He was listening to an older man who stood beside him talking earnestly, but his attention was focused on the room before him. Robin saw him nod at something his companion said as his eyes continued to scan the crowd, his handsome face flushed and frowning. She caught his eye and waved. He beckoned to her with a hand that held a sheet of white paper, and she made her way toward him, dimly aware of Richard O'Gorman following in her wake.

"I've been looking all over for you," she told Morgan. "I'm so happy for you." She leaned over and kissed him lightly on the cheek.

Morgan received the kiss calmly. "Thank you," he replied formally. "Robin, this is Ray Goetz. Ray's head of marketing at Hudson and Company. Ray, this is Robin Kennedy. Previously known as"—he glanced at the page in his hand—"Rosie McGee."

"What?" For a moment, Robin thought she'd misheard him.

"*Mrs.* Rosie McGee," he repeated bitterly. "That *is* your real name, isn't it? No relation to the Kennedys at all, as it turns out."

Robin felt light-headed. The moment she'd dreaded for so many years had finally arrived. The lies had caught up with her at last. She wished she could sink into the ground and disappear.

"You all right?" O'Gorman put a solicitous hand on her swaying shoulder.

The room began to dissolve. I'm going to faint, Robin thought. Good. Then I won't have to deal with the humiliation. . . .

"Give her some air," O'Gorman was saying. "Get some brandy."

Robin was never exactly sure what happened next. All she knew was that somewhere deep inside she suddenly realized that it didn't matter. Her real name, the fact that she'd lied about her background, none of it mat-

tered anymore. It probably never had. So her name had
once been Rosie McGee; so what? Don't you dare faint,
she scolded herself. Don't you dare. The room began to
stabilize. A new strength coursed through her. She was
no longer the whipped puppy that had gotten off the
Greyhound bus all those years ago. She had earned the
right to call herself Robin Kennedy or anything else
she chose.

Someone offered brandy, but she pushed it away and
smiled tremulously. "I haven't eaten all day," she heard
herself murmur. "I'm afraid that, and all these people,
made me feel a little faint. Now, what were you saying
about the Kennedys, Morgan?"

Morgan frowned uncertainly. "I researched your genealogy. I thought it would make a nice surprise for you,
to know how you were related to the Kennedy clan."
He waved the paper at her. "But it seems there's no
trace of you or that riverboat gambler father of yours.
You're no relation at all."

"But, Morgan, I never said I was. I mean, who cares?
This whole Kennedy connection thing was your idea, not
mine." She managed a small laugh. "As for my real
name, surely you've heard of writers using noms de
plume." She turned to wink at O'Gorman, who nodded.

"Ann Landers, Suzy Knickerbocker . . ." the *Observer*
columnist agreed. "Although personally, I don't think
there's anything wrong with Rosie McGee."

"You're right. There isn't," Robin agreed. "It's taken
me awhile to realize that." She turned back to Morgan.
"Is there anything else in that paper of yours you want
to ask me about?"

Morgan's confusion was evident. This wasn't going the
way he'd expected. He'd been both furious and disappointed when he'd read the report. The connection he'd
thought he'd had to the Kennedy money had vanished,
and so had Robin's social cache. He'd been taken in,
made a fool of, and by whom? A dumb little hick from
Nowheresville, Texas. The idea of public humiliation was
very appealing. He'd been sure she would scream or
faint, beg him not reveal anything more. But she didn't

seem embarrassed in the least. Damn her, she was handling it beautifully. *He* was the one who was looking stupid. He crumpled the paper into a ball and thrust it into his pocket.

"Nothing more?" Robin asked sweetly. "Then I'll just go and have a word with some of the guys before I leave. I've gotten to know the Comets pretty well over the past few months," she told O'Gorman. "A great bunch of guys. I'm so happy for them." Turning back to Morgan, she touched him lightly on the cheek. "And for you, too, of course."

She began moving past him toward the entrance hall where several of the players were clustered on the staircase. But Morgan grabbed her elbow and swung her around toward him.

"I'd like a little word with you first," he said tightly. He smiled dismissively at the circle that had gathered around them, and watched as they began to move off. Behind Morgan's back, O'Gorman rolled his eyes at Robin and pantomimed that Morgan had been drinking. Morgan tightened his grip and piloted her through the entrance gallery and into the deserted hallway beyond.

"So you've gotten to know my players pretty well," he said, his voice dripping with sarcasm. "And you've gotten to know Adam Salt pretty well, too, haven't you? In fact, it seems you've gotten pretty friendly with a lot of people recently."

Robin pulled her arm away. "What are you implying?" she demanded.

"Implying? Oh, I'm not implying. I'm saying it right out. It took me awhile to realize why you've cooled toward me. You're having an affair with Adam Salt, aren't you?"

Robin flushed. "That's not true." But her indignation was undercut by the awareness of her growing attraction to Adam.

"You're probably sleeping with Kenny Reese, too," Morgan declared.

"You're mad."

"I heard Kenny and Salt talking in the gym. It seems

you convinced him to consult Salt for some medical problem. Why would Kenny ask *you* about something like that, and not the team doctor? And why would you suggest he see Salt if there's nothing between you?"

"Your mind's in the gutter, Morgan. Kenny was having headaches. They've stopped now."

"Thanks to the miraculous curative powers of your lover."

"I never—"

"Rosie McGee's lover."

The glass jumped in Robin's hand, showering Morgan's face, shirt, and jacket with club soda. With an oath, Morgan jerked back, then leaned in and slapped her hard. Robin gasped and stepped back. For a long moment they stared at each other. Then Morgan slumped back against the wall and put his head in his hands. "I'm sorry," he murmured. "I had no right ... I'm sorry."

"Forget it," Robin told him, keeping her distance. "Apologies and flowers won't work anymore. You want to know why I've cooled toward you, as you put it? It's because you've been treating me like shit, and I won't stand for it."

"I've been under a lot of stress lately," Morgan whispered. "The deciding game was coming up ... and then my secretary quit ..."

"I'm sorry you've been having a rough time," Robin said. "But don't take it out on me."

Morgan pulled a linen hanky from his breast pocket and dabbed at the wetness on his lapel. "Then, on top of all my other problems," he continued as if she hadn't spoken, "I suddenly learn you're not who you said you were ..."

"My past is not your problem," Robin said firmly. "Besides, all that was a long time ago. If your researcher is any good, you'll know exactly why I decided to put some distance between myself and my past."

Morgan nodded. "I guess I can understand that. But it was quite a shock."

Robin shrugged. "I don't know why you built up that whole Kennedy thing in your mind in the first place.

Look, I'm sorry if what you've learned about my past has hurt you. But I'm not sorry I changed my life. I'm proud of it. And I'll tell you something else: I'm through being a victim. So if you want us to remain friends—"

"I thought we were more than friends."

"We were, once. But—" Robin hesitated. "I think we should work on being friends for now, Morgan. If you can treat me with respect, if you can curb this violent streak you seem to have developed . . . Well, then we'll see." But Robin knew they could never go back to the way things had been. Nor did she want to, now that she'd met Adam.

"Deal," Morgan said softly, extending his hand. Robin took it reluctantly, and he grasped it firmly, then pulled her toward him. Before she realized what was happening, his mouth was on hers, his tongue probing her lips. His other hand came around her, crushing her body against his.

With a violent wrench, Robin broke free. "For god-sake, Morgan," she exclaimed angrily as she backed quickly away from him. Her face burned from the scrape of his cheek, unshaven since morning.

"I'm sor—"

But Robin was already halfway down the corridor, heading for the gallery, the front door and freedom.

Morgan felt the fury build in him, driving out desire. Bitch, he thought, staring after her retreating figure. As he watched, Kenny crossed the hallway, heading for the living room. "Kenny," he called. "Hang on a second." Kenny turned and waited as Morgan hurried down the hall to him. The coffee Connor had poured into him had done its work. Now he grinned, expecting his boss to thank him yet again for the grand slam in the sixth inning. Instead Morgan scowled at him. "What's this bullshit with you and Adam Salt?" he demanded, his face an angry mask.

Kenny's smile froze. "What are you talking about?"

"I know you consulted Salt for some medical problem. I overheard you two talking. What the fuck do you think we have a team doctor for?"

"I, uh ... was having these headaches, and Miss Kennedy suggested ... that is, I thought ... Hey, it was nothing. I feel great, the headaches are gone. ..."

"You go see Burt Gross on Monday, understand? Have a complete checkup. You got that?"

"I don't need to, dammit. I'm perfectly—"

"That wasn't a suggestion," Morgan roared. "It was an order."

"I won't," Kenny shouted. "There's nothing wrong with me."

Attracted by the raised voices, several people appeared from beyond the curve of the staircase, Connor among them.

"The hell you won't," Morgan shot back. "Who do you think you are?" Only the best player we've got, a tiny voice said, but Morgan ignored it. "You may be in line for Most Valuable Player," he bellowed, "but you still work for me."

Kenny's face went red. "Well, you can take your contract and shove it up—"

"Gentlemen, gentlemen, please." Connor stepped between the two men. "We're all a little overexcited this evening. Let's just calm down and—"

"Fuck you, Connor," Kenny said hotly. "And fuck—oof."

"He's had a helluva day, Mr. Hudson," Connor said, elbowing Kenny in the ribs again. "Let's just cut each other some slack, okay?" He looked anxiously from one to the other.

Morgan shook his head, but his burst of anger was already dissipating. "Damn kid," he muttered. "Make sure he sees the doctor." He stalked off toward the living room.

"But there's nothing wrong—" Kenny began.

"I know that," Connor hissed. "But make an appointment anyway, okay? Keep the boss happy."

"I've got a full day Monday."

Connor looked after Morgan's retreating back. "Well ... the old man's so pissed, he probably won't even remember this conversation." He looked around at the ring of worried faces. "Come on, guys," he exclaimed. "This is supposed to be a celebration. Go celebrate."

Kenny grinned. "You really think I'll make MVP?"

"Unless Hank Aaron comes out of retirement," Connor told him, "yeah, I think you've got a shot." He was relieved when everyone laughed.

Chapter Nineteen

"There's something I have to tell you."

Adam sprawled on his clay-colored sofa, his feet on the stone coffee table, carefully considering the statement Robin had just made on the phone. She'd refused to be drawn, asking only that she be allowed to interrupt his Saturday with a visit to his apartment. As if he'd refuse. As if he wasn't absolutely delighted.

But what could it be? Had she learned something at the party, something important about the supertraining? Had Morgan or Kenny or Connor taken her into his confidence and spilled a few beans?

The kettle was whistling, and he went into the kitchen and turned it down to a low simmer. Then he loaded a tray with cups and saucers and a small pitcher of milk, and carried them out to the living room. He decided to wait until she arrived before making the tea, otherwise it would stew and turn nasty. Adam was fond of tea and rather particular about its brewing and consumption. He also had great faith in its restorative powers, and Robin had sounded stressed. Back in the kitchen again, he sorted through the cupboards, unearthed a half-empty package of chocolate biscuits, and began arranging them on a plate. An unpleasant thought occurred to him: perhaps she'd decided to marry Morgan. But surely she wouldn't rush over to his apartment to tell him that. It must be something else. Something about the supertraining. He went and set the biscuits beside the tray, then checked the room carefully. She hadn't been to his apartment before, and he wanted it to look nice for her.

Gargantua was investigating the milk pitcher and he

shooed her away. "I know it tastes better from people dishes," he told the cat sternly, "but we're expecting company." He settled himself on the sofa again and the little cat jumped into his lap, purring. She can't be marrying Morgan, Adam thought fiercely as he stroked the cat's soft orange fur. I don't want to lose her.

The intercom buzzer sounded and Gargantua leaped down and headed for the door, her tail and ears signaling friendly curiosity. Adam gazed at the cat fondly, remembering how, when they'd first become roommates, Gargantua would hide every time the buzzer rang.

Adam spoke briefly to the doorman through the intercom, then opened the apartment door in anticipation of Robin's arrival. Soon he heard the elevator open, and she came walking down the hallway toward him. She wore a simple ankle-length blue dress in a fashionably crumpled material that moved around her body in a way Adam found most provocative. As she drew near, he could see the obvious tension in her face. He gave her what he hoped was a chaste but welcoming kiss—no sense in rushing things—and was surprised to feel her lean against him. He held her close and realized she was crying.

"What's wrong?" he asked softly, but she shook her head and held on. He stroked her hair and held her gently. They stood that way for some time. At last, Robin pulled away. Tears stood in her eyes.

"I'm sorry," she said. "I didn't mean to throw myself at you like that."

"Any time," Adam assured her. There was a long red scrape along one cheek. "What happened to you?" he asked, touching the mark gently.

"It's part of the story. Not the most important part."

"Come on in," Adam said. His arm still around her waist, he guided her into the spacious apartment. "How about a cup of tea?"

Robin smiled tremulously. "I'd love one." Adam settled her on the sofa and a small orange fur ball immediately launched itself into her lap, purring loudly. "Who's this?"

"My roommate," Adam explained. "Her name's Gargantua."

"Very appropriate." Robin ran her fingers through the cat's fur. "She's a sweet little thing." Spying the pitcher on the coffee table, she looked over at Adam. "Okay if I give her some milk?" He nodded, a bemused expression on his face. Robin took a saucer from under one of the teacups and filled it from the pitcher. Setting it on the floor, she took the cat gently from her lap and put her down next to the saucer. Gargantua gave Robin's hand a friendly lick and began lapping at the milk with enthusiasm. Robin laughed. "She likes me."

"Who wouldn't?"

Robin sighed. "Maybe *you*, when you hear what I've got to say."

Adam's face sobered. "I'll just make the tea. Then we can talk." He disappeared into the kitchen, returning with a brown teapot on a tile trivet. "Darjeeling," he said as he poured.

"Smells delicious."

Adam sat down next to her and they drank their tea in silence for a while. He was determined not to rush her. At last she set down her cup and turned to him. "I'm an impostor," she said. His left eyebrow rose questioningly, but he didn't speak. "My real name is Rosie McGee."

" 'A Rosie by any other name ...' Uh, sorry about that. But I can see why you might want to change it."

"You can?"

"Sure. I mean, there's nothing wrong with the name Rosie McGee. But Robin Kennedy's a terrific pen name." He smiled at her. "So you chose to write under a different name. So did George Sand. Is that all?"

"No, that's not all." Robin took a deep breath. "I need to tell you about who I was before I became Robin Kennedy. Don't worry," she added, seeing his face, "I'm not an ax murderer. I haven't done anything illegal. All I did was invent a new past for myself, because the old one was so painful, and so ... grim. Changing my past gave me the confidence to change my life. But the past has a way of catching up with us, doesn't it?"

The cat gave the empty saucer one last lick and bounced up onto the sofa. She looked from one human to the other, then stepped daintily onto Robin's lap and curled herself into a contented circle.

Robin glanced at the cat and smiled. "Over the years," she continued softly, her face becoming serious again, "I've built up a whole series of lies about my past. Once you start, it's hard to stop. Impossible, in fact. Morgan had my genealogy traced. He thought it would be fun to see how I was related to the Kennedys. Of course I wasn't. He was furious." She touched her cheek. "Please understand that the stories I made up were only about what my life was like before I came to New York. Everything since then is absolutely true. It was only the past I needed to escape." Robin paused, searching for the right words. "I also want you to understand that I didn't come here today because Morgan found out about Rosie McGee and I was afraid you would, too. The truth is that ... I really like you, Adam. I respect you and I value your friendship. You've become ... important to me. I would have told you the truth sooner or later, even if Morgan hadn't stumbled on it. In fact, it's been bothering me a lot lately." She paused. "I hope you can believe that."

Adam studied the sleeping cat for a moment, then took Robin's hands in his. "Robin or Rosie or whoever you are, there's a distinct possibility that Gargantua and I may be falling in love with you. We both see qualities in you we value and trust. Intelligence. Empathy. Honesty. Yes, honesty," he assured her, seeing the surprise in her face. "You've always been straight with me about your relationship with Morgan, and your suspicions about the supertraining. In fact, I've been less than honest with you in that regard; I've had doubts about the Comets from the beginning." He thought a moment. "Aside from your name, you've never really told me much about your past. You said you came from the South ..."

"I do."

"And that you grew up on Tex-Mex." He grinned at her. "I know that's true; I've seen you eat." She gave him a small smile. "That's better." He squeezed her hands encouragingly. "Aside from that, you've told me nothing. Apart from your name, you haven't lied to me at all. And even your name isn't really a lie; it's the name you're known by, now; the name you write under." He looked deeply into her eyes. What he saw there reassured him, not that reassurance was needed. "You must have had some pretty good reasons to deny your past. I'd like to hear them. Not because I'm planning to judge you, but because I care about you. I want to know everything about you."

Robin could feel the tears forming. She blinked them away and began to speak. She told him about her alcoholic mother, her abusive stepfather. She described her attempts at self-education, efforts that had ended with her marriage to Tommy McGee. She told him about becoming pregnant and then miscarrying when Tommy had beaten her during one of his drunken rages. She talked about her feelings of despair and self-doubt, of her determination to escape the fate of her mother and sisters, to create a new life for herself. By the time she'd finished, she was weeping and Adam was holding her close; tears stood in his eyes as well.

"If you don't . . . don't like me anymore, I'll understand," Robin whispered. "I'll just get up and go."

"And wake up the cat? I won't hear of it." Robin gave him a small smile as he wiped at her tears with his hanky. "What you've told me makes me like you even more than I did before," Adam told her as he kissed her forehead. "I'm proud of you. And you should be proud of you, too. You have nothing to apologize for. What you did was very hard. And absolutely necessary."

"That's not how Morgan saw it."

"I'm not Morgan." He fingered the red streak on her cheek. "Did he hit you?"

"Not exactly . . ."

"Let me get something to put on it."

"No, just hold me. Please." Robin nestled closer. "Adam?"

"Yes?"

"It's all over between Morgan and me."

"I'm very glad to hear it," Adam said sincerely.

"And not just because of the Kennedy thing. I've been avoiding Morgan for some time. He's been acting really strange . . . he attacked me in his office one day, and his secretary had to rescue me."

"Nice guy," Adam said dryly.

"Actually, he *is* a nice guy, that's what's so awful about it. He used to be gentle and understanding . . . But since he's been taking the supertraining—I didn't tell you that, did I?"

"I figured as much," Adam said. "I saw him at the Pro Club, coming out of the training room. So Morgan's started acting like the superplayers, huh?"

Robin nodded. "But even if his behavior isn't really his fault, I don't want to be around him."

Adam studied her for a moment. "You didn't tell him . . . ?"

"Of course not. You and I had an agreement. But that's another reason I'd like to get to the bottom of this thing. I'm sure Morgan has no idea what's happening to him, and I feel guilty about not warning him."

"I thought it was over between you two," Adam said, frowning.

"It *is*. It would be, even if Morgan weren't acting so badly toward me. It's just that it feels sort of . . . immoral, not to tell him he could be at risk."

"I know how you feel. But of course we don't really know whether the thalamic hormone is actually being administered in some way, or if its presence in Kenny's spinal fluid is merely a reaction to something else."

"It *is* too early to go public," Robin agreed. "We'll learn more if no one knows we suspect anything."

"I wonder why they're giving Morgan the supertraining," Adam mused.

"I assume because he owns the Comets."

"I guess so, only . . ."

"What?"

"I don't know. Connor said the only reason Barrett chose to give his technique to the Comets was that he was a Comets fan. And he only gave it to three of their players. Barrett had complete control of the technique, and I just can't see him being persuaded to give it to anyone else, even the team's owner."

"Maybe Morgan had some kind of hold over Barrett."

"You mean money? I'm sure Morgan was paying Barrett plenty, but I can't imagine him threatening to remove his superplayers if Barrett didn't give him the training, too. No, Barrett had to know the money would be paid whether he gave Morgan the training or not. Morgan needed Barrett, not the other way round." Adam looked thoughtful. "I wonder why Barrett chose the Comets? He was a Brit, he hadn't been here very long ... and his game was rugby. I'd have thought football would have more appeal for him. Why baseball? Why the Comets?"

"Maybe Connor was wrong," Robin said thoughtfully. "Maybe Barrett didn't go to Morgan; maybe Morgan went to Barrett. They both attended Cambridge University although at different times. Morgan says he didn't know Barrett back then, but I suppose he could have heard about Barrett when Barrett came to the States, maybe through his ties with Cambridge. He could have learned what Barrett had invented ..."

"I suppose it's possible," Adam allowed.

"And then there's Connor. What's his role in all this?"

"Good question."

"So you see why I have to stay in touch with Morgan."

"I don't think that's a very good idea," Adam said slowly. "It could be dangerous. He's already attacked you."

"Don't worry, I'll keep my distance. But Morgan's a lead we can't afford to drop. For one thing—"

Adam kissed her lightly on the lips, interrupting her.

"I'm tired of talking about Morgan," he said. "I want to talk about us."

"Okay."

"And dinner. It's nearly nine. Are you hungry?"

"I don't know ... a little, maybe?"

"There's a bistro around the corner. Or we could order in." Their eyes met.

"Order in," Robin said softly. "It's a shame to disturb the cat."

Much later, as they sat propped against the pillows of Adam's big sleigh bed, watching the late news and eating tepid Peking duck, Robin sneaked a fond glance at Adam's strong, handsome profile. Something wonderful had just happened, something that hadn't happened to her in many years. Was it his body, or his technique, or the love she saw in his eyes? Well, yes, it was all of those things, she decided. But even more important was the release, the freedom she felt at having told the truth at last. No more fear of discovery, no more false expectations. No more pretending. Rosie McGee and Robin Kennedy were one at last. And Adam loved her.

Chapter Twenty

Dave Hirsch, junior counsel at Downing, Turkewicz, and Neese, counted the people gathered around Ben Harvey's long marble conference table with some amusement. Two clients, seven attorneys. He leaned over to his friend and fellow lawyer Sid Frankel. "How many attorneys does 'it take to screw in a lightbulb?" he whispered.

Frankel smiled back. "I give up. How many?"

"How many can you afford?"

Alan Downing glared at them.

It had taken nearly an hour to review the contract they'd all verbally approved several days earlier. But this was the moment of truth, when the two parties would actually put ink to paper. And all seven attorneys were keenly aware that whatever their clients signed today would have to be lived with. Or litigated.

"Okay, Ben," Downing said, flipping over the last page of his copy of the agreement. "With those small changes we just wrote in, I'm fine with this. Tom?" He looked over at his client, Tom Wachtel, who nodded. A small gray man in a nondescript suit and tie, Wachtel looked more like the proprietor of a local pharmacy than the major industrialist he was. Dave Hirsch winked broadly at him. Downing gave Hirsch a stony stare, but Tom Wachtel grinned. Everybody know Tom was getting a terrific deal. Downing turned back to Ben Harvey. "You have the training guarantee?"

"Right here." Harvey had been Morgan's attorney for nearly ten years. A round-faced man of fifty-four whose wild white hair and round eyeglasses made him resemble a wise if slightly demented owl, Ben Harvey was one of the most highly regarded contract and litigation attorneys in the city. Now, his attention still fixed on Downing, he held out his right hand and one of his senior partners at Harvey, Schwartz, & Sidney, an intense woman in a serious suit, slapped a folder into it. To his left, one of the two lower-ranked attorneys he'd invited to sit in nodded thoughtfully while the other put a large check mark on a list attached to the Lucite clipboard in front of him. This was a major deal, and firepower counted.

"It says that Connor Egan guarantees to continue training the superplayers for a minimum of three years from the contract date," Harvey announced. Everyone already knew that, of course, but Harvey was a belt-and-suspenders man. He opened the folder, removed three of the four copies of the signed guarantee, and passed them across the table to Downing. "A brief description of the training is included. It is my understanding that your client has seen it and can attest to the accuracy of the description." Downing nodded and passed copies of the guarantee to Wachtel and Hirsch. They all began to read.

In the ensuing silence, Ben Harvey stood and stretched, then went to the coffee setup on a credenza some distance from the conference table and poured himself a fresh cup. He wasn't happy about the sale he'd been asked to preside over. Wachtel was getting much too good a deal. Morgan rose and joined him at the coffee urn, his face tight with controlled excitement. "Thanks for pushing this thing through so fast," he said.

Harvey shrugged. "It wasn't hard. Wachtel's as eager to close as you are. He figures any day now, you're going to come to your senses." He added cream and sugar and stirred. "No second thoughts?"

"I need the money," Morgan stated. "I told you that."

"I know, I know. Still, you'd get a better price if it were known the Comets were on the block."

"I can't let Felicity find out. She'd take me to the cleaners."

"She has no right to any part of this deal. We can defeat any action she brings."

"I haven't got time for legal maneuvering," Morgan protested. "Defending an action could tie up the money for months. I need it now."

"Well, it's your decision." Harvey glanced over at the group around the conference table as he sipped his coffee. "I don't know how long you're going to be able to keep this thing quiet, though. Even with that confidentiality clause."

"We'll just have to hope," Morgan replied. "It's only for a few weeks. Just until after the World Series."

"You think the league owners are going to keep their mouths shut until then?" Harvey scoffed.

"I told them the deal would go sour if anyone talked," Morgan explained. "They approved the sale because they like Wachtel, they know he's a straight shooter, and he's promised not to take the team out of New York. They know if they queer this deal and Wachtel walks, they could end up with a bastard like"—Morgan named a widely disliked major league ex-owner, currently reputed to be shopping for a new team—"or some guy who wants to move the Comets out of the city. It's to their own benefit if they can keep the sale quiet until after the Series."

The attorney shrugged. "Let's hope they can. More coffee?"

At the table, Alan Downing was conferring with his client. "This accurately describes what you saw?" he asked softly, pointing with the tip of his silver pencil at the description of the supertraining in the letter of guarantee.

"It seems accurate, yeah."

Downing shook his head. "I never did understand all the New Age stuff. Wouldn't have believed it worked." He studied his client. "You're absolutely sure you want to go through with the purchase?"

"You bet." Tom pushed the guarantee back toward

Downing. "The team is red hot, they just took the pennant, and at ninety million, they're cheap."

"Another ten million if they take the Series. Which they will."

"Still a good price, and you know it."

Downing nodded. "Just checking. And speaking of checks . . ."

"Right here." Tom took a slim white envelope from his inside jacket pocket and passed it over to his attorney.

Morgan and Ben Harvey returned to the conference table. "Guarantee look okay to everyone?" Harvey inquired.

"Fine."

"Then we're all set. Yes, Chris?" He turned to the intense young woman on his left.

"The medical releases."

"Of course," Harvey said, looking annoyed. "You have the medical releases for the three superplayers?"

Now it was Downing's turn to extend a hand toward his assistant, who handed him a sheaf of papers encased in a clear binder. "All in order," he said, handing it on to Harvey. He'd been puzzled by this request to have the superplayers examined by a physician of Wachtel's choice, prior to signing. But Harvey had explained that Morgan Hudson was very sensitive to the unfortunate sense of mystery in which the press tended to shroud the superplayers from time to time, and he wanted Wachtel to be absolutely confident that Freeman, Reese, and Sanchez were all in excellent health. Wachtel had been favorably impressed, and had readily agreed.

Harvey had also been puzzled by this request of Morgan's, and in fact had attempted to talk him out of it, but Morgan had been adamant. "I don't want Wachtel coming back to me later on, saying the contract's no good because there was something wrong with the superplayers when he bought the team." Harvey's eyebrows rose, but he said nothing. "Not that there *is* anything wrong," Morgan added hurriedly. "It's just that there's been so much weird shit in the press. One of those guys gets a cold or something and can't start the season, and I get sued."

"I doubt that would happen," Harvey had told him.

"Maybe so, but I want independent evidence showing that the superplayers are just fine, and I want that evidence made part of the sale contract. I want Wachtel to attest to the fact that he's satisfied about the health of the superplayers."

Harvey had studied Morgan carefully. "Is there something here I should know?" he'd asked at last.

"Absolutely not," Morgan had stated. "Hell, I'm taking the training myself. I just can't afford for this deal to go bad. I really need that money, Ben. And I have no intention of giving it back."

Now Harvey passed the binder to Morgan, who skimmed through it and nodded. The attorney leaned back in his leather chair and smiled at the faces around the table. "You have the certified checks?" Downing patted the white envelope Tom Wachtel had given him and nodded. "In that case, gentlemen," Harvey announced, "I believe it's magic time."

Robin sat at her desk, attempting to marshal her thoughts. Before her lay a legal-size yellow pad; a thin black marker lay dormant in her hand. Her instincts finally unclouded by romantic notions about Morgan, she had decided to organize what she already knew about the Comets, and work out exactly what questions Connor could help her answer. But it was hard to concentrate. She'd arrived home around nine that morning, having had very little sleep. Not that she regretted one second of the incredible weekend she and Adam had spent together. Their repeated lovemaking had washed away the past, and with it, any residual feelings of personal and sexual inadequacy. She felt cleansed, renewed, and very much in love.

When Adam had dropped her at her apartment and taken the taxi on to his office, Robin had felt surprisingly energized, and determined to do some work herself. Perhaps she'd learn something interesting she could share with Adam at dinner that evening. But despite the pot of coffee she'd consumed during the past two hours, she was finding it hard going. It wasn't lack of sleep that was interfering with her mental processes; it was joy. Once again, her thoughts began to drift ...

The sudden shrill of the phone brought her back to earth with a start. "I had a couple of minutes between patients and I wanted to hear your voice," Adam said softly into her ear. "I miss you already."

"I miss you, too."

"This weekend was ... well, it was probably the most incredible experience of my life."

"Probably?" Robin teased.

"Definitely."

"Yes, for me, too."

"Robin?"

"Mmm?"

"About the weekend ... I want you to know that it wasn't just the sex. Although the sex was probably—uh, definitely the most ... er, what I'm trying to say is, I really care about you. In fact, I think I uh, er ..." He trailed off.

"I feel the same way," Robin said softly.

"You do?"

"Yes, I think I uh, er, you, too. Probably."

"Probably?" It was Adam's turn to tease.

"Well, let's see what happens tonight," Robin said wickedly. "Then I'll decide."

"You're going to put me in the hospital," Adam protested, laughing. "Not that I'm complaining or anything. Have a seat, Mr. Silverman."

"What?"

"Sorry, light of my life," Adam explained. "My torn ligament's arrived. Gotta go."

"See you tonight."

"I'll count the minutes. One, two, three ..." He disconnected.

Still busy, Morgan fumed. He slammed down the receiver in annoyance and half rose, banging his shin on the leg of the conference table. Cursing out loud, he flung an empty coffee cup through the air. It shattered on the end of the marble table, shards flying. What in hell are you doing? a voice inside asked. He froze, shaking slightly, then shamefacedly went around and collected the pieces of the cup. He deposited them in the wastebasket, then slumped back down in his chair again. These feelings of rage were on the increase, and they were beginning to frighten him. He'd never considered himself a violent man. He thought about Freeman and Reese, and felt a frisson of fear. Don't be stupid, he told himself. Wachtel's independent medical reports had all been negative. It was just stress. God knew, he had enough of that in his life at the moment.

He gazed around at the empty conference room. Should he try the number again? Maybe give it another five minutes. He had to wait for Ben Harvey to cut the check, anyway. It would take several days for Wachtel's payment to clear into Harvey, Schwartz, & Sidney's client account, and several more for their people to work up the legal fees and compute Morgan's net. But, much to Ben Harvey's annoyance, Morgan had insisted on taking a postdated check with him. "Estimate the legal fees high," he'd told them, "and pay me the difference when you've done the numbers. I want to take a check for the bulk of the money with me today." He didn't explain how vital it was that he show that check to certain of his creditors. Now he fingered the signed sale agreement, gazed out the conference room window, and smiled. Ninety million. He should be celebrating, not smashing up the china. He grinned to himself. You pulled it off, boy. You're practically home.

No sooner had a broadly smiling Robin finished her conversation with Adam than the phone rang again. *People* magazine wanted a few final revisions to the article she'd turned in three weeks before. Putting the editor on hold, she pulled the most recent version of the piece from the file cabinet, then scrabbled around in the desk drawer for a pencil to mark it up. Why did pencils always roll to the back? She tried to open the drawer wider, but it jammed and refused to move. She reached in; a card of some sort seemed to be stuck back there. Damn. She grabbed an edge, yanked, and brought forth a wrinkled piece of thick, heavily embossed notepaper. Tossing it onto the desk, she rolled the drawer all the way out, found a pencil, and apologized to the waiting editor. Their conversation was brief, the changes minimal. Piece of cake, she thought. She swung around to the computer table that was set at a right angle to the desk, and booted up the Mac. She'd make the changes now and fax it off.

As the program loaded, she reached for the crumpled note card she'd pulled from the drawer. The raised white-on-white initials were so elaborate, so florid, they were impossible to read, and it was only when she unfolded the note and saw Felicity's signature that she remembered what it was. When Felicity had called Robin to apologize for having been the cause of Morgan's learning about their friendship, she'd followed it up with this little note. In it, Felicity had apologized again, reassured Robin of her friendship and support, and renewed her suggestion that they get together for lunch some time. Undecided how to respond, Robin had thrust the missive into her desk drawer and forgotten about it. Now, as she smoothed it out, she again admired the thick paper, the rich and complicated embossing. She could just make out the *F,* but was that an *R* between it and the collection of curlicues that formed what had to be an *H*? Stationery like this must cost a fortune, she thought as she shoved it back into the drawer. Now that she and Morgan were no longer dating, there was no reason she shouldn't have lunch with Felicity. And yet, as long as she was determined to stay on Morgan's good side, perhaps it wouldn't be politic.

Turning to the computer, she took up the *People* article and began typing in the few necessary corrections. She'd finished and was printing it out when the phone rang yet again. Half hoping it was Adam, she lunged for it. But the voice on the other end was not the one she'd hoped to hear.

"You're very popular this morning." Morgan's voice boomed cheerfully. "I've been trying to reach you for twenty minutes."

Go to hell, Robin wanted to tell him. Get lost. You're always apologizing, and then you treat me like shit again. Besides, I'm involved with Adam now. You and I have nothing to say to each other on any level. Instead, she took a deep breath and held her tongue. Staying in contact with Morgan was vital to their investigation. She'd explained her strategy to Adam yesterday, and although it was obvious he wasn't thrilled by the idea, he'd accepted the usefulness of it. If Morgan hadn't called her, Robin reflected, she would have had to call him sooner or later. This way was better, but not much.

"Again, I'm really sorry about the other night. It was wrong of me to spring that Kennedy thing on you. But I really thought you'd get a kick out of it. I had no idea you weren't, uh, you were actually—"

"Rosie McGee."

"Right. And, I, uh, also made some terrible accusations about you and Kenny and Adam. Of course, I know it couldn't possibly be true." Robin felt herself blushing. "I don't know what comes over me sometimes," Morgan continued. "I get so angry these days. Must be stress. Anyway, I always seem to be apologizing, but do you think you could forgive me one more time?"

"I don't know what to say, Morgan," Robin replied carefully. Too quick an acceptance would seem strange. "You really hurt me."

"I know, I know. Let me make it up to you."

"Morgan, I—"

"Just come to the World Series with me. The first game's this Saturday in Philadelphia. You've tracked the Comets story since the beginning. It's only fair that you should be there for the big finish. Come as a reporter, as a friend. After that, if you feel we can try again . . ."

"You really want me to keep on with the story?"

"Of course. It's all but finished anyway, isn't it? That rough draft I saw. That was it, right?"

His question hung in the air. "Uh, yes, of course it was," Robin replied slowly. "I was just, uh, waiting to see how the Comets finished the season."

"Then you'll come to the game with me?"

"Yes, I'd love to," Robin assured him, her voice ringing with false enthusiasm.

"Good. It'll be like old times."

Robin sighed. "No, Morgan. That's exactly what it won't be like. Please."

"Okay, okay. Just come. I'll pick you up in the car."

Trapped in a car with Morgan Hudson? I don't think so. "I'll fly down and meet you at the stadium," Robin said quickly.

"If that's the way you want it," he replied, sounding disappointed. "Uh, no chance of dinner before then?"

"I'm awfully busy these days," Robin told him. "Another article, some freelance advertising . . ."

"Good for you." Morgan hesitated. "Uh, how's Felicity these days?"

"What?"

"I guess maybe I was wrong to get all worked up about you two being friends. Have you seen her lately?"

"No, Morgan," Robin replied stiffly. "I haven't seen Felicity since the party that started all this. Frankly, I don't plan to."

"Good." Morgan sounded relieved. "Um, there's one more thing I have to ask. How did you happen to suggest to Kenny that he see Adam Salt?"

What the hell is he after? Robin wondered. "I met Kenny at the stadium one day, with you," she explained carefully. "He and I got talking and he mentioned he was having headaches. I suggested he talk to Adam because . . . er, Adam's really into sports, and, uh . . ." God, this sounds lame. "The truth is, Kenny was afraid you might bench him if you thought he was sick, and I knew Adam would keep his confidence."

"You should have told me."

"Yes, I see that now," Robin said mock-contritely. "It

was wrong of me not to. But fortunately, it turned out to be nothing. And the headaches went away."

"Probably just stress."

"Yes, that's what Ad— Dr. Salt thought, too."

"Well, if you're sure I can't take you to dinner—or lunch perhaps? No? Well, I'll look forward to seeing you in Philly on Saturday."

"It's very exciting," Robin said, feeling she should show a little more enthusiasm.

"Isn't it? Listen, Robin ... or Rosie, or whoever you are: I miss you. I don't care whether or not you're a Kennedy." Not now that I've got my ninety million. "I hope we can work things out."

"Morgan, I—"

"Don't say anything now. Just come to the game. Then we'll see."

Robin sighed. This was awful. "Morgan, I have to tell you—"

"Tell me what?"

Robin hesitated. If she said what she was longing to say, she'd blow her insider status for good. "I'm really hoping the Comets will win the Series," she finished lamely.

"So am I. See you then. And if you change your mind about dinner, call me, okay?"

"Okay."

Morgan disconnected and Robin slowly lowered the receiver. Whether it was the time of day or the rush of adrenaline produced by the conversation with Morgan, she found she was getting a second wind. So Morgan had decided she was still on the Comets story. Perhaps he thought he was throwing her a sop, dangling the story to get her to come to the game with him. Never mind; she'd use it. Right now, in fact. Leaving the article in the printer tray, she paged through her notebook, then reached for the phone and dialed the number of the Pro Club.

Why was Robin's story really taking so long to finish? Morgan wondered. He'd seen a rough draft several months ago, but nothing since. Had Robin really put it away until the end of the season, or was she still gathering information? If the latter, why had he not been informed, or involved? And what had she learned?

He was glad he'd managed to persuade her to come to the first game. It wasn't as useful as dinner, but it kept the contact going. He had to stay close to her. He had to find out what she knew. If only he hadn't let his temper run away with him. If only he'd controlled himself, that day in his office. Well, what was done was done. He could handle damage control with the best of them.

And then there was Salt ... Just what was Robin's relationship with the good doctor? And was he still involved with Robin's story? He hit the intercom button and spoke briefly to the receptionist, then scribbled the number she gave him on a scrap of paper. Taking up the phone again, he began to dial.

"Morgan Hudson on line three, Dr. Salt."

"Hudson? What the hell—never mind, Pat, I'll take it." Adam punched the flickering button on his office phone. "Mr. Hudson? Adam Salt."

"Dr. Salt. Adam. I know you're busy, so I'll just take a moment. I'm calling to invite you to the World Series."

Chapter Twenty-one

Robin stood pressed against the rough stone exterior of the Pro Club, a gym bag slung over her shoulder. Her second wind was wearing off fast, and with the return of her earlier tiredness came a distinct nervousness. What she was about to attempt was a far cry from the interview with Connor she'd requested when she'd dialed the Pro Club nearly an hour ago. But as the telephone receptionist was explaining that Connor was in training sessions until three, a better idea had come to her. "Never mind," she said. "I'll check my schedule and call again tomorrow." If she moved fast, she could be in and out of Connor's office before his sessions were over.

Now she stood to one side of the Pro Club's solid front door, wondering what idiocy had possessed her. Search Connor's office? I must be mad, she thought. What if someone finds me there? What will I say? She thought of Connor's muscular torso, his huge, strong hands, and shuddered. Well, she'd just have to invoke Morgan's name. Say that she'd changed her mind and decided to wait for Connor in his office; that a member had been leaving and he'd held the door open for her. The last part, at least, would be true. It was the only way she could think of to get inside the place.

The best strategy was not to get caught, she decided. But time was growing short; it was two thirty-five. Maybe she should forget it. Just go home, change her clothes, and wait for Adam. She was about to head back down the stone steps when the oak door swung soundlessly open. She grabbed it without thinking and slid inside.

"Hey, you can't—" began the startled young man who had emerged.

"Forgot my key card again," Robin exclaimed over her shoulder. "Late for my session. Connor'll kill me." She was into the lobby, the door shut firmly behind her, before he could react.

She stood for a moment, waiting. Would he hit the intercom button and report her? She listened carefully, but heard no voices. Satisfied, she turned and looked around the small, empty lobby.

The elevator stood open and ready, but she headed for the stairway she spied through the windowed door off to one side. She'd be a sitting duck on that elevator; at least she could run down the stairs. Or up. Although who besides Connor would know she wasn't a member? The club was small but not that small. In the partially concealed stairwell, she quickly pulled off her sneakers and stripped off her jeans to reveal the tight fuschia exercise pants she'd worn underneath. She crammed her feet back into her sneakers and the jeans into her gym bag. From the pocket of her white T-shirt she took a bright headband and tied up her hair. Then she slung the gym bag over her shoulder and started up the stairs.

Unlike the lobby, the stairs were uncarpeted, but her sneakers made no sound on the bare cement. Did anyone really monitor the video camera transmissions? she wondered as she climbed. Would someone be waiting for her on one of the hidden landings? She stopped and listened, but could hear no door handle being turned, no footfall on the stone steps. She took a deep breath and continued upward.

The metal doors at each level were painted orange and marked with large numerals in black paint. Connor's office was on the fourth floor, she recalled. Just three months had passed since she'd come here for her tour of the supertraining room, but it seemed like a century ago.

Just short of the third-floor level, the door above her opened and male voices spilled out onto the stairs. She

swung around and flew back down the stairs as they
descended above her. At level two, they exited, laughing
as they pulled the door shut behind them. Next time,
don't run, Robin told herself. Members obviously use
the stairs; act like a member and nobody'll think twice.
She began to climb again, her heart pounding.

She paused just above level three to catch her breath,
then continued upward. What if someone were in the
waiting room outside Connor's office? What if his sessions had been canceled? I'll simply say I've changed my
mind and decided to interview him today after all. In
gym clothes? Shut up, she told herself fiercely. Just get
on with it. Slowly, she opened the orange door and
stepped inside.

All was quiet beyond. The waiting area was unoccu-
pied. Robin walked forward. Built-in storage closets
took up most of the available wall space; she could see
cartons of mineral water, stacks of towels, hand weights.
Ahead, the wall of glass gave a dizzying view of the
entire gym with its cantilevered platforms and catwalks.
To one side of the wall of glass, an open landing gave
access to the gym below. On her left was Connor's office,
the door ajar. She put her hand on the door, then froze.
Was it her imagination, or had she heard a creak? She
stepped backward and collided with a warm, firm body.

"May I help you?" a female voice asked.

Robin jumped back and swung around. A tall, muscular woman stood before her. "Mr. Egan's in a session,"
the woman said, frowning. She was dressed in white
warmup pants and a T-shirt that said PRO CLUB STAFF in
gold letters above the pocket. A pin-on name tag identified her as Greta. She carried a sheaf of papers, and a
plastic stopwatch hung from a red ribbon around her
neck. "What did you want with Mr. Egan?" she demanded, eyeing Robin suspiciously.

"We're out of water on level two," Robin replied
quickly. "Someone said it was up here. I thought Mr.
Egan . . ."

Greta sighed. "They're supposed to check the supplies

three times a day. I'll have some sent down right away. Sorry."

"No, it's all right. I'll just take a couple with me, if that's all right. Uh, where—?"

Greta gestured toward the supply closet. "Help yourself. What level was that?"

"Uh, two."

"I'll take care of it." Greta paused. "Are you new here? I thought I knew everyone." Robin nodded. "I'm Greta." Her handshake was firm and businesslike. "And you are . . . ?"

"Uh, Rosie. Rosie McGee."

"Nice to meet you, Miss McGee. Take what you need and I'll have more water sent down." She watched as Robin went to the open supply closet and took two of the large plastic bottles. "You okay on towels?"

"Just fine."

"Well, have a good workout." She smiled briskly and disappeared into Connor's office.

Now what? Robin thought. She turned toward the stairwell door, then changed her mind. Greta had come up behind her, so she'd obviously entered through the stairwell door; there was a reasonable chance she'd leave the same way. And surely she wouldn't spend long in Connor's office. She was probably just dropping off some papers. And if she left soon, there would still be a little time . . .

Robin went to the open landing and looked out over the gym floor. It certainly was impressive. She stepped down onto the open catwalk and knelt; craning backward, she could see that she was now out of view of anyone on level four, though highly visible to people below. But who would question a woman in workout clothes, tying her sneaker? Slowly she untied her shoe and tied it and untied it and tied it again. When she heard the faint metallic clunk that told her Greta had left the way she'd come, Robin rose and retraced her steps.

Connor's office door was now swung closed. She pushed it open, stepped inside, and closed it again behind her. It was nearly two forty-five. She'd have to hustle.

She cast a longing look at the computer—with more time, it would have been the first place she'd have looked—and turned her attention to the white metal file cabinet instead. Its contents proved disappointing: a yellow Pendaflex folder for each member containing the original application, training records, and sundry information. Presumably Connor hadn't thought it was worth his time to enter such information into the computer. She went to the desk. Much to her surprise, the drawers weren't locked. Obviously no secrets here, she thought. The center utility drawer held the usual paraphernalia: pens, paper clips, blank petty cash vouchers, assorted small change. The contents of the top side drawer were similar: pads, membership applications, credit card charge slips. The desk's built-in file drawer held green suspension folders, and at first she assumed they were the records of special members, but a quick glance told her these were Connor's personal files. Not very exciting all the same, she thought, walking her fingers past "Club-Telephone," "Club-Electricity," and "C.E.-Expenses." C.E.; Connor Egan? That was more promising. She pulled the file. Copies of monthly expense reports, the most recent in front, were neatly marked with the dates Connor had received reimbursement. Robin leafed through them. The past three or four months were fairly standard. How far back do these things go? she wondered. Flipping the file over and starting at the back, she found herself staring at reports beginning nearly a year ago. She looked more closely. Air travel to Puerto Rico, Colorado Springs, Detroit, Phoenix ... Did that mean anything? Phoenix was easy; the Comets' spring training took place in Arizona. But Connor had begun traveling to Phoenix in December. And Puerto Rico? Colorado? Colorado ... Kenny Reese's family in Colorado Springs. But how could Connor have known Kenny last November? He'd only joined the team this past spring. Perhaps Connor had scouted him. But that didn't make sense, either. Connor was a fitness expert, not a professional baseball coach. . . . Well, she'd puzzle it out later. It was five to three now, and she had to hurry.

She replaced the expense file and looked hurriedly through the rest of the file labels: 'Club-Laundry,' 'Club-Allied Maintenance,' 'C.E.-Employment Contract.' Hmm. She pulled out the contract file and scanned the three-page document inside. According to the date of the agreement, Connor had been hired some twelve months earlier by a company called Pro Club For Men. Robin paused; why did that name ring a bell? She seemed to associate it with something beyond the gym itself, but what? And why the For Men part? Had Barrett originally planned to restrict the membership, then changed his mind? The employment contract was straightforward, and she thrust it back in the drawer and drew out a folder labeled only "Lease." Had Barrett rented, not owned, the Pro Club premises? And why should such a lease be in Connor's files? But one glance told her she was mistaken; it was Connor's lease, not Barrett's. Connor had recently taken up residence in Barrett's old apartment. That must have taken nerves of steel, she reflected. The lease, in the name of Pro Club For Men Corporation, stipulated that the nominal rent was waived in exchange for services rendered. She flipped to the signature page. Presumably Barrett's executors had signed the lease; it would be interesting to see who they were. But the document had been signed by an attorney.

The loud buzz of the phone intercom made her jump. "Connor? Can Gary take the van for a private at five? Les Wilkens just called. Connor? Are you there?"

Not here yet, but no doubt on his way, Robin thought, hastily stuffing the lease back into its folder and slamming the drawer. Ten past three; for godsake, *move*. She scurried out of the office, pushing through the metal orange door just as a tall, white-haired figure stepped onto the landing from the catwalk below. She was halfway down the cement stairs when she realized she'd left the bottles of water on Connor's desk.

                         *   *   *

"Just one more week, Austin," Morgan said firmly. He sipped his Scotch and stared across the table at his chief financial officer. "Stall them."

"I've *been* stalling them. I'm running out of excuses."

"Send them seats to the World Series. Invite Tully to watch the game from the owner's box." Tully Regan was one of their major suppliers of chemical compounds.

Austin Price shook his head in disgust. "Those guys are only impressed by cash, Morgan. You know Tully. He'll say, 'Pay my bills and I can buy my own god-damn seats.' "

Morgan smiled. "Yeah, that's exactly what he'd say." He broke off a piece of his roll, buttered it, and put it back down on his plate. "I realize things have been rather ... unsettled lately," he said, his face becoming serious again. "But I guarantee—"

"Unsettled?" Price interrupted. "The divisional managers are in my office every day, complaining about the lack of product on the shelves. The plant guys say chemical shipments are being delayed because our suppliers— Tully's not the only one—haven't been paid. The ad agency's threatening—"

"Screw the agency," Morgan told him harshly. "Look, the suppliers will be paid next week, we'll beef up the distribution, everything will be fine. Eat your fish."

But Price remained glum. He'd been delighted to be appointed CFO of Hudson & Company at the tender age of thirty-one. But four years of Morgan's seat-of-the-pants management style had worn him down. And his boss's obvious inability to delegate had afforded Price far less control than his job description had implied. Now, despite all evidence to the contrary, Morgan was assuring him that their creditors would be paid, next month's payroll would be met, and profitability would rebound. It all sounded a little too much like the Psychic Hotline. "Can't you give me something concrete I can take to them, so they'll believe I'm not bullshitting them again?"

"Tell them there's money coming into the company

next week, a lot of money. But its source is highly confidential."

"Not good enough," Austin told him firmly. "They just won't go for it."

Morgan took an envelope from his pocket. "This might help," he said. He drew out the Harvey, Schwartz, & Sidney check and waved it toward Price. "It's postdated. And some of it's got to be used to pay off that goddamn loan from my ex-wife." Austin nodded. He recalled how embarrassing it had been for Morgan to explain that transaction to him, how Morgan had practically sworn him to secrecy despite the fact that it was right there in the company records. "Still," Morgan continued, "Tully won't know that."

He passed the check over and Price repressed a gasp as he looked at the amount. How in hell had Morgan been able to raise that kind of money, all of a sudden? As he stared at the check, one way came to mind, but he brushed it aside. Morgan would never sell the Comets. He loved those guys. Price grinned across the table at his boss. "Can I show this to Tully? Can I leak it?"

"That's the idea. But keep me out of it."

"Of course. Uh, Morgan?"

"Yes?"

"About this check. Er, how . . ." Morgan's eyes bore into his, daring him to ask. Austin Price flushed. "Never mind," he said. "It's really none of my business."

It was nearly eight-thirty when Robin arrived at Monsoon, refreshed after a brief rest, though she'd been too keyed up to actually sleep. Despite the torrential rain, Amsterdam Avenue thronged with diners and shoppers. The restaurant was new to her, and crowded, but Adam had managed to secure a table for four, and he waved to her as she sloshed her way past the line at the door.

"I hope you didn't mind my asking you to meet me here," he apologized as she edged between the wooden tables to join him. "I was in the OR until an hour ago. Emergencies happen in my line of business."

"Mine, too," Robin assured him. "No problem. Al-

though you could have arranged for better weather."
She pushed her damp hair out of her eyes and smiled
at him.

He took her hand. "You look beautiful, wet or dry."

"So do you." She smiled. "But—Vietnamese cooking?
I thought the Southwest was your thing."

"Don't want to get typecast," he said. "Ever been
here?" She shook her head. "The food's like nothing
you've ever tasted. You'll love it."

A waiter appeared with menus and took their drink
orders. As soon as he had gone, Robin turned to Adam
with barely controlled excitement. "Ask me where I was
this afternoon," she said. "You'll never guess."

Adam pretended to study her. "The hairdresser?"

"Oh, very funny. No, I was—"

"Only this man and this restaurant could coax me out
on a night like tonight," said a voice.

"Agnes." Adam rose. "You remember Robin?"

"Of course. The friend of the man who owns the baseball team, is it not?" She smiled, proud of her memory,
but the expressions on their faces told her something
had changed. "I have put my feet into it, yes?"

"Not at all." Robin smiled at the older woman. "It's
just that Morgan and I are no longer an item."

"She's traded him in for a racier model," Adam explained. "Someone younger, with more hair, better conversation, exquisite taste in restaurants . . . but I boast."

Oh ho, Agnes thought; good for Adam. She beamed
at them.

Adam turned to Robin. "Agnes called just as I was
leaving," he explained. "She said she had some news, so
I suggested she join us."

"News?" Robin asked. "What's happened?"

Agnes eyed the hovering waiter. "Why don't we order
first?" she suggested. "Then we can talk."

"I recommend a huge assortment of appetizers, followed by the coconut custard," Adam said.

"You always recommend that," Agnes chided him.

"I like it," he replied. "I think you will, too," he
added, turning to Robin. "Will you put yourself in my

hands?" Robin nodded, and Agnes smiled at the look that passed between them.

From the corner of her eye, Robin caught Agnes's eye and flushed. "But only if you include the beef sate," she told Adam quickly, turning her attention to the menu. "Number seventeen."

When the waiter had gone, Agnes set down her beer. "Now I shall tell you what has happened," she announced.

"Uh, Robin has some news, too," Adam said quickly. "She got here before you, so I'm afraid she takes precedence."

"No, please," Robin said. "I'm too curious. Go on, Agnes."

"Well, some time ago, as you both know, I injected several groups of my laboratory rats with that mysterious thalamic hormone I isolated from Kenny's spinal fluid." Adam and Robin nodded. "And the rats, they continued being the same rats. Nothing unusual happened to them. Naturally, I was very disappointed, but there it was. These things happen. Then, a week ago, I went to California for a conference. The weather was beautiful, I met some old friends, and I decided to stay through the weekend. I came back today and I checked the rats, and—what do you think?"

The waiter began covering the table with plates of fragrant food. "Taste this," Adam said, handing Robin a skewer of chicken. "Dip it in the peanut sauce—"

"I checked the rats," Agnes repeated loudly, "and the rats were not as I had left them. Ah, now I have your attention. Yes, they had changed. They had become—" Agnes paused for effect—"super rats." She reached for a shrimp dumpling and popped it triumphantly into her mouth.

Adam grinned at her. "Super rats, Agnes? Able to leap tall mazes in a single bound?"

"Yes, Adam, exactly so. They go through the mazes much faster. They learn repeated actions faster. I tried them with a primitive little test I invented specially for them, using a lightbulb and an electric shock, and their learning and reaction times are off the scale."

"That's great," Adam exclaimed. "Now we have the link."

"The link, yes," Agnes agreed. "And also we have the rages." Adam set down his chopsticks. "The rats are fighting one another," Agnes continued. "Suddenly one rat attacks another, and just as suddenly, it stops. Tomorrow I will perform more tests, do some dissections, make some slides and so forth. But I am certain what I will find. The rages are seizures arising in the cortex."

"Shit."

"And there is one other thing." Agnes selected a shrimp dumpling, dipped it in sauce, and ate half of it. "One of the rats is acting ... peculiar."

"Only one? I thought you said—"

"More peculiar, I should have said. Different. Crazy. It has the rages, yes. But it also exhibits other unusual behavior from time to time. It is subtle, you understand. But it ... how do I say this? It occasionally loses touch with reality."

Adam grinned. "How does a rat lose touch with reality, Agnes?"

But Agnes did not return his smile, "It occasionally reacts inappropriately to simple situations and objects that are highly familiar. It is the only rat with this ... problem."

"Which means?" Adam asked, fascinated.

"It is possible that, in certain cases, perhaps where a particular brain is more sensitive to chemical stimulation, the huge amounts of nitric oxide in the cortex cause misfiring along the neural pathways, erroneous communication. You follow?" Adam nodded. "This interference with the neural circuitry of the brain, this miscommunication, results in a mismatch between the neural circuitry and established patterns of reality."

"You mean the rat is crazy?" Robin asked.

"Just so. But this is an atypical reaction. For the time being, I believe we should concentrate on the more generalized behavior—the rages and physical improvements—

that are common to the rats and the superplayers." She popped the rest of the shrimp dumpling into her mouth. "These are delicious."

"So what do we do now?" Robin asked.

"Now we will wait," Agnes told her, "and see what happens next."

"What do you mean?" Robin asked. "I thought everything had already happened."

"Everything we know about, yes. But this thing moves faster with rats than with people. Whatever happens next will happen first to the rats."

"Jesus."

"Indeed," Agnes said dryly. "Now, Robin, I have interrupted what you were about to tell Adam, and I apologize. Please go ahead."

Robin chewed a mouthful of seaweed salad thoughtfully. "Well, I'm not sure whether anything I found in Connor's office today is really important, but—"

"Connor's office?" Adam stared at her. "You were at the Pro Club?"

Robin nodded. "They told me Connor would be in training sessions most of the afternoon, so I sneaked in and searched his office."

Adam's brow furrowed with concern, but Agnes laughed. "I like this girl," she announced. "How did you do it?"

"Don't encourage her," Adam said.

"Of course I shall encourage her," Agnes said. "Young women today need spirit." She turned to Robin. "Tell me everything."

Robin described how she'd gotten into the Pro Club, her encounter with Greta, and how she'd barely escaped without being caught. She found that telling it after the fact made it all seem rather amusing, and she soon had them laughing. But as she began to describe the files she'd found in Connor's desk, their faces grew more serious. "Do any of those trips mean anything?" she asked. "I mean, anything important?"

Adam thought for a moment. "The Arizona spring training connection is obvious. As to why Connor went out there, well, he could have been sent to work with the players, help get them in shape."

"Or to work with only three of the players," Robin said.

Adam nodded. "That's probably more like it," he agreed. "He must have set up some sort of temporary training facility. And the Colorado Springs trip is obviously linked to Kenny Reese. But why would he start Kenny's supertraining before Kenny joined the team?"

"Maybe Kenny *had* joined the team by then," Robin said. "Or maybe they wanted to see if the training would work before they signed him. We'd need to see Kenny's contract to know for sure, but I think it's obvious Connor was working with Kenny well before spring training started."

"It took only two weeks for the hormone to affect my rats," Agnes said. "It might take longer with people. A month, six weeks ... That would fit with your timing, wouldn't it? December, January ..."

"Otis Freeman comes from Detroit," Robin said, "so that explains that trip. But Ernie Sanchez comes from Florida, and he's been with the team for several years. So where does Puerto Rico come in?"

Adam smiled. "That's easy. Ernie plays winter ball in Puerto Rico. Connor probably set up a temporary facility down there, too."

Robin sighed. "Nothing mysterious after all."

"Afraid not. Did you find anything else?"

"There wasn't much time," Robin reminded them, "and I'm afraid I didn't even try to get into his computer. I did find out that Connor's renting Barrett's old apartment, though." She shivered. "Better him than me."

Adam looked up from his seaweed salad. "Now that's interesting. Who's he renting it from?"

"The same corporation that signed his original employment contract: Pro Club For Men."

"For men? But the club has women members."

"I know. It seemed strange to me, too. And there's

something about that name ... Anyway, Connor's living there now."

"I wonder ..." Agnes began. They looked at her expectantly. "Do you not find Connor's position in all this rather ... interesting? He is an employee of the Pro Club. With Barrett dead, he alone is privy to the secrets of the supertraining. He moves into Barrett's old apartment weeks after the man's death ... I wonder what his relationship with Barrett really was."

Adam raised an eyebrow. "You mean, the son Barrett never had?"

"Or the one he did."

Adam laughed. "Nice idea, Agnes, but highly unlikely."

"I wonder whether Connor could have benefited from Barrett's will in some way," Robin mused.

"A way that would give him a motive to murder Barrett."

"But the police cleared him."

"True, but—"

"Children, children," Agnes broke in. "You have overlooked the biggest question here. Is Connor taking the supertraining himself?" They stared at her. "He is very involved with his physical condition, yes? So you, Adam, have told me."

"Agnes and I had a long phone conversation after she found that hormone," Adam explained to Robin. "She insisted I tell her everything."

"I'm glad you did," Robin told him. She looked across at the older woman. "We need you, Agnes."

Agnes nodded, pleased. "You do," she agreed. "So my question remains: is Connor taking the training?"

"How can we know that?" Adam protested.

"You are often at the Pro Club, Adam. Have you observed any rage behavior? That seems to be a constant among the superplayers. Has Connor been having temper tantrums?"

"Not that I've noticed," Adam said. "He always seems pretty even-tempered. Even when he gets annoyed about something, like a piece of equipment being used incorrectly, he always manages to keep his cool."

"It is too bad no one else has been given this training," Agnes reflected. "We have only the baseball players for comparison. And the rats, of course."

"Uh, there is someone else," Robin said. "Morgan Hudson."

"Morgan's been getting the training?" Agnes exclaimed.

"He started back in August. As owner of the Comets, he put pressure on Barrett to give it to him. He wanted to win the tennis championship at the country club. See, he'd come in second or third for years, and he was determined ..." She broke off. "Anyway, he won." Adam touched Robin's cheek. Only a faint remnant of the angry red scrape was still visible. "Yes," she continued, "he did get moody and angry, sometimes. He was always sorry afterward, but ..."

"Four out of four, not counting the rats," Agnes said gleefully. "No rages, no supertraining. I think we can assume that Connor has decided to abstain."

"Maybe he can't give it to himself," Robin suggested. "Maybe he needs someone else to—"

But Agnes shook her head. "Surely he could use the strange machines you described, Adam, and watch the video screens and all that, without any help. But he does not do it. So I ask myself, why not? What does he know?"

"Connor's on my list," Robin said. "I'll get Morgan to set up an interview with him, see what I can pry out of him. That was actually my original plan for today."

But Adam was shaking his head. "No way," he told her firmly. "Maintaining contact with Morgan could be dangerous."

"But he's our best lead," Robin protested. "He's my access to people like Connor."

"It's too risky," Adam insisted. "I think you should stay away from him. Don't go to the game on Saturday."

Robin stared at him. "How did you know I was going?"

"Morgan called and invited me, too. He made sure to tell me you'd already accepted. I thought it prudent to turn him down. Cordially, of course."

"But why would he invite you? He barely knows you."

"Fishing expedition?"

"Maybe. I think he suspects there's something between us. And he overheard you and Kenny talking in the Pro Club locker room. He knows I referred Kenny to you about his headaches. Of course I assured him you'd found nothing."

"All the more reason this strategy of yours could be dangerous."

"There'll be tons of people in the owner's box on Saturday," Robin protested. "And I'll slip away as soon as the game's over. Believe me, I have no intention of getting caught alone with Morgan Hudson. I just want to stay close to the action." She paused. "Agnes, why don't you come with me?"

"But I know nothing of baseball."

"It'll be a helluva game to learn on," Adam told her.

"And how will you introduce me?" Agnes asked Robin. "I do not think the presence of a medical research scientist will thrill Mr. Hudson."

"We'll think of something," Robin assured her. "Please come." The waiter had removed the empty plates and set down dishes of coconut pudding and thick white mugs of tea.

"Well, why not?" Agnes decided. "It will be an adventure of a sort." She spooned up some pudding, her expression turning thoughtful. "Now that you say Mr. Hudson is taking the supertraining," she mused, "I find there is another thing that puzzles me: Why should he know less about the training than Connor?"

Robin stirred her tea meditatively. "Morgan's rich," she said slowly, "and he considers himself worldly and sophisticated. But being worldly and being a dupe are not mutually exclusive."

"Meaning?"

"Maybe he's being used."

"By whom?"

Robin shrugged. "I have no idea. But Morgan *is* taking the supertraining, and Connor's not."

They finished their pudding in silence, watching the rain pelt down outside. When the waiter had poured another round of tea, Agnes rose. "It has been a most interesting evening," she told them, putting some money on the table. "Delicious, too. But regretfully, I must now leave you. No, Adam, you are generous, but I insist on paying my share." She shrugged into her long olive-drab slicker and pulled the hood over her head. "We all have much to think about."

Robin nodded. "You'll call if there's any change in the rats?"

"Of course, immediately."

"Does that mean you're expecting something to happen?" Adam asked.

But Agnes would not be drawn. "All we can do is wait and see."

As it turned out, they didn't have to wait long.

Chapter Twenty-two

Friday, October 1

The small furry body lay rigid and contorted, the red eyes open and staring. Adam nudged it with a pencil. "Spastic paralysis," he said softly.

Agnes nodded. "Yes, that's what I thought, too."

"And the others?"

"This is the first. It was lying in the bottom of the cage when I came in this morning. I called you immediately."

"The first? You expect more deaths?"

"Don't you?"

Adam shook his head, not in disagreement but in resignation. A feeling of helplessness swept over him. "Any chance it could be an anomaly? That it could be only this one rat that's affected?"

"You know better than that." Agnes beckoned to a white-coated assistant, who carefully placed the rat's body in a plastic bag and carried it to the refrigerator that stood against one wall of the animal laboratory. "I'll have a look inside this afternoon," Agnes said. "See what the brain is like." She shrugged. "I'm sorry, Adam."

"Yeah, me, too." He thrust his fists deep in his pockets and wandered over to the window. The view, out over the black-tarred roofs of the neighboring brownstones, was uninspiring, but he wasn't really focusing. In his mind's eye, he was seeing a young baseball player in a smart blue blazer checking out the chemistry section of the local bookstore.

Agnes went and stood beside him. "There was never

really any doubt in my mind about what would happen," she told him. "I hoped, but . . ."

"All the rats exhibited the same clinical symptoms?" Adam asked, knowing the answer. "The brain lesions, the—"

"—cortical seizures. Yes." Agnes put her arm around Adam's shoulder. "There's always the chance that it could affect humans differently. Have any of the players exhibited weakness or trembling in their legs or arms?"

"Not that I know of."

"Well then, maybe it'll be different with them."

"Maybe."

"Can you make him stop?"

Adam shook his head. "I tried. Several times. Kenny refused. Funny thing is, I understand how he feels. I think I'd probably have refused, too."

"Yes, but that was before . . . this."

"Do you really think if Kenny, if any of them, stopped now, it would make a difference?"

Agnes thought for a moment, then shook her head. "Probably not. Once the rages start, the damage to the cortex has probably progressed too far. But you mustn't blame yourself, Adam. It was already too late when Kenny first came to you about his headaches." Adam nodded. "And of course," she continued, "we don't know how long the hormone remains active, once it's in there. Even if Kenny had stopped the training months ago, it might not have made any difference."

"Once it's in there," Adam repeated. "We don't even know how it gets in there."

"The brain could produce it in reaction to some external stimulus."

"Like that New Age crap? I don't think so, Agnes. Do you?"

"Frankly, Adam, I don't know. The brain's a very mysterious organ."

"You said that about the thalamus."

"It is true of both. There is still so much that is unknown to us."

Adam sighed and turned away from the window. "So

what the *hell* do I do now?" he asked of no one in particular. "Call Kenny and tell him to get his affairs in order? Call the baseball commissioner and tell him to cancel the World Series? Hell, I can't tell him whether this hormone is originating inside the body or outside. I can't prove it's even connected with the Supertraining, except circumstantially." He began to pace. "Unless I can do a spinal tap on Sanchez and Freeman—oh yes, and on Morgan Hudson, too—I can't even prove the hormone's present in anyone except Kenny. And even if the owner of the Comets were to give me permission to stick a large, painful needle into his best players the day before the first Series game, what the hell could I do with the results, even if they were positive?"

"Adam—"

"Maybe the fucking hormone's got *nothing* to do with the Supertraining. Maybe it's some goddamn chemical that's leached into the goddamn water!"

"Are you finished?" Agnes demanded.

"Unless you have anything to add."

"I do. You must keep digging."

"I'm out of ideas, Agnes."

"Nonsense. Apply the scientific method. Trace it back."

"How do you mean?"

Agnes took his arm and led him out of the animal lab and back to her office. "Robin's covering the current situation," she said. "Morgan, Connor, and so forth. I like her very much, by the way. So much nicer than Helen."

"Faint praise."

"I didn't mean it that way and you know it." Agnes seated herself behind her desk and gestured toward a chair beside it. "Sit." Adam sat. "Robin's dealing with the here and now," Agnes continued. "Why don't you see what you can find out about the 'then'?"

"The 'then'?" Adam gave her a lopsided smile.

"Really, Adam, you are very obtuse today. Think. Barrett arrives in New York with a unique training system for turning good athletes into great ones. How did he know it would work?"

"Maybe he didn't. Maybe he tried it out on the Comets first."

"Would Morgan Hudson allow that? Allow some unknown Englishman to use his beloved Comets as guinea pigs for an untried technique? Would he do that without some kind of proof, some assurance that it would work?"

"Proof? You mean ... Barrett might have used the technique before?"

"Exactly. He might have had a trial run with it before bringing it to Morgan. So you need to concentrate on Barrett. What do you know about him?"

"Not much. He was British. He'd been confined to a wheelchair for years. He had a degree in biochemistry. He was an ex-jock ..."

"Jock?" Agnes asked, puzzled.

"Athlete, Agnes. It comes from the word 'jockstrap.' "

"Ah. And a jockstrap is ... ?"

"Um, it doesn't matter."

Agnes regarded him with amusement. "So Barrett was a jockstrap. Anything else?"

Adam shook his head. "But Robin might know more. Morgan may have spoken about him."

"Use my phone." Agnes pushed the instrument toward him.

Quickly Adam explained the situation to a distressed Robin, and then broached Agnes's idea of his attempting to dig into Barrett's background. Robin was enthusiastic but not sanguine about her ability to help. "Morgan never really talked about him," she said. "In fact, the only time I remember us discussing him at all was when he was murdered." She thought for a moment. "I remember thinking a degree in biochemistry was a strange qualification for a gym owner to have. And ... oh yes, I asked Morgan whether he'd known Barrett at Cambridge."

"Morgan went to Cambridge, too?"

"Yes, but some years before Barrett. And his degree was in economics. They never met." Robin sighed. "How awful it must have been for Barrett. Trapped in his wheelchair, unable to defend himself against his murderer."

"It must have been tough for Barrett—a cripple—to train athletes to do what he couldn't."

"Yes, that was sad. He'd been a great athlete as a young man, a real star, apparently, but his spine was crushed during a rugby match. They carried him off the field and he never walked again."

"When would Barrett have first arrived at Cambridge?"

"Let me think ... Morgan's forty and Barrett was three years younger ... Fourteen, fifteen years ago, maybe?"

"You've been a great help," Adam told her. "More than you know. I'll tell you about it tonight." He hung up quickly, already making plans. Rugby. Cambridge. Biochemistry. If Cambridge was where Barrett had first developed his technique, perhaps secret human trials were made there. And since rugby was Barrett's game ... "Agnes, you're a genius," he declared. "Mind if I call my office?" He was already dialing. "Hello, Pat? I need you to cancel, well, everything for next Monday ... better cancel Tuesday, too. Fred Fenton can cover for me. Say I had a family emergency. I don't know; make something up. Oh, and book me on a flight to London tomorrow evening. That's right. No, it's kind of complicated. Thanks; you're a trouper. I'm leaving for the office now; be there in fifteen minutes." He replaced the receiver. "Thanks, Agnes. I really appreciate your help with this whole messy business."

"It is nothing," she assured him. "An interesting challenge."

"Well, I'm very grateful. Who knows? Maybe I'll learn something that can make a difference to Kenny and the others." He rose. "Now I'd better get moving. I'll call you from Cambridge and let you know how I'm getting on."

Agnes held up her hand. "A moment, please. What are you planning to do when you get to Cambridge?"

"Well, I thought I'd—"

"—march in and ask them for the names and phone numbers of everyone who has played rugby for Cambridge for the past fifteen years?"

"Something like that, yes . . ."

"And of course they will simply give them to you." Agnes shook her head. "You are very charming, Adam, but not that charming. No. You will call Tibor. I will give you his number."

"Tibor."

"A very dear friend who teaches microbiology at Cambridge. Once he asked me to marry him. So flattering. But I refused. Oh, don't look at me with those cow eyes, Adam. I have never regretted it for an instant. Tibor is a dear man, but . . . well, you will meet him, and you will see." She thumbed through her Rolodex and scribbled several numbers on a square yellow Post-It. "Call him at home, as soon as you get back to your office. There's a five-hour time difference, remember." Adam nodded, somewhat bemused. "Tell him I said he was to do the footwork for you."

"The legwork?"

"Foot, leg . . ." Agnes waved a dismissive hand. "Tell Tibor I said that tomorrow he must look through the records of the rugby players at Cambridge; you will tell him which years. Say that you will call him from Heathrow when you land, to hear what he has found. Then you can decide what to do next."

"Yes, ma'am." Adam grinned. "Anything else?"

"Yes, one thing. I know it looks bad," Agnes said with an involuntary glance in the direction of the animal laboratory, "but don't give up hope. Who knows what you may discover at Cambridge?"

Adam studied her. "Are you telling me you really believe we can save Kenny and the others?"

"Believe? No. Hope? Always." She reached over and patted his hand. "Go to England. Learn everything you can, and quickly." She paused. "And if we cannot save Kenny, perhaps we can avenge him."

Chapter Twenty-three

Saturday, October 2—World Series, game number 1
The owner's box was packed, the air smoky and charged, as Robin and Agnes stepped through the door. She'd purposely timed their arrival to precede the start of the game by mere minutes.

"I was afraid you weren't coming," Morgan said, enveloping her in a welcoming bear hug. "Sandy, you remember Robin, uh, Kennedy." He spied the older woman and scowled. "Who's this?"

"Agnes Havacek is a ... colleague of mine from the ad agency," Robin explained as she disentangled herself from his embrace. "She's a real Comets fan and this is such a thrill for her—"

Morgan frowned. "You didn't tell me you were bringing a friend," he said ungraciously.

"Please forgive me," Robin began nervously, but Agnes moved forward and put her hands on Morgan's shoulders. As tall as he, she looked reverently into his eyes, then kissed him firmly on each cheek. "It is such an honor," she proclaimed, her accent suddenly thickening, "such a great, great honor. How I have longed to meet you, the owner of my beloved Comets. What miracles you have wrought! How we admire you in Hungary!"

Morgan's expression brightened. "How very kind," he murmured. "I didn't realize Hungarians followed American baseball."

"Oh yes," Agnes assured him. "And we play, too, although our rules are somewhat different. I tell you, Mr. Hudson, in Hungary, you are quite the celebrity!"

Morgan smiled. "How, uh, very charming. Er, how long have you lived in America?"

"Eleven years," Agnes announced. "For eleven years I am writing advertising about Toyota cars. 'You asked for it, you got it!' That is mine." Behind Morgan's back, Robin rolled her eyes at Agnes, but he seemed to find it all perfectly believable. "And also I write for Domino's Pizza."

"And do you find it difficult, writing in English?"

"Not at all," Agnes replied. "I write of feelings, of emotions. The love of the sunroof, the yearning for two free toppings. Such things are the same in every language, are they not?" She gazed at him adoringly. "Ah, your photos do not do you justice. Robin is a lucky young woman."

"You're very kind." Morgan beamed at her. These European women really understood men, he thought. "Uh, help yourself to some champagne," he offered. "And there's plenty of food—" The first notes of the national anthem rang out. "My God, here we go! Come on, Robin." Grabbing her hand, he hurried her toward the front of the glass box.

Agnes smiled grimly and pushed her way through the crowd to join them. "You allow that I sit with you?" she asked, sliding beneath Sandy Napier's descending bottom and effectively unseating him. Ignoring his growl of protest, she leaned across Robin to their host, her eyes wide and innocent. "They will be thrilled in Budapest," she exclaimed, "when I tell them I am here with the great Morgan Hudson. And after the game, you will introduce me to these famous superplayers of yours, yes? Such a great honor . . ."

"Yes, of course," Morgan agreed absently, his attention fixed on the expanse of green below, the intercom phone in his hand.

Agnes gave Robin a triumphant smile.

"I can't believe he bought that ridiculous act," Robin whispered.

"Ridiculous? Not at all. Everybody likes to be flattered. Now look down there and tell me what is happening."

The Comets were running onto the field, resplendent in crimson and white. With an encouraging roar from seventy thousand voices, the first game of the World Series began.

The team seemed determined to give no quarter, in the field or at bat, and their spirits were high. It was quite amazing, Robin thought, the way the three super-players had inspired a middle-of-the-league team to greatness.

The first inning was a walkover, and it only got better. Fans went wild as Kenny homered in the third inning and again in the fifth. Philadelphia played well, but they were no match for Freeman's lightning moves and cannon arm. Sanchez powered through inning after inning on the mound, strong, confident, and inspiring. And the runners kept coming home . . .

A strong comeback by Philadelphia in the seventh inning wasn't enough to break the Comets' hold. The score stood at fourteen to eight in favor of the Comets going into the ninth, and ten minutes later, the team had taken their first World Series game.

Players and coaches rushed onto the field. The noise in the owner's box was deafening. Morgan grabbed Robin and kissed her, and Agnes grabbed Morgan and kissed him, too. He laughed and hustled them both down to the clubhouse.

The boisterous scene beneath the stadium had become very familiar. The press was out in force. Everyone was high on the win. Players in various stages of undress were shouting, laughing, banging each other on the back. Robin soon lost Morgan in the crowd, but a sweaty-faced Jim Warfield shouldered through the throng to pump her hand.

Robin glanced at her watch; five-thirty. Five hours before Adam's flight departed for London. Tonight would be the first time in a week they'd slept apart.

"Miss him already?" Agnes asked, her expression teasing but kind.

Robin nodded. "Not that there isn't plenty to do while he's gone. Arrange to talk to Connor, for one thing."

"And Felicity, too, perhaps," Agnes suggested. During the flight to Philadelphia, Robin had told her of their brief friendship, and how Morgan's anger over it had been her first real experience of his disintegrating temperament.

"You think she knows something about the Comets?" Robin asked, surprised.

Agnes shrugged. "There are few secrets between husband and wife. Even when they have separated, the secrets they shared remain. Felicity is no longer fond of Morgan. Who knows what she would be willing to reveal?"

"But Felicity hates baseball," Robin replied, remembering. "She mentioned something about team sports being as boring as team players."

"Well, invite her to lunch and ask her anyway. Or would that be uncomfortable for you?"

"Actually, it would be quite easy. Felicity seemed very eager to get together the last time we spoke. Of course, that was weeks ago . . ."

Agnes frowned. "You don't find it strange that a man's estranged wife would go out of her way to befriend his new lover? Pardon me, Robin, but we are both adults."

Robin flushed. "She didn't actually go out of her way," she protested. "It just sort of happened."

"Really."

"She's awfully nice, and a lot of fun." She hesitated. "But yes, I have wondered why she's been so eager to be friends. Maybe I'm her way of keeping tabs on Morgan . . . and two can play that game, right?"

Agnes nodded.

"Now that I think of it," Robin continued thoughtfully, "when Morgan invited me to the game today, he asked whether I'd seen her. He seemed relieved when I said no."

"Interesting."

"Maybe. Or maybe just Morgan being his usual paranoid self."

"Either way," Agnes said, "it can't hurt to talk to her."

"I guess. Of course, if Morgan finds out . . ."

Agnes shrugged. "What good is an inside track if you don't use it?"

"You're right. I'll call her from the airport. Maybe she's free tomorrow. The sooner, the better."

"Absolutely. And now I would be grateful if you would introduce me to Kenny Reese. Do you think we can find him?"

"Finding him isn't the problem," Robin told her with a laugh. "It's getting anywhere near him. Hang on."

Taking Agnes's hand, she managed to fight her way through the thick crowd surrounding the young player. Kenny seemed pleased to see her, and welcomed them both into the circle around him. Soon he and Agnes were chatting together like old friends.

"I think I'll escape before Morgan notices I'm gone," Robin whispered to Agnes after a few minutes. "Are you ready to go?"

"No, I think I prefer to stay awhile," Agnes replied. "I find it all quite fascinating. And young Mr. Reese is delightful." She smiled, but her eyes were sad. "Give Adam my love."

Robin nodded and turned away, and found herself face-to-face with Morgan. Had he overheard Agnes's words? But no; he was smiling. "Your friend is very amusing," he said, glancing in Agnes's direction. "A little . . . scatty, but such old-world charm." He put his arms around Robin's waist and pulled her close. "I've missed you," he told her urgently. His speech was slurred, his face flushed. His breath smelled unpleasantly of Scotch.

"Just friends for now, Morgan. Remember our deal?" Robin kept her tone light and bantering.

"Yes, of course," he agreed, immediately loosening his hold on her. "See? I'm really trying to behave myself." He gave her an appealing look, but his eyes were dark.

A group of people, Connor Egan among them, pushed past, laughing. Connor turned and gave Morgan a thumbs-up. "Way to go," he called out, and the other applauded. "The series in four!"

"Christ, it's an incredible feeling," Morgan exclaimed, warming to the praise. "We *will* take the series. I can feel it."

"It must be very exciting," Robin agreed.

"Unbelievable. Nothing like it in the world." He gestured at the celebration in progress around them. "God, I'm gonna miss all this next year. Old Tom Wachtel better treat my boys right, or by God—"

"Tom Wachtel?" Robin repeated the name of the famous industrialist. "What do you mean?"

"Sold the team," Morgan told her, lowering his voice. "Sold the Comets. Very confidential." He leaned against her, his breath hot in her ear. "Got my hands on some of those Wachtel millions. Don't tell a soul." Suddenly he pulled away, frowning. "Shouldn't have told *you*." He paused. "It's confidential, you understand?" He glared at her. "You tell anyone, I'll kill you." Robin gasped. Suddenly his face broke into a huge smile. "Scared you, didn't I?" he leered. "Booga, booga."

"I think you need some coffee," Robin said tiredly.

"Coffee? At a cele ... celebration? I need a drink. Nurse!" Morgan lurched in the direction of the bar.

Okay, I'm out of here, Robin thought. But she paused long enough to watch Morgan push his way across the room, the sea of humanity parting for him, then closing in his wake. Why would Morgan sell the Comets now, when they were finally winning? Why now, when they were profitable at last?

Well, the talk on the street said his business was failing. He probably needed the money. Nothing mysterious about that. If anything, it was sad.

"You're not leaving?" Jim Warfield exclaimed as she pressed past him toward the exit. "Party's just getting started."

"I need a little air," she lied, and quickened her pace. Soon everyone would be drunk with exhaustion, drunk with success, or just plain drunk. Unconsciously she wiped her hand across her mouth; she could still feel the pressure of Morgan's lips on hers. If she hurried, she might catch Adam before he left for the airport.

Chapter Twenty-four

Sunday, October 3—World Series, game number 2

Adam pulled his bag from the overhead compartment and set it on the empty seat beside him as he waited for the aircraft doors to open. The flight had departed Kennedy at eleven-thirty in the evening, and he'd had only four hours of fitful sleep before the flight attendants had turned on the lights and served everyone the prepackaged, reconstituted breakfast. He yawned deeply as he adjusted his watch. Ten-thirty in the morning, London time; back home, dawn was breaking, and Robin would still be asleep. People began shuffling toward the front of the plane, and Adam stepped out into the aisle and joined the slow-moving line. He hated overnight flights. They always reminded him of his residency.

Once in the terminal, he found a telephone and dug out the phone number of Agnes's erstwhile love. It amused him to think of Agnes as a young, romantic girl. He wondered why their relationship had been broken off. Had Agnes really refused Tibor's offer of marriage, or had he fallen for someone younger and more beautiful? Adam leaned against the inside of the phone booth, fantasizing. Tibor had been tall, strong, fiery-haired. A brilliant thinker. A silver-tongued orator—in Hungarian, of course. Tibor had been the great love of Agnes's life. She'd never gotten over him; he was the reason she'd never married. Because of Tibor, Agnes now climbed mountains and dived deep beneath the sea, but she could never forget ...

You're punchy from lack of sleep, Adam told himself.

Make the damn call. He dialed the number. The phone was picked up after only one ring.

"Dr. Salt? It is you? Your flight was comfortable? You arrived on time? And the food was not too bad? I am so glad." Not exactly silver-tongued, Adam reflected, but it had been a long time ago. "Now then, to business," Tibor continued. "I am pleased to inform you that I am the bearer of good news."

"Yes?" Adam drew a small pad from his jacket pocket. "What have you got for me?"

"I have examined all eleven years, starting from fourteen years ago and working forward." Tibor chuckled. "The registrar was very reluctant, I can tell you. But I invented a most wonderful story for him. You will love it, Adam. Let me tell it to you. I said that a former student of mine was pursuing a statistical project and had asked for my assistance. He had been quite a scholar here at Cambridge, I said, and had recently come into some money, so naturally felt it my duty to—"

"Uh, Tibor, can we save it for another time? I'm running on empty here, and—"

"Of course, of course. I am so very sorry. At any rate, the man allowed me to peruse the records. And so I was able to extract the required data. I have analyzed it, codified it, alphabetized it, and—"

Agnes, I wronged you, Adam thought. You live the way you live because you want to. And Tibor is a well-meaning but excruciating bore. "I don't mean to sound ungrateful," he said aloud, "but for me it's only five-thirty in the morning, and I'm standing in the middle of Heathrow Airport—"

"Again, forgive me. Let me cut, as you Americans so colorfully say, to the chase. I have the names you seek: Cambridge's greatest rugby players for all those years. But the players of thirteen years ago are particularly interesting, I think."

"Why's that?"

"Patience, Adam," Tibor said, sounding just like Agnes. "One of those players became a doctor, like yourself. Two went into business. All three of these men completed their courses here at Cambridge and were awarded their degrees. I have their current locations and phone numbers. You can speak with them whenever you like."

"Great," Adam said, clicking his pen. "Give them to me one at a time." Tibor did so, and, resting the small pad on his knee, Adam laboriously recorded the information.

"You have written it all?" Tibor asked.

"Yes."

"The phone numbers as well?"

"Yes, Tibor, yes."

"Good. Now I will tell you about the fourth man."

"I'm delighted you decided to call me at last," Felicity told Robin, leaning back in the green brocade chair. "I know how difficult Morgan can be about some things." A bowing, tailcoated waiter served their brunch choices: a Caesar salad for Felicity, curried chicken for Robin. Felicity rewarded him with a bright, impersonal smile. "Don't you adore the Plaza?" she asked Robin. "So New York."

Robin nodded politely. In fact she found the Palm Court rather touristy. Perhaps Felicity had chosen it to impress her. The idea was vaguely insulting.

"And how are things going with you two lovebirds?" Felicity inquired, elegant brows arched. "The divorce will be final in a few months. Have you chosen a date? Oh, don't look so shocked, my dear. I finished with Morgan a long time ago."

Had she really? Robin wondered. Agnes had been right; this buddy act of Felicity's was a little unusual. Was it really Felicity's way of keeping tabs on a man she still secretly cared for? Or was it something more? Well, whatever was behind Felicity's interest in her, Robin realized that being taken into the woman's confidence meant maintaining the myth of her own coupleship with Morgan.

"I promise you, it's true," Felicity insisted. "I wish

you all the luck in the world." She paused. "I'm afraid you'll need it."

"What do you mean?"

Felicity sighed. "I hate to be the bearer of bad tidings," she said, "but ... well, I hope you earn a good salary with your writing, my dear, because Morgan is broke." She speared a lettuce leaf on her fork, cut it neatly in half with her knife, and ate it, glancing at Robin to see how she was taking the news. When Robin remained silent, Felicity continued. "Perhaps 'broke' is not quite accurate. But his financial situation is fairly desperate. Hudson and Company is dead in the water and I doubt he could interest a buyer, let alone an investor, with the company debt at its current level. Not that I've ever known much about his business, but Caleb's a very reliable source of information in that regard." She took a small sip of her gimlet. "And that beautiful Hudson Valley estate? I know you've been there." Robin nodded. "Heavily mortgaged, I'm afraid. Of course he'd already run through a great deal of my money by the time we parted. That was what finally killed our marriage, you see. The relationship had been floundering for some time, but when I refused to let the man continue to milk me dry ..."

"I had no idea," Robin murmured.

"Of course you didn't," Felicity agreed. "How could you? You were so trusting, so loyal. How could you know what a bastard the man was? The way he uses people, uses his relationships with them. Like that glowing article you wrote for *Fortune* ..."

"But I barely knew Morgan back then."

"It was wonderful publicity," Felicity continued as if Robin hadn't spoken. "It painted a far more solvent picture than was true, and helped him stave off his creditors for a while." Robin recalled thinking the same thing herself. "This fabulous season the Comets are having helped, too. And the new article you're writing will do him no harm. You've been very useful to him. And then there's your name ..."

"My name?"

"Kennedy. As in *the* Kennedys. Oh, you don't have to be coy with me. Morgan told Sandy Morrison all about your black sheep of a father, and telling Sandy is like telling the *Enquirer*. I believe Morgan was going to try to trace your genealogy, get you a nice dowry. Anything come of that?"

Robin shook her head.

"Well, you can bet he's working on it. Believe me, my dear, I feel awful having to tell you all this. But did you really believe Morgan was interested in you for yourself?"

Robin felt herself redden with anger. She had no love for Morgan these days, but this broadside attack was insulting to both of them. Had her entire relationship with Morgan really been nothing but opportunism? Sure, he'd used the media for his own purposes, but didn't most people in the public eye? And hadn't that *Fortune* piece been good for her own career, too? As for the Kennedy situation, Morgan now knew that she came from nothing, yet he was still pursuing her.

"I've wanted to warn you for some time," Felicity was saying. "I really do consider you a friend, and I hate the idea of a friend of mine being, well, manipulated."

Manipulated? Robin thought furiously. And just what did Felicity think she was doing, with her insults and accusations? Was the country house really heavily mortgaged? Was Morgan's company really dead in the water? The man was no prince, but he didn't deserve to be vilified like this. "I've heard rumors that Hudson and Company's got some financial problems," she shot back, "but no one's suggesting the company's actually going belly-up."

"Caleb's suggesting it. To everyone he meets, as a matter of fact."

"But that's not fair," Robin protested hotly.

"Fair? Face it, dear, the man's a loser."

"I'm sure he can turn things around," Robin argued. "Now that he's sold the Comets—"

Felicity gasped. Her face paled. "He's sold the team?"

Damn, Robin thought. Stupid, stupid. "It's only a

rumor," she said quickly. "I never should have mentioned it." Her face grew hot; she was mortified. How could she have betrayed such a confidence? She'd played right into Felicity's hand. "I doubt it's even true ..." she stuttered. "Please don't repeat—"

"Calm yourself, dear," Felicity said soothingly. "Your secret is safe with me." She was all smiles again, although her fist gripped the gimlet glass so tightly, the knuckles whitened. "But you must be very, very careful about what you say from now on. And to whom. It could be ... dangerous."

"You tell anyone and I'll kill you," Morgan had said. But he'd been joking; he'd even said so. "Isn't that a tad dramatic?" Robin asked, trying for a brittle, sophisticated tone but managing only to sound annoyed.

"You're angry with me," Felicity said sadly. "You're in love with him, so you think I'm the world's biggest bitch. Perhaps you suspect I'm still in love with him myself. Yes, I can see that you do." She reached across and patted Robin's hand. "Nothing could be further from the truth. The fact is ..." She glanced around furtively, then leaned across the table toward Robin. "The fact is, I've become rather frightened of him." She drained her gimlet and looked around for the waiter, waggling her glass at him for a refill before turning back to Robin. "I had hoped the financial situation as I described it would have put you off him—that and the way he's used you. No, don't object, just listen. I was hoping, for your sake, that all that would discourage you. But I can see I'm going to have to tell you the real reason I'm so concerned about your union."

The waiter arrived with Felicity's drink, and she waited until he'd left before she spoke again. "This isn't easy for me," she began. "But I feel for you. You're young, you're a bit naive ... yes, you are; it's one of your endearing qualities." She smiled warmly. "In some ways, you remind me of myself, too many years ago. So I feel compelled to tell you something I haven't told another soul in this world." She took a swallow of her drink, then set the glass down again. "On the night Paul

Barrett was murdered, Morgan came to my apartment to discuss the terms of our divorce settlement. Our respective attorneys had been going back and forth for weeks, and I felt if the two of us could just sit down together ... Anyway, in the course of the discussion, Morgan asked me to lend him some more money. He promised to repay me when he sold the Comets. He said that if the Comets won the World Series, he could sell them for enough to repay the loan and recoup his other losses, too. He even had a potential purchaser, he said. But it all hinged on winning the World Series. That was why I was so surprised just now, when you said the team had been sold. The Series has just begun. How could he have sold the team already?"

"It was just a rumor," Robin protested, but she could see Felicity wasn't buying it. How could I have slipped like that? she asked herself as she sipped her mineral water. Her appetite was gone, and the curried chicken lay congealing on her plate.

"Not hungry?" Felicity asked solicitously. "How about a cappuccino, then?"

"Uh, sure." The waiter was signaled, and Felicity ordered the coffees as Robin sat frowning. Why had Morgan told Felicity the Comets sale hinged on a World Series win? It was the league pennant that counted; the Series was just the icing on the cake. Perhaps he'd done it to postpone repaying Felicity's loan. Well, she wasn't about to reveal any more of Morgan's secrets; she'd done enough damage. Besides, it was none of her business.

"Anyway," Felicity resumed, "Morgan must have left my phone number with that dreadful Jack Ridley, because a call came for him while we were talking. He gestured that I should leave the room, that he wanted privacy. Of course I left immediately, but, well, you've seen the apartment. It's not that big." She paused as the coffees arrived, added sweetener to her cup, and continued. "I could hear him arguing with whomever was on the phone." She leaned across the table again. "I heard him say, 'You can't stop now,' and 'What about the team?' The person on the phone said something in reply, and Morgan started pleading; well, half pleading, half shouting. 'I need a few more months. Just a little more time. You owe me that much.' Or words to that effect; I can't remember exactly." She lowered her voice. "It was Barrett on the phone. I'm sure it was."

"Barrett wanted to stop the supertraining?"

"That's what it sounded like. But let me tell you the rest. When Morgan told the other person—Barrett—that he owed him that much, Barrett said something that seemed to enrage Morgan even further, because he shouted 'You told me it was safe! You bastard!' There was another little pause, I remember, and then Morgan yelled, 'That's blackmail,' or 'You can't blackmail me.' Something like that. Then he slammed down the phone and headed for the door. I—"

" 'You told me it was safe ...' " Robin repeated. "You're sure that's what he said?"

Felicity nodded, her eyes frightened. "Anyway, I tried to stop Morgan from leaving. He was absolutely furious, and I was so scared. I knew what he was capable of, in such a mood."

This was the second time Felicity had implied that Morgan had a violent streak, Robin mused. Yet, until the supertraining had begun affecting him, she herself hadn't seen that side of him at all. Was Felicity lying? And if so, why? "He was going to Barrett's apartment?" she asked, knowing the answer.

"Yes. I begged him to let me go instead, to let me talk to him. But he wouldn't hear of it. He went charging out into the night."

"I don't understand ... Why would you offer to go and talk to Barrett if you didn't even know him?"

Felicity's eyes narrowed for a tiny moment; then she shrugged. "I said the first thing that came into my mind, really," she answered easily. "I just wanted to stop him. He looked so ... so violent, so crazed. And the next day, the newspapers carried the story of Barrett's murder." She shuddered. "Even though they arrested that player, the one whose jacket was found in Barrett's apartment, I've always wondered whether it was really Morgan who murdered him.''

"Have you told the police?"

"Of course not," Felicity exclaimed. "After all, he was my husband; technically he still is. And of course I had no actual proof."

"But if you believed he'd committed murder . . ."

"How could I be sure?" Felicity countered. "I suppose if they hadn't released that ballplayer, I might have come forward, but . . . Anyway, you see why I say that Morgan's dangerous."

Robin shook her head as though to clear her growing confusion. "I don't understand," she said, looking questioningly at Felicity. "Why would Morgan kill the man who held the key to the superplayers? Wouldn't that be self-defeating? Whatever he may be, Morgan's not stupid."

"No, he's not stupid. But look at it this way. Barrett wanted to stop the training. Morgan couldn't afford for him to do that. He'd already told me that selling the team would solve his financial problems. He couldn't let Barrett stop."

"Yes, but killing Barrett *would* stop the training," Robin said without thinking.

Felicity looked sharply at her. "But it didn't, did it?" Robin shook her head. "Apparently Barrett was no longer as necessary to the technique as he'd been in the beginning."

"Do you think Morgan realized that?"

"Who knows? I think he just acted out of desperation. He was raging when he left my apartment. He probably tried to convince Barrett to continue, and then killed him when he refused. Horrible. I can't bear to think about it."

Robin's mind was whirling. Was it really possible? Was Morgan a murderer?

"I don't suppose he ever discussed the supertraining with you?" Felicity asked casually.

"No, never," Robin answered.

"Good," Robin's chin jerked up. "I mean, good for *you*. Knowing too much could be dangerous."

Robin sat back in her chair, sorting out her thoughts. " 'You told me it was safe,' " she repeated. "Barrett must have told him the training technique was harmful, dangerous in some way. So how could Morgan continue to allow the players to keep getting it?" Tears formed in her eyes as she thought of the dead rat in Agnes's lab. "That would be a form of murder, too."

"Murder?" Felicity stared at Robin. "Oh, I don't believe for a minute the technique's harmful. The players are all fine, aren't they? No, Barrett was obviously lying. Remember, Morgan shouted something about blackmail. Barrett must have been trying to blackmail Morgan, to get more money from him. Not that there was any more money to get."

The waiter approached with a leather-bound book containing their check. Robin fumbled in her handbag for her wallet, her tears falling faster. Felicity dug into her purse and extracted an expensive-looking hanky. She handed it across the table. "Better to face it sooner than later," she said gently. "I'm afraid he's played us both for suckers, my dear. So much for true love."

Robin smiled through her tears. "It seems a shame to use this," she said, admiring the rich antique lace.

"This old thing?" Felicity laughed at her use of the cliché. "It's ancient; part of my trousseau. Time to retire it." She smiled encouragingly. "Go on; mop up. Here's to better days."

Robin unfolded the hanky and began to raise it to her face. In the corner was a tiny embroidered monogram. She blinked to clear the mist of tears from her eyes, then gasped in astonishment. Unlike the florid embossing on Felicity's stationery, these letters were perfectly legible.

About the time Robin and Felicity were sitting down to brunch in New York, Adam was navigating his small white rental car between hedgerows lining the narrow road to Nether Lees. The drive had taken longer than Tibor's optimistic estimate of five hours, due partly to

Adam's determination to stay awake, which had meant numerous stops for food and coffee, and partly to the exaggerated caution he found necessary to employ in his attempt to stay on the left side of the road. The steady rain in which he'd left London had gradually diminished to a light drizzle. All at once the hedgerows fell away, and the Cornish coast rose up beside the road, impressive and beautiful. Four miles, a sign proclaimed.

How would he approach the man? What would he say? The local pub would have a phone directory, he supposed. He could stop and call. But for some reason, he disliked the idea. Fuller might refuse to see him. Presumably the secret had been well-guarded. It might be guarded still. Better simply to arrive.

He was through the town and past it before he realized the short parade of drab houses beside the road had been Nether Lees' main street. He slowed, looking for a place to turn the car around. Some distance ahead was a small stone church. He headed for it, turning off onto its short drive and pulling into the small cobbled yard. An elderly priest looked up from the plants he was setting out along the grassy border, and stared after him. Adam swung the car around. The vicar had straightened up and was coming toward him.

"Afternoon," he offered.

Adam stopped the car and rolled down the window. "A little wet for that kind of work," he observed, smiling.

"This is England, friend. If you wait for dry weather, you'll never get anything done." He glanced at the rental car. "You lost?"

"Not exactly." A parish priest would know where the Fullers lived, he thought. He shoved the gear shift into park, pulled on the hand brake, and got out. The damp air was chilly. "I'm looking for a family named Fuller," he explained. "Any idea where I can find them?"

The vicar eyed him warily. "Fuller?" he repeated.

"Andrew Fuller," Adam replied. "My name is Adam Salt. I'm a doctor in the States, and I'm involved in a research project on athletes and, uh, how they, er, age.

We're doing a comparison of England and the U.S. I understand Mr. Fuller was a terrific rugby player for a brief period at Cambridge. I was hoping he'd allow me to involve him in my study."

"Andrew Fuller, you say . . ." The man's face was troubled. "Andrew . . ."

"Yes, Tibor Radovic at Cambridge gave me his name, but he couldn't find any current information on him, just his old address—his parents' address, I guess it must be. There's no current record of—"

"No, there wouldn't be," the vicar said sadly. "Not after all these years." He looked at Adam sharply. "I'm Father Mayle." He extended his hand and Adam shook it. "Let me show you something, and then we can talk. Better switch the engine off, Doctor. We may need a little time." The old priest waited patiently as Adam did as he was bid. "No need to lock it. Not around here."

Father Mayle led him around the side of the church and along a narrow path. Ahead Adam saw a small graveyard, the headstones low and mossy. Beyond, the cliffs rose against the sea. Adam shivered in the chill mist; he suddenly knew what Mayle would show him.

The ground squelched beneath their shoes. Beads of water settled on Adam's eyelashes; he blinked them away. The priest led him into the graveyard, threading his way slowly between the markers. He stopped in front of one, then stepped aside so that Adam could bend down and read it.

"It was a day much like this, when we buried him," Father Mayle said softly. "A sad, wet day."

"What . . . happened to him?" Adam asked tentatively, rising. Would the priest tell him? Did he even know?

The old man made the sign of the cross over Andrew's grave, then turned to face Adam. His white hair was heavy with rain, but he seemed not to notice. "An unusually severe case of cerebral palsy, Doc Trelawney said; he was our local man. Gone now, I'm afraid; lost him to pneumonia six years ago."

"Andrew had severe cerebral palsy?" Adam repeated,

surprised. "How did he ever become a first-rate rugby player? How did he manage to play at all?" It didn't make medical sense.

"Came on suddenly, Trelawney said," the older man replied. "The boy never showed any sign of it before. It hit him all of a sudden." The priest sighed deeply. "Come; let's get in out of this rain." The two men walked slowly out of the graveyard and back toward the church. "He'd just finished his first year at Cambridge," the priest said softly, his eyes cloudy with remembrance. "He'd always been a good player, but at Cambridge, he just bloomed. Made the first fifteen halfway through the year. Absolutely unheard of." The rain was increasing again, and the cliffs played hide-and-seek in the mist. "In August, Andrew came home to stay with his parents for a while before the start of the new term. The local boys organized a scrummage, of course, and we all went along to see him. Ah, how that boy could play." They stopped at the car. Adam could feel moisture trickling down inside the collar of his trenchcoat. "It was during the match that it happened," the priest continued. "He was running down the pitch, the lads baying at his heels. Then suddenly he stopped and sort of trembled. Next thing we knew, he was on the ground, twitching. Doc ran up, and so did I; everyone did. His eyes were staring out of his head, and his body was convulsing. Then suddenly he lay still. They took him off to the local hospital in his father's car, but ... he was gone."

"And Trelawney was certain of his diagnosis?"

Father Mayle shrugged. "Maybe he was and maybe he wasn't. The family was dead set against an autopsy. Besides, the boy was gone. Knowing the cause wouldn't have brought him back." He put his hand on Adam's arm. "Come up to the vicarage and have a cup of tea," he said. "Catch your death in this weather."

People bustled up and down the steps and strolling tourists stopped to gawk at the famous facade, as Robin and Felicity parted company in front of the Plaza Hotel. "I know I've distressed you," Felicity apologized yet again as she gave Robin an air-kiss. "But truly, I fear for your safety. Why don't you come to dinner with Caleb and me? He knows lots of people, and—" She broke off at Robin's frown. "Too soon? Well, never mind, just come. I'll call you." Robin managed a nod. "*À bientot.* The doorman will get you a taxi."

"I think I'll walk awhile," Robin replied, feeling slightly patronized.

"I understand," Felicity said sympathetically. "So much to think about. Well, off you go, dear. I think I'll just pop into Bergdorf's." With a wave of her fingers, she turned and walked south toward West Fifty-eighth Street.

Robin set off in the opposite direction, crossing Fifty-ninth Street and heading north along Fifth Avenue on the Central Park side. It could be a coincidence, she thought. She'd never known Felicity's maiden name. But Felicity had said the handkerchief had been part of her trousseau. So couldn't that mean . . . ? It was unthinkable, yet it also made sense in a twisted sort of way. She paused; was there any way to check it out, to confirm or refute her suspicion? No, none she could think of; not here. Perhaps Adam would be able to come up with something when he called from England. She continued up the tree-shaded street, her mind rife with speculation

Felicity stopped at the corner and retraced her steps, watching Robin's retreating back until it disappeared beyond the trees. Then she reentered the Plaza and made her way to a row of phone booths. Slipping inside one, she dialed hurriedly from memory. "Out of the office?" she exclaimed angrily to the person on the other end. "How long for?" The answer seemed to mollify her. "Of course," she replied more temperately. "It completely slipped my mind. Well, as soon as he gets back, tell him it's important that we talk immediately." She listened for a moment. "Oh, he has my number," she assured the woman. "And yes, he bloody well *will* know what this is in regard to."

"More tea?" the vicar inquired. "Another cake?"

Adam accepted both. "This is very kind of you," he

said gratefully. His coat had been hung in the hall to dry, his muddy shoes wiped with yesterday's newspaper, and the Ceylon tea and toasted teacakes had both warmed and restored him.

"Nothing like a cuppa on an afternoon like this," Father Mayle said, glancing out of the mullioned window at the rain bucketing down.

Adam took a large bite of the buttery teacake. "You were describing the funeral," he prompted.

"Yes, the funeral . . . a small local affair, it was. Family, relations, friends . . ."

"No one from Cambridge?"

"A handful," Father Mayle replied. "He'd only been there a year. And of course, his two Cambridge friends from Nether Lees."

"From here?"

"Yes. Funny how often one travels miles from home only to meet someone from one's own village. Of course, their being some years older than Andrew, they wouldn't have known him growing up. Different social circles, too. Small towns can be rigid that way. But at Cambridge, they seem to have taken him under their wing."

"They?"

"Strange, that," the vicar continued. "I would have thought being Andrew's friend would have brought back too many painful memories for him . . . But I was telling you about the funeral," he reminded himself. "All funerals are sad, of course, but this one, well, it seemed particularly unfair." He shook his head. "First, one fine young athlete crippled for life in a rugby scrum, and then Andrew suddenly taken. Seeing that wheelchair brought it all back . . ."

"Wheelchair . . . ?" Adam repeated stupidly, setting down his cup.

"Yes, and he'd been so full of life just three short years before. Still, he'd turned into some kind of scientific genius up at Cambridge, so they said; at least he had that. I remember his wife had quite a time getting the wheelchair up the church steps . . ."

"He was married?"

"Yes, and a pretty thing she was. Solid county family—not a very old one, but plenty of money. She was three years older than he was. We were all surprised when she married him."

"You knew her?"

"I baptized her," Father Mayle replied. "She was born here; they both were. Felicity Wells she was, before she married Paul Barrett."

Chapter Twenty-five

Robin turned on the TV while waiting for Adam to call. Two-thirty New York time was what they'd arranged, and the thirty-block walk from the Plaza to her apartment hadn't taken up all the slack. The second World Series game had begun half an hour before, and already the Comets were ahead by three runs. Robin hurriedly exchanged her navy blazer, patterned silk shirt, and gray wool skirt for an old pair of jeans and a baggy sweater. Then, getting a soda from the fridge, she settled down in front of the television.

"Well, the boys were on their best behavior yesterday, Ron. No one wants to get thrown out of the game at this point."

"Of course with the Comets, best behavior's a relative term, Jim." Laughter.

"You mean, when Reese struck out in the seventh and started grabbing bats from the rack and hurling them out onto the field?"

"Well, he was understandably disappointed." More laughter. "Okay, here's Hendershot, the Falcons' pitcher, stepping up to the plate ..."

"He's not a strong hitter. But with a little luck, he could—"

"Hey, what the heck was that? Did you see that?"

"Hendershot's down. Ernie drilled him in the shoulder. I can't believe—"

"I think that was payback time, Jim, for when Hendershot clipped Freeman's wrist in the second inning. Uh oh, here comes trouble ..."

"The Falcons are mad, Ron. I haven't seen a dugout empty that fast since—"

"Here come the Comets ... The officials are trying to separate them, but—"

The phone rang and Robin jumped for it. "Adam?"

"Hiya, sweet knees. You won't believe—"

"What? Hang on a second while I lower the TV," Robin interrupted, reaching for the remote. "Listen, I had lunch with Felicity today, and when she gave me her hanky—never mind why—the initials on it were FWB. This is going to sound crazy, but do you think the B could stand for Barrett?"

Silence. "There goes my surprise," Adam said.

"What? You mean, it's true?"

"It's true all right. She married Barrett sixteen years ago, just before he started his graduate work at Cambridge. He was crippled in that rugby game five months later."

"You've been busy."

"I spent the afternoon with the parish priest in Nether Lees," Adam explained. "The good vicar seems to think Felicity married Barrett to escape the boredom of the place. She'd already turned down half the single men in the county; said she wouldn't spend her life stuck out in the country. Barrett had already completed his undergraduate work at a local university and been accepted at Cambridge. He was brilliant, apparently. Felicity had no interest in furthering her own education, but she probably had a romantic idea of life as a wife of a Cambridge fellow." He paused. "Barrett and Felicity befriended an undergraduate at Cambridge. His name was Andrew Fuller. He came from their hometown, and guess what? He played rugby."

"You talked to him?"

"That would have been difficult. He died at the end of his first year. Quite suddenly and rather mysteriously. Look, are you sure Felicity didn't meet Morgan at Cambridge?"

Robin thought back to her first lunch with Felicity, when she'd referred to her 'terminally boring childhood' in Cornwall. "I suppose she could have lied about having met Morgan in London," Robin said slowly. "But Morgan's three years older than Barrett. If she married Barrett—sixteen years ago, you said?"

"That's right."

"Well, Morgan would have been," she calculated quickly, "nearly twenty-five then. I can't be sure, but my guess is, he'd left Cambridge by the time Felicity and Barrett arrived. She said she escaped to London on the weekends, and that rings true. She probably found Cambridge as dull as Nether Lees; not at all what she expected. And of course, when she'd married Barrett, she hadn't expected to spend her life with a paraplegic. No, the lie was that she was escaping from Barrett and Cambridge, not Cornwall."

On the television, the brawl had been contained and the game had resumed. Ernie Sanchez made the third out with runners on first and third, and the side was retired. Simms, batting first for the Comets at the top of the fourth inning, led off with an infield single.

"Felicity and Barrett . . ." Adam mused. "I guess you were right about Morgan having been used."

"I don't know who's using whom, anymore," Robin replied, keenly aware of having been used herself. "Obviously, they're all involved in this thing. But Morgan was the one reaping the profits from the special training technique, not Felicity. In fact, when I told her he'd sold the team—"

"He *what*?"

"He sold the Comets to Tom Wachtel. It's supposed to be a secret until after the World Series. Anyhow, Felicity went white. Apparently Morgan borrowed money from her, promising to pay her back when the Comets were sold. And you know what else Felicity told me? She thinks Morgan killed Barrett."

"Jesus. Why?"

"Barrett was threatening to stop the Supertraining. He tried to blackmail Morgan for more money. She heard Morgan talking to him on the phone in her apartment.

He shouted at Barrett that he wouldn't be blackmailed, and then he ran out the door."

Adam digested the information. "I'd say that puts an end to your strategy of staying close to Morgan, wouldn't you?"

"Yes. If it's true."

"You think she's lying?"

"God, I don't know. She's obviously not the world's most truthful person, but I can't see why she'd lie about something like that. And she seemed genuinely frightened."

"Has she gone to the police?"

"No. She says he's still her husband, after all." Robin was silent for a moment. "I sometimes wonder whether she's still in love with him, whether she's trying to put me off him so she can work at getting him back."

"That's her problem," Adam said, "and his. It's not yours. Stay away from them both."

"I guess you're right. Only . . . I just can't see Morgan as a murderer. It doesn't feel right."

"He's been doctoring his players with lethal hormones. That's close enough."

"But I don't think that's what Barrett was doing," Robin protested. "He's taking the training himself, don't forget."

Adam sighed. "I know, I know."

"You sound tired."

"I am. I'm sick and tired. We have three players whose lives are at risk, and a World Series underway that's obviously illegal. And I still don't have the evidence I need to tell Dennis to call it off."

"Dennis?"

"Dennis Locke. The baseball commissioner. He's the one who got me involved in this mess." He gave a prodigious yawn. "God, I'm beat."

"Get some sleep."

"I will. Robin?"

"Mmm?"

"How about packing a bag and going to stay with Agnes?"

"Agnes? Why in the world—"

"It might not be a bad idea for you to disappear for a while. Keep a low profile."

"I'll think about it."

"I know what that means. Look, I'm flying to Cambridge in the morning. Tibor says that when Barrett took a sabbatical to come to New York, he left all his papers and stuff locked up in his office. Tibor thinks he can get us a peek at them. I should be back in a couple of days. Don't do anything rash."

"Rash? Moi?"

"Very funny. How's the game going?"

Robin turned up the volume and held the phone to the TV speaker.

". . . the most overrated statistics are batting average and earned run average. Run production is what really counts."

"That's right. A .400 hitter—"

"Don't see many of those, these days—"

"—strikes out six times out of ten. If he makes those six outs *with* men on base, and gets his four hits *without* men on base, he's still a .400 hitter, but he's not driving in the runs, so—"

"Speaking of run production, how about that Kenny Reese? He's sure driving them in today. If you've just joined us, the score is New York Comets eight, Philadelphia Falcons four, going into the sixth inning. Freeman's on deck, and—"

"Did you hear?" Robin asked, reclaiming the receiver. "Comets, eight to four, top of the sixth."

"Wish I could get excited about it."

"Get some sleep."

"I will. Call you from Cambridge. Don't know what time it'll be."

"That's okay. We never shut."

"I love you."

"Me, too."

Robin lowered the phone and switched off the television. What now? she thought. Do I just sit and wait until Adam comes back? What if he doesn't find anything in

Cambridge? Adam was probably right about avoiding Morgan, but there was one other person who held the key to the supertraining technique. She reached for the phone again, and dialed the Pro Club.

"Mr. Egan's out of town until tomorrow," the receptionist told her.

Of course, Robin thought; he'd stayed on in Philadelphia for the second game. "Could you check his schedule for me, please? I only need twenty minutes or so."

"Well, I don't know . . ."

"It's important," Robin urged. "I'm a friend . . . a very good friend of Morgan Hudson."

"I'll just check his desk calendar and call you back," the woman said, suddenly helpful.

"I'd rather hold," Robin told her. She pictured the woman rising from the appointments desk in the basement, hurrying into the elevator, entering Connor's office . . .

"May I put you down for one o'clock?"

"That was fast."

"I'm in Mr. Egan's office. My line goes into his phone, too. Is one o'clock all right?"

"Perfect," Robin told her. "And thank you."

"Thank *you*, Ms. Kennedy."

Morgan's name certainly got people moving, Robin thought as she hung up. Well, there was nothing else she could do today. She made herself an iced tea, turned on the TV, and watched the Comets win the second game of the World Series.

Chapter Twenty-six

Monday, October 4 (travel day for the Comets)
Ten minutes before one, Robin stood at the door of the Pro Club, waiting to be admitted and rehearsing her story. "I'm doing a series of profiles about people involved in the training of professional athletes, and who better to start with than—"

"Ms. Kennedy?" Robin turned toward the intercom box, then up at the security camera mounted above it. "I'm afraid Mr. Egan's had to cancel."

"What? But we specifically arranged—"

"Yes, I know. But he had an important meeting come up at the last minute. Perhaps you could come back later?"

"How much later?"

A pause. "Maybe around two? I'm awfully sorry . . ."

"Not your fault. Two will be fine. As long as you're sure that won't get canceled, too."

"Absolutely not. Uh, would you like to wait downstairs at the juice bar?"

Robin hesitated. A Starbucks had opened on the corner across the street, and a hot chocolate seemed more appealing than carrot juice. "I don't think so, thanks. I'll just come back."

"Thank you for understanding."

"Of course."

Robin went across to the coffee bar. The day was sunny, but with a taste of autumn coolness in the air.

"So you think we'll get it?" the counterman asked as he took her order. A strong tropical storm was sweeping up the Florida coast, and unless it veered out to sea, New York was right in its path.

"What's the latest forecast?"

"Mostly watch and see," he told her. "But there's talk of having to postpone whatever's left of the World Series, if it hits."

"Must be expecting quite a blow."

She took her chocolate to the counter, and sat idly people-watching. How was she going to kill a whole hour? Perhaps she'd buy a magazine. She had gone to the door and was scanning the street for a newsstand when she spotted him getting out of a taxi. Instinctively she shrank back, but Morgan never turned in her direction. Instead, he ran up the steps of the Pro Club and began searching in his trouser pockets for his key card.

So she'd lost her one o'clock appointment to Morgan. Great. If Connor mentioned it to him, she could kiss her two o'clock meeting good-bye as well. She was about to retreat back inside the coffee bar when an elegant blonde got out of a parked car and hurried up the street toward the club. Recognizing her, Robin abandoned her chocolate and moved forward. She heard Felicity call out to Morgan, but couldn't make out the words. Averting her face, Robin crossed the street and went cautiously toward them, hugging the wall of the corner building. A small alleyway separated it from the club premises, and she slipped inside, positioning herself so she could hear, and partially see, the two people on the steps.

"Didn't you get my messages?" Felicity called.

"I got them," Morgan answered shortly. He glared at Felicity as she climbed the steps toward him.

"Then why didn't you return my calls? I waited all morning. I finally had to charm your secretary into telling me your schedule."

"I can't talk to you right now," he replied testily. "I'm busy." Stupid temp. He'd fire her as soon as he got back to the office. He inserted his key card and pushed the door open. "I'll call you later, okay?"

But Felicity grabbed his elbow. "Now, Morgan."

"Forget it." Shoving her aside, he stormed into the club. But Felicity was quick. She lunged for the closing door, flung it open again, and followed him inside.

Robin stepped from her hiding place. Oh, to be a fly on the wall inside the Pro Club right now, she thought. Something must be brewing. According to Morgan, he and Felicity rarely if ever spoke. What could be so important that she would run him to earth at his gym? Well, it would be easy enough to find out, Robin decided. She climbed the stairs and rang the bell. "I've decided to wait in the juice bar," the told the disembodied receptionist. "No thanks; I know the way." The door lock clicked open, and Robin crept quietly inside.

The elevator stood open; Morgan obviously hadn't used it. He must have taken the stairs, with Felicity in hot pursuit. She edged a look through the small window: nothing. Cautiously, she pushed through the door.

Voices echoed in the cinderblock stairwell, but the content of the conversation was unclear. Robin moved upward, passing the door to level two and stopping just before the half-landing that divided each level.

"You've been avoiding me, haven't you?" she heard Felicity say. "And I know why."

"Don't be stupid," Morgan replied testily. "I've been in Philly for the last two days, and— Oh, go ahead and get it over with. What's so important it can't wait?"

Their voices seemed to be coming from one landing above. They must be standing just this side of the door to level three, Robin decided. As long as she stayed where she was, they couldn't see her.

"I want to talk to you about the Comets."

"What about them?" Morgan growled.

"I want my share of the Comets sale money," Felicity demanded. "And I want it now."

Shit, Robin thought, her face growing hot. I should have known.

"I've already told you I can't sell the team until after the World Series."

"Bullshit. Robin told me you've already sold them. So pay up."

"What? *Robin* told you?" Morgan's voice grew loud and angry. "What the hell kind of conspiracy is this?"

"Never mind her. I want my money."

"There *is* no money. I may have told Robin I was *planning* to sell, but—"

"Don't bullshit a bullshitter, my dear," Felicity said, her voice low and dangerous. "Pay me or else."

"Or else what? You'll have Caleb horsewhip me on the steps of the New York Stock Exchange? I've heard enough." Robin heard the metal door creak open, then slam shut again.

"No, you don't," Felicity said. "You'll stand here and listen. Either I get that money within twenty-four hours, or I tell all. And 'all' includes your part in the murder of Paul Barrett."

A brief silence descended. "Barrett's murder?" Morgan sounded more puzzled than angry. "What are you talking about? Otis Freeman killed Barrett."

"Otis Freeman was released, remember?"

"The evidence was too circumstantial to hold him, sure, but I always believed ... his jacket, Barrett's diary ... Who else could have done it?"

"Who else indeed," Felicity replied dryly. "I'm sure the police would be extremely interested to hear about what happened in my apartment that night. How Barrett called you at my place, and you went running to the Pro Club—"

"What are you playing at?" Morgan demanded, angry now. "*You* were the one who went running over there. You insisted on going; you said you knew how to calm Barrett down. I only followed later, when you didn't come back. I kept ringing his bell but he didn't answer. Finally I saw you coming out of the front door of the Pro Club, and you said—"

"I know that, and you know that," Felicity told him crisply, "but no one else knows that. So it's your word against mine. And if the truth about your wonderful superplayers should happen to come out at the same time, your word wouldn't be worth shit, now would it?"

She paused. "Why don't you think about that. But don't take too long. Twenty-four hours."

"No one would ever believe— Come back here, you bitch!"

Robin scrambled down the stairs as Felicity descended, Morgan close behind. So Felicity had lied about Morgan having gone to calm Barrett down. Why? Was it just to keep her past relationship with Barrett a secret, or was there a more urgent reason? If Felicity had been the last person to see Barrett live, might she also have seen the murderer? Or . . .

Think later, she told herself firmly. Move now. Shoving the level two door open, she dashed inside, pressing herself flat against the wall as the heavy door closed behind her with a thunk. Had Felicity seen her? Had Morgan? If she could get to the catwalk leading down to the gym floor . . . She hadn't taken more than a few steps when the door behind her banged open, and a strong hand gripped her arm and swung her around.

"Of course," Morgan said. "Who else?"

"I was just—"

"Shut up." He frog-marched her back into the stairwell, slamming the door shut behind them. "What are you trying to do to me?" he demanded furiously.

"I have an appointment with Connor at two, and I—"

"The Comets sale was confidential," he shouted, his voice ricocheting off the concrete walls. "Confidential. I told you that."

"I'm sorry." Robin flushed. "I didn't mean to. It just slipped out."

"It just slipped out," Morgan repeated nastily. "And who did it happen to slip out *to*? Only my goddamn ex-wife who is now threatening to implicate me in murder— I don't suppose it would do any good to tell you that anything you heard Felicity say just now is also confidential." He released her arm and grabbed her by the shoulders. "This is all your fault. *Yours*," he repeated, shaking her violently. Suddenly he stopped and shoved her away from him in disgust. "Well, she's won. I'll have to pay her. Goddammit," he exclaimed, his voice rising again. "She'll take every dime I've got."

"But if you're innocent—"

"Of *course* I'm innocent," he raged. "Hell, you heard me remind her *she* was the one who went to Barrett's that night, and you heard her agree. But if she starts spreading rumors about the superplayers, she could get the Comets sale invalidated. I'll be ruined. God*dam*mit!" Almost dizzy with frustration and rage, he turned toward Robin, his arm raised threateningly.

"Morgan, no!"

He hesitated, then slammed his fist into the cement wall instead, roaring with pain. Robin backed away, her eyes wide. Morgan stared down at his bloody hand, his whole body shaking, then collapsed back against the wall. Robin began edging toward the door to level two.

Morgan raised his head to look at her. Defeat and resignation showed clearly in his face. "Wait," he whispered through his pain. "Please."

"Is it broken?" she asked, still keeping her distance. "They must have a first-aid kit around here."

He flexed his fingers painfully. "Hurts like hell, but no, I don't think so." He lowered himself heavily down on the steps, then looked over at Robin. "Don't be afraid," he said tiredly. "I didn't kill Barrett."

"Who did?" But Morgan merely shook his head. "Morgan, why would Felicity try to implicate you in the murder?"

"Ah, she's just trying to blackmail me about the Comets money."

But Robin shook her head. "I don't think it's that simple. You should know that she told me that same story at brunch yesterday. She also implied you've always had a violent streak."

Morgan's head jerked up. "She did?"

"Yes. And it wasn't the first time. Why would she do that?"

"I ... I can't imagine." He seemed completely bewildered.

Robin thought furiously. The conversation she'd just

overheard between Morgan and Felicity indicated quite clearly that Morgan was never inside Barrett's apartment that night. She felt very relieved. Despite his fits of temper, she'd never believed he was capable of murder. So why would Felicity suggest to Robin that Morgan was a murderer? Surely she couldn't be all that jealous of Robin's relationship with him, or hate Morgan quite that much. Think, she told herself. There was no evidence that Otis had really been at Barrett's that evening. His jacket, sure, and his name in Barrett's diary. But no fingerprints, no witnesses ... "What time did you see Felicity come out of the Pro Club?" she asked Morgan.

"God, I don't know ... around eleven, I guess. She said she'd calmed him down and he'd agreed to continue the training."

"Then Felicity would have been the last person to see Barrett alive," Robin thought out loud. "Aside from the murderer, that is." A thought hit her, and as she looked at Morgan, she could see that it had hit him, too. "You don't suppose ... ?"

"Anyone could have moved that jacket," Morgan said, his excitement building. "And written Freeman's name into Barrett's diary. She knew his handwriting well enough—" He broke off, frowning, but Robin touched his shoulder.

"It's all right," she said. "I know she was married to Barrett."

Morgan started. "How?"

"It doesn't matter. Anyway, you can ignore Felicity's threat to implicate you. I heard her admit she was the one who went to Barrett's apartment that night."

He smiled at her gratefully, but the smile faded. Felicity still had a potent weapon. If she went public with what she knew about the supertraining ... His brow furrowed. Of course, there was one solution, if he dared take it. But first ...

He rose, cradling his throbbing hand. "The time for lies is over," he told Robin earnestly. He looked around at the concrete walls. "We can't talk here. Come back to the town house."

"I'm not sure that's such a good idea."

"I don't blame you for feeling that way," he said sadly. "I haven't given you much reason to trust me lately." He sighed. "If it makes you feel any better, Jack Ridley's there. My personal assistant, remember?" Robin nodded. "He lives with me. I won't even use my key, so you can see him open the door before you walk in." He gave her a gentle smile and took a few tentative steps toward her, wincing at the pain in his hand.

"You should see a doctor."

"Later. This is Adam Salt's kind of thing, isn't it? Orthopedics? Hey, don't be so jumpy; I meant it nicely. You thought you were doing the right thing, sending Kenny to him." He paused. "And I forgive you for leaking the Comets sale. Rumors were already flying at the stadium yesterday. Felicity would have heard about it by now, anyway." His handsome face radiated honesty and goodwill. "Please come back with me. To tell you the truth, I'm looking forward to getting some things off my chest. I haven't been sleeping well; even saw a doctor about it." He held out his good hand. "There's so much we need to discuss."

"Well . . ."

"Just friends, I promise." But still Robin hesitated. "Please," he said gently. "You already know about Felicity and Paul. You deserve to know the rest."

"All right."

"Magnificent, Tibor," Adam enthused, staring at the towering gothic spires of King's College Chapel and the flamboyant architecture of the gatehouse guarding the college's front court. "Inspiring." Cambridge was indeed very beautiful, but after an hour of trotting around it in the wake of this short, round, balding academic, he was running out of adjectives.

"The first establishment of the educational community at Cambridge dates back to the thirteenth century, you know," Tibor droned as they entered the Tudor gatehouse. "Peterhouse, the first college for scholars at Cambridge, was founded by the Bishop of Ely in 1284." He

paused briefly to point out the massive arched windows
that rose along the side of the chapel. "I do not bore
you, I hope?"

"Not at all," Adam replied bravely.

"I am so pleased."

"What college was Barrett associated with?" Adam
asked as they emerged into Trinity Lane.

"Sidney Sussex," Tibor replied. "Founded in 1596.
Much restoration work was performed upon it in the
early nineteenth century. Barrett did his graduate work
there, but he did his research in the department of biochemistry. He attained the rank of reader." Adam
looked at him questioningly, and he continued. "At
Cambridge, there are lecturers, readers, and professors.
Unlike other British universities, there are no senior
lecturers."

"I see. And then eighteen months ago, this highly respected academic up and announced, 'I'm on holiday
starting Monday'?"

Tibor smiled. "His application for a sabbatical *was*
rather sudden. The biochemistry department had to do
some fancy footwork, I believe the expression goes, to
try to accommodate his request 'to travel, to study, and
to pursue a variety of personal and academic interests.' "
Adam's left eyebrow arched questioningly. "I was fortunate in obtaining a copy of his application," Tibor explained modestly.

Adam eyed him with new respect. "But they did manage to accommodate him?"

"Oh, yes. Barrett was a valued colleague."

"And all these years, he's been doing his own research
projects under the auspices of the university?"

"The biochemistry department, yes. Research is of
major importance here. Cambridge has given the world
more than sixty Nobel prizewinners during this century."

"Impressive."

"Isn't it?" Tibor agreed. "I've taken us a tad out of
our way this morning, but I didn't want you going back
to New York without having seen the splendor that is
Cambridge."

"Wouldn't have missed it," Adam assured him.

"Excellent. So now let us go to Mr. Barrett's office in Tennis Court Road and see what we shall see. They tell me no one has been inside since he left, aside from the cleaning staff."

"I'm very glad to hear it."

Tibor took a key from his pocket and dangled it in the air. "To procure entry to friend Barrett's inner sanctum, I'm afraid I was less than forthcoming about our true purpose," he explained. "Should we encounter a member of the biochemistry faculty, it is possible that he or she may greet you as Dr. Adam Barrett, and offer condolences on the untimely passing of your dear British cousin."

Adam grinned. "Tibor, you have hidden talents."

Tibor smiled primly. "I am so glad you do not object." He hesitated. "There is another matter I would like to mention. When Agnes requested that I assist you, I of course agreed unquestioningly. I have known and, er, admired the lady for many years." His brown eyes grew soft and soulful. "She may have told you that once I had hoped ..." He sighed deeply. "Ah well. What I desire to say to you is this: I have no wish to pry, you understand. But if you could be a little more precise in regard to what you are hoping to find, I could perhaps be of greater assistance during our search of Paul Barrett's possessions."

Adam laughed. "You're absolutely right, my friend. But first let me give you a little background. Actually, it's quite a story."

Chapter Twenty-seven

"See? I promised you a chaperon," Morgan told Robin with a smile as Jack Ridley ushered them inside the limestone town house. "Jack, make us some drinks, will you? My hand's killing me."

"What happened?" Ridley followed Morgan and Robin into the living room.

"Caught it in a door," Morgan told him briefly.

"Shouldn't you put some ice on it?" Robin suggested, seating herself in a wing chair.

"I suppose so," Morgan replied. "Actually, I have some painkillers upstairs. Will you excuse me for a moment? Jack, get the lady a drink, will you? And fix me a vodka and tonic."

"Of course." Morgan disappeared up the staircase and Ridley went to the built-in wet bar. "What can I get you, Miss Kennedy?"

"A mineral water if you have any, thanks."

Ridley handed Robin her drink and left her to her thoughts. Had she really spent yesterday morning in the Palm Court with a murderer? A chill ran through her. Felicity, a murderer. Was it possible? Yet, as she reviewed it in her mind, it all seemed to fit. Barrett threatened blackmail. Felicity, realizing that any sale of the Comets, from which she'd been told she'd get a large chunk of money, was dependent on the continuation of the supertraining, rushed off to deal with Barrett. And when she couldn't dissuade him, she killed him. Had she gone there planning to murder Barrett, or had she acted impulsively, out of rage and frustration? Robin preferred to believe the latter, though it hardly mattered now.

Once the deed was done, Felicity attempted to frame Otis Freeman, retrieving the distinctive jacket he'd left in the gym, and writing his name into Barrett's diary. When a worried Morgan met her coming out of the Pro Club, she assured him that Barrett had agreed to go on with the training and had been alive and well when she'd left his apartment. It had never occurred to Morgan that Felicity had been lying. Why should it? How many people would suspect even a thoroughly disliked ex-spouse of being capable of murder? The only part of the hypothesis that still bothered Robin was why Felicity would kill the man who held the key to the supertraining. She remembered asking Felicity that very thing when she'd implicated Morgan: Wouldn't killing Barrett stop the training? "But it didn't, did it?" Felicity had replied.

Her thoughts were interrupted by Morgan's return, his hand wrapped in an iced cloth. "Sorry to leave you on your own like that," he apologized. Retrieving the drink Ridley had left for him on the wet bar, he came and sat across from Robin. "Let's start at the beginning. But I need a promise that you won't reveal anything I say until after the Series. Whatever mistakes I may have made, it wouldn't be fair to screw things up for the players." He took a large sip of his vodka. "And I'm not sure how much of this I want you to write about, either, okay? This is all off the record until I say otherwise."

Robin nodded. "I know I let you down with Felicity and the Comets sale—"

Morgan waved away her apology. "That woman has a knack of bringing out the worst in people," he said with a crooked smile. "You didn't stand a chance. Need a refill?"

"Not yet, thanks."

"Okay, from the beginning ... When Felicity and I met in London, she never told me she was married. She divorced Paul Barrett soon after we met, but I never knew anything about that. We lived together in London, then married when we moved to New York. That was over twelve years ago." He paused, drank, continued.

"Then about two years ago, maybe a little more, Barrett contacted her. He'd known about me even though I hadn't known about him. Seems he'd kept tabs on us, all those years."

"Creepy."

Morgan shrugged. "I guess. He'd never gotten over her. Besotted with her, actually. She could do that to people. Anyway, he'd learned I'd bought the Comets and that they weren't doing so well. He told Felicity he was developing a training technique that could create super athletes, but he needed money to perfect it. He wanted to offer it to me. I'd tried everything I could think of to bring the Comets up in the league: new manager, new players, new coaches. Nothing was working. I figured I'd gamble on this thing, whatever it was."

"Why you?" Robin said. "He must have hated you. Why would he want to make you rich?"

"Who else could he take it to?"

"If it were a legal, acceptable training technique, anybody," Robin responded.

"What are you implying?" Morgan demanded.

"Come on, Morgan," Robin said tiredly. "You said the time for lies was over."

Morgan sighed. "The truth is, Barrett didn't describe his technique, and I didn't ask. He said he was offering it to us for old time's sake—"

"Oh, please."

"—and for a great deal of money. He said that since the Comets needed it so badly, he figured I'd be willing to pay through the nose. He was right about that. I paid him a lump sum to reserve the supertraining technique exclusively for the Comets players. I funded the on-going development. I provided the money to open the Pro Club and get the training started . . ." He swigged down the rest of his drink. "Here, let me get you another." He took their empty glasses to the bar and began to mix fresh drinks.

"But you must have known what he was doing was illegal," Robin prompted.

"You saw the training room," Morgan challenged. "Did it look illegal to you?"

"No, but Barrett was a biochemist. You knew some kind of drug was involved."

"I didn't," Morgan replied angrily, turning back from the bar. "And I still don't. I'm trying my best here, Robin, but don't put words in my mouth. As far as I know, there has been no wrongdoing."

"You mean as long as you don't actually know the specifics of the wrongdoing, you're innocent, is that it?" Robin replied hotly.

"It isn't like that at all," Morgan protested, turning back to the bar.

Sure it is, Robin thought; it's exactly like that. How could anyone be so morally bereft?

Morgan set their fresh drinks on the coffee table between them, and Robin took a long pull at hers. "The last thing we need is a rumor that there's anything illegal about the superplayer training," he said more calmly. "Sure, it would be bad for me. But you know whom it would really hurt? Your friend Kenny Reese. And Otis Freeman. And Ernie Sanchez. The whole team, in fact. Managers, coaches, everybody. Anyway, the baseball commissioner's office was all over the place in April, and again last month, and they gave it a clean bill of health." He took a large swallow of his drink, then shook his head sadly. "You know how I love those guys. How can you, of all people, accuse me of doping my players?"

"I never said *you* were doing it," Robin murmured.

Morgan's head jerked up. He set down his drink and stared at her, his eyes narrowing slightly. Robin could feel her face flush as he studied her. Uncomfortable under his gaze, she picked up her glass and sipped at it. Morgan had added a lot of ice, and the mineral water was nearly finished when she set the glass down again.

"Robin ..." He leaned toward her across the low table, his face tight. "If you know something I don't, you owe it to me to tell me. Don't leave me holding the bag. If there's something wrong, I want to make it right."

"What do you mean?" she asked, trying to look innocent.

"I think you know what I mean. Back in June, you began consulting with Adam Salt about your article. You even took him into the supertraining room. The two of you have obviously become friends, because you sent Kenny Reese to him."

"I sent him to Adam because he deals with a lot of sports figures—"

"For knees, not headaches. Didn't we agree that the time for lying was over?" Morgan's eyes were full of sorrow and regret. "I honestly don't know what Barrett was doing. I didn't want to know. But now I do. I want to do the right thing," he told her earnestly. "Please help me make things right. Tell me what Adam found."

Robin felt his eyes boring into her. The intensity of his stare made her feel a little muzzy. "I think . . . maybe you should ask Adam."

"Please, Robin. Tell me. I took the training myself, remember. What did he find?"

"He found . . . a hormone," she said softly.

"What kind of hormone?" Morgan asked, an expression of astonishment on his face.

"It's . . . something new."

"But how did Adam find it? A blood test?"

"No, a spinal tap. He found it in Kenny's spinal fluid."

Morgan rose and began to pace. "Does he know how it got there?" he asked over his shoulder.

"No, that's just the trouble. He doesn't know if Kenny's the only superplayer who has it, or if the others do, too. He can't even tell if it was put there on purpose, somehow. But it seems likely."

"Does it? Why? What does this hormone do?"

"It seems to speed up reactions in the brain. You actually think faster."

Morgan turned to face her. "And Adam thinks this hormone is part of the supertraining. Is that it?"

Robin shook her head. "He doesn't know. He suspects it is, but ..."

Morgan collapsed heavily onto the sofa. "God, I can't believe it," he muttered. "I had no idea. Do you think I should withdraw the Comets from the World Series? Would that be the right thing to do?"

"I don't know ..."

"No, that wouldn't be fair to the guys. They've worked so hard to get where they are. Not just the superplayers; everybody connected with the team. Besides, Adam isn't sure about the hormone, right?" He looked over at Robin hopefully. "You said he doesn't know whether the other superplayers have it. Maybe it isn't part of the training at all."

Robin opened her mouth and shut it again. Talking seemed rather an effort.

"Look, tell Adam I want to help," Morgan assured her, wringing his hands. "Ask him what he thinks I should do. If it's within my power, I'll do it." Tears stood in his eyes. "I'll stop the Supertraining right now. I know the evidence isn't anywhere near conclusive, but that would be the prudent thing to do." Robin nodded. "The Comets deserve their chance for a World Series win. But after the Series, we'll get to the bottom of this thing. That I promise."

"And you'll stop taking the training yourself?"

"Of course, of course." He looked over at Robin fondly. "You look beautiful but exhausted."

"I am tired."

"Well, it's been quite an afternoon."

"Morgan, I'd like to ask you something. On a completely different topic."

"Shoot."

"Well, something's been bothering me. About Felicity." For some reason, she was finding it hard to string her words together. "Assuming she murdered him. Barrett. She knew he controlled the supertraining. That kept the Comets winning. She told you ..." Robin yawned deeply. "She told you Barrett had agreed to keep it going. But that wasn't true."

"Apparently not."

"So why did it keep going?"

"I'm not sure—"

"If someone—Felicity—wanted Barrett to keep the training going, which was why she went over to his apartment in the first place, how could she risk killing him? Killing him would have had the opposite effect. At least, it should have."

"But Barrett wasn't necessary to the continuation of the supertraining, not anymore," Morgan said. "Connor Egan . . ."

Their eyes met. "Could Connor and Felicity . . . ?" Robin wondered aloud.

"They could . . . they did! Robin, you're brilliant." He stared at her for a long moment. "I'll be right back."

Robin leaned back into the enveloping softness of the wing chair. She reached out a hand for her drink, then remembered it was empty. Connor and Felicity; of course. She berated herself for having been taken in by Felicity's charm and false friendship. No wonder she'd told Robin Morgan was both desperate and violent; she was setting him up as the murderer. Morgan and I have both been dupes, she thought. Dupes and dopes . . .

"How are you feeling?"

She hadn't heard him come back into the room, but Morgan was leaning over her solicitously. "I must have dropped off for a minute." She smiled weakly. With an effort, she rose from her chair and stood there weaving.

Morgan frowned. "You don't look well. Maybe you should rest for a while."

"No, I'm fine." She took a few steps forward and stumbled against him.

He caught her and gently lowered her back into her chair. "Just rest."

"I want to go home now," she mumbled.

"Of course," he agreed kindly. "Whatever you say." He watched her eyelids flutter and close. Soon she was snoring softly. He gathered up the glasses they had used and carried them to the wet bar, where he washed them thoroughly, then dried them and put them away. The vial of prescription sleeping pills that he'd brought downstairs wrapped in the cold cloth around his hand now lay concealed under a small towel. He retrieved it, slipping it into his trouser pocket.

A glance at the figure in the chair confirmed that Robin was deeply asleep. With a tiny nod of satisfaction, Morgan went down the hall to his office. He pushed aside the drape and looked out at the evening. The sky was clear, but a halo ringed the moon. Tomorrow's game would be played as scheduled, but the following day's was iffy, Jack had remarked as he'd thanked Morgan for this unexpected evening off. Well, better get busy, he thought. There's a long drive ahead. He turned away from the window and began shredding papers.

"More tea?" Tibor offered.

"One more cup and I'll start wearing a bowler and talking funny." Adam sighed and surveyed the small, crowded room in which they'd spent the last seven and a half hours. "Didn't this guy ever throw anything away?"

"Apparently not. But that is to our benefit, I think."

"I suppose you're right. If we had about a hundred and fifty years to sift through it all." He walked his fingers through the file labels in front of him. "A Study of the Intracellular Manifestations of Ion Channel Opening in Vascular Endothelium—"

"I've already been through those," Tibor interrupted.

"All of them?" Tibor nodded. Adam got up from his cross-legged position on the floor, flexed his cramped legs, and went to the small leaded window. It was late; lights twinkled strangely in the distorted glass of the panes. He turned back to the work at hand. He'd consciously avoided the stack of old, dusty cartons, nearly to his waist, that stood beside the window. Now he lifted the lid of the topmost carton and glanced inside. "How about 'Examination papers and student theses for the academic year 100 B.C.'?"

"I have already reviewed the material from 100 B.C.," Tibor told him with a smile. "Do you have anything earlier?"

"You've been through all this, too?"

"Just the top one. It was accessible."

Adam muscled it off the stack and set it down, then checked the carton beneath it. "More of the same ... old exams and student papers ..." He lifted it off and dropped it on the floor with a bang. "What have you got?"

"All these cartons contain Barrett's work on various research projects," Tibor said. "Notes, experimental observations ... But these projects are worlds away from what we are looking for." He placed the lid carefully back on the carton and pushed it aside. "I think we should concentrate on the older files."

"Well, these are old," Adam said, uncovering the last box in his stack. "Students' doctoral theses ... exam questions—" He broke off.

"Yes?"

"Come and look."

"You have found something?" The chubby microbiologist levered himself up off the carton on which he had been perched.

"I'm not sure," Adam said slowly. "But these aren't Barrett's students' theses and research papers. They're his own. And they seem to go way back."

"Ah. That becomes more interesting."

Dust rose as they attacked the carton. "These are from Barrett's earliest days," Tibor said happily. "I know the name of this professor. He retired years ago."

"Look. Here's a lecture Barrett gave on—" Adam broke off. Tibor was staring at a thick sheaf of bound pages. "What is it?"

"A minute ... Yes, of course. This is what we seek. Part of it, at any rate."

"What is it?"

"You have told me, Adam, that you could not understand how this mysterious hormone, if administered from outside the body, could have passed through the blood-brain barrier. Here is how." He handed the pages to Adam with a flourish. "Barrett was working on a way to alter the chemical composition of the hormone to enable it to bypass the blood-brain barrier." Adam was silent. "You are not happy?"

"Yes, I'm happy, Tibor," he said, cradling the research papers. "I'm appalled, but I'm happy." He paused. "Well, I guess that's it."

"That is enough? That is all you need?"

Adam shrugged. "I'd like to find the original thesis, too—the one in which he discovered the thalamic hormone and its effect. But it doesn't really matter. We've got the link." He sneezed several times. "I guess I'm just overwhelmed by the evidence that Barrett was actually drugging those poor kids," he told Tibor sadly. "I mean, I suspected it, I knew it, but because I didn't see how it could be done, I kept hoping I was wrong . . ."

Tibor put an arm around Adam's shoulder. "I understand," he said. "But at least now you can make sure it will not happen to any other young men, yes?"

"Yes," Adam agreed. "Absolutely." He began flipping idly through the pages. "There's one thing I still can't quite figure out. Kenny claims he wasn't given any injections. And the hormone couldn't have been ingested. So how was it administered?"

Tibor took the research papers from Adam's hand and turned back to the first page. "If we consult this manuscript in an organized manner," he said pointedly, "perhaps it will tell us." He seated himself and began to read.

Adam wandered back to the window and stood staring out at the distorted view. Would there be anything in that paper that could save Kenny and the others? And if so, was there time?

"How very curious," Tibor said suddenly. Adam swung around to face him. "There is nothing definitive, you understand," Tibor cautioned. "This is a preliminary paper; more work, a great deal more, would have been done. No doubt that is locked away somewhere. But what we have here is . . . suggestive."

"Of what?"

"You mentioned injection and ingestion. Both those means of administration assume the hormone as a liquid. Or perhaps as a soluble solid." Adam nodded. "But our friend Barrett seems to be concentrating his efforts on a gas."

Adam's brow furrowed. "The nerve endings in the nose go directly to the brain," he said slowly. He thought of the special training room, and the New Age techniques. It was starting to make sense. . . .

Tibor placed the manuscript carefully to one side. "Shall we go on?" he asked. "Or do you want to stop for dinner and then return?"

"As long as we're here," Adam said, aroused from his reverie, "let's see what else is in this damned box."

One by one, they examined the rest of Barrett's early research papers, pitching them onto the floor as they went; all were unconnected to the thalamic hormone research Barrett had secretly conducted. "That's it, then," Adam said at last, removing the last of the papers, a torn, coverless thesis, from the bottom of the carton and tossing it onto the pile. He put his hands on his hips, arched his aching back, and stretched.

"Yes," Tibor said. "This is it." Something in his tone made Adam turn toward him curiously. Tibor had retrieved the torn thesis and was staring at it. Now he waved the pages at Adam triumphantly. "Here is the original thesis you described. The discovery of the thalamic hormone itself."

"Are you sure?" Adam asked doubtfully, taking the stapled report from him. "There's no title page."

"The first paragraph is quite clear," Tibor replied. "See for yourself." He handed the report to Adam and began scrabbling around in the loose pile of discarded papers on the floor.

"You're right. This is it!" Adam agreed with rising excitement. "Don't worry about the title page," he added, glancing over at Tibor. "I must have ripped it off when I picked up the report lying on top of it."

"But we must be complete."

"Come on, Tibor. We've got what we came for." Adam waggled the two research documents in his direction. "These are enough. The cover doesn't matter. Let's just clean up and get out of here." He began scooping papers back into the carton.

"Please stop doing that," Tibor said firmly. "It is most important that you take with you the full document— Ah, here it is. I knew it could not have gotten very far. 'The Effect of the Administration of Extracted Thalamic Hormone on the Production of Nitric Acid in the Cortex and the Resulting Increase in the Rate of Interneural Cortical Communication.' Just so. Only . . ."

"Only what?" Adam asked testily, his hand outstretched for the torn and wrinkled page.

But Tibor continued to stare at it. "There is something here I do not understand. All that," he gestured at the mound of research papers they'd removed from the carton, "all of Barrett's early work goes back thirteen, fourteen years. Yet this paper is dated seventeen years ago, before Barrett arrived at Cambridge."

"Well, how could Barrett do that kind of research before he'd ever—"

"He couldn't. He didn't." Tibor's face was solemn as he handed Adam the title page. "This research paper was written by Morgan Hudson."

Chapter Twenty-eight

Tuesday, October 5—World Series, game number 3

Robin awoke slowly. Her head ached. Her mouth felt
dry and cottony. Her eyes were sticky with sleep as she
forced them open. She gasped. Where was she?

She jerked upright with a start, and was suddenly
dizzy. She closed her eyes for a moment, and when the
dizziness had passed, opened them again and looked
around. The narrow brass bed on which she sat was covered with an expensive-looking floral print quilt. A white
wool blanket had slipped off onto the floor; presumably,
she'd been covered with it during the night. The room
was small but beautifully appointed: deep-pile carpeting,
polished antiques, and expensively framed prints on the
walls. A faint lemony light crept tentatively through the
gauzy curtain of the dormer window. A glance at her
watch told her it was just after eleven in the morning.
Robin stood up, ignoring the roiling of her stomach, and
crossed the small room to look out. Some three miles
off, beyond intervening fields and copses, she could see
the Hudson River.

Morgan, you bastard.

She was fully dressed in the dark brown slacks, pale
sweater, and loafers she'd worn the day before; presumably he hadn't raped her in her sleep. Not that he
wouldn't have been capable of such an act, she
thought furiously.

She turned from the window and surveyed the room.
A small partly opened door revealed a tiny bathroom.
A larger, more solid door, leading to what was presum-
ably the hallway, was closed. When she went over and

tried the handle, she was not at all surprised to find that it was locked. The ornate white-and-gold telephone that stood on the bedside table was dead.

Finally alert enough to be frightened, Robin banged on the door and yelled for help. No one answered. The house must be deserted. Certainly, Morgan wouldn't be here; he'd be on his way to Parker Stadium.

A small table in one corner held a tray. On it were a thermos of coffee, a cup and saucer, and several sandwiches wrapped in plastic, their 7-Eleven price stickers still attached. Wedged under a sandwich was a hastily scribbled note. "Don't panic," Morgan had written. "Will return tomorrow evening. Once the Series is over, you can write whatever you like about the Comets. But for now, I can't afford any more leaks. Please understand. Please forgive me."

Robin's hand shook as she poured the lukewarm coffee into the delicate china cup. Don't panic, she thought. Right.

The taste of the strong black coffee was reviving, and she went back to the tray for another cup. Her eyes lit upon the note once more. "Once the Series is over, you can write whatever you like." That was nonsense, of course; Morgan couldn't possibly allow her to write a word. Not now; not ever. But how could he stop her? He couldn't keep her locked up here forever ... Of course not, she thought. And he doesn't intend to. The cup fell from her fingers.

No one knew she was here. No one even knew she'd gone to Morgan's town house except Jack Ridley, and for all she knew, Ridley might have helped load her unconscious body into Morgan's car. She had to get out of here before Morgan came back.

Her headache had returned; had he spiked the thermos of coffee as he had that drink he'd prepared for her last night? Her heart was beating fast, too fast, as she searched the small room for a weapon with which to defend herself when he came, a tool with which to smash down the solid oak door and escape. But the scant furniture was delicate and spindly. She dumped the tray onto the floor, coffee and all, picked up the small, light table and smashed it into the door. The table splintered, and nothing happened to the door.

Don't panic, she kept telling herself. Don't. Panic. She could feel her limbs growing heavy. She went to the dormer window, trying to remember the layout of the house. The Hudson River lay to the west, of that she was sure. And Morgan's bedroom faced west; she recalled they'd had drinks on the terrace leading off from it one evening, watching a glorious sunset. That terrace should be just below this room. If she could manage to get down to it . . .

The roof below the dormer window was slanted but not severely. If she could force the window, there was a chance she could creep backward along the roof and drop down onto the terrace below. How big a drop was it? She had no idea. But anything was better than staying here.

She tried the window, but it was sealed shut. She could feel herself growing weaker; anything she was going to do had to be done right now. She grabbed a chair and smashed the window. She went and got the white blanket and slung it onto the sill, then pulled over the bedside table. Standing on it, she climbed out of the window onto the small roof. Shards of glass cut through the blanket as she turned around and clung to the sill for a moment before inching backward toward the overhang. The incline was steeper than it looked, and progress was slow, but at last her foot touched something: a gutter. That would give her a handhold as she hung over the terrace below. God, how far below? She shifted her body sideways for a quick look; it didn't seem too bad, but she'd have to hit it feet first. Her hands scrabbled on the tiles as she attempted to get her feet downslope again. Her head was getting muzzy. She stubbed her knee on the gutter, then thought, my knee? The realization that she was sliding came too slowly. Her hands clawed frantically at the rough tiles, then grabbed for the gutter. Then everything went black.

*　　*　　*

"So Morgan's degree was in biochemistry, not economics."

"Correct," Professor Grant said in his whispery voice. He smiled at his two visitors. "I remember him as a brilliant student. He had a degree in chemistry from an American university, but came here to do his doctoral work in biochemistry. I was rather surprised when he told me he'd decided to forego his dissertation and enroll at the London School of Economics. Ah, Martha, my dear. Could we have a little more coffee for our guests?"

"Please don't trouble," Tibor told the plump, white-haired woman who had entered with another plate of cookies. "I'm afraid we must go soon."

"No trouble," she chirped, retrieving the nearly empty coffeepot and heading back to the kitchen.

"It was very kind of you to see us, Professor Grant," Adam told the gaunt figure in the rocker.

"My pleasure, Doctor," the professor replied. "I quite enjoyed our chat about the old days. The usual response I get to my little stories makes me feel a bit like the Ancient Mariner." Adam smiled. "I've been retired for nearly thirteen years, you know."

"Yes, so you said."

"I'm repeating myself again, am I?" The old man sighed. "I'm afraid at my age I tend to dodder a bit. Feel free to stop me. Where were we?"

"You were saying that you were surprised that Morgan Hudson gave up science for industry," Adam reminded him gently.

"Did I say that? The truth is, I was and I wasn't. Young Mr. Hudson had always been more interested in the practical applications of his work, the financial rewards. Pure research didn't interest him. He was after money. So how did he turn a Cambridge education into cash?"

"He founded a toiletries company," Adam explained. "Patented formulations for treatment shampoos, skin care products . . ." Professor Grant's face clearly showed his disgust; surely such a fine education could have been put to better use. "I'd always assumed Morgan had bought the patents to his products, or had them developed for him," Adam mused. "It never occurred to me he'd created them himself. One last question: Did Morgan Hudson know Paul Barrett, do you recall?"

"Good heavens, no. Mr. Hudson was living in London by the time Paul came to us." He selected a cookie, broke it into several pieces, and chewed one thoughtfully. "Paul wouldn't have cared for Mr. Hudson's attitude toward research. Paul is, er, was—I can't believe he's gone. So sad. New York is such a violent city." He leaned forward and sipped his coffee, holding the cup carefully in his thin and shaking fingers. "Paul loved research for its own sake. It was knowledge he sought, not material gain."

Adam rose from his chair. "You've been most helpful, Professor. We mustn't impose on you any longer."

"That's why I was puzzled," Grant continued, "when Paul came and asked me about Morgan Hudson."

Adam lowered himself back down again. "He what?"

"He'd heard about Hudson from someone, he said, and was curious about him." He paused, remembering. "Paul was a little unsettled at the time. His wife had been spending a lot of time away from Cambridge as I recall. Family matters, I believe. She left him, eventually. Pretty woman. I wonder whatever became of her ..."

Adam waited, but Grant remained lost in contemplation. "Uh, you were saying Paul Barrett asked you about Morgan Hudson's work ..." he prompted.

"Not so much his work ... He seemed more interested in Hudson the man, wanted to know what I thought of him, what he was like." He paused. "Paul was always rather ... eccentric. Obsessive and secretive and ... Well, he'd been through a lot." Grant sipped his coffee. "And he was such an original thinker."

More than you know, Adam thought grimly.

Tibor looked meaningfully at his watch; Adam's train left in twenty minutes. It would take nearly an hour to travel down to London, then another hour to taxi across the city and out to Heathrow to catch his flight home.

It was a flight they both knew he couldn't afford to miss. There was a big storm coming up the East Coast of America, the airline's telephone agent had advised them that morning, and Adam's transatlantic flight might well be one of the last to land before Kennedy Airport was shut down.

Adam stood and, thanking Grant for his time and memories, he and Tibor took their leave. With the professor's little wife waving them good-bye from the front step of their cottage, Tibor fired up his small Japanese import and stomped heavily on the gas pedal. "Of course I will drive you to the station," he insisted as they careened down the narrow street at a frightening speed. "You are very, very late." Adam promptly made a long and rather embarrassing speech thanking Tibor for all his invaluable assistance, before lapsing into a meditative silence.

Now he sat clutching the case containing the two old research papers, deep in thought, as the countryside flashed by.

So Barrett had learned that Felicity was seeing Morgan Hudson in London. Had he hired a detective to follow her on one of her many supposed trips home to Cornwall? Or had Felicity dangled Morgan's name in front of him, taunting him with his inability to hold her?

It hardly mattered. The result was that Barrett had become obsessed with the man who was stealing his wife. And as he'd traced Morgan back through his time at Cambridge, he'd found the abandoned thesis, abandoned because Morgan could think of no commercial use for the hormonal effect he'd discovered.

But as Dr. Grant had pointed out, Barrett was an original thinker. He'd found a way through the blood-brain barrier, and come up with an imaginative application for Morgan's hormone: rugby. The sport Barrett had loved. The sport that had crippled him.

He'd befriended Andrew Fuller, a young rugby player from his hometown, and secretly administered the hormone to him. The technique had worked brilliantly, but

Fuller had died. Had Barrett grieved? Or had he always considered the boy expendable?

Soon after, Barrett had watched his wife, who knew nothing of his obsession with her lover, go off to London to live with the man whose discovery he had stolen.

And he'd hidden the hormone research away. And he'd waited.

The unsettled weather was making everyone uneasy. At Parker Stadium, fans glanced up at the leaden sky and wondered whether they should run home and tape up their picture windows, as meteorologists were suggesting. Even the players seemed uneasy; several fights had broken out in both teams' locker rooms before the game, and another in the Comets dugout during the third inning. On the mound, Ernie Sanchez was battling a rising wind, testily shaking off signal after signal from the catcher.

In the owner's box, the mood was strained. There was champagne, there was food, and the Comets were ahead by two runs. But Morgan seemed edgy, and his edginess was infectious.

"Where's the lovely Robin Kennedy?" Sandy Morrison asked. "Haven't seen her since Philly."

"She couldn't make it," Morgan answered shortly, keeping his concentration on the field below. "I haven't seen her since Philly, myself." He paused. "Actually we broke up."

"Too bad. Well, plenty of fish in the sea and all that."

"Shut up, Sandy."

"Say, can I have her phone number? Wouldn't want all that talent to go to waste."

"Fuck you."

Below them, Ernie Sanchez sent a pitch streaking across the plate an inch from the batter's nose. The batter hit the ground, and Ernie wheeled to make the double play at second and first. The crowd went wild, stamping and shouting. This was more like it. Next up was Anderson, a great clutch hitter, and as he strode up to the plate, the stadium quieted. One strike . . . two . . .

On the third pitch, Anderson blasted the ball to deep center, and the spectators gasped. But Otis Freeman was already heading back for it. He leaped straight up and plucked it out of the air for the third out, and the Comets trotted in from the field for their turn at bat.

Sandy Morrison looked over at Morgan. "You're prickly today," he commented. "I was going to invite you to join Britt and me for dinner tonight. Celebrate today's game."

"They haven't won yet," Morgan said moodily.

"They will. How about it? A pre-hurricane bash?"

"I'm going out to High House right after the game," Morgan replied. "Got a helicopter waiting. With this storm coming in, I want to make sure the place is safe." He drained the strong vodka tonic he'd poured himself, relieved that his hands had finally stopped shaking. He'd contained the damage. Everything would be all right.

"How about lunch tomorrow, then? We'll all huddle together and ride out the storm in sybaritic splendor."

"Afraid not. Now that the fourth game's postponed a day, I'll probably stay out at the house until Thursday morning."

"Want some company?"

"No."

"Well, how about—"

"Watch the game, Sandy, or get out."

Sandy shrugged and poured himself more champagne.

First up for the Comets was Martinelli, who hit a double off the wall. He was followed by Agua, who grounded out. Kenny Reese was up third, with Simms on deck. Kenny ripped one down the third base line for another single, then turned it into a double by stealing second. Morgan shouted with joy. Not one eye was on the sky now. The Falcons' pitcher shook off a signal, then lobbed the ball in tight and fast, grazing Simms's elbow. Tossing aside his bat, Simms jogged over to take his base. And then Otis Freeman hit a triple and brought everybody home.

*   *   *

More than half the TV sets in the country were tuned to the World Series, and Felicity's was no exception. She reclined against the sofa pillows, staring at the screen. The sound had been turned way down, but the images were clear: the Comets were about to win their third straight game. Felicity sat motionless, her eyes unblinking. A small green Perrier bottle stood on the coffee table. The ice had melted in the glass beside it; a soggy section of lime floated in the tepid remains.

Though deeply flushed, her lovely face was placid, her demeanor calm. One arm was thrown carelessly across the sofa, the other folded in her lap. Her tweed skirt rested demurely on her knees, and the rolled collar of her pink silk blouse had been pulled up to conceal the livid purple bruises on her neck.

She didn't shout with joy, as many did, at the Comets' seven-to-five victory over the Falcons, not did she curse. She moved not a muscle, uttered not a sound.

Morgan had explained the situation most convincingly to her that morning. The very force of his argument had been impossible to resist, and she had tacitly relinquished all knowledge of secrets, hidden or revealed. With brute strength and grim determination, Morgan had presented his case, and ensured her eternal silence.

It was nearly dark when Robin opened her eyes and peered around groggily. She lay on the flagstone terrace, shivering in the chill wind. Her knee was badly bruised and when she tried to stand, her ankle twisted painfully. She remembered scrabbling for the gutter as she slid off the roof. She must have held on long enough to slow her drop to the terrace below, and landed feet-first. Thank God for that.

Her watch was cracked, but the second hand was still revolving. It showed ten past six; why was it so dark? She tucked her arms around her for protection. The wind was increasing; trees writhed and leaves danced in circles on the manicured lawn. The hurricane, she suddenly remembered. The hurricane was coming, and so was Morgan. The game would be over by now. She had very little time left. Fear sent adrenaline coursing through her body. She went to the edge of the terrace and looked down. The ground seemed very far away. No way she'd survive that drop. She'd have to break the French doors and go through Morgan's bedroom to the stairway.

The terrace was bare of furniture; presumably it had been taken inside in anticipation of the storm. But several branches had blown onto the terrace. If she could use one to make a hole big enough for her to slip her hand inside and undo the lock . . . Choosing the thickest of the branches, she attacked the plate glass again and again, to no avail. Tossing the battered branch away, she leaned against the wall, exhausted. It was obvious she wasn't going in that way.

A glance at her watch told her the effort had cost her twenty minutes. Frantically, she looked around. The terrace didn't run the length of the house, only the length of the bedroom. A small window was set just beyond the end of the terrace. Morgan's bathroom? She leaned over the railing for a closer look. The glass looked thinner than that of the French doors. She went and retrieved the branch. Leaning out over the railing again, she smashed the pane, then knocked out the shards clinging to the frame. She climbed up on the railing and wavered there, her body pressed against the rough wood siding of the house. Now or never, she thought. She stretched her body across the small but perilous drop and half leapt, half fell across the window frame. Glass raked her stomach as she pulled herself into the room. Using the toilet lid to stop her slide, she tumbled onto the carpeted floor.

The light helicopter bucked and reared as it approached the local airport. Morgan was glad they were finally here; he was beginning to feel sick.

"Keep your head low when you get out," the pilot shouted through the earphones as they descended. "I'm lifting off as soon as you're clear."

"Got it," Morgan assented. He couldn't blame the man for wanting to get home fast. It was bad up there.

"That your ride?" The pilot thumbed toward a black car, the only sign of life at the closed airport.

"I certainly hope so."

"Set you down as close as I can."

"Thanks."

The driver, suddenly aware of the copter's arrival, flashed his lights, the twin shafts cutting through the gloom like knives.

She'd twisted her ankle again, going in over the sill. Working as fast as her shaking hands would allow, Robin bound it up with strips from one of Morgan's shirts, then lifted her sweater and smeared her stomach with antibiotic cream from his medicine cabinet. Her hands were cut and bleeding. She rinsed them to remove the shards of glass and gave them a light coating of the same cream, rubbing off the excess on a towel. In his closet she found a black slicker. It was miles too big, but would offer some protection against the elements if she was still at large when the hurricane struck. Then she hurried out of the room and down the stairs.

At the bottom, she paused. Morgan's study was along here somewhere. Was it worth a fast search? You're nuts, she told herself, but she ran down the hallway anyway, shoving open the doors on either side.

"Congratulations on today's game, Mr. Hudson," the driver said, peering into the rearview mirror at his distinguished passenger.

"Thanks," Morgan replied tersely. He was in no mood for conversation.

"I was workin' today, but I listened to it on the car radio. Your boys're gonna take the Series for sure."

"Hope so." Just shut up and drive, he thought fiercely.

"You were lucky to get in tonight. Airport's been shut down for hours. Gettin' too rough up there for a small plane."

"I guess."

"Helicopters must be different, huh?"

"Maybe."

"You own it?"

"No."

Silence.

"Beautiful place, High House."

"Thanks."

"Yep, beautiful place. Hate to see it damaged, this thing hits. You board up your windows?"

"Not yet."

"A lot of folks already boarded up their windows."

"Uh-huh."

" 'Course, it's falling trees that do the most damage. You've got some fine old trees right next to the house, haven't you?"

"Yes."

"You get a lotta rain, it loosens up the roots, and then the wind comes along, and, bang! There goes your roof."

"Uh-huh."

"Well, good luck, Mr. Hudson. You get in any trouble, you just call the Chester fire brigade. If the phone lines're still up, that is. Here we are."

Robin stood staring at the scene in Morgan's den. A confusion of file folders covered the rosewood desk, their contents spilling out onto the floor. Worms of shredded paper overflowed the wastebasket. If there had been anything to find here, there wasn't anymore. She bent and examined a thin ribbon of paper from the bin. The shredding process had been efficient. She was too late.

A sudden stab of light made her blink and gasp. Through the window she could see a car, its headlights on high beam, swinging toward the front of the house. Morgan was back.

She ran for the rear of the house, vaguely remembering a kitchen and a back door. She fumbled to free the catch, and stumbled out onto the rear lawn, tripping on some low plantings in the dark. Struggling to her feet,

she circled around toward the front door, keeping close
to the house for cover. She saw Morgan reach for his
wallet and begin counting off bills. While his head was
down, she ran across the open space between the house
and the beginning of the tree-lined drive, then tucked in
behind the trees to tighten the makeshift ankle support.

The bang of the front door got her moving again. It
wouldn't take long for Morgan to discover her escape.
Could he tell how long she'd been gone? Would he follow on foot or in the Mercedes station wagon he kept
in High House's three-car garage? Lights swept past her
as the car that had delivered Morgan now sped away in
the darkness. Robin hurried over the rough ground just
inside the treeline. The driveway connected with a
county road, small but reasonably well-traveled. If she
could reach it before Morgan found her, if there was
anyone moving out here tonight, if she didn't look too
frightening with her bandaged ankle and huge black
slicker, she could thumb a ride to ... anywhere else.

Morgan rushed out of the house, furious and frightened. How in hell had she managed to get free? How
long had she been gone? Was she already telling the New
York City police about her abduction? No, surely not.
The blood on the windowsill was still sticky. He stood
rooted with indecision. Maybe she was hiding on the
grounds. He started around the house at a run, the small
object he'd snatched from the desk drawer bouncing
heavily in his pocket. He ran past the swimming pool,
then stopped short; this was hopeless. The car, he
thought. He'd hunt her down with the car. He ran for
the garage.

Robin stumbled out onto the county road. The sky
was pitch black now, and the wind tore angrily at her
clothes. She forced herself along the road, trying to put
some distance between herself and Morgan's driveway,
and prayed for a ride. The road was the main connector
for a string of small towns along its length, and despite
the darkness of the evening, it was only a quarter past
seven. People were making last-ditch attempts to stock

up on food, or trying to beat the storm home. Within minutes, two cars had appeared, but they'd both ignored her outstretched thumb and swept past her.

Morgan wrenched the estate car around the turning circle and sped down the drive. A quick search of the grounds had revealed nothing. Where could she be?

More lights. Robin ran from her hiding place and stationed herself in the center of the road. The small truck screeched to a halt.

"You crazy, lady?" the driver yelled, sticking his head out of the window.

"I need a ride."

"Where to?"

"Anywhere. Please."

The young man sighed and shrugged his shoulders. "Okay," he said. "Get in."

All the way to New York, Morgan cursed his luck. She was gone, gone. Well, he'd find her. He'd find her and—

Rain was spattering onto the windshield as he arrived at Robin's apartment. The doorman hadn't seen her since he'd come on duty at four. Did Morgan want to leave a message? Morgan did not. The story was the same at Adam's building; no one had seen him for days. The doorman thought he was away on a trip somewhere. Morgan rolled up the window and stomped on the gas.

Connor was just closing up the Pro Club when Morgan announced himself on the intercom. "Never expected to see you here tonight, Mr. Hudson," Connor said, ushering Morgan into his office. "There's a big storm—"

"Screw the storm," Morgan said succinctly. "We're closing down the Pro Club. As of right now."

"We're what? But we can't. Our members—"

"Reimburse them for the unused time on their contracts."

"And ... the supertraining?"

"That stops, too, effective immediately. I'm going to overhaul the whole place, gut it, rebuild ..."

"But it's great just the way it—"

"Well, it'll be even better. We'll open again next year. Hey, don't look so worried, kid. You'll still have a job, you can keep right on living in that great apartment upstairs."

"But what'll I do when you're rebuilding?" Connor protested. "I can't work."

"That's true." Morgan considered. "Well, I wouldn't want to lose you to the competition." He winked conspiratorially. "So why don't I hire you as a kind of design consultant? At your regular salary, of course. I'll even throw in a little bonus."

Connor brightened somewhat, but confusion still showed in his face. "But the superplayers," he protested. "They need me."

"Of course they do," Morgan agreed soothingly. "Say, how would you like to join our Comets family as a trainer?"

Connor's eyes narrowed slightly. "There's a rumor going around that you sold the team."

Morgan assumed an expression of pure astonishment. "Sold the Comets? Sold my boys? Why would I want to sell a world champion team? Hell, you can't believe rumors like that." He studied the young man for a moment. "Listen, why don't you come on down to Parker for the fourth game? As my guest. Watch it from the owner's box. See the guys make history."

"That'd be great, Mr. Hudson."

"Excellent." He reached across Connor's desk and patted his shoulder. "You're a good man, Connor. I promise I'll take good care of you." Connor nodded. "But it's vital that you lock up the club right now—"

"That's what I was doing when you—"

"I mean for good. Lock it up for good. Admit no one. Tell them we're closed for renovations."

"Whatever you think best . . ."

"Good." Morgan rose. "Well, I've leave you to it. No, you don't need to see me out."

"Uh, Mr. Hudson?"

"Yes, Connor?"

"I really appreciate everything you're doing for me."

Morgan smiled at him. "You've got a golden future ahead of you, Connor. As long as you do precisely as I say."

Chapter Twenty-nine

Wednesday, October 6

"Is she up yet? I have to get to the Pro Club, and I don't want to leave without talking to her."

Agnes shook her head. "I'm surprised you're not still sleeping, yourself. Pounding on my door at three in the morning . . ."

"I didn't pound," Adam replied. "I rang your bell like the gentleman I am."

"And when I didn't answer, you pounded. Never mind, I forgive you."

Adam grinned. "Thanks. Is that coffee I smell?"

Agnes nodded. "Help yourself." She followed him into the kitchen and he poured out cups for them both. "You were very lucky you were able to land last night," she said. "Have you seen it?" She gestured at the driving wind and torrential rain outside the window. The city had caught the edge of the hurricane as it headed out into the Atlantic, but that was quite enough.

"We were the last plane in," Adam said. "The passengers applauded when we touched down." He gulped the hot coffee gratefully. "Thanks for the air mattress. When I got your message that Robin was here—"

"You're welcome. The mattress is not very comfortable, but it is better than the floor."

"It was fine." He refilled her cup and then his own. "Maybe I should look in on her again."

"Let her alone, poor child," Agnes told him sternly. "She's completely exhausted. As you saw last night, her ankle is not tender, not swollen. As for the scratches, they will heal. Let her sleep."

"Did she say what happened to her?"

"She was too exhausted to talk." Agnes sipped her coffee. "There is brown bread on the counter and butter in the fridge. Eggs, too."

"I'm not very hungry."

"I am." Robin stood in the doorway, her smile bright despite the shadows under her eyes. "Was it you who bandaged my hands?"

Adam hurried to her. "Yes, while you were sleeping. What happened to you?"

"I've been drugged, I've been kidnapped, and I haven't eaten for a day and a half. Other than that, I'm fine. Those eggs you mentioned sound good, Agnes."

"Drugged?" Adam repeated, astonished, as he helped her into a chair. "Kidnapped? By whom, for godsake?"

"Felicity told me that naïveté was one of my most endearing qualities," Robin said ruefully. "Pour me a cup of that coffee and I'll tell you both how stupid I've been."

They'd finished the eggs and were halfway through a second pot of coffee by the time she reached the part about hitchhiking to New York in the rain, learning from her doorman that someone fitting Morgan's description had been asking for her, and finally arriving at Agnes's door at midnight. She turned to Adam and said, "Well, that about covers it. What did you find at Cambridge?"

Adam shook his head in disbelief. "You could have been killed. You would have been, if you hadn't—"

"Well, I wasn't. Now let's hear your story."

"First I want another look at that ankle," Adam countered. "And I ought to check those scratches again, too."

"Only if you can doctor and talk at the same time."

"Do my best. And then we're calling the police."

"Not so fast," Robin told him. "You're not ready to call the baseball commissioner, but you want to tell the police, which means the newspapers, all about it? Besides, this is my story, remember? If anybody's going to break it, I am."

"I *am* ready to call Dennis Locke," Adam said slowly. "Let me tell you what I found at Cambridge ..." He took her quickly through the search of Barrett's office, and the conversation with Professor Grant. Agnes had had a brief overview the night before, but she listened intently.

"But if Morgan actually discovered the hormone," Robin reflected, "how could he have taken the stuff himself?"

"I don't think he knew the whole truth about Barrett's application. I bet he still doesn't. Morgan's original research was purely theoretical. He never ran any clinical trials."

"But Barrett did do some testing, you said. On that rugby player. So he knew."

"Oh, Barrett knew, all right, but he'd have been nuts to tell Morgan. Not if he wanted to sell him on the scheme. Morgan might have accepted—did accept—administering illegal drugs to his players. But killing them would have been counterproductive."

"But how could Barrett be sure Morgan would be receptive?" Agnes asked. "He could have turned out to be a man of honesty, a man of morals. I truly believe most people are."

"Well, that was a chance Barrett was prepared to take," Adam replied. "What did he have to lose? He had an inside track to Morgan through Felicity. And he knew Morgan was the one person who'd understand the hormone therapy idea; he'd discovered it himself."

"Yes, but—"

"Hear me out. Barrett was obsessed with Morgan, and very bitter. He must have nursed his hatred for years. He'd been keeping tabs on them both ever since Felicity left him, so he knew Morgan had bought a baseball team. He also knew about Morgan's financial difficulties. But Morgan had a business, investments . . . and there was Felicity's money, too. Barrett probably figured Morgan could raise the money if he had to. And he was right."

"And how did this horrible Mr. Barrett plan to deal with the lesions, the rages, the spastic paralysis?" Agnes asked angrily. "He knew what the hormone would do."

"Maybe Barrett believed he could fix all that," Adam replied, "if he threw enough money—Morgan's money—at it. And if he couldn't—and we know now that he couldn't—he must have planned on leaving Morgan and Felicity holding the bag. He'd kept a pretty low profile all along, remember. He could simply disappear for a while."

"So if the scheme worked," Robin said, "Barrett would get rich. If it failed, he'd get revenge. He must have loved it when Morgan asked to take the supertraining, knowing what he knew." She thought for a moment. "So when Barrett called Morgan that night to say he couldn't fix the side effects, he was telling the truth."

"That would be my guess. One last little dig in the ribs with the long knife before he disappeared, leaving them to face the heat."

"And so Felicity killed him," Agnes said, "in a fury over being deceived."

But Robin shook her head. "Felicity would have wanted him alive, so they could turn him into the fall guy." She thought back to her brunch of several days before. "I think she was convinced Barrett was trying to blackmail them, that he'd invented imaginary side effects to pressure them into upping the ante."

They listened to the rain beating against the windows.

"So you are now ready to talk to your friend the commissioner," Agnes said at last.

"Yes," Adam replied. "But first, I need to get to the Pro Club—no, I'll take Dennis with me, so he can see for himself."

"And what will you show him?"

"The delivery system, I hope," Adam replied. "Only . . ."

"Yes?"

"I still can't figure out how or where that hormone is being made. It's not the sort of thing you could whip up in your kitchen, is it, Agnes?"

She smiled and shook her head. "No, one would need a specialty lab."

"I suppose it's traceable, eventually. Invoices, deliveries made to the Pro Club ..."

"Not to the Pro Club," Robin reminded them. "To the Pro Club For Men, remember?" The kitchen phone rang, and Agnes went to answer it. "That name's sounded familiar to me ever since I read it in Connor's files," Robin mused. "If I could just get hold of my notes from that first article I did on Morgan ..."

"Not today, you can't," Adam told her severely. "As your medical advisor, I advise you to stay put."

"It's Pat," Agnes announced, her face serious. "There's been a break-in at your office. The place has been ransacked. And the contents of Kenny Reese's file are missing. She got your message about flying home yesterday, and she's been calling everybody in your Rolodex this morning, trying to find you."

"Shit." Adam lunged for the phone, listened, then spoke briefly. Replacing the receiver, he turned back to the two women. "It happened late last night, the security people say. I left my pager at home when I went to England, and then I came straight here from the airport ..." He headed for the front hall. "Pat called the office from home this morning, and the service told her. So she came on in, God knows how." He pulled his jacket from the closet and shrugged it on. "Robin, call Dennis Locke for me, will you? Pat has the number. Tell him to meet me at the Pro Club in an hour. I'll stop by the office and calm Pat down, then I'll head on over."

"What if he's not in his office? A lot of people aren't working today."

"Locke lives in the city, somewhere downtown. If he's not in the office, call his home. The number's unlisted, but Pat has it. Tell Dennis I'll be inside the Pro Club, waiting for him. And that I expect him to swing his weight around and get us into the Supertraining room." He put his hands on Robin's shoulders. "And you stay here, okay?"

"Maybe," Robin replied.

"She's kidding, right?" Adam appealed to Agnes, who merely shrugged.

"I'm going to the Pro Club, too," she announced.

"With those hands? And everything that's happened?"

"I want to be there," Robin insisted, "when you show Dennis whatever it is you suspect is in that training room. I think I've earned it. And this is my big story, don't forget." She grinned at him. "Locke and I will *both* meet you there."

Adam gave a theatrical sigh. "Reporters," he said. "They never let up."

Chapter Thirty

"I need to talk to Dennis Locke. It's urgent."

"Sorry. The commissioner hasn't shown up yet this morning," the male voice replied. "Don't know if he will. I'm just here to pick up some papers. Can I leave a message for him?"

"Please. Tell him Adam Salt said to come to the Pro Club as soon as possible. It's very important. Put the message someplace he'll be sure to see it when he comes in."

"Okay," the man said doubtfully, "but I can't promise he'll get it. Have you tried him at home?"

"That's my next call," Robin told him. "Here, let me give you my phone number, in case he wants to call me back."

Adam dug in his drenched pocket for his key card while the wind whipped his trenchcoat around his dripping trousers. His shoes were soaked, and, umbrellas being useless in such weather, his hair dripped water down the back of his collar. Fortunately the key card was plastic. He tried to shove it into its accustomed slot beside the door, but the card wouldn't fit. Strange. He tried again, then bent and looked into the slot. A piece of metal had been fitted across it just inside, effectively blocking its use. Curious.

He pressed the bell, looking up at the video camera. Maybe the place was closed because of the storm. But Connor was living in Barrett's old apartment now, wasn't he? He should be around here somewhere. Adam rang and rang, but got no answer.

Slowly he descended the steps. He had to get in, had to get Locke in, too. He tried the handle on the garage that held the training van; not surprisingly, it, too, was locked. He fought the wind back along the Pro Club's frontage. Was there a back door? A side door? He remembered the narrow alley that cut between the club and its nearest neighbor to the left. He peered down its dark length, then took a few tentative steps inside. The wind immediately lessened, although the rain still fell.

Halfway down, he spotted a dull red glow. Hurrying toward it, he discovered an alarm system panel set beside a steel door. A push button was set beneath the red light. He pressed it, keeping his finger on it for a good ten seconds.

"Who's there?" A male voice, annoyed and sleepy, boomed through the intercom box.

"Connor? Is that you? It's Dr. Salt. Adam. I guess you're closed because of the storm, but—"

"We're closed for good," Connor told him tersely.

"What? You mean, permanently? When did this happen?"

"Yesterday."

"So that's why my key card didn't work. Look, can I come in? It's wet out here."

"No. No one's allowed in. We're renovating."

"Not today, surely," Adam protested. "Look, I need some, uh, stuff from my locker. Important medical stuff." Renovating, my ass, Adam thought. Getting rid of the evidence is more like it. I've got to get in there. Now.

"Sorry, Dr. Salt. We'll be clearing out the lockers next week, sending everything back to people."

"I can't wait that long, Connor," Adam said. "I need that material right away. There are medical reports, and, er, test results. I've got a very sick patient who's just been admitted to the hospital, and if I don't have that information, he could die." Was he laying it on too thick? "Come on, Connor, let me in. There's a hurricane happening out here."

"Oh, all right, Dr. Salt," Connor said grudgingly. "Go around to the front. I'll come open the door."

It took an ill-tempered Connor several minutes to descend to the lobby and admit Adam. "You're soaked,
Dr. Salt," he said disapprovingly, jangling a large key
ring.

"Yeah, it's a little damp out there. Well, sorry to
bother you, Connor. Go on back to, uh, whatever you
were doing. I know the way."

"I better go down and turn on a couple of lights for
you," Connor said glumly. "Black as night, down there."
Selecting a key from his ring, he preceded Adam down
the stairs, keying on every other light switch as he went.
"Afraid it's kind of a mess," he apologized as they
stepped into the partly lit locker room. "I was doing a
little . . . reorganizing last night."

Adam stared at the scene around him. Large pieces
of equipment had been dragged out of the special training room and now lay in various states of disassembly,
blocking access to the benches and lockers. The appointments desk, usually covered with a clutter of papers and
schedules, was completely clean, and the bulletin board
mounted beside it was bare.

"Which locker is yours, Dr. Salt?" Connor asked.
"Over there? I better shift some of this stuff for you."
He set down his key ring and began dragging a large
section of metal tubing away from the wall of lockers.

"Let me help," Adam offered. "Here, I'll take this
end—" He broke off. Was it his imagination, or was a
strange blue light spilling out from behind the freestanding locker wall that concealed the door to the supertraining room. "Uh, that'll do fine, Connor," he said. "I can
manage the rest."

Connor shrugged. "If you're sure . . ." He placed his
bulky fists on his hips, arched his muscular back, and
yawned. "Sorry to be so grouchy, but you woke me up.
I didn't get to sleep until around five this morning. You
sure you're okay down here on your own?"

"Absolutely. Won't be a minute." Adam gave him a
thumbs-up and began clambering over pieces of equipment toward his locker. Connor watched him for a moment, then retreated back to the stairwell. Once Adam

heard the stair door click shut behind the trainer, he made a fast U-turn and headed for the supertraining room through the litter of metal tubing. The door was indeed ajar; with the Pro Club closed, Connor hadn't expected visitors. Checking his watch, Adam calculated that Locke should be arriving in about twenty minutes. The doorbell rang at the appointments desk, he knew; he'd seen the secretary admit members who'd forgotten their key cards. Wedging open the heavy door, he slipped inside the forbidden room.

"... please leave a message after the beep, and I'll call you back ..."

Where could the man be, in such a storm? Robin thought frantically. She left an urgent message about meeting Adam at the Pro Club, along with Agnes's phone number, and then tried Locke's office again. This time she got an answering machine. Discouraged and concerned, she left the same message a third time. Where was that man?

Dennis Locke was drinking bad coffee and cursing. "Dammit, Ed, *I* got here. Why couldn't anybody else?"

The deputy mayor sighed. "Be fair, Dennis. You're only a ten-minute walk from City Hall. Half my staff lives in Jersey, Long Island, Westchester ..."

"And the other half?"

"Hey, *I'm* here, aren't I?" Ed Silver retorted. "The mayor's here."

"My meeting was not with the mayor. It was with you and Jerry and Brian and Marcy—"

"So what should I do, fire them because they didn't come to work in a hurricane? Let's just reschedule." Silver reached for his desk calendar. "Next Monday? Three o'clock?" Locke grunted an assent. "More coffee?"

"You call that rat's piss coffee?" Locke shrugged into his yellow slicker, showering water on everything within a four-foot radius. "I'm going back to bed. Never should have left it."

"I'm sorry, Dennis."

"Yeah, well, you owe me."

"Uh, you want to use my phone, check your office?"

"What the hell for?" Locke grumbled. "Whole fucking city's shut down. Nothing's gonna happen today."

The long, narrow, blue-lit room was much as Adam remembered it, with the addition of some clutter and minus the equipment Connor had removed during the night. The giant video screens hung, dark and silent, above him. The pale wood floor was bare, its thick mats stacked high along one wall. Boxes of supplies—athletic tape, ace bandages, clear plastic vats of energy tonic— had been dragged out of storage and shoved into a corner. One of the MIE machines was still installed; another lay partially disassembled. Behind its half wall, the control console was dark.

Adam thought back to the training as Connor had explained it that day when he and Robin had been given the fifty-cent tour. Blue-light therapy, meditation and breathing exercises, biofeedback ... He raised his eyes to the high ceiling and studied it carefully. Yes, it was certainly possible ...

Connor reached the second-floor landing before he remembered his keys. He stomped back down the stairs, tired and annoyed. Well, Salt should be finished by now; he could let him out and turn off the lights at the same time. But when he reached the locker area, Salt wasn't there. He hadn't left, had he? No, there hadn't been time. Connor found and pocketed his keys, then glanced around, puzzled. Where could the man be? He checked the john, the showers, and the juice bar, then returned to the locker area. Pieces of equipment still blocked the section of lockers Adam had claimed as his. Connor frowned; how had he gotten the locker door open without shifting them? Well, apparently he had; he'd grabbed his stuff and gone. Funny Connor hadn't passed him on the stairs— A thought hit him. He remembered having left the Supertraining room unlocked last night. He'd been tired, it was late, the Pro Club was locked up. Could Salt have wandered in there for a look?

No harm done if he had, Connor reflected. He'd seen it all already. He stuck his head inside the training room; no Salt. Well, maybe he'd left, after all. Unless— A chill ran through him. He'd been doing some work in the storeroom last night; Morgan had insisted on it. He was sure he'd locked up when he'd left, but . . . Shit, if *that's* where Salt was— Connor hurried across the room, his heart thumping, but when he reached the small, unobtrusive door, he was relieved to find it closed.

Maybe he should check inside, just in case. He scrabbled inside his T-shirt for the strangely shaped key that hung from a long gold chain around his neck, and unlocked the cluttered room. Everything looked the way he remembered leaving it. With a sigh of relief, Connor walked back out into the training room, leaving the storeroom door open. So Salt had simply grabbed his papers and rushed out, he thought. Not surprising, really; hadn't he said it was an emergency? Might as well finish up in here, now that he was awake, he decided. No one would be picking up oxygen cylinders today, so he'd cart out the equipment first. A box of tools stood beside the partially disassembled MIE machine. Connor selected a screwdriver and went to work.

Behind the wall of mats, Adam peered out, waiting for his chance.

"Silver? Remember that favor you owe me? I want to collect."

"Already?"

"Immediately. I need a car and driver—"

"You kidding, Dennis? On a day like this?"

"Come on, Silver. If the mayor needed a car, you'd get him one."

"He already has one."

"Well, if he needed *another* one. Don't play dumb with me, Silver. I know you can do it."

"Where are you?"

"I'm at home." Locke gave him the address. "I need to go to a place called the Pro Club."

"What for? You gonna work out?"

"Very funny. I've suddenly got a very important business meeting."

"So use your own car service. Or the subway."

"The subway's flooded, and the car service doesn't answer; none of them do. Look, I know you City Hall boys have clout. Find me somebody."

"I don't know ... it could take awhile. And you're not on the city payroll, Dennis. It wouldn't be official business."

"Yeah, well, I'm gonna make it my official business to come down there and kick your ass, Silver. That official enough? Now get me that goddamn car."

Dennis Locke banged down the receiver, then picked it up again and dialed another number. "Robin? Dennis Locke again. Look, I'm doing my best, but this storm has everything at a standstill ... subways, buses ... I put pressure on a guy I know at City Hall—Ed Silver, the deputy mayor. He's getting me a car, so you can tell Adam I'm more or less on my way. No, I don't know how long, but soon, I hope. You, too? How? Well, I guess you can do the fifteen blocks on foot, but you'll be soaked to the skin by the time you get there. Yeah, I guess it *is* that kind of day. See you later."

Connor dragged the metal armrests out into the changing area, then stood and stretched. The wrecking crew would be here tomorrow morning to start tearing down the supertraining room, Morgan had said. It was sad, Connor thought; the end of an era. He'd miss the guys. Then he thought of Morgan's offer of a spot on the Comets training team, and brightened. He went back into the blue-lit room, started for the other MIE machine, and stopped. The storage room door was closed. Funny; he remembered leaving it open.

Brow furrowed, Connor went over and gave the door a tiny push. It swung noiselessly inward a few inches, and Connor peeked in. Adam Salt, his back to the door, was examining one of the long chrome cylinders.

Connor's first instinct was to go charging in and pull Salt away. But then what? He forced himself to back off, instead. Maybe the cylinder would mean nothing to Salt. Maybe Salt was just curious. Maybe he should simply go in and ask Salt to leave. But what if he refused? What if he'd already found— No, this was Morgan's call, not his. He turned and left as silently as he had come.

Some of the cylinders were chrome, others were painted green. All had the words "OXYGEN—CAUTION—CONTENTS UNDER PRESSURE" stenciled in large letters on their sleek bulk, but only the green tanks bore the tag of a well-known supplier of medical gases. The chrome ones were silent as to their point of origin.

Adam turned and gave the rest of the small room a cursory initial inspection. Several portable oxygen units—self-contained masks and small tanks—lay on an otherwise empty shelf. Adam recalled Connor mentioning oxygen therapy as part of the training. He recognized the compact units; EMS workers routinely carried them. Nothing suspicious there.

Below the shelf, several lengths of black hose snaked along a counter running along one side of the small room. A cursory examination of the coupling at one end of a section of hose showed that it was designed to connect to the top of the metal canisters. The other end had a smaller coupling. Where did it fit? Adam wondered. He spotted a narrow door on the wall separating the room from what he calculated was the garage. The lock was a standard key-operated cylinder; nothing fancy. That made sense, he decided; the garage was merely the entrance and exit point for the compressed gas cylinders. The presence of the hoses suggested that the delivery system was somewhere right in this room.

Pushing the hosing aside, he examined the walls, but found no outlet. Beneath the counter were two cabinets. Adam opened the doors and peered in. The cabinet to the left was empty. The other contained first-aid equipment, plastic thermoses emblazoned with the Pro Club logo, spare towels ... and behind that, a discreet metal cover which, when lifted, revealed an inset connector housing just the right size for coupling on the black hose. Next to it was a small heavy-duty switch; its three positions were marked "On," "Off," and "Exh."

Well, Locke and his people could trace the whole thing back inside the wall. In Adam's mind, there was no question what they'd find. The switch controlled the flow of air to the ventilation ducts in the supertraining room. The "Off" position would allow a normal airflow, the same cooled air that flowed throughout the gym. "On" opened a shunt in the duct work to allow the contents of the large metal cylinders, fed by hose into the connector housing, to infiltrate the training room. And "Exh" would fire up a strong exhaust system to clear it from the room after each session.

Biofeedback, my ass, he thought. No wonder Kenny and the others had no idea drugs were part of the supertraining plan. The hormone, in the form of a compressed gas, had been secretly pumped into the training room, probably during the meditation and breathing exercises.

Breathe in through your nose to a count of ten; really inflate those lungs. Now breathe out slowly through your mouth. Let the nerve endings in your nose carry the molecules of Morgan's discovery, of Barrett's brilliant adaptation, directly to your brain. Breathe them in, and they will improve your game beyond all understanding. Making you incredibly quick. And undeniably dead.

"He's *where*?" Morgan roared, his voice bouncing off the walls of his town house living room. "I told you to lock up the place. How the hell did he get in?"

"He left some important medical papers in his locker, and—"

"And you let him in? And you *left* him down there?"

"It was only for a second. I—"

"Are you crazy? Are you fucking nuts?" Morgan was beside himself with rage. Robin had said that Adam knew about the hormone. If he was inside the storage room, he undoubtedly knew the rest.

"What should I do?"

"Shut up. I'm thinking." One more day and it all would have been gone, Morgan thought furiously. The cylinders, the tubing, the whole damn place. No one would have known for sure. No one could have proven anything. But now . . . And had Robin told Adam about her abduction, or was she still wandering around in the storm? I should have taken care of her when I had the chance, he thought. Well, those two have left me no choice. "Lock him in," he ordered.

"What?"

"Lock Salt inside the training room."

"Hey, wait a minute. I didn't sign on for—"

"Listen to me, Connor. You want to keep that nice apartment? You want that cushy training job next year?"

"Well, yes, but—"

"Then do as I say. Lock him in there." Morgan thought for a moment. Assuming Adam and Robin were in this together, which seemed obvious to him now, he just might get lucky. "And if Robin Kennedy shows up," he ordered, "I want you to put her in there, too."

"But I can't just—"

"I'm not going to hurt them," Morgan said soothingly. "Robin's my girlfriend, remember? Didn't you see her with me in Philadelphia?"

"Yes . . ."

"I just want to talk to the two of them. Explain things to them, so they'll understand, and not make any trouble for the team. I'm sure Adam has no idea what he's looking at, in there. They're just curious."

"But if you only want to talk, why do I have to lock—"

"Because I'm afraid Adam might misunderstand what you've let him see," Morgan replied. "He might just go charging out of there. All you have to do is hang on to him until I get there. Okay?"

"You're coming over?" Connor asked hopefully.

"Of course I am. You didn't think I'd leave you to handle this mess on your own, did you? You've made a bad mistake, letting Adam in there, but I told you I'd take care of you, and I will. Now I want you to write down the number of my car phone and call me if there's any more trouble."

"Uh, okay." Connor fished a pen from the desk drawer and scribbled the number on his hand. "But I still don't see—"

"You don't have to see," Morgan told him, his voice suddenly angry. "Just do it."

Frowning, Connor lowered the receiver. Then he sighed, shrugged, and went and locked the training room door.

Chapter Thirty-one

"I'll be perfectly safe," Robin assured a worried-looking Agnes as she struggled into Morgan's black slicker. "Adam will be there. And Dennis Locke."

"And Morgan Hudson?"

"He's back at his country house until tomorrow, his office says. Can you lend me a pair of gloves? I look like the mummy's curse."

"Maybe I should come with you."

"I really think it would be better if you stayed here. Your phone is our only communication link."

Agnes nodded. "Well, make sure Adam has actually arrived before you set one foot inside that place," she cautioned.

"Don't worry. I've learned my lesson." Robin glanced outside: the rain was still sheeting down, but the wind seemed to have diminished a little. "They're still predicting this thing will move out to sea by midnight?"

"Yes. And that the World Series will resume tomorrow afternoon."

"I wouldn't bet on *that,*" Robin said grimly.

Morgan ran from his town house to the Mercedes station wagon he'd parked just down the street. No one was bothering with alternate-side-of-the-street parking rules today. Yanking open the door, he threw himself inside and fired up the engine, then roared down the street, cursing aloud.

Traffic was light but the streets were flooded and slippery as he sped toward the Pro Club. Adam was contained; that was good. But silencing Adam wouldn't work unless he could silence Robin, too. Where was she? Could he use Adam for bait? Whatever he did, it would have to be done fast. Jack Ridley thought he was still in the country; his office believed the same. Connor knew his true whereabouts, of course, but Connor could be dealt with, one way or another. In fact, couldn't the whole mess be blamed on Connor? Yes, a case could definitely be made for Connor and Felicity having been in cahoots, as Robin had suggested. It wasn't true, of course, but if Morgan acted decisively today, who would be around to dispute it?

"Yes, Ms. Kennedy, Dr. Salt's here," Connor told her. "He's downstairs waiting for you. Please. Come in."

Robin stepped through the door into the lobby. "Is Dennis—uh, anyone with him?"

"No, he's alone." Connor's eyes narrowed. "Is he expecting someone else?"

"Not exactly. That is, I thought Adam might be bringing a friend of his. Uh, to look around. Maybe sign up."

"We're not taking any more members," Connor announced, leading her down the stairs. "The Pro Club's closed."

"Closed? Since when?"

"Yesterday. We're going to renovate, make it even better." Connor preceded her through the juice bar and into the locker area. "Dr. Salt's just through here."

Robin followed him around the freestanding lockers. "In the supertraining room?" she asked, surprised.

"Yeah. He wanted to look around," Connor told her. "Nobody else is here today, so I figured, why not?"

Well done, Adam, Robin thought. I don't know how you talked him into it, but well done. "I see you've already begun dismantling things back there," she commented as they approached the closed steel door. "When do you expect to reopen—"

But Connor motioned her to be quiet. "Extraneous voices confuse the voice lock circuitry," he explained. Keeping his eyes on her, he reached over and pushed a button set into the wall beside the door.

Robin stepped back, suddenly suspicious. Why was the door locked? If the club was empty, and Connor had allowed Adam into the training room, why had he locked the door after him? She backed away, frowning. "Tell Dr. Salt to come out and talk to me," she said. "I'll be waiting in the lounge."

Connor went after her. "He wants you in there," he insisted, grabbing her arm.

"Then let him come out and tell me himself," Robin insisted, breaking free. She was running now, dodging the scattered pieces of equipment, but Connor was faster. He grabbed her arm again, yanked her around, and began dragging her back toward the training room door. She pulled against him but he was much too strong. She made a grab at the scattered equipment, try-ing for an anchor, and a long metal bar, part of an arm-rest, came away in her hand. The scratches on her palm protesting through Agnes's climbing gloves, Robin swung the heavy bar at Connor's knee. It connected, and he howled with pain, loosening his grip.

Twisting away, Robin ran for the stairs, not daring to look behind her. As she topped the first flight of steps, she could hear the stairway door slam open below her, and Connor's voice shouting. Then she was through the lobby and out the door.

"What do you mean, she *was* there?" Morgan shouted into the car phone.

"It's not my fault," Connor told him in an aggrieved tone. "I almost had her. I got her downstairs and told her Salt wanted her in the training room."

"And then?"

"I guess she got nervous when she saw me start un-locking the door. Anyway, she ran. I grabbed her but the bitch practically broke my knee."

"So where is she now?"

"I don't know. She ran out."

"Goddamn you, Connor." Morgan pounded the steer-ing wheel in frustration. "How long ago was this?"

"Just now. I called you right away, like you said. My knee's really bad, Mr. Hudson. Maybe I should—"

"Fuck your knee, Connor. You stay right there. Don't move, you hear me?" Morgan slammed down the receiver, furious at this new turn of events. It should have been so simple, but now— As he swung around the corner toward the Pro Club, a figure in a large black slicker ran diagonally across the narrow street, heading away from him. The slicker looked familiar. Yes! he exulted. We're back in business. He gunned the engine and headed straight for her.

The wind and rain masked the sound of the oncoming car, and it was nearly upon her when the roar of its engine caused Robin to glance back over her shoulder and discover the black Mercedes bearing down on her. She raced for the small space between two parked cars and slipped between them as the station wagon scraped alongside, laying long dark scratches down their sides.

Crazy New York drivers, Robin thought angrily as she stumbled to safety. But as the car flashed past, she recognized Morgan's profile. Heart pounding, she did a one-eighty and headed back up the one-way street. If she could reach the broad avenue that ran at right angles to this narrow side street, she could duck into one of the stores.

Morgan wrenched the car around in a tight U-turn. Ahead were a series of small unblocked driveways that serviced the built-in garages of the small houses lining the street. He chose one, and using its access, turned onto the sidewalk behind Robin. Standing on the gas, he came up fast behind her, but she ran out into the roadway again, still heading for the avenue.

Cursing, he swerved back into the roadway, too, sideswiping a tree and wrenching off the protruding fender of a parked car in the process. The fender clattered in his wake as he tore along, heading up the street against the flow of traffic, wild eyes fixed on the fleeing figure.

A bakery truck rounded the corner, moving fast. The driver yelled when he saw the Mercedes coming at him, and swerved to one side, horn blasting. Reluctantly,

Morgan shifted his attention from the running figure to the oncoming vehicle. His eyes widened in horror as he fought the wheel around, just missing the truck. The station wagon spun out of control, smashing against cars on either side of the road before coming to rest about four hundred yards down from the Pro Club. The bakery truck driver, having escaped unscathed, took one look in his rearview mirror and kept going.

Morgan's head hurt where he'd banged it on the side window; the Mercedes was a mess. I'll say it was stolen, he decided. My car was stolen, officer. I never lock the garage. I haven't driven the car myself for weeks. It was stolen. He shoved at the buckled door with his shoulder until it sprang open, and clambered out.

Hopeless to go after Robin on foot, he decided. He still had Salt, though—if Connor hadn't fucked that up, too. There must be some way to use Adam to draw her back. Damn Connor, he thought angrily. Wrapping his coat around his body, he ran for the Pro Club.

Connor admitted him, an ice bag strapped to his knee. Morgan offered no sympathy. "Salt still in the training room?" he barked. "At least you didn't screw that up." He followed the limping Connor down the stairs. "How can we use him to get the girl?"

"Miss Kennedy?" Connor stopped and looked back at Morgan. "I thought she was your girlfriend."

"She was; now she's trouble," he growled. "And you, you dumb shit, you let her get away."

"It wasn't my—"

"Shut the fuck up," Morgan told him. "Don't you see what you've done? It's no good taking out just one of them. We need to get rid of them both."

"Get rid—?" Connor swung around to face Morgan. "Hang on a minute. I didn't sign on for any rough stuff. Whatever your fight is with those two, count me out."

"Oh, no," Morgan told him, eyes blazing. "You're in it, Connor, right up to your eyeballs."

"The hell I am," Connor retorted angrily. "I just do what I'm told, that's all. I run the gym, I give the training—"

"A real innocent, aren't you?"

"Aw, I don't need this shit," Connor said, elbowing past Morgan. "You do what you want. I'm out of here."

The report echoed up the stairway; the bullet, intentionally fired wild, dug itself into the wall above them. "I suggest you reconsider," Morgan said in the silence that followed the shot. His voice was dangerously calm; the pistol, now pointed at Connor's stomach, didn't waver. "Walk past me very slowly. Go through the door and into the lounge. That's right. Can you feel the gun in your back? Good. We're going into the training room."

"Ed Silver, please. It's very important. My name? Robin Kennedy, but it won't mean anything to him. Tell him I have to reach Dennis Locke. It's very important. Yes, I'll hold ..."

"Miss Kennedy? Ed Silver. Yes, I did provide Mr. Locke with a car and driver, but— A car phone? I doubt it. No, I really don't know whether the car service uses a two-way radio to talk to the drivers. Well, I can try. What's the message?"

"Tell him ..." Robin hesitated. She had to alert Locke and get help, without revealing too much to Silver. "Tell him we've run into some trouble at the Pro Club. Tell him I think we're going to need some backup. And tell him to hurry."

"Dr. Salt. Such a pleasant surprise."

"Sorry I can't say the same."

"Do sit down." Morgan motioned toward the MIE machine with his gun. "You, too, Connor. Over against the wall."

"I thought Connor was supposed to be on your side," Adam said conversationally. He glanced over at the trainer, who glared at him. No help there. Morgan did not reply. "No friends left, huh?" Adam turned back to Morgan. "Felicity hates you, Barrett's dead ..."

"Barrett was never my friend."

"Truer than you think," Adam said. Stall, he told himself. Keep him talking. Locke would be there any minute, and he'd insist on seeing the training room; Robin would have instructed him to do so. Morgan would have to let him in. And he wouldn't dare pull a gun on the baseball commissioner. Would he?

Morgan was regarding him with suspicion. "What do you mean?"

"I've learned a lot about Paul Barrett recently. How he built on your hormone discovery, turned it into a gas, found a way through the blood-brain barrier, and offered you the chance to turn three Comets players into superstars."

"I don't know what you're talking about."

"But I wonder," Adam continued, ignoring the interruption, "whether you know about Andrew Fuller."

Morgan shrugged. "Name's familiar."

"Fuller was the first player to reap the benefit of your friend Barrett's hormone therapy. Thirteen years ago."

"Oh, him. Yeah, Paul told me about him. A great success."

"Yes. But then he died. Barrett ever tell you how?"

"Cerebral palsy, I believe."

"Really." Adam paused. "I understand Barrett was trying to blackmail you, claimed the technique had side effects he couldn't control. He threatened to stop the Supertraining, maybe even threatened to go public."

"Robin told you?" It was Adam's turn to shrug. "Yeah, he did," Morgan conceded. "But it was all bullshit. He just wanted money."

"Still, Barrett controlled the training. And he knew too much. So Felicity went over there to try to change his mind. She talked to him for a couple of hours and then killed him."

"Robin's got a big mouth," Morgan grunted.

"Lucky for you. Otherwise, people might think you murdered him."

"Why not Otis Freeman? His jacket was there, his name—"

"Felicity set him up. But you must know that now. Here's how I see it: You got worried when she didn't

come back, so you came over here and rang the side
doorbell, the one for Barrett's apartment."

"How do you know about that door?"

"I didn't, until today, when I went looking for a way
in here, to ... pick up my stuff. Anyway, when the bell
rang, Felicity panicked—she didn't know it was you—
and decided to leave through the front door of the Pro
Club. Of course, both you and Felicity knew about that
door from the apartment into the gym. She went down
through the gym and happened upon Otis's jacket—he'd
left it on a bench—and that gave her an idea. She took
it up to Barrett's office and scribbled his name in the
desk diary. Then she went back through the gym and
sneaked out the front door. She met you and told you everything was fine, that she'd calmed Barrett down and the
training would continue. The following day, you were genuinely shocked to hear about the murder. And then Otis
was arrested. Didn't you have any doubts?"

"Why should I have?"

"Just curious." Where was Dennis? What was taking
him so long? "So you and Felicity decided that Barrett
was just blowing smoke; there were no side effects.
That right?"

"Of course. Anyway, I don't know anything about any
hormones. Barrett said the technique was based on meditation, mental image enhancement, alpha waves ..."

"That right, Connor?" Adam asked laconically. But
Connor only glowered.

"And you've been feeling okay lately?" Adam turned
back to Morgan. "No headaches? No sudden feelings
of rage?"

"If you're trying to scare me, forget it," Morgan
growled. "I know about the mood shifts. Took me
awhile to figure it out, but that's all they are—mood
shifts. So don't plan on offering me some miracle cure
to try and save your skin, Doctor. I know better."

"Do you?" Adam turned from Morgan to Connor.
"How come you never took the training?" he asked.
"Did you know something Morgan didn't?"

"Divide and conquer?" Morgan walked toward Adam,

the gun pointed at his chest. "I don't think so. Connor, go get a few rolls of that athletic tape over there, will you?" He motioned with the gun. Connor scrambled up and did as he was told. "Now tape him to the MIE." He waggled the gun. "Hurry up." Reluctantly, Connor began taping Adam's hands to the armrests. "His legs, too."

"Don't do it," Adam told Connor. "You're next."

"Don't listen to him," Morgan said. "This is a chance to redeem yourself, Connor. Don't you want that training job with the Comets?"

"The Comets have been sold," Adam said.

"He's lying! Haven't I always been your friend? I gave you the apartment, all that money—"

"Morgan's no friend of yours, Connor," Adam told him urgently. "Right now he's probably trying to think of a way to hang this whole thing on you: drugging the superplayers, murdering Barrett—"

"Shut up!" A bullet whined off the metal stanchion next to Adam's head. Where the fuck was Dennis Locke?

"You bastard!" Connor charged Morgan, his eyes blazing. "Blame it all on me, huh? Well, I'm not—" The gun spoke again, and Connor collapsed, his hands clutching his bleeding side.

"Get back against the wall," Morgan ordered.

"He can't," Adam said. "Untape my hands. Let me help him."

"Forget it."

"Don't you understand? He'll bleed to death."

"And you'll be next, if you don't shut up." Morgan waved the gun threateningly. "The only reason you're still breathing is so I can use you to lure the lovely Robin over here."

"Forget it."

"A surgeon works with his hands ..." Morgan mused. "Don't be so negative, Dr. Salt. I'm sure we can work something out."

As Robin huddled under Starbucks' awning, watching the Pro Club and willing Dennis Locke to appear, a plain blue Ford rounded the corner and pulled up in front of the club's garage. At last, she thought, racing across the street. But the tall, husky man who emerged was a stranger to her. He glanced over at the battered Mercedes. "You know anything about this?" he called to Robin as she approached.

"No . . . Yes. That is . . . Did Dennis Locke call you?"

"Yes. Are you Robin Kennedy?" Robin nodded. "I'm Phil Lorenzo. Dennis said to meet him here, that you were in some kind of trouble. That it?"

"Only part of it—" Robin began. "We need to get inside the—"

"Phil?" Locke called as he stepped from the Lincoln Town Car. "I really appreciate this. Robin?" Locke turned to shake her hand. "I see you two have met. Phil and I go way back to his early days on the force."

"The force?"

"Police force," Lorenzo explained. "I retired two years ago."

"He traded his badge for a private detective's license," Dennis told Robin. "And he's always been a real baseball fanatic. So I figured he'd be the perfect person to give us a hand with this thing."

"Baseball?" Lorenzo glanced up at the Pro Club suspiciously. "This wouldn't have anything to do with the Comets, would it?"

"He's a big fan," Dennis explained. "Your grandchildren enjoying those World Series tickets?"

"Yeah, I owe you," Lorenzo said. "Look, it's wet as hell, and I've got about a million things to do back at the office. Will somebody please tell me what I'm doing here?"

"Connor Egan—he's the manager of the club—has Dr. Adam Salt trapped inside the training room," Robin explained quickly. "He tried to drag me in there, too, but I got away. Then Morgan tried to run me over." She gestured toward the abandoned Mercedes. "We need you to help us get Adam out."

"What the hell—? Dennis, you didn't tell me—"

"I didn't know."

Lorenzo turned to Robin. "What did Adam say to you? Did he ask for help?"

"I didn't actually see him, but Connor said he was there. He said Adam wanted to talk to me inside the training room. But the training room door was locked, which worried me because there was no reason for Connor to have locked that door. So I ran out. That's when Morgan tried to run me down."

"So you didn't actually see Adam in there? Or talk to him?"

"No . . ."

"So he might not be in there at all."

"Salt did tell me to meet him inside the Pro Club," Dennis broke in. "He was definitely planning to come here."

Lorenzo sighed. "How many people did you actually see inside the Pro Club?" he asked Robin.

"Only Connor. But Morgan's probably inside, too, now."

"And Morgan is . . . ?"

"Morgan Hudson. He owns the—"

"—Comets, yeah I know." He shot Dennis a questioning glance, but the commissioner shrugged. "Did you see any weapons?"

"No, nothing," Robin replied. "Connor just grabbed my arm."

"And it didn't occur to either of you to call the police." He rolled his eyes in exasperation.

"I felt the need for . . . discretion," the commissioner explained. "Salt has some sensitive information for me, and there could be more involved here than I'm ready to go public with. Hell, your PI license'll probably scare them into releasing Adam," Dennis continued persuasively. "We're dealing with the owner of a major league ball club and a personal trainer, not hardened killers. Can't we give it a try?"

Lorenzo sighed and turned to Robin. "You're sure you didn't see any weapons?" Robin shook her head. "And only one, maybe two people?"

"That's right."

Lorenzo shot Dennis a baleful look. "The things I do for friendship," he growled. "Okay. Let's ring the bell and see who answers."

"Please, Dr. Salt. Help me."

Adam's eyes were misty. "I wish I could," he said. "Morgan?" But Morgan smirked and shook his head. "Keep pressing your hands on the wound, Connor. Try and control the bleeding."

"It hurts," Connor moaned. "It hurts."

"You really are a bastard," Adam told Morgan furiously. "Well, you'll get yours. The same hormone that's killing your players is killing you, too."

"I don't know what you're talking about," Morgan replied. "The hormone's not lethal. It causes mood shifts; so what? We're shutting down the training room; nobody's taking it anymore. No more hormone, no more mood shifts. End of story."

"Not quite. What you call mood shifts are actually cortical seizures."

"So? I stop taking the hormone, the seizures go away."

"It's not that simple. The cortical seizures are caused by lesions in the brain, permanent damage caused by the vastly increased nitric oxide levels."

"You telling me I've got brain damage?" Morgan snorted derisively.

"I'm telling you that Andrew Fuller died of spastic paralysis, not cerebral palsy. Caused by your thalamic hormone. Just like the rats in Agnes Havacek's lab."

"Agnes Hav— Isn't she the advertising writer Robin brought—?" Morgan's face darkened. "You son of a bitch!"

"I didn't know," Connor moaned. "I swear, Dr. Salt. I didn't know it was dangerous. Barrett told me what to do, how to hook up the tanks, but I never knew what was in them. Barrett said it was safe."

"Then why didn't you take it yourself?"

"I hate drugs. Even when I'm sick, I don't like to ... I don't use recreational chemicals, I don't smoke ... or drink." He groaned and clutched his side. "It interferes with the mantra, the meditation. But I swear, I didn't know the stuff would hurt the guys." His face was contorted with pain. "They paid me so much money," he whispered. "I knew it was wrong, what I was doing, but ... they paid me ... so much ... and it was supposed to be ... safe."

Morgan looked from Connor to Adam, his eyes hot and angry. "This is bullshit," he said. "I'm not dying."

"Wait and see."

"Yeah, well, you're going first." He hesitated. "A murder-suicide, I think. You and Connor. Yes, that's it. You were getting too close to the truth, except you thought I was behind it all, when in fact it was Connor. Connor and Felicity. You came here and told Connor what you knew, and he locked you in the training room, tied you up, and killed you. Then, racked with remorse, he shot himself."

"In the stomach?" Adam scoffed. But Morgan only shrugged. "And do you really think Felicity will sit still for that? She'll sing like a canary."

"Poor Felicity was murdered yesterday," Morgan replied calmly. "Strangled. I shall be so distraught when they come and tell me."

Adam's eyes widened. It suddenly hit him that Morgan had slipped over the edge. He recalled the rogue rat in Agnes's lab, and how Agnes had postulated that if the cortex was especially sensitive to chemical stimulation, the toxic amounts of nitric oxide caused misfiring and miscommunication along the neural pathways, interfering with the brain's ability to evaluate and respond appropriately to established patterns of reality. Morgan was one of those cases. The supertraining had driven him insane.

"Due to Connor's carelessness, you've had plenty of time to inspect the tanks in there," Morgan was saying. "Doubtless you've discovered the hookup point for the ventilation system. Perhaps the door to the garage, as well?" Adam didn't reply. "That's how we take the cylinders in and out. But you've probably already figured

that out. Not that it matters." Pocketing his gun, Morgan
rifled Connor's pockets and retrieved the key ring, while
Connor groaned in pain. "That setup in there will let
me pump anything I want to into this room," he continued. "Let's consider what's available: oxygen . . . hormone gas . . . carbon monoxide . . . I think carbon
monoxide will do very well. It's quite painless, I'm told.
If you two gentlemen will excuse me, I'll hook up the
hose and start the van."

"Now what?" Lorenzo demanded. He'd been ringing
the bell for several minutes without result.

"Can't you drill through it? Or batter it in?" Dennis
asked.

"I don't carry equipment like that around with me.
Besides, it's called breaking and entering."

"Isn't there anything else we can do?" Robin asked
urgently. "Break a window? Something?"

"Any other way into this place?" the detective asked.

Robin looked around. "There's the garage . . ."

But Lorenzo was already heading down the stairs
toward it. "That your car and driver?" he called to Dennis over his shoulder. "Get rid of him."

Locke bounded down the stairs to dismiss the driver,
and Robin followed. He put his arm around Robin's
shoulder as the car drove off. "Phil Lorenzo's the best,"
he said. "Don't worry. We'll get him out."

Lorenzo inspected the garage lock. "Standard hard-
ware," he repeated. "Hey, sounds like somebody's running a vehicle in there." He banged on the garage door
with his fist. No reply. He turned and hurried back to
his vehicle and popped the trunk open. "We'll have that
off in a minute," he promised.

Morgan stood in the middle of the training room, one
of the portable oxygen units strapped to his face, and
the small pistol back in his hand. He surveyed the scene
before him with manic enjoyment. He removed the mask
for a moment, and spoke. "How're you feeling, gentlemen? Getting a little sleepy?"

Connor lay motionless on the floor, barely breathing. Adam, still pinioned to the MIE machine, stared at Morgan through glassy eyes. "You're a dead man, Hudson," he snarled.

"After you," Morgan said pleasantly.

"We're in!" The garage door was flung open. "What the hell—? Kill that engine, Dennis," Lorenzo ordered. He went around to the rear of the training van and ripped the hose from the exhaust pipe. Fearfully Robin followed the hose with her eyes. It led through a partly open door into a small room. "And stay back, both of you." His hand on his holstered weapon, Lorenzo moved cautiously through the open door.

Morgan went over and kicked Connor gently with his foot. "One down," he said. He turned back to Adam. "Isn't this when you're supposed to tell me I'll never get away with it?"

But Adam merely shrugged. "You're dying," he whispered. "You're already dead." He rested his head against the cool metal. "You just don't know enough to lie down."

"You never give up, do you? Still trying for a last-minute reprieve. 'Oh, Dr. Salt, only you can save me . . .'"

"I can't save you," Adam murmured. "No one can. And I don't give a shit . . ." His eyes closed, and his head lolled onto his chest.

Morgan wandered over and looked down at him. He pulled Adam's head up by his hair, studied his face, then let his head drop again. Nearly there, he thought, as the ragged breathing became fainter. He switched off the oxygen tank valve and took off his mask. Time to head back upstate and work on his alibi. He sprinted for the door to the locker area, then stopped. For the suicide thing to make sense, Connor would need to be shot in the head at close range, and the gun pressed into his hand. He knelt beside the dead trainer and fired.

"Freeze!" a voice shouted. "Throw down your weapon. Put your hands in the air—"

Morgan turned and fired again, diving behind the wall of exercise mats as Lorenzo returned his fire. "Throw down your gun," Lorenzo repeated, his weapon trained on the mats. "Give it up."

Robin struggled free of Dennis's protecting arm and ran through the storage room. "What's happening?"

"Get her the fuck out, Dennis," Lorenzo shouted. "We've got an armed man in here." Locke grabbed Robin's arm and pulled her back. "And Dennis?"

"I'm here."

"Get on my car phone and call for some goddamn backup. And an ambulance."

With a cry, Robin pulled away from Dennis and raced across the room to Adam. Ignoring Lorenzo's shouted order to leave, she knelt down and began untaping his arms. He looked so pale. My God, he's dead, she thought. He's barely breathing. She looked around frantically, spotting the portable oxygen unit Morgan had abandoned. She raced over and retrieved it, then quickly fitted the mask over his face and twisted the valve open.

"Throw down your gun and kick it over here," the detective shouted. "Don't make me shoot you." A fusillade fired into the ceiling was the only reply.

Slowly Adam opened his eyes and looked around. "Don't speak," Robin whispered. "Just breathe." She finished untaping his arms, then knelt and went to work on the tape around his calves. Despite the fresh air flowing into the room, she was starting to feel a little wobbly.

"Where's . . . Morgan?" Adam gasped.

"Over there." Robin gestured toward the stack of exercise mats. "He's got a gun."

"I know." He stood, holding on to the exercise machine for support. "He shot Connor." He lurched toward the fallen trainer and knelt down. Ripping the shirt away, he felt for a pulse, then saw the terrible head wound and knew it was hopeless. "He's gone."

Lorenzo glanced over and saw Adam was mobile. "Will you people please get the hell out?" He, too, was beginning to feel the effects of the bad air.

"Backup's on the way," Dennis reported, breathless. "EMS, too. Come on, Adam. Let's get you out of here."

Adam slowly got to his feet, and Robin and Dennis helped him toward the door.

"Adam!" Morgan's voice echoed in the high, narrow room. "You still alive?"

"Yeah. Disappointed?"

"Keep moving," Lorenzo ordered Adam.

"Were you telling me the truth?" Morgan asked, sounding woozy. "Am I really dying?"

Adam stopped, leaning against Robin for support, and pulled off the oxygen mask. "We isolated your damn hormone from Kenny's spinal fluid. Gave it to rats. Rats are all dead."

"Rats aren't people," Morgan replied.

"You're forgetting Andrew Fuller."

"Fuller died of cerebral palsy."

"Believe that if you want to," Adam said tiredly.

"Well . . . Barrett improved it since then."

"If he told you that, he lied. The rats died exactly the way Fuller did. Spastic paralysis. Saw them myself."

"But Kenny's all right."

"Not according to his MRI. Matter of time. Goddamn you, Morgan." Adam's voice broke; tears filled his eyes.

"You're not hearing this," Dennis told Lorenzo firmly.

"But there must be something you can do . . ." Morgan's words floated out from behind the wall of mats. "Reduce the level of nitric oxide, reverse the brain damage—?"

"I wish there were," Adam told him. "Not for you, but for the others. They don't deserve to die like that. They didn't choose to drug themselves into playing better ball; that decision was made for them, without their knowledge or consent. The only bright spot is that you'll die the same way they will. Morgan? Are you listening?"

"You're sure about this? There's no way back?"

"No way back. No way out."

Silence. "There is one way out," Morgan said.

The gunshot was loud in the narrow room. It burned the ear and seared the brain, its echo bouncing from wall to ceiling to floor, mingling with the faint sirens of approaching ambulances.

"Morgan?" Lorenzo called. "Morgan?" Cautiously the detective approached the mats, his weapon at the ready. "He's dead," he reported. He turned to Dennis, his eyes blazing. "I could have been killed. We all could." His fury mixed with confusion as he looked from Dennis to Adam to Robin. "What the fuck just happened here?"

Dennis took a deep breath. "A deranged intruder broke into the Pro Club. He tied up Dr. Salt, shot this guy, tried to gas them both. And killed Morgan Hudson when he came to their aid."

"Bullshit," Lorenzo said.

"I had an appointment to meet Robin and Adam here at the club. Robin eluded the intruder and got a message to me, and I called you. At the time, we had no idea the situation was so serious." Lorenzo was shaking his head as he listened. "It was all over by the time we got here. Isn't that right, Robin?" Robin looked from the commissioner to Adam and back to Dennis. "If you say so," she agreed, frowning.

"Forget it!" Lorenzo growled. "What about Morgan's car out there?"

"It was stolen," Robin suggested. "By the intruder. He'd been stalking Morgan . . . he hated the Comets . . ."

"This is nuts!"

"Please, Phil," Dennis begged. "If the truth about this"—he gestured at the carnage around them—"comes out, the rest will, too. The drugging of the players and a lot of really bad stuff. The sport will never recover from the scandal. And it'll blacken the names of three young ballplayers who don't even know what's been done to them."

"Forget it, Dennis."

"Phil, if you want your grandchildren to ever enjoy a baseball game again, go with me on this. At least for now."

"The evidence won't support a bullshit story like

that," Lorenzo replied angrily. "Hudson's fingerprints are all over the hose, the van, the doorknobs—"

"The intruder held him at gunpoint, made him do it before he shot him."

"Using Morgan's own gun? No, it'll never fly—"

Dennis approached Morgan's lifeless body. Repressing a shudder of disgust, he picked up the pistol, wrapped it in his handkerchief, and shoved it into his trouser pocket. "The intruder must have taken the gun with him when he escaped."

"They'll yank my license. They'll kick my ass from here to— Escaped how?"

"Through the gym," Adam said. "Up into Barrett's apartment, down the stairs and out through the alley." Outside, squad cars and ambulances were pulling into the street, their sirens dying.

"Who else knows about this? Any of this?"

"Only the people in this room," Adam said. "Everyone else is dead." Robin opened her mouth, but the look on Adam's face warned her to close it again. He'd be responsible for Agnes's silence.

"How about those three superplayers?"

"They're innocent bystanders in all this," Adam said. "And besides . . ." He shook his head, tears welling up. "No, it's just us. There's nobody else."

Lorenzo stared hard at his friend. "I've known you a long time, Dennis. Our wives play bridge together. I can't believe you're asking me to do this." He paused. "You could actually live with this? You think it's *right*?"

"Right?" Dennis repeated, his broad face creased with tension. "Is it right that the lives of three young men should be destroyed for something they had no part in, no knowledge of? Is it right that an entire team should be dishonored, that baseball itself should be defamed, all because of one man's greed?" He shook his head. "All I'm asking for is a little time. Time to hear what Adam knows, to think about what's best for everybody." He sighed. "If I believed in divine retribution, I'd tell you the guilty have already been punished. At any rate, they're gone." He looked pleadingly at Lorenzo. "This situation we have here, it's not typical of baseball. Most players, owners, coaches, they're honest, moral people. A few bastards, sure, but not this." He hesitated. "Buy me a little time, Phil. Twenty-four hours. You know I want to do the right thing. Give me a day to figure out what that is."

"You're putting me in a helluva position," Lorenzo growled. "I'd have to be crazy to go along with you on this one."

"Well, that kind of depends, doesn't it?" Dennis said. Outside, two police officers, their weapons drawn, were entering the garage.

"Yeah? On what?" the inspector demanded.

"On how much you love baseball."

Chapter Thirty-two

Thursday, October 7—World Series, game 4

"Pro Club For Men," Adam said softly, staring at the paper in his hand. "So that's how he did it."

Robin had been up early to retrieve her notes from the original Morgan Hudson article. Now she and Adam were snuggled in his sleigh bed, a tray of coffee, melon, and breakfast rolls beside them. Adam reached for a croissant, scattering flakes across the papers spread out on the coverlet.

"I thought the name sounded familiar," Robin said triumphantly. She reached for a crimson folder bearing the Hudson & Company logo in shiny white letters. "Pro Club For Men was a small, unprofitable division of Hudson and Company," she explained as she leafed through the pages. "Here it is: 'Pro Club For Men: A line of skin care products built around the concept of a spa experience for men.' The ads featured testimonials by famous athletes."

"Sounds familiar."

"No kidding." Robin smiled at him. "Well, the skin care products bombed, and the division ceased operation some years ago, but the trademark's still current. The name and the famous athlete concept gave Morgan the perfect front for Barrett's technique." She sipped her coffee. "Mmm, good."

"Hazelnut." Adam thought for a moment. "I bet that's how they covered the isolation of the hormone. Hudson and Company funded it under the Pro Club For Men label, just as if it were a shampoo in development. That's how it would have been carried on the books."

Robin nodded. "And as long as no paperwork existed linking the division to the Pro Club itself, it would look like another experimental, unmarketed product." She paused. "So Hudson and Company did the isolation?"

But Adam shook his head. "It's very doubtful. Their R and D wouldn't be up to that kind of technical work. Besides, Barrett must have kept the process under tight control. How else could he have threatened to cut off the supply of the stuff, the way he did? No, Barrett either contracted for the isolation through a specialty lab, or he did the isolation himself—he was quite capable of doing it. That could have been part of his deal with the lab: time and facilities and no questions asked. And Hudson and Company wrote the checks."

"But if that's true, how could the training continue after Barrett was killed?"

"Several of the cylinders I found at the Pro Club were still full. They probably stockpiled it. The hormone would stay stable for a good three, four months, under pressure." He speared some melon with his fork, chewed and swallowed. "And after he sold the Comets, Morgan wouldn't need the stuff anymore." He selected a sweet roll and carefully broke it in half.

"I'm glad your appetite's returned," Robin told him. "You had me worried, yesterday."

"I had us both worried." He hugged her. "I'm glad you and the cavalry showed up."

"It was a rather unorthodox way to get a story, I admit," Robin teased him as she kissed his nose. "But as you yourself said, we reporters never let up. Better get dressed. The game starts in an hour."

Dennis Locke sat in his reserved seat at Parker Stadium, looking out over the field. The flag, at half-mast in honor of Morgan Hudson, killed during a break-in at the Pro Club the previous evening, flapped lazily under an overcast sky.

He rose for the "Star-Spangled Banner," then sat and watched the Comets run onto the field, their crimson-

and-white uniforms bright against the turf, their energy and their hopes high.

He knew what he should do: stand up right now, stop the game, and declare the Philadelphia Falcons this year's World Series winners. But if he did, he'd have to explain why, and that 'why' could kill professional baseball, and destroy the lives of every member of the Comets team—players, managers, coaches, trainers. Who'd believe that none of them knew the superplayers were being drugged?

Beside him, Phil Lorenzo sat hunched in his seat, brow furrowed, eyes fixed on the outfield. They'd arranged that if Dennis decided to stop the game, he'd immediately introduce Lorenzo who would then announce that new evidence had come to light and that Morgan's gun had been recovered. The detective shifted in his seat, wishing he'd been out of the office when Locke had called yesterday. Then the game started, and he lost himself in it.

Lorenzo had loved baseball ever since he could remember. As a kid, it had kept him off the streets and out of trouble. He'd been pretty good, too; not good enough for pro or even semipro ball, but good enough to develop a little self-esteem, for once. Soon he'd traded pickup games for a spot on a neighborhood team organized by the Police Athletic League....

Stop the game or let it continue? Dennis weighed his choices, as he had throughout the previous, sleepless, night. The superplayers didn't knowingly use drugs, he thought. They didn't know they were being medicated. On the other hand, how can I let the record stand, knowing what I know? But the Pro Club is closed for good, he told himself; the people behind it are dead. He looked around at the packed stadium, the thousands of happy faces, and sighed. Was Phil right? Did he owe it to the fans to stop the game and tell them the truth? Or did he owe it to them *not* to?

A section away, Adam shouted gleefully as Rick Simms scooped up the grounder and threw to second for the out, all in one smooth movement. Simms had never been a great fielder, but this season he'd improved tremendously. And he wasn't the only one. Heart, not hormones, Adam realized, had won the Comets their pennant race, and had brought them to this fourth World Series game. The superplayers, great as they were, hadn't done it alone. If they won today, the whole Comets team would have earned their victory. Whatever Dennis's decision, Adam resolved that he himself would have no part in taking that victory away from them.

He glanced over at Robin. "Exciting, isn't it?"

Robin nodded. "The best. It's going to make a fabulous story. I can't wait to start writing."

Adam sighed. "I meant the game. You can't write the story. Not unless Dennis goes public first."

Robin's shoulders drooped. "I know. I keep hoping he'll stand up and stop the game." She glanced toward the commissioner's seat. "I worked hard for this story, Adam." She hesitated. "But then I think about Kenny and the guys, and I hope he won't."

By the seventh-inning stretch, Dennis still hadn't made up his mind. He and Lorenzo stood and sang "Take Me Out To The Ball Game" along with everyone else, but Phil's expression was strained, and he avoided Dennis's eyes. Locke understood what this cover-up was costing Lorenzo; he wondered if their friendship would ever be the same.

The commissioner looked around at the capacity crowd: parents and kids here to enjoy a rare afternoon of family fun; teenagers excitedly trading statistics and opinions; young children, wide-eyed with excitement; everyone thrilled at the opportunity of seeing their heroes in the flesh.

And they were heroes, every one of them, Locke thought. The Comets and the Falcons both. This was the American Dream. It didn't matter where you came from, as long as you could play. Your ability, your talent, your heart: that was all that mattered. How many kids had dreamed the dream? How many had been inspired by it? He glanced over at Lorenzo; he knew Phil had been one of them.

The Comets were playing great ball, but the Falcons, determined to avoid a Series shutout, were fighting hard. At the end of the ninth inning, the game was tied up, seven to seven, and after two outs in the bottom of the tenth, the score had not changed.

The crowd roared its support as Kenny Reese came up to bat, but Adam sat quietly, a worried look on his face. Kenny's game had become more erratic every inning, and sitting this close to the action, Adam had seen him grimace in pain as he'd trotted in from the field. He thought of Agnes, now searching for a way to mitigate the deadly effects of the hormone but doubtful it could be found in time.

The first pitch was low: ball one. The second barely clipped the corner of the plate, and Kenny went for it: strike one. Adam groaned. Ordinarily, Reese would have held back. A superb clutch hitter, Kenny was known for biding his time until he got the pitch he wanted, and then walloping the ball hard. What the hell was he thinking? Kenny let the next pitch go: another ball. Then suddenly he dropped his bat and stepped back, grabbing his head with his hands. Shit, Adam thought; here we go. The crowd quieted, and the home plate umpire stepped toward him. But as quickly as the pain had come, it receded. Kenny shook his head, looked around, waved off the head coach who had started toward him from the dugout, and grabbed his bat. Giving an experimental swing or two, he spat and stepped up to the plate again. His face was ashen but his mouth was a grim, determined line as he locked eyes with the pitcher, daring him to give him something he could hit.

The pitch came in like a freight train and Kenny hit the ground. Ball three. The fans screamed abuse at the guy on the hill, but Kenny simply stood up and brushed himself off, taking his position again, his eyes blazing. And here came the one he was waiting for: a change-

up he could read like a book. The impact of bat on ball
was so strong, the wood split apart. Tossing the stump
aside, Kenny headed for first as the crowd turned their
heads in unison to follow the trajectory of the ball as it
streaked obliquely across centerfield and over the left
field fence.

Comets came pouring out of the dugout onto the field,
shouting and pounding one another on the back, as
Kenny loped around the bases. In the stadium, the
crowd was going wild, stamping, yelling, hurling objects
onto the field. Police officers rushed to assist security
guards trying to hold back groups of young men who
were scaling the wall separating the seats from the field.

Adam rose and watched as Kenny rounded third,
stumbled, recovered, and moved forward again, but
more slowly. His teammates ran beside him, cheering.
Suddenly Kenny grabbed his head again and stopped.
Pain bent him double, but he pulled himself erect and
forced his feet to keep moving forward. He was nearly
home when he staggered and collapsed heavily, his body
twitching. A gasp went up. Was he ill? Was he dead?
Was this some kind of stupid joke?

Slowly, Kenny's hand, the fingers stiffly clenched in
spastic seizure, appeared from beneath his crumpled
body. Inch by inch, his arm stretched out toward home.
Slowly his fingers uncurled as he reached blindly for the
base. The stadium went silent as Kenny's fingers inched
across the brown dirt toward the plate. As he touched it,
his body gave a final convulsive shudder, and he lay still.

A wave of fans broke onto the field, sweeping aside
the police, security guards, and stadium officials who
rushed to contain them. Reporters and television crews
joined the frenzied crowd, which barely parted for the
ambulance that sped out onto the grass.

Dennis Locke, his face a stark mask, surveyed the
cameras clustered around him. "I have an announcement," he said. Off to one side, Phil Lorenzo sat
slumped in his seat.

"What happened here today . . ." Locke paused, visibly

struggling with himself. "The game we have just seen . . ." He scanned the faces around him: so many children. So much hope.

"This year's World Series is a symbol of the American Dream," he proclaimed. "The Comets came from behind to win their first league pennant, and, today, their first World Series. They won despite the death of their owner Morgan Hudson, who was tragically killed last night when he went to the aid of the manager of the Pro Club during a robbery. And now, tragedy has struck again: Kenny Reese is dead.

"But the Comets are not one man, be he player, owner, manager, or coach. The Comets are a team. Teamwork brought them victory. And teamwork will see them through this dark time, as well. Baseball—" He glanced over at Lorenzo, who was staring out at the empty field. "Baseball represents the best in all of us: dedication, talent, good sportsmanship. Respect for others regardless of their race or creed. Working together for the common good.

"Wherever he is, Morgan Hudson is looking down on what his team has accomplished here at Parker today. And he's smiling."

"I'm going to be sick," Robin announced, "if I have to listen to any more of that drivel."

Adam put his arm around her shoulder. "I know it sounds a little mawkish, but there's a lot of truth in what he says."

"I meant the drivel about Morgan being a hero."

"He's only doing what he has to do."

Robin nodded, her eyes filling with tears. "Poor Kenny. Poor everybody."

"Let's get out of here."

Arms around each other, they made their way past the press cluster and out into the parking lot.

"I suppose that's the end of my big scoop," Robin said regretfully.

"It's the best way."

"I guess." She looked up at him mischievously. "Maybe I'll write it as fiction. A short story for *Playboy*?"

"Don't even think about it," Adam told her. He took her in his arms and kissed her deeply.

"Okay, you smooth-talking cowboy, you've convinced me," she gasped, laughing. "But you have to admit, it would have made one hell of a story."